The Fallen

Star

Jessica Sorensen

For information:

http://jessicasorensensblog.blogspot.com/

Cover Photograph by Shutterstock
Cover Design by Mae I Design and Photography
www.maeidesign.com

The Fallen Star — Book 1
ISBN 978-1461052142

Chapter 1

*In the midst of a dark forest, haunted by the winter's chill, I
found myself running for my life. My feet thudded heavily
against the snow as the thunderous roar of the yellow, glowing-
eyed, black-cloaked monsters chased after me.*

*I shoved helplessly through the brittle pine trees, leafless
branches clawing at my flesh. Snow flooded my sneakers, soaking higher and higher on my jeans with every step I took. My
heart pounded furiously. My lungs grew tight, about to collapse
from exhaustion. The air dipped colder. Fog swirled everywhere.
They were close, so close I could feel their icy breath down my
neck. That's what they do—they drop the temperature so drastically the air instantly bruises over with ice. And if they catch
me, I am a goner. Their chilled breath would strangle me to a
hypothermic death in a heartbeat.*

*I threw a frantic glance over my shoulder, struggling to
keep my numb legs moving. Flickers of yellow flooded through
the trees. A sheet of ice crackled over the ground, nipping at my
heels. I tore my gaze away, forcing myself to run faster.*

*"Gemma, there's no use running." The man's voice rum-
bled through the night. It was the same voice that always showed*

up right before the monsters captured me. "No matter what you do, you'll never escape."

The sound of snapping twigs and crunching footsteps echoed nearer. My muscles seized up, leaving me no choice but to slow to a lethargic jog. A cool breeze swept my skin as ice-cold fingers wrapped around the back of my neck and yanked me backwards, my bones popping in protest.

I let out an uncontrollable whimper and opened my mouth to scream, but only a whisper escaped. I flung my weight forward, squirming and kicking and fighting to break free with every ounce of strength I had in me. But it was useless. My arms and legs moved in slow motion. My blood rushed cold, my veins darkening, mapping my skin with bluish-purple lines.

"I told you there was no point." A tall, husky man appeared in front of me. The black-hooded monster's bony fingers dug deeper into my skin. "Like I said, you won't escape." He grinned, the kind of grin that would have sent chills down my spine if I hadn't already been freezing to death.

The golden moonlight spotlighted down from the night sky, highlighting a white scar scuffing his left cheek. His black hair matched his dark, hollow eyes. "Finish her off," he commanded.

The black-cloaked monsters crept out from the trees, their yellow eyes gleaming hungrily toward me. I tried to scream again as ice whipped through my body. I heard a deep laugh as I felt myself falling. Then everything went black.

Chapter 2

I woke up, gasping for air, my disoriented mind still thinking I was sprawled out on the forest ground, freezing to death from the monsters' deathly touch. That the tan walls forming my bedroom were just an illusion.

I bolted upright in my bed, my pulse racing as I untangled myself from my sheets. Beads of sweat trickled down my skin, sticking my t-shirt to my back. I rubbed my eyes and blinked a few times, seeing if my room stayed in place. Nothing budged and I relaxed. It had been a dream, just like it had been the night before, and the night before that.

I inhaled slowly, letting my racing heart settle, as I climbed out of bed, the carpet feeling cold against the soles of my bare feet. I wrapped a blanket around me and treaded softly over to the window. The soft pink glow of the sunlight spilled over the snowy mountains, kissing the tips of the pine trees. The very pine trees that I had just been running through, and where I would keep running through every night in my nightmares.

Of course, my nightmares were just the tip of the iceberg in the madness that had overtaken my life. When I was awake, I had much bigger problems to deal with than monsters attacking me. Real problems. Ones I couldn't blink away.

It all began right before I started having my way too realistic dreams. Back before I had been able to dream at all.

Okay, so you're probably thinking I'm a total nut job. But before you go jumping to any conclusions, let me explain.

I wasn't always the girl that I am now. *Terrified*—the word meant absolutely nothing to me. In fact, almost everything meant nothing to me. My mind was as blank as a sheet of paper—there was zero going on inside. I could still walk, talk, breathe, and function; I just couldn't feel any emotions. *Ever.* Crazy, I know. But at the time, I could have cared less.

Then about a month ago, something inside me changed. The day had started out just like any other day. I had been going through my morning routine of getting dressed for school when, out of nowhere, I felt a prickling sensation on the back of my neck. Confused, I ran over to the mirror to check for any bumps or marks on my pale skin. But there was nothing there except my normal specks of freckles.

Dismissing it to my imagination, I grabbed my backpack and headed downstairs to get some breakfast. That's when I felt the strangest thing—this overwhelming sadness building up inside me. Seconds later, I was crying, real tears and everything.

It was weird.

Up until then, at least as far back as I could remember, I had never experienced anything like the prickling sensation before. From then on, my life was never the same. The prickle would show up and *bam*, I would be bouncing with happiness. Or boiling with anger. Or...well, you get the picture. And once I felt an emotion, it never left me. In the beginning, I really struggled to keep all of my newfound emotions under control. There was this one awful incident at school when I had this sudden outburst and started bawling right in the middle of Mr. Belford's lecture on Plate Tectonics. People stared at me like I was a freak, which is understandable. I mean, only a freak would cry over shifting plates.

I had done quite a few searches on the internet, trying to figure out what was happening to me, but I found nothing remotely related to what I was going through. Apparently, whatever "it" was was one hundred percent original. Which was great. Just great. My life would be so much easier if—

My alarm shrieked, startling me so badly I actually jumped and spun around.

Man, my nightmares were making me jumpy.

I hit the off button. *It's time for school. Ugh.* School was so my least favorite part of the day. My past inability to experience emotions had kept me detached from everyone

7

and everything, which resulted in my current life being a friendless one. This had been fine when I couldn't feel, because I had no idea what I was missing. But now...well, let's just say that for someone who has no friends going to school is like dangling a piece of bacon in front of a dog's face—pure and utter torture. I hated watching everyone walk around in their little cliques while I stood on the sidelines alone.

I tossed my blanket on the bed and put on a pair of jeans and a black t-shirt. I ran a brush through my long, tangled brown hair and pulled it into a ponytail. Then I went over to the full length mirror on the back of my bedroom door and did a quick glance over. My legs were way too long, my skin far too pale, and my eyes...they were violet. Yes, weird, I know. But it fit right in with everything else that had to do with me.

Downstairs in the kitchen, Marco and Sophia—my grandparents, who have insisted I call them by their first names—were already there. Sophia stood over the oven, pans hissing, as the smell of bacon filled the air. Marco sat at the table, the morning newspaper opened up in front of him.

The room was small and brightly lit, making the yellow walls nearly blinding. Add that to the teal cupboards and the room had this sort of funhouse effect going on in it.

I grabbed a bowl from the cupboard and took a seat at the kitchen table.

Marco peered over the newspaper at me, his black oval rimmed glasses sliding down the brim of his slightly crooked nose. "Gemma," he mumbled with a subtle nod.

I strained a smile.

I've lived with Marco and Sophia since I was one, after my parents passed away in a car accident. That's all I know about my parents—how they died. I asked Marco and Sophia about them a few weeks ago after the crazy prickle thing had traced its way down my neck. To say my grandparents freaked out was putting it mildly. They had gone ballistic, yelling that I was never to ask about my parents again. And when I shed tears and screamed back, things got even worse. Finally, I ended up storming off to my room. Since then, our already strained relationship has worsened. We barely talk to each other, which I guess isn't that big of a change since we barely talked before.

Over the last few weeks, I had been trying to make some sense out of why they refused to speak about my parents. All I could come up with was that maybe talking about my parents was too painful for them. Either that or they didn't like me.

It wasn't just my asking about my parents that had Marco and Sophia acting crazy. Every time I was near them and showed emotion, I could sense them cringing. Evidently, they preferred the old hollow me. I don't know why, though. I didn't. They never even asked me about my sudden ability to feel either. I mean, if you had a child that had been an emotionless zombie for most of her life, then suddenly she did a complete 180 in the emotional department, wouldn't you celebrate and talk about it instead of getting pissed off?

I know I would.

But since Marco and Sophia chose to say nothing about it, I opted to keep the prickly sensation to myself. Besides, I had a gut-wrenching feeling that if I did mention it to them, I would be buying myself a one-way ticket to the Psych Ward.

"Do you want some bacon?" Sophia's voice yanked me out of my thoughts.

The bacon sizzled as she tapped her foot on the tile floor. She reminded me of one of those women in a 1950s TV series; her auburn hair pulled back into a bun, a crisp white apron tied over her floral dress.

"Sure," I said, starting to get to my feet. I wish we could be closer. Yes, I knew I should be grateful that I had grandparents who fed me and put a roof over my head. And don't get me wrong, I am. But it would have been nice if they would at least talk to me more than what was required. Or maybe give me a smile once in a while. Was that too much to ask? "But I have to go start my car first."

"Marco already did that for you," she said curtly.

"Oh." I turned to Marco. "Then—"

The sound of the chair grinding against the tile floor cut me off. Marco rose to his feet, all tall and mighty like.

10

He folded his newspaper and tucked it under his arm. "I'm going to um..." He trailed off and hurried out of the kitchen.

He did that a lot—mumbling to himself or walking away mid-sentence. He was a retired salesman, but it was hard to picture since he couldn't carry on a conversation for more than a minute.

The spatula clanked as Sophia tossed it on the counter. "Go get a plate and come get some then." Her nippy tone was my signal to hurry up and get out of her hair.

So I did, rushing over and piling a few pieces of bacon on a plate, along with some eggs. Then I ate my food so quickly that I nearly choked twice.

Once I finished choking my food down, I trampled across the snowy driveway, climbed in my faded blue Mitsubishi Mirage, which made a loud clanking noise every time I pushed on the gas pedal, and headed off to school.

Marco and Sophia had given me the car six months ago when they decided that they were tired of driving me to and from the bus stop, which was about a ten-mile drive each way.

I live in a very small, very spread out town called Afton. It is known for two things: its infamous elk horn arch made of real elk antlers, and its hobby of accumulating snow nine months of the year. Now, I was in no way, shape, or form a fan of either the snow or the cold, so living here was like a polar bear trying to live in Hawaii—unbearable and very unpractical.

When I graduate in a few months, I am packing my bags and moving to some place warm and one-hundred percent mountain free.

Today, the normally poor road conditions were even worse due to the temperature being five below and freezing everything in sight.

Forced to drive at the pace of a snail, I managed to play through almost the entire CD of Taking Back Sunday—one of my favorite bands—before arriving at school. I parked my car right as the bell shrilled from inside the school and reverberated its way outside. I grabbed my bag, scrambled out of the car, and barreled across the skating rink parking lot.

As I reached the sidewalk, I had to stop because the prickling sensation made an unannounced appearance on the back of my neck. It was poking at my skin like a tattoo needle. I held my breath and waited. Each experience was like opening a present. I never knew what feeling was going to consume me. Or whether I would like the feeling or want to exchange it for something else.

A few seconds ticked by, but no new feelings came. Well, except for the feeling that I wasn't alone, which I wasn't. There were a few people lurking out by their cars, and a girl in a neon pink coat was sprinting like mad for the glass entrance doors of the school. Obviously she was trying not to be late, which was what I should have been doing. But I couldn't get my stupid feet to budge, as if the soles of my pink and black DC shoes had melted to the sidewalk. Then, suddenly, I saw him; a guy, ambling across the parking lot as if he had all the time in the world. My heart did this little fluttery thing that I had never felt it do before. *Whoa.* Even from a distance, I could tell he was gorgeous. The way his dark brown hair scattered messily over his head, but in an intentionally-done-perfect kind of way. His bright green eyes reminded me of clovers and flourishing springtime leaves. He wore a pair of dark blue jeans and a black hoodie. I guessed him to be tall, but I couldn't say for sure unless I got closer to him. He had to be new here because if I had seen him before, I probably would have remembered. No. Scratch that. I *definitely* would have remembered him.

But he didn't seem to notice me at all. Which was a good thing, I guess, since I was standing there, staring at him idiotically as he made his way across the sidewalk and strolled past me.

The prickle showed up again, this time filling me with a very overpowering urge to run after him. I had to admit, I probably would have too if the tardy bell hadn't rang and knocked me out of my prickle-induced-gorgeous-guy trance.

I flinched and shook my head. What was I doing standing out in the freezing cold, gawking at some random guy, when what I needed to be doing was getting my butt to class.

I rushed toward the entrance of the school, barely catching up with the new guy as he swung the door open. He stepped to the side and held it open for me, very gentleman-like. I bit my bottom lip nervously as I walked by him. I swear my heart was hammering so loudly in my chest that he had to be able to hear it.

Okay, so I don't know why I did the thing that I did next—it was very unlike me. I mean, I usually keep my head down and my eyes glued to the floor during school hours. But when I suddenly felt compelled to look up at him, I actually did. And boy was I in for a real shock. And I'm not talking about the emotional kind of shock. I'm talking about a literal shock. A blaze of electricity fired through my body like I had stuck my finger in an electrical socket. I froze, my eyes widening. What the heck? Was I going insane? First the prickling sensation and now this—what was wrong with me? If I wasn't careful then I was going to end up in a mental institution.

I felt the zap again and let out a gasp. The feeling momentarily took me away until I realized I was standing in the middle of the doorway, staring at the new guy with my mouth hanging open. I would have been completely mortified too, except to my astonishment—and my relief—his bright green eyes had widened and were locked on mine, and it almost looked like he could feel the electricity too.

My pulse raced as sparks of static nipped at my skin. The more we stared at each other, the more the electricity ignited, and I could almost feel my skin melting. So many different feelings were pouring through me simultaneously: confusion...desire...intensity, I couldn't think straight. I felt an invisible tug, drawing me to him, and before I even knew what I was doing, I took a step toward him.

Like a light switch, his expression slipped into a glower. "Do you mind?" he said, sidestepping around me and letting the heavy metal door slam painfully into my elbow.

"Ow," I said, rubbing my arm. "What the heck?"

He shot me a glare and a different kind of intensity burned in those beautiful green eyes of his. Intense hatred. My mouth dropped open as I watched him turn his back on me and walk down the hall without another glance back.

Chapter 3

Never in my life had I ever had a crush before. Although I wasn't even sure if what I was feeling toward the new guy qualified as a crush. If a crush was something that could cause a strange mix of emotions to bubble up inside me and leave me incapable to stop thinking about the new guy then yep, I had a crush.

All during first and second period, I tried to process what had happened—what on earth that electric feeling could have been. But trying to make sense of it had gotten me nowhere. It was about as confusing as the prickle and my newfound emotions and my reoccurring nightmares.

Wow. My crazy list just keeps getting longer and longer, doesn't it?

I was fairly spaced out for most of my morning classes, but like usual, I managed to get through them unnoticed. This was a good thing, since I heard zero of what my teachers were talking about. I thought I would eventually snap out of it, but even when third period rolled around, my brain was still lacking in the focus department, making me question if I was ever going to be able to think clearly again.

Why, you might be asking, did third period matter? Well, because third period was when I had astronomy, which was my favorite subject. Even during my emotionally detached days, I still was able to gaze up at the night sky, full of twinkling silver stars, and appreciate the beauty of the sight. However, the way I look at the stars now, and the way I looked at them before I could feel, are two entirely different experiences. Back then, I felt like I had been obligated to look up at them, as if some unseen force I had no control over bounded me to do so. Whereas now, I gaze up at them with a desire to...belong...or be part of them. The first time I ever felt happy—and I mean *ever*— was when I had been lying in my bed, staring out my window, watching the stars shine harmoniously with one another. The prickle had shown up, and I unexpectedly found myself smiling. All this warmth and happiness started swelling up inside me. The very next morning, when I entered the planetarium-style astronomy room, that same feeling of happiness filled me again. Ever since then, I always perk up when it is time to go to astronomy class.

Today, however, I felt completely out of it, and conjuring up any happiness seemed like it was going to be a challenge. There was just too much going on inside my head.

I arrived to astronomy with plenty of time to spare, which was typical for me since I had no one to talk to between classes. I made my way up the stairs to the very top of the mini planetarium, and sat down at my usual table, the one in the very far back corner where most of the loner kids tend to sit. I took my book out of my black messenger bag and hung my bag on the back of my chair. To kill some time—and to attempt to focus on something else besides the new guy, who I hadn't seen since he let the door bang me in the elbow—I did a quick skim-through of today's chapter. It turned out to be a lame attempt though, since all I ended up thinking about was how gorgeous he was, how much hatred his bright green eyes had when he'd walked away from me, and the electricity that hummed against my skin when I was near him. I swear I could still feel the sparkling sensation lingering on my skin.

The bell finally rang and class began. Mr. Sterling started taking roll. I barely paid attention, not even looking up when my name was called and I replied, "Here."

After he finished with roll, Mr. Sterling moved on to the announcements. Typically, it was a tedious task, but today it took a turn for the surprising.

"Alright, everyone, I have a few things to discuss before we start class." Mr. Sterling cleared his throat, trying to shush the whispering that had suddenly combusted amongst everyone. I still had my eyes glued to my book, only half listening as he continued, "First off, I'd like to announce that we have two new students joining us today."

Did he just say new students?

My head whipped up. Mr. Sterling was standing behind his podium, sporting a wrinkly grey suit and a red
striped tie. And holy crap, standing next to him was Mr.
New Guy himself. He had a bored expression on his face,
his arms folded across his chest, his bright green eyes
sparkling beneath the florescent lighting.

The sight of him made my heart skip a beat. I let out
an unintentional gasp and quickly flung my hand over my
mouth, wanting to smack myself in the forehead for reacting so ridiculously.

Kelsey Merritt—aka the head cheerleader who sat at
the table in front of me—turned around and shot me one
of her infamous you're-such-a-loser looks. Up until a couple of months ago, she didn't even know I was alive. And
honestly, I kind of preferred the old way, because her
knowing of my existence equaled getting thrown dirty
looks and nasty comments. Luckily, I wasn't much of a re-
actor; at least on the outside anyway. But today, I didn't
even react on the inside because my mind was fluttering
with a billion different thoughts that I could scarcely process. Like why the sight of this guy was making me react
this way. Because right now, all I could think about was
how beautiful his eyes were and how I had the strongest
urge to run my fingers through his messy, yet perfect, dark
brown hair. And how he—

All of a sudden, he looked right at me, his eyes full of
the same hatred I had seen in them earlier. I blinked and
sank back in my chair, the corners of my eyes burning with

tears threatening to spill out. I sucked in a slow breath. I would not let some guy make me cry. I wouldn't.

"This is Aislin Avery." Mr. Sterling gestured towards a girl standing on the other side of him. She was short and slender with golden blonde hair. And she had the same bright green eyes as the new guy. She was dressed in a pink sweater, jeans, and fur trimmed boots. I instantly got the impression she would probably soon be friends with Kelsey Merritt. Which, I know, is very judgmental of me.

I really shouldn't assume things about people.

"And this is her brother Alex Avery," Mr. Sterling said, motioning at the new guy.

Alex Avery? The name sounded vaguely familiar. Why though? I mean, it wasn't like I was the kind of person who ran into so many people that I couldn't keep track of their names. Besides, even if I was, I would have remembered him. Still…the sound of his name sent me into a *déjà vu* moment.

"Now we just need to find you two a seat," Mr. Sterling said, scanning the room for some empty chairs.

There were two empty seats at my table, but I wasn't sure how I felt about them sitting by me.

I wasn't sure how I felt about anyone sitting by me.

Kelsey Merritt's hand shot up in the air.

Mr. Sterling sighed. "Yes, Kelsey."

She flashed her pearly white teeth at him and twirled her platinum blond hair around her finger. "I was just going to say that Alex can sit at my table."

How nice of her since she shared a table with her two best friends, Anna Miller and Sarah Monroe—both could pass as her clone I might add—and there were no empty chairs for her to offer up. I scowled at the back of her blonde head, suddenly feeling very territorial of Alex. And yes, okay, I knew I in no way had any claim over him, but apparently, when it came to him, I didn't have any control over my actions.

"Actually, that won't be necessary, Kelsey," Mr. Sterling replied. "Gemma has two vacant seats at her table. They both can sit there. That way, no rearranging will have to be done." He pointed a finger at me and instructed Aislin and Alex to "Go ahead and take a seat back there."

It was at this very moment that the people I'd gone to school with for the last twelve years decided to notice me. The weight of their eyes felt heavy, and I found myself wishing I possessed the power to temporarily make myself invisible. The prickle on my neck let me know I was experiencing my first anxious moment. I shrank down in my chair and focused on the table.

I stayed with my eyes down until a small stack of books landed on the table with a thump.

"Hi." The girl—Aislin—smiled as she sat down. "I'm Aislin."

I gave her a small smile. Did I forget to mention my people skills sucked big time? "I'm Gemma."

She smiled again, unzipped her bag, and pulled out a pen and a notebook.

The chair next to me slid out and Alex sat down in it. I held my breath, waiting for the electricity to attack again. I waited. And waited some more. But the electricity seemed to be a no show.

Strange.

Mr. Sterling began his lecture on sky charting. I scratched a few notes down, but my attention kept drifting to Alex. He wasn't doing anything, not even taking notes. He was leaning back in his chair, his arms resting behind his head, his eyes half opened. He looked like he could have cared less about class, like it didn't matter whether he failed or not.

In the middle of my staring, Alex turned his head toward me, his eyelids lifting open. Our eyes met and I froze, unable to breathe. And then... he glowered at me.

I would have loved to have told you that, at that very moment, I decided to stop acting like a fool over a guy who obviously despised me, and in response to his hateful glare I fired one right back at him. But if I told you this, I would be lying. Because all I did was look away.

Yep, I'm a big chicken.

Class moved on so slowly it was unbearable. The electricity stayed MIA, which had me questioning if I had imagined the whole thing. Perhaps when I felt it this morning I had been overly exhausted, and my mind had been playing tricks on me. My sleep had been super crappy due to the reliving-of-my-death-over-and-over-in-my-nightmares thing.

Then again, maybe I was just losing my mind. There did seem to be many things happening to me that could qualify me as being on the brink of insanity.

But right as the thought crossed my mind that I might be going off the deep end, I felt it—a spark. Soft at first, barely tickling at my fingertips, but growing stronger as it surged up my arms and down my back. I had to catch my breath as my body *hummed* with heat.

I stole a glance at Alex, curious if he showed any signs of being able to feel the electricity. He looked bored. Absolutely, one hundred percent bored. He stared lazily ahead at the front of the classroom, where Mr. Sterling was yammering something about stars and their positions and...I don't know, his words sounded far off and distant.

With Alex seeming so relaxed and calm, I assumed there was no way he could feel the electricity. I guess the strange, electric feeling was a one-sided thing. Of course it was. It was me, after all, we were talking about here—the Queen of Freakiness.

But then again...as I peered closer at Alex, I noticed his hands were clenched rather tight. And the line of his jaw looked as if he was biting down hard. So maybe I wasn't alone. Well, either that or Mr. Sterling's lecture was painful for him to listen to.

As Alex ran his fingers tensely through his hair, he caught my eye. I should have looked away. I mean, how many times could I get caught staring at him before he declared me a stalker? But once my eyes met his, looking away was impossible, like an invisible force had magnetized my gaze to his.

My heart thumped deafeningly inside my chest as I stared at him with wide eyes. He didn't look away either. He didn't even so much as blink, this half serious, half afraid expression on his face, as if he wasn't quite sure what to think about the situation.

I wasn't quite sure what to think about the situation either.

Time seemed to come to a standstill, electricity spiraling through my body, heating my skin hotter and hotter. I felt like I was floating, yet suffocating at the same time. I could barely breathe. In fact, I couldn't breathe. The room had started to sway from my lack of oxygen. That was when I realized I was holding my breath.

Whoops.

I sucked in a breath of air.

Alex blinked, breaking our gaze. Immediately, he flung his attention back to the front of the classroom. I watched him, confused and somewhat sad. Why I felt these things, I couldn't say. Well, at least about the sad part. The confused part was totally understandable. Electricity that buzzed between two people. What could be more confusing than that?

But which one of us was causing it? If I had to guess, I would say it was me since weird seemed to be my middle name. Although, if I was the one causing it, why did I only feel it when I was around him?

"Alright, everyone go ahead and begin." Mr. Sterling's voice rose over my thoughts.

Great. Go ahead and begin what?

I casually peeked over at Aislin, trying to figure out what the heck I was supposed to be doing.

"Well." She flipped open her book. "How should we do this?"

I stared at her blankly. *Do what?*

Sensing my confusion, she said, "We're supposed to be working on the review questions as a group."

"Oh," I said idiotically. Note to self: start paying better attention. "Um...we could just divide the questions between the three of us, I guess."

"Is that how you usually do it when you work in a group?" she asked.

"Sure," I told her, holding back a laugh. Work in a group? The only time I ever worked in a group was when teachers forced me to work in one. And since this class went by the sit-wherever-you-want-and-work-with-the-people-at-your-table option, guess what? I never worked in a group. *Ever.* Because I sat alone.

All the time.

"Why do we have to work together at all?" Alex interrupted, his voice as sharp as glass. He glared at me, his eyes so full of hate I nearly melted into the back of my chair.

"Alex, knock it *off,*" Aislin hissed. "I mean it. Be nice."

Well, at least I wasn't the only one noticing his hatred for me.

He shook his head. "We don't need to work together just because the teacher suggested it."

My jaw dropped. Okay, so I know I'm a little weird and everything, but what the heck had I ever done to him? I mean, besides stare a little? Okay, well, maybe a lot. But hey, staring never hurt anyone.

Aislin leaned toward him and lowered her voice. But I could still hear her. Hello, I was sitting right next to them.

"Alex," she whispered. "I don't know what your problem is, but you need to stop. *Now*."

After that, it got quiet. The awkward kind of quiet where no one speaks and the silence is almost maddening.

"You know what," Alex said, slicing me with a glare, "I think I'm going to take off early." He shoved his chair away from the table and got to his feet.

Aislin reached up and caught him by the sleeve of his grey thermal shirt. "Alex, sit down."

He yanked his arm away from her, threw his book in his bag, and hurried down the stairs. He went straight to Mr. Sterling's desk and said something. Mr. Sterling gave him a nod and he left, bumping his elbow on the doorway on his way out.

For a moment, I just stared at the doorway. There were so many different feelings pouring through me, half of them new. Hurt, anger, pain, longing. It was too much.

My brain felt like it was going to explode from the over-load.

"I'm so sorry," Aislin apologized. "He's just been moody lately with the move and everything."

"Oh." I tore my eyes off the doorway and focused on her. "Okay."

She frowned. "Are you okay? You look like you're going to be sick."

"Huh?" I shook my head. "No, I'm fine." I faked a smile, pretending like it wasn't a big deal. That I didn't feel like I was going to throw up. That my heart didn't feel like it was breaking. That a guy I barely knew, who hated me, wasn't tearing me apart. But it was. It really, really was.

Chapter 4

So if I thought my life had been strange with the not-
being-able-to-feel-prickle-up-the-neck-and-suddenly-you-
can-feel thing (I really need to give it a name), then I had
no clue what strange meant. Over the last few days the
word "strange" had taken on an entirely new meaning.

First off, Alex did not like me. And that was putting it
mildly. When he looked at me, half of the time it was as if
he was staring into some far off place—like I wasn't even
there. And the other half of the time, the brightness in his
eyes darkened with utter loathing.

It sucked.

Why he felt this way about me still remained a mys-
tery. The only reason I could come up with was that
maybe he blamed me for the fact that every time he sat
down at our table in astronomy, the electric sensation
sparked up.

So where did this leave me? Nowhere basically. For
the time, my brain had taken up temporary residency in
the Land of Confusion.

Regardless of my problems, life still moved on. School
moved on. Mr. Sterling started pushing more and more for

group participation, like he could tell Alex and I were having issues and wanted to force us to work them out with each other. But how was I supposed to work out my issues with Alex when I wasn't sure what the issues were?

It didn't matter though, because Alex wasn't having any part of it. He refused to work on any of the assignments as a group, crossing his arms like a two-year-old and not doing anything.

It was Friday when things took a shift in a different direction. Mr. Sterling had passed out a deck of cards with the constellations printed on them in gold ink. Now, as a group, we were supposed to be holding the cards up for one another and trying to identify them, but doing so required all three of us to work together. Instead, Alex had half of the cards and was identifying them to himself. He looked exceptionally good today, dressed in a dark grey Henley and faded jeans, his hair scattered messily just like always. But I was trying my best not to focus on how good he looked. And, let me tell you, it was working out real well for me too.

Across the table, Ailsin sat texting away on her cell phone, her pink manicured nails hammering away at the buttons as she disregarded the assignment entirely. Over the last few days, I caught on that this blasé attitude seemed to be a trend for her, like she didn't care about her grades.

The rest of the cards were on the table beside my elbow. I had been doodling an inartistic rose on the cover of my notebook, daydreaming for the last fifteen minutes about what it would be like to be normal, while the electricity flowed lightly across my skin; a continuous reminder that normal was something I would never be.

As I added the thorns to the stem of my rose, Mr. Sterling appeared by our table, holding a pink slip of paper in his hand. Startled by his sudden appearance—and the fact that I wasn't doing what I was supposed to—I dropped my pen. It rolled off the table and landed on the floor as I scrambled to grab a card and pretend I had been working on the assignment the whole time.

He frowned disapprovingly at me and set the pink slip down on the table in front of Aislin. "This came from the office for you."

She snapped her cell phone shut and flashed him an innocent smile as she gathered up the paper.

"No more texting," Mr. Sterling mumbled, adjusting his tie as he walked away.

Aislin read the paper and then announced, "I have to go to the counselor's office."

Alex dropped the card he was holding and it floated to the floor. "What for?" His voice came out loud, his words rushed, causing a few people to shoot curious glances at us. Alex leaned closer to Aislin and lowered his voice. "Why do you have to go?"

"I don't know." She shrugged and handed him the paper. "It doesn't say why. It just says I have to."

Alex skimmed the paper over, then crumbled it into a ball and tossed it on the floor. It brushed down Nina Monroe's long blonde hair during the downfall, and she turned around, her eyebrows furrowed as she ran her fingers through her hair.

Aislin flashed an apologetic look at her and scooped up the ball of paper from off the floor. "Jeez, Alex," she said, smoothing out the creases. "You really need to stop freaking out about the tiniest things."

Alex rolled his eyes. "And you need to stop butting into my business."

Aislin pointed her finger at him as she got to her feet. "Be nice while I'm gone. I mean it." She grabbed her phone and trotted down the stairs, the curls of her golden blonde hair swinging across her back.

Just like that, a tension-filled bubble formed around Alex and me. Electric sparks danced all over my skin. My heart was like a jackhammer in my chest, feeding my already growing concern of how much more my heart could take before it would explode.

I needed to concentrate on something else.

I plucked a card from the deck and tried to center my attention on the gold dots forming the constellation. Right away I knew it was Andromeda, but still flipped the card over to check the answer. Yep, Andromeda printed in bold black letters on the back. I slipped it underneath the bottom of the deck, took another card from the top, and stared at the set of gold dots. This one was a little bit trickier, which was a good thing because figuring out the answer took more of my attention. I could feel my heart rate slowing down and my body relaxing. But then Alex began tapping his pen on the table over and over and over again. I don't know if he was doing it just because, or if he was attempting to get under my skin. If it was the latter then it was working.

At first, the tapping noise was only mildly annoying. But the movement seemed to be stirring up more and more sparks inside me. My heart began to speed up again. My head started pounding. I massaged my temples with my fingertips, taking a deep breath before I looked up at Alex.

My plan was pretty simple. I would give him a death stare until he stopped tapping his pen. I ran into a bit of a problem, though, because when I looked at him and our gazes met, my mind blanked out. I ended up just staring at him like an idiot gaping at their celebrity crush.

Alex stared back at me with this semi-intrigued, semi-panicked look on his face. What he was finding so intriguing was beyond me. The electricity? Me? Or maybe he found it interesting that he was making me feel the electricity? I always assumed it was me causing the electric sensation, but maybe I was wrong.

Alex and I continued to stare each other down like we were having a staring contest or something. Alex, for some reason, seemed to find it entertaining. The amused smile playing at his lips proved that. I was torn between wanting to slap that amused smile right off his face and leaning over and pressing my lips to his. Yeah, I know, definitely something I should not be thinking.

"Gemma. Alex."

I blinked and realized Mr. Sterling was standing beside our table, a stern expression on his face.

How long had he been standing there?

"Can I speak with you two in the hallway...*now*?" he asked, but it wasn't a question that was allowed to be answered with a no.

"Alright," I muttered at the same time Alex said, "Okay."

Alex kept his eyes glued on me as he rose to his feet. I stood up too, and we followed Mr. Sterling down the stairs and out into the hallway.

I found the situation very unsettling. The hallway was empty and silent. Mr. Sterling looked irritated. I had never been in trouble before, but I was getting the impression that this was going to be my first time.

"I was wondering if there was a problem between you two?" Mr. Sterling asked.

I shook my head. "No." I mean, what was I supposed to say? There's this really strange electric feeling buzzing between us, and despite the fact that Alex hates me, I can't seem to hate him back. Yeah, that wouldn't make me sound crazy at all.

Mr. Sterling stared heavily at us—his attempt, I assumed, to be intimidating. The thing was, he just wasn't a very intimidating teacher. In fact, he had a reputation for being a real softy and letting things slide.

"It just seems like there isn't a lot of group interaction going on," Mr. Sterling said, his attention focused on me. "Now, Gemma, I expected you to be a little more welcoming to Aislin and Alex since they're new here."

My jaw dropped. *What!* Was he kidding? "I-I'm not...I mean I—"

He held his hand up, silencing me. "I don't want any excuses. What I want is for the three of you to work together and get along."

My jaw tightened as the prickle stabbed at the back of my neck. I was pissed; more than pissed. I was downright furious. I burned the hottest glare I'd ever summoned up at Alex. He pressed his lips together to, of all things, hold back a grin. Apparently my anger was another thing that entertained him.

I clenched my hands into fists. I have never been a violent person before, but if Mr. Sterling hadn't been standing there, I might have hit Alex. Well, okay, that was a lie. But in the imaginative part of my brain I would have.

"Now, we have a fieldtrip coming up pretty soon and working in a group is a very big part of it," Mr. Sterling continued on, oblivious to my outrage. "So I want you two to get to know each other by working on the other assignments as a group." His gaze wandered back and forth between Alex and me like he was waiting for us to promise we would.

34

But I was too irritated to make such a promise.

"Alright," Alex said, his eyes flickering in my direction. "We will."

I had to hold back an eye roll. What was this "we" crap? I wasn't the one going out of my way to hate someone I barely knew.

"Good," Mr. Sterling said with a pleased smile. He opened the door to the classroom. "Now I'll let you two get back to the assignment."

Grinding my teeth, I stepped back into the classroom and made my way back to my table. Kelsey Merritt awarded me with one of her infamous you-are-such-a-loser looks as I passed by her, and then batted her eyelashes at Alex. In spite of how mad I was, I still felt a wave of relief as Alex turned his head away from her.

But I hated that I reacted that way.

I hated that Alex had that much control over my feelings.

I dropped down in my chair and watched Alex as he shuffled the deck of cards like he was getting ready for a game of poker. He cut the deck once, twice, and then tapped it on the table, aligning the cards evenly with one another.

"Alright." He slid the deck of cards at me. "You hold them up and I'll tell you the answers."

I raised my eyebrows questioningly. Was he being serious? Because I thought when he made the agreement with Mr. Sterling, he made it as an empty promise.

I eyed the deck of cards warily, wondering if it was a trick. If I picked one up and showed it to him, would he laugh at me because I actually thought he wanted to work with me? Or was he just trying to be cooperative?

There was only one way to find out.

Reluctantly, I grabbed the deck of cards and flipped the top card over.

"Cassiopeia," Alex answered indifferently.

He was correct, so I nodded and slipped the card under the deck. I lifted up the next one at the exact time the intensity of the electricity decided to ascend a notch.

"Ursa Major," he said. Then very condescendingly added, "Or the Big Dipper."

The sparks blazed as I held up another card.

"Ursa Minor." He caught my eye. "Is something wrong?"

Although my heart was racing, I managed to sound composed. "Nope. Nothing's wrong."

He rolled his eyes, and my anger simmered as I showed him another card.

"Andromeda." He shook his head. "This is so ridiculous."

Okay, that was it. Enough was enough. A few choice words burned at the tip of my tongue, but I bit them back. "You know what, you're right. This is ridiculous." I tossed the card I was holding onto the table and slumped back in the chair. "If you don't want to work with me, then fine. Maybe you should just leave again." The prickle poked at my neck, but whatever emotion was trying to emerge was smothered by my anger. "You don't even know me, yet you hate me. Just like that. You never even gave me a chance." I shook my head. "Yeah, you're right. This is ridiculous."

Wow. Where had that come from? It was so unlike me. Normally I was quiet. I held back saying a lot of things to the point that it felt like my chest was going to burst from the pressure.

As soon as I was done with my little speech, I wanted to take it back. Yeah, he deserved it. He possibly deserved worse. But still, I should have been the bigger person.

He cocked an eyebrow, his expression hovering somewhere between shock and curiosity. "That's quite the temper you have."

"You're the one that has the temper," I mumbled, and then quickly bit down on my tongue to stop myself from saying anything else.

He watched me closely, his expression softening as he leaned over the table. "Okay, here's the deal. I'll make you a promise." He paused. "I promise I won't be a jerk anymore." I was about to relax until he tacked on, "At least for the rest of class, anyway."

I shut my eyes and shook my head. What kind of a promise was that? Better yet, what kind of person said something like that? *The gorgeous kind*, I thought as an afterthought. Instantly, I wanted to smack myself on the head. What was I doing, thinking that way about a guy who clearly hated my guts?

I pulled myself together before opening my eyes. "Fine. Whatever. Sounds good."

For the rest of class, we worked together in peaceful harmony. We took turns holding up the cards. There were no more fights or stare-downs. To an outside observer, the situation probably appeared normal. Of course, they couldn't feel the sparks constantly spiraling and swirling in my body, a silent reminder that things were far from normal.

They weren't even close.

When the bell rang, I darted off to the library to eat my lunch. It was my typical lunch routine. Yes, it was a weird spot to eat lunch, especially for someone in high school, but I didn't have any friends, and sitting alone in an overly crowded cafeteria was my only other option.

There were always a couple of other kids eating lunch in the library. Sherman, this guy with extremely curly hair and tons and tons of freckles, was a regular. There was also Mrs. Bakerly, the seventy-something-year-old librarian.

"Hello, Gemma," Mrs. Bakerly greeted me from behind the counter. "How are you today?"

"Good," I replied. A total lie, but I didn't need to share that with her. I adjusted the handle of my messenger bag higher onto my shoulder. "How are you?"

She smiled brightly. "I'm good."

Smiling back at her seemed like such a huge project, but I managed to force a small one. Then I started off toward the far back corner of the bookshelves, my regular spot to hide out and eat my lunch. I selected the book I had been reading from off a shelf before settling down on the floor. Using my bag as a pillow, I relaxed against the shelf and opened the book to the page I had left off on from the day before.

The book told a story of a girl who had a superpower. It got me wondering what it would be like to have a superpower of my own. What if I could have been some extraordinary person with the ability to help the world, instead of a loner/freak girl? Or what if I had the power to, let's say, shield invisible, out of control, electric sparks?

I sighed. It was such a nice thought.

My stomach growled and in the silence of the library the sound was nearly deafening. I dug a granola bar out of my bag and a can of Coke, then commenced reading. I made it about halfway through a paragraph when I heard voices from the other side of the shelf. Whoever it was, was speaking too quiet for me to make out any of what was being said, yet still loud enough to distract me. I popped my neck and tried to block the voices out. It worked until I heard my name, as clear as day. "Gemma." At first I thought someone was trying to get my attention. But when I realized this wasn't the case—since no one was around—I wondered if whoever was chattering away on the other side of the shelf was talking about me.

Now, I know eavesdropping is very bad. And I did feel a little bit bad for doing it. But who on earth would be talking about me? Me, Gemma Lucas, the invisible-barely-known girl that hardly spoke to anyone?

I had to know.

I scooted forward, straining my ears to listen.

"You shouldn't have left me there alone with her," a voice grumbled. It was a guy's voice, deep and almost recognizable.

"What was I supposed to do?" It was another voice—a much higher voice—which belonged to a girl. "If we want to blend in, we have to act normal. If I get called to the office, I have to go. You should start doing this too, especially when you're around her. I know we're not supposed to get close to her, but still…it's called tack. She's not stupid. She can probably tell there's something going on."

Were they talking about me? If so, who were *they* exactly?

My skin began to tingle with a low buzz of electric static, and I had my answer. Alex. He was on the other side of the shelf. That meant that the girly voice most likely belonged to Aislin.

This revelation sparked my curiosity even more. Holding my breath, I inched closer to the shelf.

"You don't understand." Alex's voice dipped lower. "Something weird is happening between me and her."

"What do you mean?" Aislin asked.

"I'm not really sure how to explain it." He paused. "It happened the first day we came here. I felt this weird electric feeling when she walked by me. And it keeps getting worse the more I'm around her."

So they were talking about me. Wow. It was amazing what eavesdropping could do. It made me want to listen more. But how long was I going to be able to listen without being noticed? All it would take was for Alex to feel the tiniest buzz, and I would be caught. He hadn't felt it yet though, so...

"Have you told Stephan about it?" Aislin asked.

"No," Alex snapped. "And I'm not going to. He already has too much to worry about. The last thing he needs is to find out that Gemma is causing some kind of electrical static thing."

Before I could stop myself, I let out a gasp. Crap. My muscles tensed as I sealed my mouth shut.

"Yeah, but if it has something to do with the prophecy, he would want to know," Aislin told him.

It seemed like they hadn't heard me. I quietly exhaled, my muscles relaxing a little...Hold on. Rewind. Did she just say prophecy?

"Why would that have anything to do with the prophecy?" Alex said, clearly annoyed. "It's not about the prophecy. It's about her. She's causing it."

"You don't know that for sure. Maybe you're the one who's causing it," Aislin suggested. "I mean, I know I don't feel anything like that when I'm around her. For all you know, she might not even feel it."

"Trust me, she does," Alex said with confidence.

I pulled a face. How could he be so convinced I felt it? *Ugh*. He was so sure of himself. Of course, my constant gasping and inability to breathe when I was around him might have been a bit of a giveaway.

"Alex, I really think you should—" Aislin started.

Alex shushed her. "Just a second."

"What is it?" Aislin whispered.

The air ceased to an eerie standstill. Had he felt the electricity? If he had, I was so busted.

I scrambled to my feet and reached for my bag.

"Gemma, can I help you find something?"

I jumped back, my pulse racing with fear. But it was just Mrs. Bakerly. She had a small stack of books in her hands, and she was looking at me with wide eyes. My alarmed reaction must have scared her or something.

"No, I'm fine." Why oh why did she have to say my name? "I was just looking to see if I could...um...find something good to take home with me?"

"Well, if you need anything," she slid a book onto the shelf, "just let me know."

"I will," I told her.

She smiled and walked away.

I whirled my attention back to the other side of the shelf—back to Alex and Aislin. Had they figured out I had been listening to them? Were they waiting for Mrs. Bakerly to leave so they could, I don't know, jump me or something? Yeah, the idea sounded as stupid to me as it might to you, but hey, you never know.

I couldn't hear anything. My hands shook as I peeked through a sliver of space between two of the shelves. They were gone. Great. Now I had no clue whether they discovered I had been listening or not. Although I was pretty sure they had, which seemed like a very bad thing.

This sucked.

One good thing that came out of the situation, though, was that I learned a valuable lesson. If you're going to eavesdrop, don't get caught, especially when the people you were eavesdropping on just might be a little off of the rocker.

The stuff they were saying...it was so weird. Like straight out of a science fiction novel weird.

I shook my head and sighed. Something was going on and I needed to find out what.

Chapter 5

Like always, when I went to bed that night, I got sucked into my reoccurring nightmare—the one where I was being chased by the glowing-yellow-eyed, cloaked creatures in the middle of the forest. But the ending took a turn in a different direction.

After the monsters captured me, the man with the scar stepped underneath the light of the moon and transformed into someone else.

Alex.

His green eyes glimmered hauntingly in the shadows of the night as he grabbed me. But instead of freezing to death, I burst into flames. I woke up dripping in sweat. And for a split second, I was convinced I really was on fire. So convinced that I checked my body for burn marks.

Everything was becoming too stressful, to the point where I considered breaking down and telling Marco and Sophia everything. About Alex and Aislin. About the electricity. Even about the prickle and my feelings. But when I went downstairs to tell them, Sophia had pierced me with a glare before I could even get the words out, and I was quickly yanked back to reality; the reality that I had no one. No one to talk to. No one to help me.

Over the weekend, I tried not to worry about stuff, but it was a worthless effort. So I decided to search the internet for…well, I wasn't exactly sure what I was looking for, but I hoped I would know when I found it. Most of my research centered on Alex and Ailsin. But when I typed their names into the search engine, I got nothing. They didn't even have a Facebook page. Then again, neither did I. But really, who was I going to add to my friends list?

After awhile, I gave up and moved on to the electricity. Again, my searches brought up nothing. It was just like when I tried to find out about the prickle. There was a bunch of scientific stuff, but nothing remotely similar to what was happening between Alex and me.

So after hours of research, I still had no clue what was going on.

These unsolved mysteries left me with a massive sense of dread. I wasn't excited to go to astronomy on Monday. I even went to the extent of trying to fake sick so I could skip out on going to school. But that plan went to crap because Sophia hadn't bought my lame acting attempt at having the flu.

Thus, here I was, entering the astronomy classroom, my chest feeling like it was going to cave in on me at any moment. And just my luck, Alex and Aislin were already at our table. They were engaged in what looked like a very heavy conversation. I could tell by the seriousness in their expressions, and how they were leaning in like they were trying to create a barrier between themselves and everyone else around them. I could only guess what they were talking about.

I gave myself a quick mental pep talk. *You can do this. You aren't the one who should be nervous.* I straightened my shoulders and started up the stairs. I swear my shoes felt like they weighed a hundred pounds each. With every step, my breathing shortened.

For a moment, I thought I might faint.

Alex and Aislin didn't notice me until I sat down. Then they stopped talking. I avoided eye contact with them as I unzipped my bag and took out my book. But I could feel their eyes on me, watching me like hawks.

After I dragged out the process of taking my stuff out of my bag, I snuck a glance at Alex. He had on a black hooded jacket, and the color of his bright green eyes seemed to look a little darker today. Although it could have been from the death stare he was giving me.

I amazed myself when I actually glowered back at him. I think I might have shocked *him* too, because his death stare twisted into a look of puzzlement.

Aislin acted the absolute opposite of Alex. Her smile shined almost as much as the diamond necklace she was wearing. "Hi, Gemma."

By her overly cheerful tone, I could tell she was feigning being nice to me. I decided to play her little game, and

I politely smiled back at her. However, I think it came off more twitchy and nervous than I wanted.

Aislin, however, was a pro, her smile never faltering. "How was your weekend?"

"Great," I lied, sounding grumpy.

"Alright, everyone," Mr. Sterling said, clapping his hands together. "Let's get started."

And that was the last thing I heard. I tuned everything out as the electricity ignited and preoccupied every inch of my concentration. To make things even more distracting, Alex started staring at me. It sucked and made me squirm around uncomfortably.

The bell finally rang and class was dismissed. I quickly collected my things and shoved them into my messenger bag, feeling thankful that Mr. Sterling had been in one of his discussion modes and had left no time for group work.

I stood up, ready to bolt for the door right as Mr. Sterling decided to make an announcement.

"One more thing before you go." He waited for everyone to settle down before continuing. "As a group, I want you to complete a project. It can be any topic of your choice, just as long as it relates to astronomy. It's worth thirty percent of your grade, and you'll have to spend some time out of class working on it." He ignored the moans and groans that filled the room. "I will need you to tell me a basic idea of what your topic is going to be by tomorrow. There are more specific instructions in this."

He held up a packet of papers. "Make sure you pick one up as you leave class so you can start brainstorming ideas. That's it. Class dismissed."

A group project? Great. I swung the handle of my bag over my shoulder and dashed for the door, not slowing down until I made it safely to the corner of the library.

I couldn't find the book I had been reading—the one about the girl that had a superpower. After searching for several minutes, I finally spotted it lying sideways in front of the Encyclopedias, which were on the top shelf. Now, I was tall, but not tall enough. Even on my tiptoes, with my arm stretched out as far as it would go, I still came up inches short. I was just getting ready to make a jump for it, when an eruption of electricity rippled up my back.

I jolted backward.

"Need some help?" Alex asked, watching me with patronizing eyes.

I had to collect myself before I spoke so my voice would come out even. "No. I'm good."

He stepped closer and nodded at the shelf. "Which one are you trying to reach?"

"I—that one," I stammered, pointing at the book. Then I rolled my eyes at myself. *Get it together, Gemma.*

He reached over my head, the scent of his cologne fluttering in the air. In height, he had me by about four or five inches, and he grabbed the book effortlessly. "Here you go."

"Thanks." I took the book from him, being extra careful not to let my fingers touch him. If just being near him made my body buzz, I could only imagine what touching him would be like.

Without saying goodbye, I weaved my way through the maze of bookshelves until I was back at my normal spot. I was very aware that Alex had followed me, but was trying hard to ignore him.

I sat down on the floor and got comfortable.

He stared at me, clearly irritated. "I didn't just come here to get your book for you."

I opened the book up. "Then why did you?"

It got quiet. The only sound was coming from me flipping through the pages of the book.

"Aislin had me track you down," he said suddenly. "And since you seem to like hiding back here so much, I figured I'd find you here."

And there it was. The thing I was waiting for—for them to say they knew I had been eavesdropping on their conversation and had heard all the bizarre things they had been talking about.

Totally dumfounded on what to do or say, I kept searching through the book. The pages fanned my face with a cool breeze that felt nice against my heated skin.

Alex stole the book out of my hands.

"Hey." I grimaced.

He snapped the book shut. "Aislin wants to know if you'll meet us here after school so we can come up with an idea for our project." He spoke every syllable slowly, as if he thought I was slow.

That was it? That was all he wanted?

"Well, can you?" he asked impatiently.

I wanted to tell him no because I really, really didn't want to be around either one of them. Well, that was stretching the truth a little since, right now, every nerve in my body was pulling toward him. But that was because of the electricity. The stupid, obnoxious, make-your-mind-go-all-fuzzy electricity.

"If you guys want, you can just pick a topic without me," I offered, hoping he would say yes.

He shook his head. "Nope. We're supposed to work together as a group."

I raised my eyebrows accusingly. "I'm guessing you probably really don't give a crap whether we work on it as a group or not."

"Oh, I don't," he assured me. "But Aislin does."

I narrowed my eyes at him as I got to my feet. "Fine. I guess I'll be there then." I stuck out my hand. "Now, please give me back my book."

He pressed his lips together, took an unnecessary step toward me—totally invading my personal space—and placed the book in my hand. As he moved his hand away, one of his fingers brushed against mine. Whether it was an accident or not, who knew? But the smug smile on his face was making me think he probably did it intentionally, perhaps to try and torture me to death. And torture it was.

Not the chain-you-up-in-the-basement-without-any-food-or-water kind of torture, but more like the want-it-so-badly-lose-your-mind-because-you-know-you-can-never-have-it kind.

My hand shook as I fought to stay calm. I knew the worst thing to do was to let him see how much of an effect his touch had on me. On the inside, however, my body was going wild. My heart was erupting. My blood was racing. At that moment, I wanted nothing more than to be close to him.

For a split second, I thought I saw Alex's eyes widen, building my hope that maybe the touch was having the same effect on him. But it happened so quickly, I couldn't be certain if it actually happened. And before I knew it, he turned his back on me and left without saying another word.

What did my life used to be like? That was the question that ping-ponged through my brain during the rest of the school day. What had my life been like before I'd been able to feel? Before Alex had come along? Before the electricity had shown up? Oddly enough, even though the majority of my life had been spent without all of this, it didn't feel like it. In fact, my pre-feeling, pre-Alex, pre-electricity days seemed like such a long, long time ago.

But what was life without feeling, really? Nothing. And maybe that was why I was having a hard time remembering.

My last class of the day was a big crap-fest. I was called on three times, which has never happened to me before. But for some reason—who knows, maybe Alex's touch had left my skin glowing—I was the opposite of invisible. At least to Mr. Montgomery, my seventh period English teacher, who continued to call on me.

Gemma, can you tell us what one of the major themes is in Shakespeare's *Romeo and Juliet*? Gemma, what is the significance of the poison in the play? It wasn't like I didn't have the answers to his questions, but I hated being put on the spot. And I hated the fact that I stammered out my answers.

To top it all off, my locker got jammed, and in the middle of kicking the crap out of it, a teacher strolled by and scolded me. By the time I sank down into a chair in the library, I was in no mood to deal with any more crap. Really, I probably should have skipped out on the meeting, since Alex had the tendency to get under my skin.

I also had a major headache. My brain felt like it was boiling inside my skull. God, I was going to have to take up yoga to deal with all this stress.

I rested my head on the table. The wood was cold against my warm skin. I massaged the sides of my temples, and let my eyes drift closed. I took a slow breath and tried to bury all of my problems.

But then a current of electricity weaved its way up my spine, and I groaned as my endeavor at relaxing flew out the window.

Alex dropped his bag on the table. "Headache?"

"Yep," I replied snippily. *And it's sitting right next to me.*

"Gemma, what's wrong?" The voice belonged to Aislin.

I raised my head up. She was standing on the other side of the table, a pink purse draped across her shoulder, her forehead creased over with concern.

"She has a headache," Alex answered for me.

"I'm fine," I told her. "Really. It's not a big deal."

"Hold on, I think I have something." She retrieved a bottle of Tylenol from her purse. "Here you go."

I gratefully took the bottle, poured two in my hand, and gave it back to her. "Thanks."

She smiled and tossed the bottle back in her bag. "No problem."

I plopped them into my mouth and forced them down my throat. Hopefully they would kick in quick. If I was lucky, maybe they would also numb out the electricity along with the headache.

Aislin sat down. "Okay, so does anyone have any ideas on what we should do for our project?"

"Whatever's easiest," Alex said. Then he glanced at me and added, "And takes the least amount of time."

I rolled my eyes.

"Don't be ridiculous, Alex," Aislin said, like it was the most absurd thing ever. "We need to do a good job. I would really like to get an A. And I'm sure you would too, right, Gemma?"

Typically, sure, but right now…hmm…not so much. All I wanted right now was to leave.

"I don't mind if we do something easy." I flicked a glance in Alex's direction. "And short."

"Good, then it's settled." He leaned back in his chair and rested his hands behind his head. "We'll pick something easy."

Aislin scowled at him.

"So, what I am thinking," he continued, ignoring Aislin's scowl, "is that we could just make a galaxy map and type up a report to go with it. That way we wouldn't have to spend very much time working on it together."

"Great. Sounds good." I got up, my chair tipping backward on two legs, then falling forward on all fours again. I snatched by bag off the table and turned to leave.

"Gemma, wait." Aislin leapt up from her chair. She put her hands on her hips and pinned Alex with an angry look. "Don't you think that project is a little too *easy*?"

He waved his hand, brushing her off. "It'll be fine."

I did a mental count to ten while I waited to see if they would say anything else. They didn't and I left.

Outside, a ghostlike fog blanketed the parking lot. I made my way in the direction of where I hoped my car was. I was still all riled up over Alex and how he had made it clear that he wanted to see as little of me as possible. I was also kind of mad at myself for not telling him off.

I was in the middle of figuring out whether or not I was walking around in circles when I was hit with the feeling that someone was watching me. Suddenly, I became hyperaware that there wasn't a single soul in sight.

I picked up my pace, my black DC sneakers thudding against the ice. It was the only sound that filled the air until a crackle rose over it. I glanced down at the ground. The ice looked like it was moving. Yes, moving, right along with the pace of my footsteps. My heart stuttered as my nightmare flashed through my mind. Me running. The monsters chasing me. Ice moving underneath me.

I ran, but not very fast since the ground was one big accident waiting to happen. I kept telling myself nightmares don't come true. Glowing, yellow-eyed monsters that kill people with their death chill aren't real. But as I felt the air abruptly descend to a bone chilling temperature, I freaked out.

I searched frantically for my car, slipping all over the ice like I was trying to be part of the Ice Capades. But I couldn't spot my car anywhere. I desperately strained my eyes against the thick fog, and then I saw it: not my car, but a flicker of yellow.

My heart stopped.

I gasped as the prickle traced the back of my neck. I had felt fear before, but this was a whole new level of fear; a run-for-your-life-or-you're-going-to-die kind of fear.

Which was exactly what I was going to do. I spun around, preparing to make a mad sprint back to the school. Except before I could work up a run, I slammed into something hard and warm and static charged. I stumbled backwards, scrambling to get my footing.

"What is wrong with you?" Alex asked, his voice a mix of irritation and concern.

I regained my balance and stood up straight. "Nothing. I'm fine."

His dark brown hair was damp from the fog, and tucked underneath his arm was a book. "It doesn't look like nothing. You look scared."

My heart drummed violently in my chest. I was scared. I glanced back over my shoulder. Nothing but fog.

"Gemma."

I turned back to Alex. "Huh?"

"Are you okay? You look a little...lost?"

I was lost. And confused. And terrified.

The air was starting to warm back up. It was still freezing and everything, but a normal freezing instead of a deathly freezing.

"I, um..." I swallowed hard, choking on the mental image of the yellow lights. Had it really been there? I hadn't actually seen the cloaked figure; just two little lights shaped as eyes. Or at least they looked like eyes. Without the overload of adrenaline pounding though me anymore, I wasn't so sure.

Alex's gaze wandered over my shoulder. "What were you looking at over there?"

"Um...nothing." There was no way I was going to tell him what I thought I saw. "I just thought I saw...a dog." I did a mental eye roll at myself. *A dog? Really, Gemma? You can't come up with anything better than that?*

He eyed me over suspiciously, and then his eyebrow arched up. "You're afraid of dogs?"

"No," I responded automatically.

"You were scared though," he pointed out. "So scared you ran into me."

"Well..." I wanted to smack myself for being such a terrible liar. I struggled to think of an excuse—any excuse I could give. "What does it even matter to you, anyway?" I snapped. "I mean, it's not like you really care."

"Yeah, good point." He shoved the book he was holding at me. "You left this in the library by the way."

I furrowed my eyebrows at the book, perplexed because I couldn't remember taking my book out of my bag while I was in the library.

"This is the part where you say thanks," he said arrogantly.

I wanted to slap the arrogance right off his pretty little face, but I didn't. I snatched the book from his hand and said, "Thanks."

He pressed his lips together and gave a quick glance behind me. "Well...drive carefully."

I gave him a funny look. Drive carefully? What was that supposed to mean? Well, I know what it means in the literal sense but...I gaped at him as he sauntered away, feeling, once again, as lost ever.

After he vanished through the fog, I ran like hell to find my car.

Chapter 6

The drive home was a blur of shapes and colors. I barely saw anything and I couldn't pay attention. My mind was still back in the parking lot where I thought I saw the lights.

My hands were sweating disgustingly as I grasped the steering wheel tightly. I was edgy and jumpy and constantly checking in the rearview mirror for any trace of yellow lights in the shape of eyes.

I wasn't exactly sure what I had seen in the foggy parking lot, but I wasn't going to take any chances. If my nightmares had crossed over into real life, then I was going to have to keep myself on high alert.

I parked my car in the driveway, jumped out, and dashed inside the house, dead bolting the door behind me. I could hear the TV humming in the living room. Marco and Sophia were home, which made me feel slightly safer. I went up to my room and locked my door. Then I sank to the floor.

This wasn't happening. This couldn't be happening. It had to be a dream. How could it not be? To find out if I was dreaming or not, I did the only thing I could think. I pinched my arm hard. It stung and a pink welt formed on my skin.

Well, that was a great idea.

I sighed, getting to my feet. I had two options here and neither one of them was appealing. The first, and my least favorite: wait it out; see what happens. The second option I wasn't too fond of either: tell Marco and Sophia. This meant risking looking like I was a total nut job. But getting killed seemed worse. So with a million knots tying their way into my stomach, I headed downstairs.

You know that feeling you get when you walk into a room and the air feels thick and heavy and you know you were just being talked about? Well, that's what happened when I found Marco and Sophia, huddled together at the kitchen table, talking quietly. I instantly got the impression they were talking about me. And by the horrified expressions on their faces when they saw me, I assumed my impression was right.

Sophia leaned back in the chair and smoothed out her grey skirt. "Do you need something, Gemma?"

I eyed her over suspiciously. "I'm not sure." Something felt off, and my insides were screaming at me to keep my mouth shut.

Marco swiped a magazine up from the table and fumbled to open it, mumbling incoherently underneath his breath.

"Well, if you don't need anything..." Sophia drifted out of her chair and roamed over to the cupboards.

I stood in the doorway, watching her closely as she moved over to the pantry, grabbed a can of tomato sauce, and fought to get the lid off.

I glanced at the clock: 4:30. A little too early to be making dinner. Yet there she was, making dinner. I turned my attention to Marco. He shook the magazine out, and then turned his back to me.

What in the world had I been thinking? I should have known better than to believe I could talk to them. I didn't even know them. Not really. I mean, for all I knew the real reason I have been living with them for the last seventeen years was because they kidnapped me. Yeah, I really didn't think that was true or anything, but until I could prove it wasn't true, I wasn't going to disregard the theory.

The next day at school, I felt like a walking zombie. I slept like crap the night before because of my nightmares. Of course, I had no trouble sleeping during biology. When the bell rang, it woke me up, and scared the crap out of me, causing me to leap from my seat and bang my knee on the desk. Not to mention my cheek had been resting on my arm, right where my studded bracelet was fastened, so now there was a sequence of dots indented into the side of my face. Which in no way made me look like a bigger dork, let me tell you. Add the humiliation factor with the giant bruise on my knee, and I felt awesome.

My next stop was astronomy. I arrived early and the classroom was empty. The emptiness immediately made me uneasy. Goose bumps sprouted all over my skin as I hung my messenger bag on the back of the chair and sat down. God, I was so tired. I needed a nap.

As soon as the first person entered, I rested my head on the table and let my eyelids slip shut. But moments later, a warm tingly sensation shot up my arms and reverberated down my back.

"Tired?" Alex remarked. I heard a chair slide out and then something landed on the table not too far from my head. His backpack, I assumed.

I didn't say anything. Nor did I look at him. I just wasn't in the mood to deal with him.

He didn't say anything else to me, and I didn't raise my head until class started. That was when I realized Aislin's chair was vacant.

"She's not here today," he said, noticing the direction of my gaze. He was wearing a black shirt, the sleeves pushed up to his elbows. He looked good. He always looked good. Too bad he was such a jerk. "She has the flu," he added.

"Oh." I frowned. So it was just him and me? Well, today ought to be fun. About as fun as watching a two hour special on fungi growth (and yeah, I've actually had to do that before). Aislin acted as our mediator. With her gone, I could only imagine how well the next forty-five minutes was going to go.

"You don't need to look so upset about it." A smirk threatened at his lips. "I'm not that bad to be around, am I?"

Afraid of what might come out of my mouth, I kept it shut.

Ten minutes into class, Mr. Sterling received a phone call. After he hung up, he made an announcement that there was something urgent that needed his attention, and he was going to take the class to the library so we could get started on our projects.

I considered ditching. Going home and taking a nap. But I couldn't muster up enough courage to go through with it. Mark Scholy and Dean Edwards did. They ducked out as soon as Mrs. Bakerly stepped away from her desk. But they didn't have to worry about a group of freaky yellow-eyed monsters showing up to kill them.

"So what do you want to work on first?" Alex asked me after we picked out a table.

I hung my messenger bag on the back of a chair. "It doesn't matter to me."

He took his cell phone out of his pocket and glanced at the screen. "Well, it doesn't matter to me either."

We both stood there, mulling over what to do next, and I caught him staring at my eyes. Not into my eyes — at my eyes. Typically when people stared at them, they were awestruck by the shocking color of violet, which bugged me. However, the way Alex was looking at them erased my normal ping of annoyance, and made my insides melt like hot butter.

Then, of course, he had to open his mouth and ruin everything. "Maybe you should go home and get some sleep. You look tired."

He might as well have told me I looked like hell.

I shot him a scowl, turned my back on him, and marched off toward the bookshelves. Not necessarily to look for a book, but to get away from him.

He followed after me. "I didn't mean that in a bad way. I was just suggesting that maybe you should get some more sleep."

"That would be nice if it were possible." I stopped in front of a shelf and skimmed the titles of the books. Realizing I was in the romance section—the last place I wanted to be—I rounded the corner to the fiction section, with Alex trailing at my heels.

"Are you having nightmares or something?" His eyes met mine, and I momentarily spaced out.

"Yes." I blinked and shook my head. "I mean no."

His smile was mocking. "Which one is it? Yes or no?"

"Yes, I had a nightmare," I snapped. "But what does it matter to you?"

He shrugged. "It doesn't."

I bit down on my tongue to stop myself from sticking it out like a three-year-old. *Don't let him get to you. Don't let him get to you.* "You know, I could just write the report for us," I said. "And then you and Aislin could put the galaxy map together. That way you and I wouldn't have to work together."

"What are you trying to do, get rid of me or something?" he teased.

"No," I answered mechanically. Wait. Where did that come from?

He grinned haughtily.

"Oh, would you just go away?" I yanked a random book from the shelf and fixed my attention on reading the back cover.

Before he could say another snide remark—because I'm almost positive he had one ready—his phone rang from inside his pocket. Instead of answering it, he silenced it. "Actually, I was thinking about cutting out early."

I should have been relieved, but for some reason I developed a nauseated feeling in the pit of my stomach. "Okay, go ahead. I won't say anything."

"Oh, I know you won't." He slid his hands into his pockets. "I was just telling you in case you wanted to come along."

I gaped at him. "You have got to be kidding."

"Nope," he said. "You really look like you could use a break."

I had no idea what to say. Although, I knew what my heart was telling me to do—*go with him.* But he hated me. I knew that. He had to be teasing me. Playing his little Alex mind games.

65

He ambled over to the end of the aisle and glanced over his shoulder, flashing me a taunting smile. "That is unless you are too scared."

I should have been—after what he just said. But for a split second—a very crucial, decision making second—I conveniently forgot about everything. How he repeatedly treated me like crap. And I magically shoved the electric feeling right out of my mind, along with the conversation I overheard between him and Aislin.

Alex disappeared around the corner of the shelf and headed back to our table. I followed after him, Kelsey Merritt and her clones throwing me dirty looks as I passed by them.

"So where exactly are you going?" I asked him.

"It's a surprise," he said, shoving his books into his bag.

Don't go, my inner conscious screamed at me. "Okay, I'm in."

He swung his bag over his shoulder, and I could hear the smile in his voice when he said, "Let's go then."

I hesitated, suddenly unsure. Was I out of my mind? Going off with him—after everything that had happened between us?

But then he dazzled me with the most beautiful, heart-melting smile—the kind of smile I have wanted him to give me since the first day I laid eyes on him—and that was that. The rational part of my brain quit working.

Without a second thought, I grabbed my bag and followed him out the door.

Chapter 7

As soon as I realized where Alex was taking me, I went into panic mode. I even temporarily contemplated jumping out of the moving vehicle.

After I followed Alex out of the library, we went out to the parking lot and climbed into his car—an old cherry red Chevy Camaro. It was a beautiful car. But a beautiful car that was taking me toward the mountains, something that I realized a little too late. Here I was alone with a guy I barely knew—a strange guy I barely knew—and I was going straight to the place where I was killed every night in my nightmares. I had really gotten myself into a mess here, hadn't I? I can't believe how stupid and irrational I was. I mean, a cute boy finally smiles at me and I forget all logic.

But there was nothing I could do about it now except strap my seatbelt on, watch the town slip farther and farther away, and keep my fingers crossed that everything would turn out alright.

I tapped my fingers anxiously on my knee. In the confined space of the car, the electricity hummed powerfully. Between that, the heater blaring, and my jittery nerves, I was starting to sweat. "So where exactly are we going?" I asked.

"We're going to two places, actually," Alex told me, down shifting the car. "But the first stop is just so I can pick something up."

I wiped my sweaty palm on my jeans. "So what's the second stop?"

He flashed me a devious smile. "That one's a secret."

A secret? Secrets were rarely good. And since it was Alex...let's just say I wasn't feeling too optimistic, especially since he was being nice. Well, nice for him, anyway. It made me even edgier than I already was, and I couldn't help but wonder if he had some kind of hidden agenda for bringing me out here.

A lump formed in my throat as I mentally cursed myself for coming with him.

He lifted an eyebrow at me. "Is something wrong? You look scared."

"What?" I shook my head. "No. I'm not scared."

"Really? Because you sure look like you are."

I fiddled with the zipper on my messenger bag, deliberating what to say. The truth. Sure, why not? "Well, I guess maybe I'm a little scared."

He slowed down the car and made a right turn off the main highway and onto a snow packed back road that laced over the foothills. These kinds of roads were the kind that the snow plows only plowed a few miles up, which meant we probably wouldn't be able to make it that far up it. Or at least the car wouldn't be able to go further. On foot, well, that was a different story.

I gulped at that frightening thought.

"So why are you scared?" Alex asked.

I shrugged, trying not to get freaked out by the sight of the trees trimming the sides of the road. Or by thinking about what might be hiding in them. "Because...well, I really don't know anything about you other than you hate me."

"I don't hate you," he told me, and oddly enough, he sounded like he was telling the truth. "I'm just moody. It's nothing personal."

Moody. So the understatement of the year.

I tore my gaze away from the trees and looked at him. He was staring ahead, eyes focused on the road. As much as I hated to admit it, the guy was gorgeous. Bright green eyes, dark hair, perfect lips. He wasn't too thin, nor too big and bulky. He was a happy medium—lean and nice.

Very nice.

A crooked smile crept up on his face as he turned his head toward me. "You're staring."

I whipped my head back toward the window, feeling like a total idiot. "No, I wasn't."

He laughed but said nothing.

A few minutes later, he was parking the car in front of an old log cabin. A crooked gray stone chimney topped the roof, and a partly collapsed deck wrapped around the bottom. The windows were boarded up, and the entire yard

70

was buried in at least five feet of snow except for a recently shoveled walkway.

He pulled the emergency brake and left the engine running. "Wait here. I'll be right back." He got out of the car, trampled up to the front door of the cabin and entered without knocking.

My nerves were bouncing as I sat in the car alone. There were trees all over the place. What if they were out there, watching me, waiting for the perfect moment to jump out and kill me? We were so far away from civilization, if something did happen, I was in trouble. I bet I couldn't even get a signal on my cell phone.

I tapped my fingers on my knee as I counted backwards from one hundred, trying to stay calm. *Breathe*, I told myself. *Just breathe.*

Thankfully, Alex came out of the cabin before I got too worked up. Light, fluffy snowflakes had started to float down from the sky and frost now laced the car windows.

"What were you doing in there?" I asked as he climbed back inside the car.

He rubbed his hands together, warming them up. "Nothing important." He flipped the windshield wipers on. "I just needed to check on something."

"I thought you said you needed to pick something up?"

He shrugged and backed out onto the road, the car's tires spinning in protest.

The snowflakes became thicker the farther up the mountain we drove. The windshield wipers were working overtime so Alex could see. Just as I was starting to worry that the car was going to get stuck, we came to a stop in the middle of the road. I assumed he was turning around since the only things around were mountains, snow, and trees. But instead, he killed the engine.

"What are you doing?" I asked nervously.

"We're here." He gestured at the scenery outside. "This is it."

I frowned. "Where are we?"

"The mountains."

I gave him a *duh* look. "I know that, but why are we here?"

"Because this is the place I wanted take you." It seemed like he was trying to tiptoe around the details of why he drove me out into the middle of the mountains.

I grew more uneasy. "You wanted to take me to the middle of the mountains."

"Yeah." He opened the car door. "But you have to get out of the car and walk a little in order to get to the exact spot I want you to see."

Get out in the middle of the woods. Was he crazy? "Yeah, I'm not sure that's such a good idea."

He shot me a quizzical look. "What exactly is it you're afraid of?"

Hmmm...What was I afraid of? How about the image of me running for my life through the trees? However, there was no way I could explain that to him. "I don't know...I really just don't feel like walking around in the snow. That's all."

"Don't worry, I promise it'll be worth it." He smiled, this beautiful, hypnotic smile—the same smile that had lured me to follow him out of the library and into his car. Before I even realized what I was doing, I was getting out of the car. But when the cold air hit my face, it knocked me back to reality. *Get back in the car.* I shivered, debating if I should do just that.

Alex took off toward a narrow path caped by leafless trees, and motioned for me to follow. I gulped, my hands shaking—from the cold or from my nerves, I couldn't tell you—and then I tromped through the snow after him.

The great thing about wearing sneakers while you're hiking through the snow is...nothing; absolutely nothing. Unless you think your feet getting wet and frozen is a great thing.

On a more positive note, it had stopped snowing.

But the air was still cold, and I was shivering so badly my limbs were aching. "How far is it exactly?"

"Not too much further," he answered. "Why? Are you cold already?"

"No," I lied. "I was just wondering."

"Okay. Whatever you say," he said, unconvinced.

"Really, I'm not," I repeated, feeling the need to defend myself.

He didn't say anything, but by the way his body was shaking, I was pretty sure he was laughing at me.

Rounding a corner, we came across a large branch, dangling low to the ground. It blocked out the entire path. Great. Going over it would take a climbing ability I so did not possess. And going around it meant wading through at least a few feet of snow. My jeans would get soaked.

I took it as a sign that we should head back. "Umm...maybe we should..." I started, but Alex was already lifting the branch over his head like it weighed nothing. The thing had to weigh a ton, though—it was gigantic.

"Go ahead." Alex gestured with his free hand for me to go underneath the branch. "Ladies first."

Part of me wondered, as I ducked beneath it, if he would drop it on me. I know the thought was ridiculous, but after everything that had happened, could you really blame me?

Although he didn't drop it on me, my hair did get tangled around it. I struggled to get my hair loose, but my fingers were too cold and numb and wouldn't work properly. Plus, my neck was tipped back in this awkward position that made things even more difficult.

"Hold on," Alex said. I could feel him moving around and then my hair being gently pulled on. He was standing so close to me and touching my hair; it made my head buzz like a beehive full of bees.

"There," he said, and my head was freed from the un-comfortable position.

I had been holding my breath the whole time, and I let it out, a white puff of smoke rising in front of my face. I quickly scooted out of the way so Alex could slip under-neath the branch and let it go.

He dusted the snow off of his hands while I smoothed my now damp hair back into place. Well, as much in place as it had been to begin with.

Alex watched me, seeming amused. "You good?"

I zipped up my coat and tucked my hands in the pockets. "Yeah, I guess."

"Alright, then." He brushed past me and headed down the trail again.

With every step I took, my heart beat fiercer. We were distancing ourselves farther and farther from the car, and the trees were becoming denser. For all I knew, any spot could have been "the spot." The spot where I kept dying over and over again in my nightmares. It was hard to tell though, because a forest was a forest. Everything looked the same. And in my nightmares, my death took place dur-ing the night, when the sky was black and the ground was a giant shadow.

I have never been in a forest in real life before. I was quickly learning that despite the stillness the air held, there was a lot of chaos. I could almost feel the things hiding out in the bushes and trees that surrounded us. Things that I wasn't sure I really wanted to see.

Every time the wind blew, I swear it was whispering *danger*. The branches of the trees canopied above me, making it seem darker than it truly was. Then there was Alex. Amazingly, he had been fairly quiet. He was too quiet, if you ask me. Maybe he was being that way because of the electricity firing between us. I couldn't be certain how much of an effect it was having on him, but personally I felt fully awake and alive because of it. Every single one of my senses felt sharp. My skin was tingling from head to toe, which helped fade out some of the cold, so I guess that was a plus.

As I was plucking a piece of a dead pine needle out of my hair, I heard a branch snap from behind me. I skidded to a halt and spun around, my gaze skimming through the trees. But I couldn't see anything but branches and snow. I was about to turn back around when a huge gust of wind whipped through the air. I heard another *snap*, this time much, much closer. *Okay, okay. It's just an animal...a deer or something.*

Yeah, maybe it was some kind of forest animal, but I wasn't going to take any chances. I whirled back around and hurried to catch up to Alex.

As I tried to catch my breath and calm down, I heard it. Not a snapping twig. No, this sound was way worse. A crackle, like the one I heard in the school parking lot the day I saw the glowing yellow eyes. Fear rocketed through me. I had no idea what to do. Turn and sprint back to the car? Try and explain to Alex what was happening to me? Neither sounded appealing.

My heart drummed in my chest as I shot a glance over my shoulder. There were only trees and snow. I turned back around, only to end up slamming straight into Alex. My forehead banged against his shoulder, and a fire ignited under my skin. I gasped, backing away from him.

Holding his hands out in front of him, he cautiously stepped away from me. "You okay?"

I nodded, rubbing my forehead. "Sorry. I wasn't watching where I was going."

"Yeah, I got that." He nodded at the trees behind me. "What were you looking at back there?"

"Nothing." My voice squeaked. "I just thought I heard something, but it was nothing."

He eyed me over, then, apparently satisfied by my answer, spread his hands out to the side of him. "Well, this is it."

"Huh?" I stared at him blankly. "This is what?"

"This is what I wanted to show you."

Funny, but my near panic attack had made me forget why we came up here in the first place. "Okay..." I glimpsed at all of the trees and snow around us. What was so special about this particular spot? It looked just like every other spot. "It's...nice, I guess."

He laughed a genuine, heartfelt laugh. The kind of laugh that made his green eyes light up. "Gemma, this right here," he pointed to a spot on the ground in front of him, "is what I wanted to show you."

For a brief second, I got lost in the way he said my name in a normal, anti-hating voice. But I quickly forgot about it when I caught a glimpse of what he was pointing at. In the middle of the crisp white snow, right between our feet, a small spot of dirt showed through like the snow instantly melted away when it landed there. And the dirt wasn't brown, but black and ashy.

I looked back up and found Alex watching me with curious eyes.

"What?" I asked. "Why are you looking at me like that?"

He shrugged. "No reason."

I shook my head. Whatever. "So what is it?" I asked, pointing at the ashy spot.

"Well…" He tapped his finger on his lips. "See, there's this legend that about twenty years ago, a star fell from the sky and landed right here." He pointed to the strange spot. "And I'm not talking about a meteorite, but an actual star."

I frowned. He had to be joking. "If a real star hit the Earth, then you and I wouldn't be standing here talking."

"Now that's where you're wrong," he said simply. "It wasn't a whole star that fell, but a small piece that broke loose when the star began to spin too quickly. And when the piece hit this spot, the snow has never been able to stick here. It's like the heat of the star is still trapped there, and it melts the snow away."

"I've never heard of anything like that," I told him. "Are you sure you're not just trying to..."

"Trying to what?"

I sighed. "Pull one over on me."

He grinned. "Now why would I do something like that?"

I rolled my eyes. "I think the real question is why wouldn't you do something like that?"

He deliberated this. "Yeah, I can see where you're coming from. But I'm not."

We both stood there for a moment, staring at one another, my blood boiling from the electric heat.

"So if this actually did happen, then why haven't I heard of it before?" I asked, breaking the silence.

"Because hardly anyone knows about it." He paused before adding, "Even some mediocre high school astronomy teacher."

"Mr. Sterling isn't that bad," I said. "And he knows a lot about astronomy."

He lifted an eyebrow. "He isn't that bad? Wasn't he the one who put you and me together in a group?"

That stung. "Yeah...but..." I had no idea what to say.

"Relax." He cracked a smile. "I'm just kidding."

I tucked my hands up into the sleeves of my coat. "Kidding about the star or Mr. Sterling?"

His smile broadened. "Mr. Sterling."

As much as I was glad to hear that, I still wasn't feeling too ecstatic about the idea that he was still trying to convince me that an actual piece of a star had fallen. The idea was absurd. A real piece of a star—I have never heard of anything so insane. Okay, I take that back. I guess I have.

"So, why is it that people don't know about this *'fallen star'*?" I asked, making air quotes.

"Well, for starters, the piece was only about the size of a baseball." He hesitated, shifting his weight to the side. "And ...well supposedly there was this secret group who came and collected it before anyone could discover it had fallen."

I stared at him like he was crazy. And, who knew, maybe he was.

"You think I'm lying." He crossed his arms and leaned in toward me. My heart reacted with a jolt that nearly knocked the breath out of me. "But I'm not."

I had to catch my breath before I spoke. "How am I supposed to know whether you're lying or not? I don't know you at all. I mean for all I know, you could be the world's greatest liar."

He pressed his lips together, pausing before he said, "Yeah, you're right. You don't know me. But taking you out here was me trying to let you get to know me." He moved in closer to me, and I could feel the warmth of his breath on my face. "But you're not making it very easy for me."

"I..." My mind clouded, and it wasn't until he moved away from me that I could think clearly and process words again. "So what you're saying is there's a group that took the fallen star?"

He nodded. "That's what I'm saying."

"So who is this group?"

"Now that's a secret I can't tell you."

I sighed. I was so confused. "So, what happens if I touch the spot?"

"Why don't you try it and find out?"

I stared apprehensively at the ashy spot. There was something off about it. The color, the charcoal texture, the way the snow didn't cover it.

"Don't worry," Alex said, "I'm pretty sure you won't set on fire or anything."

"Pretty sure," I muttered. Well, that was reassuring.

I took a deep breath and bent down, letting my fingers brush up against the spot. It didn't feel hot or anything. Not even warm. But there was something off about it. Something different, but I couldn't quite put my finger on what it was. It almost felt sparkly....or maybe it was more electric.

"Feel anything?" Alex asked.

"Not really." I let the tips of my fingers rest against the spot for a few seconds longer, then pulled my hand away and stood up. "It's not even warm."

"Huh..." He furrowed his eyebrows as he studied me over.

My pulse sped up like a bolt of lightning had shot out from the sky and zapped me in the chest. You would think after a couple of weeks of feeling the sparks I would have gotten use to it. *You would think* being the key words. But that wasn't the case. In fact, I could still barely remember how to breathe whenever I felt it.

The wind started to pick up again, twirling flakes of snow around in the air like pixie dust. The sky had become shaded with clouds. Sundown was nearing, and it looked as if a storm might be moving in.

"Well." Alex ran his fingers through his hair. "We should probably get going before it gets dark."

"Sounds like a good idea," I agreed.

I had been so swept up in Alex's story about the star that I temporarily pushed the yellow-eyed death monsters out of my mind. But when we started the walk back to the car and the silence set in, my mind raced back to the what-if's. What if the monsters were hiding out there? What if they were real? What if they showed up and tried to kill me?

Needless to say, I was beyond thankful when we made it safely back inside the car. It was then that I silently vowed to myself that I would never go up into the mountains again, unless it was absolutely necessary.

By the time Alex was turning the Camaro onto the main road, darkness had settled around us. The glow of the headlights glistened against the icy roads as we inched nearer to town. Alex and I hadn't spoken a word to each other since we headed back to the car, and I was still confused as to why he had brought me up to the mountains in the first place. To tell me about the fallen star? It seemed like a really strange reason.

"So." He dimmed the headlights for a SUV passing by in the opposite direction. "You live with your grandparents?"

"Huh?" It had been quiet for so long that his voice startled me. "Yeah, I do. But how did you know that?

He shrugged. "And you like to be by yourself a lot too, I've noticed."

"I guess." Like always, I was confused. "What's with the analysis?"

"I'm just curious...about you." He gave me a sideways glance. "I find you fascinating."

"Fascinating?" I gave him a doubtful look. "I highly doubt that. I think the word you're looking for is annoying."

He chuckled softly, shaking his head. "I already told you, I'm just a moody person."

"You can say that again." I paused, realizing it was kind of a bitchy thing to say. I made what I hoped looked like an apologetic face. "Sorry."

He laughed. "Well, there's a cute side of you."

I chewed on my lip, replaying his words. Cute? Had he meant it as a compliment?

Suddenly, the radio, which had been playing quietly in the background, cut out and static screeched through speakers. The sound was like nails on a chalkboard, and I threw my hands over my ears.

Alex hurried and turned the volume down. He pointed to the visor above my head. "Grab one of those CD's and put it in, would you?"

I lowered my hands from my ears and flipped the visor down. Oh, my word. I was in heaven. Okay, so let me explain why. I have developed a huge obsession with music over the last couple of months. An obsession that has played a bit of a part in the whole Marco and Sophia vs. Gemma showdown because, apparently, blasting music is a very rude thing to do. Sophia had threatened to take my computer away if I didn't stop listening to music. But I love music way too much to quit listening to it completely. I was in love with the lyrics, the rhythm, and the way it could sweep me away to another world.

What was exciting here was that Alex had a great selection. Chevelle, Hawthorne Heights, Dashboard Confessional; they were all such great bands.

I decided on Rise Against and slid it into the CD player. Five seconds later, the intro popped on.

"You like Rise Against?" He sounded somewhat shocked.

"Yeah." What was with all the weird questions? "Why do you sound so surprised?"

"I just hadn't pegged that about you."

"Pegged what about me? That I wouldn't like music? Or that I wouldn't listen to Rise Against?"

He pressed the skip button, skipping the CD to the next song. "That you are the kind of person who likes listening to music."

"Why?" I felt my skin warm. And it was not from the electricity. Nope, I was getting pissed. "What kind of person would I have to be to like listening to music?"

He frowned. "Gemma, I'm not trying to insult you. I'm just trying to get to know you better. That's all."

"Oh." I wasn't sure if he was telling the truth or not. He sounded like he was though. "Well, I like music, especially the soul speaking kind."

His expression fell into a look of horror.

"What's wrong?" I asked. Had I said something offensive? After all, I was a bit of a newbie at the whole socializing thing, but he was saying a lot of strange stuff too, so...I don't know.

"It's nothing." He shook his head. "Sorry." His smile returned, but it looked forced. He fiddled with the heater, turning it up full blast. Then he cranked up the volume of the music so loud the windows vibrated.

I took it as a very unsubtle hint that our conversation was over, so I stopped talking.

Neither one of us made so much as a peep until he pulled back into the school parking lot and parked his Camaro next to my Mirage, which was now covered in a thin layer of snow.

He turned the volume down and said in a polite tone, "Thanks for taking a break with me."

Matching his polite tone, I replied, "Well, thanks for the break."

"Yep, no problem."

I opened the door and climbed out into the cold night. The parking lot was empty except for my car and his. There was only a single lamppost that actually worked, so it was basically dark.

I went to shut the door, but then Alex said my name so I paused.

"Sweet dreams," he said, in a soft voice that made goose bumps sprout up on my skin.

I smiled as I closed the door. Then I jumped in my car and let it warm up just long enough for the ice to melt away from the windshield. To my surprise, Alex waited for me to leave before he did. He followed me out of the school parking lot, staying close behind me until I made a right turn onto Main Street. There, he turned left, his headlights disappearing and taking my sense of comfort right along with them.

All the lights in my two-story red brick home were off when I pulled into the driveway. It was only a little after seven, too early for Marco and Sophia to be in bed. They must have gone out for dinner or something.

I locked the back door behind me and stumbled around in the dark until I found the light switch and flipped it on. I grabbed a Coke and an apple from the fridge and headed upstairs to my room, debating whether or not to do my homework. My brain was distracted by the weird day I had. The weird day I spent with Alex.

My day with Alex.

Holy freaking cow.

A light turned on behind me.

"And where have you been?"

I whirled around, almost dropping the can of Coke.

Sophia was standing at the bottom of the stairs with her hands on her hips. She had a fluffy pink robe on, and her auburn hair was curled up in rollers. I guess I was wrong when I assumed she had gone out. But what had she been doing, waiting around in the dark for me to show up?

It was so weird.

"I was out with...a friend," I told her, knowing how unnatural the word "friend" sounded coming out of my mouth.

She narrowed her eyes. "You don't have any friends."

"Yes I do," I protested. "Sort of."

"If that's the case, then why haven't I seen any of these *friends*?"

"Maybe because I don't want to bring them over here," I snapped hotly.

A strand of her hair unwound from a roller and bounced in front of her face. "What's wrong with 'over here'?"

I gave an exhausted sigh. "Nothing's wrong with here. I don't know why you care about any of this anyway."

Her eyes widened. "I don't." She pushed past me and marched up the stairs, calling over her shoulder, "In fact, I don't care what you do at all."

Her words hurt me like a knife to the heart. I mean, I always assumed she never liked me very much, but now that she put it out there...I felt like I might cry. They didn't care about me.

No one did.

Tears stung at my eyes. *Breathe,* I commanded myself. *You will not cry.* I sucked back the tears and dragged my butt up to my room, where I changed into my pajamas and crawled into the welcoming warmth of my bed. It was early, but I was exhausted.

Outside my window, the clouds had parted. The moon smoldered against the blackness of the sky; the stars twinkled harmoniously around it. I felt that same strange pull that I always did whenever I looked up at the night sky. It made me feel like I belonged up there, shining with the stars.

Sometimes it felt like it was the only place I did belong.

Chapter 8

I had this feeling that maybe school was going to be different. Okay, so perhaps I was being a little overly hopeful, but I was still crossing my fingers that the tension between Alex and me would lessen now that we had our semi-bonding moment.

Of course, I hadn't forgotten the crazy story he told me about the fallen star. Last night, I even dreamt about it. In the dream, I was the star falling fiercely from the sky. When I woke up, I still felt like I was falling.

Honestly, I didn't mind the dream, and the break it had given me from my repetitious nightmare—it was nice to take a break from dying. And since the little parking lot incident, I hadn't seen any sign of the glowing yellow eyes roaming around in the real world, so that was an added bonus. I also decided to push Sophia's harsh and hurtful comments out of my mind. I was going to have a good day today; a good, worry-free day.

At least I hoped.

My morning went by pretty okay. Nothing too traumatic happened. I did have a bit of a concentration problem, but no one seemed to notice, and when astronomy class rolled around I felt myself getting excited. The feeling was new to me and kind of a fun one.

I took a seat at my table, feeling restless for Alex to show up so I could see how he was going to treat me. But when the bell rang, Alex and Aislin were still not there. My heart sank. Their empty chairs were a painful reminder of the old days when I sat all by myself.

"Alright, everyone." Mr. Sterling walked up behind his podium, balancing a stack of papers and folders in his hands. "Open your books to page fifty-eight while I take roll."

I sighed and opened my book.

"Worried I wasn't going to show?"

My heart just about leapt out of my throat, and my body did this weird excited spasm thing, causing my elbow to knock my pen onto the floor. I scooped it up as Alex took a seat, pulling the hood of his jacket off his head.

"No worried," I said. Great. Not only was I socially incompetent, but now my speech was becoming impaired. Deciding it might be best to keep my mouth shut, I fixed my eyes on my book.

He laughed to himself as he flipped through the pages of his book. "That sounded convincing."

I tried again. "I wasn't worried." The pitch of my voice was a little high, but at least I got all the words out this time.

He laughed again and gently tousled his fingers through his hair. "Okay, if you say so."

I opened my mouth to argue that he was wrong, but Mr. Sterling cut me off by starting his discussion.

After Mr. Sterling finished talking, he took the class to the library for some project time. However, this time he stuck around to keep an eye on everyone. I guess yesterday he busted a few of the people that had cut out early. Fortunately, Alex and I weren't one of them.

Alex and I picked out a table near the back corner. During our walk over, he informed me that Aislin was still sick so it was just going to be him and me.

"So, what should we work on first?" he asked, dropping his bag onto the table. "The map or the report?"

"Um...since we don't have any of the supplies for the map," I slid my messenger off my shoulder and hung it on the back of a chair, "I don't think there's anything else we can do except work on the report."

"Do we even know what we're doing it on?"

"No, but looking through some books might help us come up with something."

He held back a smile. "Well, that and the internet."

I glanced over at the computer station, which was crammed with people. "How about you go over to the computers, and I'll go pick out some books?"

"Sounds good to me." He headed off for the computer station.

I turned for the bookshelves. As I passed by the new release section, I couldn't help but stop and skim over what was there. Nothing was too catchy, except for one with a dark purple star on the cover. It made me think of the fallen star story Alex had told me yesterday. Out of sheer curiosity, I decided to read the back to see what it was about.

Halfway through, electricity shock-waved up my spine and I just about dropped the book.

"That doesn't look like it would be very helpful for our project." Alex came up to the side of me and leaned against the shelf.

I held up the book, showing him the cover "It has a star on the cover."

He laughed. "So it does."

"I thought you were going to look stuff up on the internet?" I asked him.

"Yeah, I was until I realized there really isn't any point of us splitting up since we haven't chosen our topic yet."

"Oh yeah, good point."

He flicked the book I was holding with his finger. "So, what's it about?"

I glanced down at the book, then back at him. "From what I read off the back, I think it has something to do with witches."

For some reason, this seemed to entertain him. "Witches, huh? You really do have a thing for the supernatural, don't you?"

I put the book back on the shelf. "I guess you could say that...but how do you know that?"

He shrugged. "Whenever I see you reading, it seems like the book is a science fiction one."

I gave him a funny look. "Have you been watching me?"

I thought I detected a flicker of panic on his face, but it disappeared before I could be absolutely sure.

"I wouldn't exactly call it watching you..." He sauntered behind me, tracing the tips of his fingers across the base of my back. It sent an eruption of sparks surging through me. "More like...observing you."

It was the first time he touched me on purpose, and it almost seemed like he did it to distract me.

I tried not to flinch at the sparks firecrackering all over my body, causing my blood to sing and my heart to pound.

Alex watched me very closely, as if waiting for me to react to his touch. It was like he thought I was going to freak out or something. I very easily could have, too. But I fought hard and managed to keep my cool.

At least, on the outside anyway.

A gap of silence passed between us. The sounds of clicking computer keys and soft chatter trailed through the air. Beneath the lights, Alex's green eyes shined like glass. It was amazing how staring into his eyes could make me feel like I was losing myself.

If it wouldn't have been for a guy—whose name I think is Jason—scooting past us, I'm fairly certain we may have stood there forever, just staring at each other.

But the Jason guy ruined the moment.

Alex sighed, seeming disappointed, and motioned for me to follow him as he headed back toward the astronomy section.

We didn't speak to each other as we searched through the titles of books. I found one on the Milky Way that sounded interesting and sat down on the floor.

"So, do you want to know what I think is funny?" Alex flopped down on the floor next to me without a book. "That we chose our project based on what would be the quickest and easiest, yet I think out of the entire class, we've probably gotten the least accomplished."

I skimmed the list of titles in the index. "That might be because we skipped out yesterday."

"Yeah...maybe." He paused. "So what is it?"

I looked up at him, perplexed. "So what is what?"

"Your fascination with astronomy." He leaned against the shelf behind him, creating a domino effect with a row of books. "I mean, you have to have some kind of interest in it since you chose to take this class."

"I guess." I closed the Milky Way book. "Well, what's your fascination with it?"

He smiled a smile that lit up his whole face. "An easy A."

I rolled my eyes and exchanged the Milky Way book for one that was about planet locations. As I turned back around, I spotted a blond girl bouncing her way up the aisle toward us. It was Kelsey Merritt. Great. I was so not in the mood to deal with her right now.

She wore a short pleated skirt and a pink sweater. She stopped just short of us, her gaze wandering between Alex and me, like she was trying to make some kind of connection as to why we would be sitting here alone together.

I couldn't really blame her, though. If I saw myself sitting with Alex, I probably would have been trying to make the same connection.

She shot me a dirty look before flashing a smile at Alex. "Hey, mind if I get back in there?" she asked, pointing her perfectly manicured finger at the row of books between Alex and me. "I need to get a book."

"Sure." Alex scooted closer to me so that we were almost touching. "Go ahead."

Of course Kelsey took it upon herself to invade Alex's personal space, kneeling down so close to him that her arm was practically resting on his leg. He scooted over more and his shoulder pressed into mine. I froze, knowing I should probably slide over and give him some room, but I couldn't seem to find the motivation to do so. Instead, I sat there, my body humming. Beside me, Alex stiffened, but he didn't move away. I felt his eyes on me, watching me. I turned my head toward him, and our eyes met. What happened next, I couldn't tell you. My mind tuned out and didn't come back into focus until I heard Kelsey's very loud and obnoxious voice—didn't she know this was a library?

"So what do you think?" she asked.

Alex and I blinked simultaneously like we had woken up from a dream.

Very reluctantly, he looked over at Kelsey. "Huh?"

Taken aback by Alex's irritated tone, Kelsey's eyes went wide. "About the project," she said, fumbling to pull a book off the shelf.

Alex raised his eyebrows at her. "What about it?"

She looked extremely upset, probably because it was the first time she had been blown off by a guy. "That it's such a waste of time."

Alex shrugged. "It's not that bad."

Kelsey tossed her hair off her shoulder. "Yeah, I guess it's not that bad. But don't you think it would be better if we could have chosen the people we wanted to work on it with?" She shot a smirk at me.

I glared at her.

"Not really," Alex said.

"Oh, well. Yeah, I guess." She tucked a book beneath her arm, got to her feet, and fixed me with another dirty look.

I suddenly felt possessed to put her in her place. "What the heck is your problem?"

I threw her off a little, a beat of silence skipping by before she found something to say back. "You're my problem," she said and stormed off, her hair swinging across her back.

I smiled at myself. Yeah, I know, I am supposed to rise above it and be better than her, blah, blah, blah. But I have been putting up with her crap for way too long.

"That was a little out of character for you," Alex commented, sliding away from me.

The space made me feel empty inside. "I think it was about time though."

"Was it?" he mumbled to himself.

He could be so weird sometimes.

"So, you never answered my question," he said, selecting a random book off the shelf.

"What question?"

"What's your fascination with astronomy?"

"Oh, that." I wasn't sure if I felt comfortable sharing the reason with him. It was kind of personal, especially because it was connected so closely to the prickle.

"Well, I guess it's because the stars are so peaceful and mysterious and beautiful." I met his eyes, which made me lose my train of thought and I ended up babbling. "Sometimes I wish I could be up there in the sky with them."

His face dropped in horror, and I instantly regretted what I said.

"What's wrong?" I asked. "Did I say something..." *Weird*?

He shoved the book he had in his hand back on the shelf and stood up. "I think I...I left my phone in my bag." Then he practically sprinted off toward the table area.

I swallowed hard. I never should have opened my mouth. I really shouldn't have.

I hung out in the astronomy section by myself until the bell rang. Then I went over to the table, carrying a few books I randomly pulled off the shelf. To my surprise, Alex was there. I thought he left, but there he was, his phone pressed to his ear.

"Yes. Uh huh. I will," he said. Seeing me, he quickly added, "I have to go." He hung up and shoved his phone into the pocket of his jeans. "So, how much longer do you think it's going to take for us to get this assignment finished?"

I set the books down on the table and shrugged, slightly irked by his brush off attitude. "I don't know. Like you said, we really haven't gotten much done."

"No, we haven't." He slipped on his jacket and zipped it up. "Okay, so here's what I'm thinking. Maybe I should come over to your house after school so we can try to finish it up."

Huh? "You want to come over to my house?" I have never had anyone over at my house. *Ever.* Especially some gorgeous guy who had the gift of making my mind blank out.

"Yeah." He spoke slowly, like I was slow, which he probably thought I was. "Is there something wrong with your house?"

"No," I said, which was sort of a lie. There was something wrong with my house. For starters, Sophia was there. "It's just that right now my grandmother and I are going through a…weird phase." I sounded like an idiot.

He cocked an eyebrow, seeming amused. "What kind of phase?"

What kind of phase? What would be the best way to explain it to him? "A yelling one," I decided. It was too complicated to even try.

He laughed. "So, is that a yes or a no?"

I sighed. "I guess it's a yes."

I wrote my address down on a piece of paper and gave it to him. He told me that he would come over around 4:30. Then he left to go to lunch. As I watched him walk out, I felt more alone than I ever had before.

I took my lunch out of my bag and headed back toward my usual loner spot, desperately wishing that I wasn't.

Chapter 9

Marco and Sophia weren't there when I got home. I was glad. If I was really lucky then maybe they wouldn't show up until after Alex left.

I cleaned my room while I waited for 4:30 to roll around. I also had a temporary loss of sanity when I played around with the idea of changing into something different. I was wearing jeans and a black tee, and they suddenly seemed so plain. But then I realized, *who was I trying to kid*? It wouldn't change anything. I would still be socially incompetent, weirdo Gemma with the freaky violet eyes. And besides, I didn't even own anything other than t-shirts and jeans.

I turned on some music and started working on the essay until the doorbell rang.

I trotted down the stairs and opened the front door. Alex stood on the porch, the hood of his jacket pulled over his head as snowflakes drifted down on top of it.

"Hi." I opened the screen door and let him in.

He stepped into the foyer, rubbing his hands together to warm them up as he glanced around at everything. There wasn't much to look at, though; a small table with a few framed pictures of Marco and Sophia on it, and a large painting of a castle by a lake.

"So, this is where you live," he remarked.

"Yep, this is where I live." I didn't mean to sound so unenthusiastic. "My room is upstairs and I figured we could go up there and work on the assignment."

"In your room?" He squirmed around uncomfortably, which I thought was odd.

I gave him a strange look. "If you want, we could work on it at the kitchen table."

He shook his head. "No, your room's fine."

I raised my eyebrows. *Okay.* I gestured for him to follow me as I headed up the stairs.

My bedroom was very plain, particularly for a teenage girl's room. I could only imagine what someone like...say...Kelsey Merritt's room looked like. Or what Aislin's looked like. There was probably a lot of pink, and a lot of photos hanging on the walls. There was nothing on my walls. I had no rugs to cover up the boring off-white carpet. The only thing that gave it any character was a bookshelf in the corner that held my CDs and books.

"So, what should we do first?" I asked as Alex glanced around at my stuff. I suddenly felt uncomfortable being up in my room alone with him.

He traced his fingers along the titles of my CDs. "Should we get the report out of the way first?"

"Yeah, we could do that. But I've already got a lot of it done."

He turned and gaped at me. "You already started on it?"

I nodded. "I worked on it while I was waiting for you to get here. I found a few good ideas and started putting stuff together. Really, there's not much left to do."

He mulled over what I said for longer than what seemed necessary. "You know, it doesn't seem fair for you to do most of the work on the report, and to also have to help put the map together."

"I don't mind," I told him. It wasn't like I had anything better to do. Plus, I loved astronomy.

He tapped his finger on his bottom lip. "No, it's not right. I think I'll just work on the map at home. That way I can make Aislin help."

Assuming he was hinting that he wanted to leave, I said, "Okay, if that's what you want to do then it's fine by me." It didn't feel fine, though. The thought of him leaving made my stomach kind of queasy.

"So…what do you want to do now then?" he asked me.

"Huh?" Had I misunderstood him? "Are you staying?"

"I was planning on it." He cocked an eyebrow. "That is, unless you don't want me to."

My heart had already been pounding, but now it was in supercharge mode, hammering so viciously that it was making me lightheaded. But not wanting to let on that my heart was reacting so excitedly, I kept cool and gave a half-hearted shrug. "No, you can stay if you want."

He pressed his lips together, stifling a smile. "Sure. I don't have anywhere else to be."

What was with him and finding me humorous when I wasn't trying to be?

He shucked off his jacket and slung it on the back of the computer chair. Then he pushed up the sleeves of his shirt and sat down backwards in the chair so that he was facing me.

I shoved my books out of the way and sat down on my bed. The music was still playing—"Ohio for Lovers" by Hawthorne Heights. The slow rhythm of the guitar overtook the silence as I struggled to come up with something to say. Being a lifetime loner, I was completely clueless on how to strike up a conversation. Sure, Alex and I had spent some alone time together, but sitting here in my room with him felt different somehow, and I couldn't seem to find any words to say to him. Perhaps it was because we were in my room.

Alone.

"So…" he finally said, breaking the silence. He rested his arms on the back of the chair and swayed it gently from side to side. "I know I've only been around you for a week or so, but it seems like you spend a heck of a lot of time by yourself."

"I guess so," I said.

"I didn't mean that in a bad way or anything," he quickly added. "I was just stating an observation... wondering why?"

"Wondering why I what? Why I spend my time alone?"

He nodded. "I'm just curious."

"I don't know..." I trailed off. Honestly, I didn't have an answer to give him. At least not one I could share without seeming like I belonged in a straitjacket. I picked at a loose string sticking up from my comforter. "It's just how I've always been, I guess."

"And it doesn't bother you being by yourself all the time?"

I shrugged, staring at the floor. "Not really. Well, maybe lately it has a little."

The room quieted except for the low hum of the music. I heard the chair squeak, and the next thing I knew, Alex was climbing off the chair and walking toward me. His hands were in his pockets, and the lack of uncertainty he carried looked out of place on him.

When he reached my bed, he slid the pile of books out of the way and sat down beside me. We were sitting so close to one another that the only thing between our knees was a whisper of air. My head started buzzing as every single one of my nerves sparked with electricity. I became hyperaware that Alex was sitting next to me on my bed. *Holy crap.*

"Where do you think the sudden change came from?" he asked, continuing our conversation right where we left off.

I had to mentally prepare myself before I spoke, otherwise I would have stammered like an idiot. "I'm not sure."

"So, what? You just basically woke up one day and decided you wanted to have friends?"

Yeah, there was no way I was going to tell him the real reason—that part of the sudden change stemmed from his arrival. "I know it's weird, isn't it?"

"Not necessarily weird, but it is kind of interesting," he said. "But I find you interesting all together."

I traced the circular pattern of the comforter with my finger, feeling extremely uncomfortable with so much of his attention fixed on me. "Trust me, there's nothing interesting about me." I was kind of lying, I guess, if by interesting he meant the stick-you-under-a-microscope-and-study-you kind of interesting.

"I think there is." He paused, casting a brief glance at my computer as the song switched. "I mean, for one thing I find it interesting how long you put up with me being a complete jerk. Not a lot of people would have done that without getting mad and telling me off."

"Oh, trust me, I got mad."

"Is that what you call it?" he teased.

"Hey," I said defensively. "Need I remind you that you're the one who said I have a temper on me?"

"Yeah, but it's more entertaining than anything else."

I crossed my arms and stared him down, trying to look as tough as I could. "Oh, really?"

He laughed. "Yeah, really."

I sighed and dropped my arms onto my lap. I guess acting tough wasn't my forte.

A funny look passed across his face, and then suddenly he was leaning in toward me. "You want to know another thing that makes you so interesting?" His low voice sent a shiver down my spine. "That you can feel this electricity thing between us but you won't say anything about it."

I swear my heart actually stopped. "I-I don't know what you're talking about."

"Yeah, you do." He leaned in closer to me. If he did it again, our heads would probably be touching. "You can trust me, you know. You can tell me anything."

As much as I wanted to believe that was true, I didn't. Yes, he was being nice to me, but I hadn't forgotten how he treated me in the beginning. Or about the strange conversation I overheard between him and Aislin in the library.

He moved even closer. Our heads didn't touch like I thought they would, but they were close. Oh God, we were so close. "Gemma, I promise, you can trust me."

Every inch of my body hummed, and my brain was getting foggy. Maybe I could trust him....

"Gemma! What are you doing?" Sophia's sharp voice cut through my thoughts like a sharp knife, and it popped the tension between Alex and me like a needle to a balloon.

I turned around and found her standing in the doorway, her hand gripped so tightly around the doorknob that her knuckles were paper white. I could only imagine how much this scene looked out of place to her.

Heck, it seemed out of place to me.

"Umm...this is Alex," I told her, motioning at Alex. "We were just working on a project for school."

She narrowed her eyes at Alex. "Hello, Alex."

Oh my God. This was so embarrassing.

Alex seemed fine, though. He held her gaze steadily.

Man, to have such confidence.

Sophia moved her eyes to me. "It's time for dinner, so you need to wrap it up and come down and eat."

I stared confusedly at her. Eat dinner with them...What the—"Since when do I eat dinner with you guys?"

She looked like she wanted to strangle me. "Since now."

"Fine," I said, my tone clipped. "I'll be down in a minute."

"Well, hurry up. I don't want the food to get cold." She shot another death glare at Alex and then stormed out of the room.

I turned back to Alex. "I'm so sorry. She's been kind of crazy lately."

He laughed softly. "Yeah...I bet." He got to his feet and grabbed his jacket off the back of the chair. "Well, I should probably go. I'll see you in class tomorrow, okay?"

I nodded. "Yeah, okay."

He put his jacket on and started for the door, but stopped in the doorway and turned around. It looked like he wanted to say something, but he couldn't find the words. Finally, he just waved and walked out.

I sat there, feeling torn. Part of me felt relieved that he left because, if he stayed I might have broken down and told him things I didn't want him to know. I almost had until Sophia walked in. The other part of me, though, wished he had stayed; felt sad that he left.

I let out a sigh. When did life become so complicated?

I got up, shut my music off, and headed downstairs for "dinner." It was weird to picture the three of us sitting around the table like a normal family. In fact, I couldn't even picture it. It was that strange. But I guess I was about to find out firsthand what it was like to be part of a family.

Halfway down the stairs, I thought I heard voices coming from the foyer. I didn't think much of it at first, until I realized who the voices belonged to: Sophia and Alex. Great. She probably cornered him and was saying God knows what.

This was so freaking embarrassing.

I sped down the stairs—I needed to end this quick. But just before I reached the bottom, I heard something that made me slow down.

"You know the rules, Alex." Sophia's tone was razor-sharp. "So you should know better than to be getting close to her."

I stopped dead in my tracks. *Rules?* What was going on?

"Yeah, I know the rules." The sharpness of Alex's tone matched Sophia's. "But need I remind you that Stephan sent me here to get some answers from her? And in order to do that, I need to get close to her."

Stephan. There was that name again. The same one I heard him mention during my eavesdropping session in the library.

"That's not what you're doing," she snapped. "You're crossing the line, Alex. A very thin, dangerous line."

"I think you're forgetting that I don't take my orders from you." Alex lowered his voice, and I had to lean forward on my tiptoes in order to make out what he said. "I'll do what I need to do in order to get her to—"

I lost my balance and, being the graceful queen that I was, stumbled forward, banging my elbow into the wall. "Ah!" I cried out, and then threw my hand over my mouth. *Crap.*

A few moments ticked by. Had they heard me? Of course they heard me. They weren't deaf.

"Gemma," Sophia called out.

Rubbing my elbow, I slowly made my way down the rest of the stairs, my legs feeling like two flimsy wet noodles beneath my weight.

Sophia was waiting for me at the bottom of the stairs, hands on her hips, her eyes a fiery bright gold. "What in the world are you doing?" she asked.

I pressed my lips together and looked over at Alex. He was casually leaning against the front door, his arms folded across his chest. He met my gaze, appearing not the slightest bit concerned. But it seemed like he should be.

I turned my attention back to Sophia. Every once in a while, when she got really, really mad, this faint bluish-purple vein would pop out on her forehead. Right now, I could see it bulging underneath her pale skin.

"I came down to get something to eat like you told me to," I told her, still staring at the vein. It reminded me of a gross bluish-purple worm.

"Gemma, what on earth are you looking at?" Sophia barked.

I flinched and shook my head. "What's going on here between you two?" I asked. "And why were you guys talking about me like that?"

She gave me a patronizing look. "Like what, Gemma?"

"Like, you know." I waved my hand in the air, trying to come up with a word to sum up what I just heard.

Alex shifted his weight away from the door and raised his eyebrows questioningly at me.

What were they trying to do here? Make me look like a crazy idiot? If they were, they were doing a pretty good job of it.

"Look, I don't know what you think you heard," Sophia said, her tone tolerant. "But we weren't talking about you. I know Alex's father, and I was just telling him to pass along a message for me."

My anger simmered. She was such a liar. "That's such bull. You were talking about me. I heard you."

She waved her finger at me furiously. "You better watch your tone, young lady. I mean it." I opened my mouth to say a few choice words that I think, under the circumstances, would have been appropriate, but she cut me off before I could even get the first one out. "Now, I don't know why on earth you think you have the right to listen in on other people's conversations, but you need to stop. Do you understand me?"

I eyed her over suspiciously. Was there a hidden meaning to her words? Did she know what happened at the library? But if she did, who told her?

I think I had a guess.

Without another word, I pushed by her, heading for the kitchen. Before I disappeared through the doorway, I glanced back at Alex.

Now he looked worried.

Chapter 10

The next morning, I woke up with red, swollen eyes.

I hadn't wanted to cry last night, but I ended up doing it anyway.

Now I could barely open my eyes.

I glanced at the clock and saw a blurry 12:10. 12:10 in the afternoon? Why hadn't my alarm gone off?

I sat up and stretched out my arms. Well, so much for school.

But why had Sophia let me sleep in? I know last night had been super intense. Still, letting me skip out on school...She never let me miss school.

I climbed out of bed put on a black long sleeve shirt and a pair of worn-out jeans, and pulled my hair into a ponytail. Then I went downstairs. It was too quiet for anyone to be home.

So, I was alone.

I wasn't sure how I felt about that.

Just to make sure, I searched the living room and the kitchen. Both were empty. And Sophia and Marco's car wasn't in the driveway. How convenient for them. Maybe that's why no one had gotten me up for school. Perhaps they were trying to avoid me so they wouldn't have to answer questions about last night.

Outside, the sky was grayed over by clouds. Not a single speck of sunlight trickled through, making everything dark and gloomy. Between the darkness and the emptiness of the house, I felt unsettled.

I flipped on the light and made myself a turkey sandwich. I decided to eat in my room because it seemed better than sitting out in the open, where anything from the yellow-eyed monsters to Sophia or Alex could walk in at any moment and take me by surprise.

Sprawled out on my bed, with the music cranked, I tried to analyze what could be going on between Sophia and Alex. They had said so many strange things. Things I was convinced had to do with me. But how was I supposed to find out for sure?

Suddenly, out of nowhere, I had an epiphany. The house was empty and I needed answers. And what better way to find answers than to snoop around a little? Yes, I know, snooping is very wrong, blah, blah, blah, but so is eavesdropping, which is something I've done on more than one occasion.

Without any further indecisiveness, I hopped off my bed and went into Marco and Sophia's room. I had only been in their room a couple of times — and never by myself. But every time, I had felt uncomfortable, and being in here now, all alone, was way worse. The place was really creeping me out. It felt like I had stepped into a cemetery in the late hours of the night instead of into my grandparents' room at midday.

Although, the creepy factor might have been coming from Sophia's perfectionist touch. Every single thing in the room was perfectly in place. Almost everything matched. The white four post bed matched the armoire and the nightstand. The pink bedspread coordinated flawlessly with the roses on the wallpaper. The bed skirt and the curtains were made of the same frilly lace. The whole room was probably about as sterile as a hospital, which had me a bit worried. If I touched something, would she be able to tell? Maybe. I guess I'd just have to be careful.

I decided to check the closet first because...well, I'm not sure why other than it seemed like just as good a spot to start with as any.

Moments later, I ran into a problem. I realized I had no clue what exactly it was I was looking for. Still, I didn't want to just give up. So I continued to search through the massive amounts of clothes hanging up in the closet, and through the shoe boxes that were stacked on the closet floor, hoping that I would know what "it" was when I found it.

But when I finished looking through everything, I came up empty-handed.

I moved on to the armoire, then the night stand. Nothing seemed out of the ordinary though. I even checked under the bed, despite the fact that I knew I wouldn't find anything underneath it.

Neat freaks never put things under their bed.

I let out a frustrated sigh. I should have known this would be a waste of time. I mean what had I expected to find? A secret letter explaining what was going on? Yeah, right. Like that would ever happen.

Nothing is ever that easy.

Giving up, I started to leave. But I slowed to a stop when I spotted a wooden bench, lined with throw pillows. There was a small latch on the front of it.

I carefully removed the pillows from the bench and then held my breath as I unlatched the lock. I half expected an alarm to go off or something, but the only sound was the hinges squeaking when I lifted open the lid.

Inside were books, old photos of Sophia and Marco in various places, a box of pressed flowers, some ribbons and cards. Nothing unusual, or at least that's what I thought until I picked up the final object—a glass swan with a bright orange beak—and noticed the floor of the bench rocked slightly. Setting the swan aside, I used the palm of my hand to put pressure on the board. It popped up on one side, and....Ta-da! A secret compartment. Whatever I was looking for had to be in there.

I removed the board the rest of the way and found a single manila envelope hiding beneath it. My hands started to sweat as I picked up the envelope. This was it. This was what would give me my answers.

I unwound the piece of string that sealed the envelope shut. The very first thing I came across were the papers stating that Marco and Sophia had custody of me.

Well, so much for my kidnapping theory.

I sifted to the next item; a piece of blue-lined paper with my name and a list of dates printed on it in red ink. I recognized the flawless handwriting as Sophia's. There were five dates total, all seeming random with no visible order. At least from what I could tell. The oldest dated back nearly fourteen years ago, and each had a check mark next to it, except for one; February 8 of this year.

My heart stopped.

I couldn't breathe.

The date was more significant than even my birthdate. February 8th was the precise date I had first felt the prickle that had released my emotions.

I felt sick to my stomach. Why would Sophia have this? And what did these other dates mean? None of them held any importance, at least as far as I knew.

I pressed my clammy hand to my forehead. I had a big, full-of-confusion headache.

But I needed to get it together and figure out more.

I took a deep breath and looked at the next paper, a cream colored one with a gold border. It was my Birth Certificate. My fingers trembled as I read my mother's name listed at the bottom. *Jocelyn Lucas.* It was the first time I ever saw her name, yet it felt as familiar as my own. It was a beautiful name. I bet she was beautiful too. My stomach fluttered with excitement as I skimmed over to the line beside it—the one where my father's name was listed. Or should have been listed. It was blank. My heart sank. Why would it be blank? Had my father not wanted me or something? No. That couldn't be it. Sophia and Marco had told me that both of my parents had died in a car accident, which meant they still had to have been together—we had to have been a family, right? I wasn't sure. I wasn't sure of anything.

I stared down at the blank line, trying not to cry and telling myself that everything would be okay, that I would figure it out. Then I heard the downstairs door slam shut. I just about jumped out of my skin. I hurried and stuffed the papers back into the folder, except the one with the list of dates on it. On a sporadic impulse, I decided to shove that one in my pocket. I set the envelope back into the secret compartment and placed the bottom board back on top of it. I piled the rest of the stuff back inside the bench, closed the lid, and threw the pillows back on, knowing Sophia was probably going to notice how unorganized everything was and would know someone had been in her room.

But oh well. I would deal with that later. Right now I had bigger problems to deal with.

I tiptoed over to the door and cracked it open. I could hear Marco and Sophia chattering downstairs. So, holding my breath, I slipped out into the hallway and padded back to my room, gently shutting the door behind me.

I let out a huge exhale. That was close. But it was worth it. I took the list out of my pocket and stared down at the dates. What did they mean? I mean, they had to be linked to one another somehow.

Not knowing what else to do, I started for my computer, figuring there was no harm in doing a quick search on the internet to see if anything came up. But before I could even get it turned on, someone knocked on my door.

My muscles seized up. Had Sophia already discovered I had been snooping in her room?

"Gemma," Sophia said through the door. "Are you in there?"

I stared at the door, frozen and mute, with the image of her on the other side of it, all red faced and pissed off, embedded in my mind.

"Gemma!" she yelled, banging on the door again.

My adrenaline soared, and I couldn't bring myself to move.

"Gemma, open this door up. Now!"

I shoved the list of dates back in the pocket of my jeans, reminded myself to breathe, and opened the door.

Yep. There she was, all red faced and pissed off.

"Could you move any slower?" she asked snappishly.

I shrugged. "I don't know. Maybe."

Her temper flared. "Next time you better hurry up."

I rolled my eyes. "Did you need anything else?"

She pushed past me into my room and gazed around like she was searching for something.

"Umm...what are you doing?" I asked, crossing my fingers she wasn't looking for the list of dates stashed inside my pocket, which right now seemed to have taken on the weight of lead.

"Are you ready to go to your field trip?" she asked, still staring around my room.

"Wha...My astronomy fieldtrip?" God, I had completely forgotten about that.

"Yes, your astronomy fieldtrip," she snapped impatiently. "It's tonight, right?"

I slowly nodded. "But I think I'm going to skip out on it." I know I had been looking forward to going to it and everything—getting the opportunity to look through a telescope was something I've wanted to do—but at the moment it just seemed irrelevant. What I wanted to do was to stay here and find out what the list of dates meant, before Sophia found out it was missing. Anyways, I skipped out on school today, and showing up at this fieldtrip would eliminate the old "I was sick" excuse.

"No, you're going," she ordered.

"Why?" I asked, eyeing her over suspiciously. "I mean, why do you even care? You've never cared before. So what's with the sudden interest?"

She fidgeted nervously, smoothing out her perfectly pressed navy blue sweater. "There is no sudden interest. I just want you out of this house for awhile. That's all."

Ouch. That stung. "Fine. I'll go for a drive then."

"No, you're going to the fieldtrip."

119

"But you just said that all you cared about was me being out of the house, so what does it matter where I go just as long as I go?" I argued. "Besides, I missed school today."

"And whose fault's that?"

"You're the one who didn't wake me up when my alarm didn't go off."

She scowled. "You're going. End of discussion."

And it was, because she left.

Bursting with anger, I kicked the door, but not hard enough to do any damage. I let out a frustrated sigh. She was hiding something. And whatever I had to do, I was going to figure out what it was.

Chapter 11

A half an hour later, bundled up in a heavy black coat, purple gloves and a matching beanie, I was climbing out of my Mirage. It was cold and dark, and I had only one lamppost to light the way to the entrance of the school. Plus, no one was around.

Needless to say, I was freaked out a little.

The icy air seeped through my clothes and burned coldly against my skin. My breath puffed out of my mouth in a cloud of smoke. I yanked my hood over my head, zipped up my coat, and sped up toward the school. I made it about halfway when I suddenly got the shivers. I would have chalked it up to the fact that it was as cold as death out here, but the flash of yellow I saw from my peripheral vision told me otherwise.

I started to jog, my eyes scanning the parking lot. The flash could have been from the headlight of a passing car. That was what I tried to convince myself until I caught sight of two eye-shaped yellow lights flashing wildly in a cluster of nearby trees.

"Oh my God," I breathed and jetted off in a mad sprint, my adrenaline pulsating like mad. The monster was back. Or maybe it had never left. Maybe it had been waiting around for the perfect moment when I would be wandering around in a dark parking lot by myself. How could I be so stupid? I was so focused on the whole Alex and Sophia thing, when really what I should have been focusing on was the fact that there were real life monsters around that wanted to kill me. And now my mistake had left me completely vulnerable.

My footsteps thudded loudly as I ran across the ice. I heard a *swoosh*, and I flicked a glance over at the cluster of trees just in time to see the silhouette of an inhumanly tall figure emerging from them.

I ran faster. The entrance door of the school was getting closer. If I could just make it inside the school, then hopefully there would be other people around and I might be okay. But as I glanced back at the monstrous creature, I saw its demon eyes blazing violently beneath the hood of its cloak, and the next thing I knew, it charged for me.

I knew I was a goner.

My skin buzzed, and then I was slamming into something solid. I screamed as I lost my balance and started to fall toward the ground. But someone caught me by the arm. I regained my footing and jerked my arm away from Alex's grip.

"What the heck were you doing?" he asked, sliding the hood of his olive green coat off his head.

I backed away from him, putting some space between us. But not too much space since the more space there was between he and I meant the less space there was between the death creature and me. "I was…" I shot a panicked glance over my shoulder. Nothing. No inhumanly tall figure. No glowing yellow eyes.

My legs felt wobbly and my hands were shaking. "Heading into the school," I told him as I walked unsteadily past him.

"But why were you running?" he asked, following after me.

My heart was beating so fast that I wondered if it was trying to escape and free itself from this madness. I know I wished I could. I was scared. More scared than I have ever been. "Just leave me alone."

"No." He matched my pace. "Not until you tell me what you were running from back there."

I yanked open the door and shot him an angry look. I wasn't in the mood for his crap. "Are you going to tell me what you were talking to Sophia about?"

"It was nothing important," he said indifferently.

I shook my head and stepped inside the warm and brightly lit hallway. Then I let the door slam shut right in his face. I couldn't deal with him right now. Not when there might be monsters skulking around outside, waiting for the moment when they could finally kill me.

***

The astronomy classroom was packed with people. Some of the people I recognized from my class. Others I had never seen before. Hold on. Let me take that back. I had seen them. Since my town's population is a mere glitch above 1,000, I basically *have seen* everyone who lives here. I just didn't know most of their names.

I headed up to my table that I sat at during class. Aislin was already there, wearing a pink fur trimmed coat. The same pink fur-trimmed her gloves and the top of her boots. She kind of reminded me of a big pink bunny. I tried not to laugh.

I was really losing it.

She was texting on her phone, but glanced up as I sat down. "Hey, Gemma." She smiled.

The polite thing for me to do would be to smile back, or at least ask her if she was feeling better since she had been sick for the last few days, but right now polite was not in my vocabulary. So I muttered a grumpy, "Hey," then sank back in my chair and stared down at the table.

"Is something wrong?" she asked.

I opened my mouth to say...well, who knew what would have come out considering the mood I was in. I didn't get a chance to speak, though, because Alex showed up and I was interrupted.

"What took you so long?" Aislin asked him, flipping her phone shut.

Alex's eyes stayed glued on me as he lowered himself into the chair. "I found Gemma running around lost and had to help her out."

I scowled at him. "I wasn't lost."

A smile threatened at his lips. "Oh, really?"

"Yes, really," I snapped and closed my eyes, trying to pretend he wasn't there and that the yellow-eyed creatures weren't real. I tried to imagine that I hadn't found Sophia and Alex discussing...whatever they had been discussing. That there was no list of dates tucked away in my pocket. I tried to pretend I was just a normal girl whose life made sense.

The problem was, I had just seen the monster right outside. And that piece of paper with the list of dates on it was practically burning a hole in my pocket. Plus, the jolt of electricity shimmying up and down my back made me hyperaware that Alex was near.

Still, I kept my eyes closed until I heard a loud clap. Then I sighed and opened my eyes.

Mr. Sterling was standing behind his podium. He wasn't dressed in his normal teacher attire; instead he was sporting jeans, sneakers, and a navy blue coat. A black baseball cap covered his bald head.

He quickly took roll and handed out a packet of papers to each table. Then everyone filed outside to the bus.

I bounced up and down, freezing and nervous as I waited in line to get on the bus. I didn't see a single sign of anything yellow and glowing, except for the bus's lights. I wasn't going to let my guard down, though. I was going to be very careful and stay close to someone at all times.

A first for me, but this was my life we were talking about here.

By the time I got on the bus, every single seat had someone in it. *Great*. Where was I supposed to sit?

The little orange lights on the ceiling spotlighted down on me and I felt like such a loser standing there, searching for someone to sit by. I had never talked to anyone besides Aislin and Alex. And Aislin was already sitting by some guy wearing a black beanie. My only other option was to sit by Alex because, of course, he was sitting alone.

As I deliberated whether or not I wanted to sit by him, I walked by Kelsey Merritt. She was sharing a seat with Anna Miller and Sarah Monroe, all of them donning white coats and pink scarves like they were eight-year-old triplets or something.

Kelsey smirked at me. "Lost?" she asked vindictively.

I should have known what was coming, but I was too distracted with the whole where-should-I-sit dilemma, and didn't notice when she stuck her leg out into the aisle right in front of me. I had very little time to react. I stumbled clumsily over her boot, but fortunately I managed to brace myself on the back of a seat.

"You're such a loser." She snickered.

The urge to slap the smirk right off her face welled up in me like a bubbling volcano about to erupt. I felt the prickle poke at the back of my neck like it was giving me the go-ahead. At least, that's how I chose to take it. I lifted my hand, preparing to strike. But before I could swing it down, a set of warm fingers caught me by the arm. Electricity glittered across my skin as Alex dragged me to his seat.

I glowered at him, but deep down—and I mean way deep down—I felt grateful. I mean, what would hitting her have solved?

Still, I felt the need to protest. "I didn't need your help." I jerked my arm away from him.

"Now, we both know that's not true." He smiled arrogantly. "What were you planning on doing exactly? Hitting her?"

"No," I lied.

He stared at me, unconvinced.

I folded my arms across my chest. "Well, so what if I was? She would have deserved it."

He laughed and shook his head. "You and your temper."

"I don't have a temper," I argued, which yes, I know, was a lie. I did have a temper. A big one. And it seemed to be getting bigger by the minute.

"I beg to differ," he said.

I rolled my eyes. "Whatever."

Then we just stared at each other. Through the sounds of people talking, I thought I could make out Aislin's laugh.

"You know," he said, leaning back in the seat, "we were getting along pretty well the other day. It seems like such a shame for us to start fighting again."

I turned to face him. "The only way that's not going to happen is if you tell me what the heck you were talking to Sophia about."

"I can't," he said simply.

"Why not?"

"Because I just can't."

"That's it? That's your answer?"

He nodded. "It's the only answer I can give you."

I threw my hands in the air exasperatedly. "But you've told me absolutely nothing."

He actually looked a little sad. "I know."

The bus jerked forward and the lights went out. Then we were off.

I turned away from Alex and tried not to think about the fact that I was about to break the promise I made to myself to never go back to the mountains. I tried to let the gentle buzz of sparks lull me into a semi-relaxing state until we reached our destination at Star Grove, a small park that resided at the bottom of the foothills. It was surrounded by tons of trees, and I suddenly wished I had gone home. After what happened in the parking lot, I should have jumped in my car, drove back to my house, locked the doors, and never left again.

But instead here I was, sitting in a bus that had taken me up to the forest. All because I let myself get distracted. If I hadn't been so caught up with trying to get the truth out of Alex, maybe I would have thought things through better and jumped off the bus before it pulled away.

But I didn't.

I wish he would just tell me what was going on. I wish I could trust him. It would be nice to have someone I could trust and be able to confide in about the yellow-eyed monsters. Yeah, it was a nice thought. But it was only wishful thinking. And whether wishes were made by blowing out birthday candles or on a shooting star, they never came true.

In a large plowed-out area in the center of Star Grove, telescopes were scattered about. As soon as we stepped off the bus, Alex darted off to the closest one. But Aislin protested, insisting that if we went up front then we would have a "better view." I'm not sure if I understood her logic, but I didn't argue because the closer to the front we were meant the farther we were from the trees.

Aislin placed her glove covered hand on top of a telescope. "What about this one? Does it work for everyone?"

Alex shook his head and let out a frustrated sigh. "You're the one who is being picky, Aislin, so just choose one already. Gemma and I were fine with the first one."

Aislin tapped her finger on her chin as she looked down at the telescope, then up at the sky, then at Alex. "Well...if this one's okay with you guys, then I'd like to use it. It's got a great view."

"Yes, it's fine." He stomped up to the telescope and twisted the knob, adjusting the lens.

Aislin sighed and retrieved the instructions from her pocket. "Who wants to go first?" she asked, unfolding them.

Alex looked at me with a familiar smile creeping across his face. "I bet Gemma would love to go first."

I rolled my eyes, but stepped up to the telescope anyway. As I rested my hand on top of it, excitement bubbled up inside me. I couldn't believe it was going to be my first time looking through a telescope.

"Which constellation am I supposed to find first?" I asked Aislin.

"Ursa Major," she told me.

I put my eye to the cold lens and twisted the knob to focus it. Even though Mr. Sterling had given a brief demonstration on how to use a telescope, I could only get the sky to look like a dark, splotchy blur with streaks of silver.

"Haven't you ever used a telescope before?" Alex asked, standing close to me, invading my personal space.

"Nope," I said flatly.

He moved even closer, reached an arm around each side of me, and placed his hands on the telescope. Sparks twinkled against my skin like stars.

I thought about jabbing him in the side with my elbow so he would move back.

My elbow wasn't having any part of it, though.

"Let me know when they come into view," he whispered, his breath feathering across my neck.

A warm shiver tickled down my spine. The good kind of shiver—the kind that steals your breath away.

Moments later, the sky shifted into focus. "I can see them," I whispered, awestruck by how beautiful the stars were.

He dropped his arms but didn't step away. I didn't care though. The view was too amazingly perfect and surreal to care. The way the stars sparkled, and the patterns they created. There was something serene in how all of them seemed to fit together, like pieces of a puzzle. A puzzle which, strangely, I felt I was part of.

As I stood there, gazing up at the stars, getting swept away, my head started to hum. At first it was only a low hum, nothing too horrible or concerning. But as the low hum swelled into a shrilling ring, I thought my head was going to explode. I dropped my hand and jumped back, suddenly feeling as if I was falling.

Then everything went black.

The next thing I knew, I was standing in the middle of a snowless field. I had no idea how I got there. Maybe I passed out and was dreaming? It didn't feel like a dream, though.

I felt very <u>awake.</u>

A gust of wind blew up from behind me, and I suddenly felt like I wasn't alone. I turned around, tall grass hissing at my legs. In the distance, I saw two figures surfacing; one tall and the other very small.

I couldn't make out their faces, but it wasn't because of the dark. A blurry haze blocked them out like bad reception on a TV screen.

"We're almost there." It was a lovely voice that spoke. Not too high or too low, and there was no denying it, the voice belonged to a woman. It sounded almost familiar, yet unfamiliar at the same time.

The smaller figure, I was almost certain, was a little girl. She walked with a bounce, excitement springing in her voice when she said, "I'm so excited."

"I know," replied the woman. "And you should be. There is a lot to be excited about."

They were only a few steps away from me now, and I waited for them to notice me standing there, but they continued by me as if I was nonexistent, and I wondered if they could see me at all.

"Hello," I called out.

Nothing.

I followed after them.

They came to a stop beside a tall oak tree. The silver glow of the moon glimmered across their blurry faces. The only details I could make out about them were that they both had long, dark hair and fair complexions. I was getting a mother and daughter vibe from them. But I wasn't an expert on the subject, so I couldn't say for sure.

"Here we are." The woman raised her hand to the sky. "See that one right there?"

The little girl's head tilted up toward the sky. "Yeah, I see it Mama."

"That one's yours," the mother told her. "That's the spot from where you fell."

Where she fell? Who? The little girl? What was going on? What was this place?"

I called out again, "Hello."

"Almost five years ago," the mother continued, my hello going unheard.

"And that was a very special day, right?" the girl asked, eagerness beaming in her voice.

"Right," the mother answered. "My very special Gemma day."

My mouth fell agape. Did she just say Gemma? "Hey," I shouted, getting closer to them. "Who are you? And where am I?"

Nothing. It was like I was invisible.

I started to freak out. I needed to know what was going on. But before I had a chance to do anything else, I was yanked backward. I gasped as the outline of the mother and daughter faded farther and farther away, until they were nothing more than a speck of light.

"Holy—" I jumped back and flung my hands over my mouth. The telescope was in front of me. My skin was humming. Snowy mountains and trees were everywhere. I was back at Star Grove. I wasn't lying on the ground passed out. I was on my feet.

I glanced around. Hadn't anyone noticed my disappearance? It didn't look like they had. Everyone seemed content in their little groups, working away on the assignment. Alex was still standing right behind me just like he had before I...I have no idea how to finish that sentence.

Alex stared at me strangely as he cocked an eyebrow. "You okay?"

Aislin was looking at me weirdly too. But neither of them appeared to be alarmed, which seemed odd since I'd just disappeared for who knows how long. Or had I? Maybe I hallucinated or something. Perhaps I dozed off. God, it didn't feel like it wasn't real though. It had felt very real—too real. Like I had seen it before. Lived it before. Maybe I had. The mother had called the little girl Gemma. But then why had I called the woman, who I was certain wasn't Sophia, Mama? My mother had died when I was one, and the little girl had to be at least four.

Confusion swarmed my brain. I started to sweat and blood roared in my ears. Tears stung at my eyes, and I had to remind myself to breathe.

"I have to go," I whispered, making to move around Alex.

He stepped in front of me and held up his hand. "Go where?"

"I...to the bus." I made another attempt to sidestep around him.

He mimicked my move at lightning speed, stopping me dead in my tracks. "You can't just go wandering off. We're out in the middle of a forest." His bright green eyes were filled with concern. It was weird.

Despite my efforts not to, I started to cry, tears rolling down my ice-cold cheeks.

Alex's eyes widened. "Are you...are you crying?"

"Um...oh, just shut up." And then I dashed past him, my shoulder slamming into his.

"Gemma, wait," Alex yelled after me.

But I kept running, not thinking about the consequences of what I was about to do as I headed straight for the bus.

Chapter 12

I found the bus door cracked open, leaving it easy to open. The bus driver was not there and the lights were off. With tears streaming down my face, I dropped down in a seat. I hugged my legs against my chest, and cried in the dark in typical Gemma style—all alone.

What was happening to me? Was I heading towards an emotional breakdown? Was I going to end up locked away in a padded cell somewhere, screaming at the top of my lungs that everything I said was true—that I wasn't crazy?

Was I crazy, though? Was any of what was going on actually real? Or was my mind pushing on the borders of sanity, conjuring up a fictional world?

Absentmindedly, I touched the pocket of my jeans where the list of dates rested. I pulled off my glove and reached in, the edges of paper grazing my skin as I took it out. Letters forming my name and the dates stared back at me.

It was real.

Tears dropped from my eyes and splattered against the paper, bleeding the red ink. Everything was so complicated. I desperately wished I could just piece it all together.

Through my blurry veil of tears, I thought I saw a flash of yellow just outside my window. With my heart thumping wildly, I leaned in for a closer look and saw a tall dark figure zipping through the pine trees at an inhuman speed, heading directly for the bus. I almost had forgotten about the monster. *Again.* I needed to get off the bus. *Right now.* Before it was too late.

I leapt out of my seat, preparing to make a mad dash back to the telescopes, where I could be safe—at least for the moment anyway. But electricity spun through my body, and I hit a dead halt.

Alex was making his way slowly up the aisle. "What the heck are you doing in here?"

"Nothing." The word rushed out. I shot a glance at the window. The tall, dark figure was gone.

He stopped just short of me, his eyes as round as two golf balls. "You've been crying."

"So," I stuffed the list into the pocket of my coat and wiped the tears off my cheeks. "People cry all the time."

"Yeah, but only when something horrible or sad happens to them." He paused, looking out the window, then back at me. "Did something horrible or sad happen to you?"

I shook my head, afraid to speak. Afraid my voice would give away my lie.

He nodded at the window. "What were you looking at out there?"

"I was looking at...the stars?" It sounded more like a question than an answer.

He cocked his head to the side, his forehead creasing over with worry lines. "But weren't you just looking at the stars through a telescope? Right before you ran off in a mad craze."

I glared at him. Insulting me was not a good idea right now.

His expression softened a little. "Gemma there's obviously something bothering you, so tell me what it is please."

I think it was the first time I ever heard him use the word please. Still, it didn't mean I was going to break down and tell him all my secrets. "There is nothing bothering me. So if you don't mind, I think I'm going to get back to the class."

I marched forward, but his hands came down on the back of the seats, keeping me from going any farther. I backed up, trying to widen the distance between us, but he matched my steps, narrowing it right back.

I tried not to freak out about the fact that I was being cornered like a cat. "Look, I don't think—" My back hit the back door.

He stopped just inches short of me and reached for my face. I flinched as he wiped away a stray tear rolling down my cheek. His fingers tingled against my skin, making me feel lightheaded and dizzy, and I had to grab hold of a nearby seat just to keep from falling over.

He raised his finger up to the moonlight speckling through the window and inspected the tear. "If nothing's wrong," he said in a voice barely above a whisper, "then, what is this?"

I felt tired. Everything was just too...heavy. I couldn't take it anymore. I sighed, a heavy hearted sigh. "It's a tear."

"Yeah, but why are tears falling from those purple eyes of yours?"

"Because I'm sad," I told him, which was the truth. "And my eyes are not purple. They're violet."

He cracked a smile, but it swiftly faded. "Sad about what?"

"I don't know." I shrugged.

It got quiet. My body sparkled electrically as he kept his eyes on me, watching me with the most intense expression.

"I knew you could feel it," he said softly.

"Feel what?" I replied breathlessly.

"The electricity," he whispered in a voice so soft it sent another good shiver down my spine.

I had to catch my breath before I spoke. "I have no idea what you're talking about."

"Yes, you do." He inched forward, the tips of his sneakers clipping the tips of mine.

Was it just me or was it getting hot in here? My thought process was melting. The world shadowed around me. I could hear my heart thrumming in my chest, and I wondered if he could hear it too.

I felt like I was slipping away.

But I couldn't slip away. I needed to remember all the lies he told. But his eyes were locked on mine, and I could feel my self-control disappearing.

He put his hand on my cheek. Every inch of my body fire-crackered with sparks. It was like the freaking Fourth of July in here, all hot and sparkly. The ceiling lights flickered on, then back off again. Alex shut his eyes and leaned in. Um...was he going to do what I think he was going to do? No. There was no way—His lips brushed against mine. I froze, unsure of what to do, but then my instincts took over. I let my eyelids close and fell into the kiss.

"Alex! What are you doing?!"

Both our eyes shot open. Alex stepped back with a deer-in-the-headlights look. I stayed where I was with my back pressed against the door.

The lights were on and Aislin was standing at the front of the bus, her eyes wide. "What the heck is going on?"

Alex stared at me as he traced his finger across his lips. The lips that had just touched mine.

Holy crap!

He broke his gaze away from me and turned to face her. "Why would you think something was going on?"

140

Aislin placed her hands on her hips and narrowed her eyes. "Alex, you should know better than to be doing something like this."

Was she talking about him kissing me? Okay, I seriously wanted to get off the bus now. "Um, yeah, I think I'm going to go back outside."

Alex's arm came down in front of me. "No, you're not."

"Um, yes, I am." I tried to push his arm out of the way, but he was too strong. "You can't make me stay here."

"Of course I can," he said.

He wasn't even looking at me, but I was pretty sure he could feel the burning glare I was giving him by the way he shifted his weight.

"Alex, I really think—" Aislin began.

Alex held up his hand. "Aislin, just be quiet."

She glared at him, but her mouth stayed shut.

He turned back to me. "Now what did you see outside?"

I folded my arms across my chest. "Nothing."

"That's bull." He was getting mad, however when he spoke his voice sounded absolutely calm. "Just tell me, please."

I thought I felt a chill slither down my spine. But figuring it was from the cold, I shrugged it off and shook my head. "No."

He took a deep breath and said softly, "*Please*. I swear you can trust me."

I could feel myself falling again—falling into his eyes. Maybe I could tell him about everything…about the monsters….about me…the chill slithered down my back again, this time feeling very slimy and snake-like. I shuddered. "What is *that*?"

He furrowed his eyebrows. "What's what?"

"It feels like there's something slimy and cold on my back," I told him, running my fingers along the back of my coat.

His gaze moved over my shoulder, and his eyes widened in horror.

"What?" I followed his gaze and my heart stopped. Frost was webbing its way across the back door. "What the—" I shot my attention to the side windows. Ice was covering them too. My foggy breath laced out in front of me.

The air suddenly felt like death.

"Aislin," Alex said, worry ringing in his tone.

I heard a loud shriek, and through the icy windows I thought I saw a flicker of yellow. I could hear Alex and Aislin talking…something about getting out of here and transporting—whatever that was—but I couldn't seem to take my eyes off the frozen window to see what they were doing. I think I was frozen in terror—literally.

I needed to get off the bus.

I tore my gaze away from the windows. Aislin was kneeling down on the ground, doing something weird with a black candle and what looked like a chunk of amethyst. What was this? Black magic time?

"I have to get out of here," I said, trying to push past Alex.

"You aren't going anywhere," Alex growled, refusing to let me by.

"Yes I am." I shoved at him with all the force I could conjure up, but he stood as still as a statue. I was on the verge of tears again. "You don't understand, I have to get off. NOW!"

"No, you don't understand," Alex snapped. "If you walk off this bus, you'll die."

"If I stay on this bus, they'll kill me!"

That caught his attention. "Who will kill you?"

Oh crap. I hadn't meant to say that aloud. But with what was happening around us, did it really even matter?

"Those things." I pointed towards the windows, where blinking eyes now flashed.

"You know what they are?" he asked, stunned.

"Of course I do." I tried to shove past him again, but it was useless. "This is not the first time I've seen them."

He closed his eyes and took a deep breath. "Aislin, they know."

Aislin, who was dangling the amethyst into the flame of the candle, froze.

143

Alex had his back turned to me. Hoping to catch him off-guard, I tried to slip by him, but he caught me by the hood of my jacket and yanked me back, pinning me against his chest.

"I already told you if you go out there, the Death Walkers will kill you," he said. "So do yourself a favor and stay put."

I almost kicked him in the shin, but something he said stopped me. "Death Walkers? What's a Death Walker?"

"Those things out there with the glowing eyes-" he raised his chin at one of the nearby windows- "are called Death Walkers. And they're called that for a good reason. They can freeze someone to death just by touching them."

"I know they can," I whispered, horror pulsating through me as I thought about the nightmares that had haunted me over and over again—nightmares I should have taken more seriously. But it was too late now. The forest was right outside and I was about to die.

My ice-cold hands were trembling. I assumed it was from my nerves until I saw that they had turned a ghastly shade of purplish-blue. "Oh my God!" I cried, shaking my purplish-blue hands. "What's happening to me?"

Alex enclosed his hand around mine. His skin felt so warm. "Try to relax," he told me. "Aislin will have us out of here in just a second."

Try to relax. Was he kidding? How was I supposed to relax when my death was waiting for me just outside the frozen walls of the bus? And how on earth did he expect

Aislin to get us out of here? With her magic candle, voodoo witch thing she was doing? Yeah, all that was doing was creating a cloud of violet-grey smoke that was starting to fill up the bus.

I shook my hand fiercely. *Please change back. Please change back. Please change back!*

"Just stay calm," Alex lulled. "I promise everything will be okay."

Yeah, I wasn't convinced.

The bus gave a sudden jerk to the side and fog began to swarm beneath the cracks of the doors and windows. The temperature shot down. My body burned—it was that cold. Feeling exhausted, I let my eyelids drift shut.

"Stayyy awwwake." Alex's voice sounded so far away. I cracked open my eyes and he hugged me against his chest, his voice reverberating in slow motion as he said, "Aislin, hurrrry uppp."

"Perrrr is calxxxx EGO lux lucisss viaaa," someone whispered. At least I think someone whispered. At this point, I could have been hallucinating.

The interior lights blinked off, and all I could see were the yellow eyes fire-flying around outside. Then a purple glow swallowed up my surroundings, and I let my eyes close as the windows shattered. I felt Alex's arm come up over my head protectively. A sharp pain ripped up my side, and I let out a scream.

The next thing I knew, I was flying through the air.

Chapter 13

I'm not sure how long I was in the air—or if I even was in the air. It was hard to tell with the thick blanket of blackness all around me. When I finally did see light again, my face was inches away from the floor, about to smack into it, hard.

And hard it sure did smack.

With my limbs aching in protest and my brain swirling dizzily, I got to my feet. I was no longer on the bus, but in a room with red walls and an ash-black hardwood floor. An L-shaped leather sofa trimmed the far back corner, and there were bookshelves all over the place. Dark curtains blocked all the windows so I wasn't sure what was outside.

"Where the heck am I?" I said.

A hand came down on my shoulder, sending a surge of electricity spiraling down my arm. I spun around, knocking the hand away from my shoulder. Alex stood only inches away from me, and right behind him was Aislin. For a split second I was overwhelmed with the impulse to run to him. But the feeling quickly dissipated as the memories of what had just taken place hurricaned though my mind. I stumbled away from him, my hands shielded out in front of me. But a razor-sharp pain radiated up my left rib, and I let out a moan as I hunched over and wrapped my arm around my waist.

"What's the matter?" Alex asked, concern lacing his voice.

I held up one hand, keeping the other on my aching ribs. "Stay away from me."

"Gemma, I'm not going to hurt you," he said, sounding very convincing. But I wasn't buying it. "You need to hold still. You're hurt."

Something warm and sticky dripped down along the back of my hand. Blood. I lifted up the edge of my coat. A small piece of glass was lodged in my skin. I gasped.

"Just relax." The tone of his voice was tolerant, not relaxing at all. He turned to Aislin. "You better go find Laylen and see if he has a first aid kit or something. Although, I'm not even sure why you brought us here in the first place."

Aislin blushed. "I wasn't trying to. It was an accident. You should just be grateful I got us out of there before..." She glanced at me and trailed off. "I'll go find Laylen," she said and whisked out the door.

"Who's Laylen?" I asked.

Alex motioned at the L-shaped couch. "Go sit down so I can look at that."

I shook my head, my hand still grasping my wounded side. "Not until you tell me where we are. And how in the world we got here. And—"

Alex cut me off. "I really don't think that's the most important thing right now, considering you have a piece of glass sticking out of your rib."

He had a point, I guess, but I deserved some answers. "Fine. I'll go sit down. But I'm not going to drop this. You *are* going to tell me what's going on."

He studied me with a curious expression. "You know, you're nothing like what I thought you would be."

"I don't even know what that means," I said hotly. "You always say things that make no sense at all."

He sighed. "Just go sit down and I'll try and explain things the best that I can."

I was stunned. Had I actually won the argument? "Are you serious?"

He nodded. "But hurry up. You're bleeding all over the floor."

After settling on the couch, I let my questions pour out of me. "Okay, so how did we get here? And what were those things back there? Those...Death Walkers? And how do you know about them? And how do you know Sophia, because I could tell by the way you two were talking that..." The way Alex was staring at me made me trail off. He looked totally baffled.

148

"Are you going to give me a chance to talk?" he asked. "Or do you want to just keep going?"

I bit my bottom lip. "Sorry. Go ahead."

He pressed his lips together and stared off into empty space. "Take off your coat."

I blinked. "What?"

He met my eyes. "In order for me to get the glass out, you have to take off your coat."

"Oh." For some stupid reason, I suddenly thought about the kiss we shared. It could barely be considered a kiss, really soft and brief like the touch of a butterfly's wings. Still, I could feel the lingering sparkle where his lips had brushed against mine.

I carefully eased my coat off, wincing as the glass shifted.

Alex took off his gloves and coat and pushed up the sleeves of his long-sleeved black thermal shirt. Then he reached for me.

"What are you doing?" My muscles tensed as I leaned away from him.

He pointed at my ribs. "I'm going to look at that."

"Oh," I said stupidly. I took a deep breath and held as still as I could.

He lifted the edge of my shirt up just enough so he could see the piece of glass sticking out of my blood-covered skin. He examined it, gently tracing a circle around the cut with his finger.

I held my breath, trying to hold in the gasp that desperately wanted to escape my lips. It would end up being the good kind of gasp—the kind of gasp that might get him thinking I was okay with everything. And I wasn't. Not by a long shot.

Finally, after what seemed like an eternity, he moved his hand away. His face looked dead serious—worried even. It made me anxious.

"Is it bad?" I asked in a high-pitched voice.

His mouth curved into a grin. "No, it's not that bad at all. The piece of glass is small, and you're barely bleeding anymore. I should be able to get it out and stitched it up without any problems." He rested back against the couch and glanced at the door. "Just as soon as Aislin gets here."

I tugged down the corner of my shirt and frowned. "That wasn't funny. You had me thinking I was seriously hurt or something."

He laughed. "Actually, it kind of was."

I glared at him. "Do you even know how to do stitches?"

"What, don't you trust me?"

I chose not to answer that. "How about you answer some of my questions?"

He frowned. "I would rather not."

"But you said you would," I protested. "I mean, is it really that bad that you can't tell me?"

"Yes," he said.

A shiver crawled up my spine. "Well, I still want to know."

He locked eyes with me. "Are you sure about that?"

I swallowed hard and nodded.

"Fine." He waved his hand. "Ask your questions."

"Okay..." My mind suddenly seemed blanked. "Um...where are we?"

"Laylen's. He's a friend of Aislin's and mine." He drew back the curtain that was behind us. "He lives in the Nevada desert."

If it wouldn't have been for the sunlight, lighting up the sky, and the golden-brown sand, dusted with cacti, that stretched as far as my eye could see, I wouldn't have believed him. But there it was, right outside the window.

"How—" I stammered. "I mean—how?"

He let go of the curtain. "That's where *all* of this becomes confusing."

"Becomes confusing? It's already been confusing for quite awhile."

"Has it?" he muttered.

I wasn't sure if it was a rhetorical question or not, so I didn't answer. "So...how exactly did we get to Nevada in just a split second's time?"

He hesitated. "Aislin transported us here."

"Transported," I said, very slowly, like the word was foreign. But the way he used it was foreign. "I remember hearing you guys say that word back on the bus, but what does it mean exactly?"

He hesitated again. "It's a form of magic."

A burst of laughter escaped my lips. "Are you being serious? Because, just so you know, magic isn't real."

"It isn't, huh?" He gestured around the room. "Then how do you explain this?"

I shrugged. "It could be a delusion brought on by the trauma of those things—those Death Walkers things—trying to kill me."

He stared at me, astounded. "So, let me get this straight. What you're trying to say is that you believe in something like the Death Walkers who, by the way, are demons, but you don't believe in magic."

"Umm...." Okay, so he had a point, but still, it was all too strange. "I don't know what I believe in."

"Well, if you can't believe in something as simple as magic, then there's no point in me trying to explain the rest of it. Because out of everything, magic is the sanest sounding thing of all."

I thought about what he said, but it still seemed unreal. "So what you're trying to say is that Aislin's a witch?"

He nodded. "But by your sarcastic tone, I'm guessing you're still not buying it."

"I'm trying." I really was. "But it's kind of hard to accept something that sounds so...crazy."

He eyed me over, causing my skin to electrify. "So tell me this. How can you accept the feeling that I know you're feeling right now, but you can't accept that Aislin's a witch? Because, on a crazy level, they're both about the same."

"What feeling?" I asked, knowing full well what he meant.

Before I could stop him, he rested his hand on my cheek. Electricity sung through my veins, and under no control of my own, I let out a gasp.

"That feeling," he whispered, the palm of his hand still cupping my cheek.

Growing up with Marco and Sophia—the two most unaffectionate people ever—I never came close to even getting a pat on the back. So Alex touching me like that felt very strange. Yet somehow, at the same time, it felt very familiar.

He dropped his hand, and we both just sat there, staring at one another.

"Okay," I finally said, breaking the silence. "I believe you so you can go on."

He forced a fake smile. "Can I?"

"Yeah, you can."

He shook his head, looking like he was trying hard not to smile, then he turned to face me. "Look, I've broken a lot of rules here."

I tilted my head to the side, confused. "What rules?"

"Nothing. Never mind," he said quickly. He ran his fingers roughly through his hair "God, how the heck am I supposed to explain to *you* how important *you* are?"

"How important *I* am?" I gave him a doubtful look. "Trust me, there's nothing important about me. At all."

"You have no idea how wrong you are." The intensity in his eyes made me shrink back.

I gulped. "I don't understand what you mean—"

"Here it is," Aislin announced as she entered the room carrying a first aid kit.

Alex practically leapt off of the couch. "Took you long enough."

Grimacing, she shoved the first aid kit at him. "It took me a minute to find Laylen."

"Sure it did," Alex said, his tone insinuating something. Something I was certain I didn't want to know.

"Whatever, Alex." She flipped her golden blonde hair from her shoulder. "And just so you know, Laylen's going to stay away until..." She glanced at me, then leaned in and dipped her voice quieter.

After that, I could only make out half of what she was saying. Being able to lip read would have come in handy right now. All I was able to catch was something about "staying away" and "blood." Maybe Aislin couldn't stand the sight of blood...I don't know.

"I guess, but she's not bleeding that bad." Alex's voice rose loud enough for me to hear him. He tucked the first aid kit underneath his arm. "Why don't you go and try to get a hold of Stephan? Let him know what's happened and see what he wants us to do."

Who was this Stephan?

"What about the other problem?" She nodded in my direction.

He shrugged. "I'm going to tell her."

"Tell her!" Aislin exclaimed. "Are you crazy!?"

Uh...Hello, I was sitting right here. Jeez people.

"We really don't have a choice," Alex said. "After what she just saw."

I wondered if they forgot I was in the room. Then again, being subtle had never been their thing.

Aislin sighed. "Fine. Do whatever you want. I'll go call Stephan." She stomped toward the doorway, but turned around before walking out. "But just for the record, this is all on you."

"Thanks for clarifying that," he said in a sarcastic tone.

She shot him a glare before stepping out of the room.

Alex came over to the couch, knelt down on the floor, and opened the first aid kit.

"Who's Stephan?" I asked.

"My father," he said without looking up.

"Your father." That sure as heck wasn't what I expected.

He grabbed a throw pillow from the foot of the couch and set it down beside me. "Lay down so I can get that piece of glass out of you and get you stitched up. And I'll *try* to explain everything while I do."

"So, by *try*, do you mean *try* to explain the whole truth? Or just the parts of the truth you want me to hear?"

He stared at me quizzically. "You're kind of difficult, you know that?"

"Gee, thanks," I replied, my voice rich with sarcasm.

He shook his head, but I caught a glimpse of a faint smile. "I'll tell you everything as in *everything*."

I lied down on the couch as carefully as I could and rested my head on the pillow.

"Alright." He rubbed his hands together. "Try to hold as still as possible while I pull out the glass."

I cringed. I couldn't help it. I took a deep breath and fixed my eyes on the ceiling, trying to think of something else. But the red color of the ceiling reminded me a lot of blood, and I was very aware of the tug as Alex removed the glass. I threw my arm over my face and shut my eyes, taking slow breaths.

"You doing alright?" he asked.

I nodded, but my ribs were on *fire*.

"This little thing right here is what was in you," he said.

I opened my eyes. In the palm of his hand was a piece of blood stained glass about the size of a quarter.

"That's it?" Sticking out of my skin, it had looked so much bigger.

"Yep, that's it." He dropped the glass into the first aid kit, and it plinked as it hit the plastic. He took out a cotton ball and poured rubbing alcohol on it. "Gemma, I'm really sorry."

His "sorry" momentarily perplexed me. Before I could figure out what he meant by it, he had already pressed the cotton ball onto my cut. It felt like someone had dumped gasoline on my skin and lit a match. I squeezed my eyes shut and bit down on my lip, trying not to scream bloody murder.

Finally, after what seemed like hours, he moved it away. "Sorry about that. I just thought it would be better if I caught you off-guard. That way you wouldn't anticipate it and try to move away."

I was in too much pain to respond.

"Now I just have to stitch it up." He tossed the blood soaked cotton ball into the first aid kit. "The cut's not very big, so it shouldn't take me that long."

"'kay," I said through my shallow breathing.

He began unwinding a spool of clear string.

"So, are you going to explain to me why you think I'm so important?" I asked, watching him unwind the string like a cat.

"Give me a second." He snipped the end of the string off with a pair of scissors. "Before I do, though, you have to promise me two things."

"Depends on what those two things are."

He gave me a look as he withdrew a shiny needle from the kit.

"Sorry." I tried again. "So what are the two things I need to promise?"

"First, you have to promise that you'll try to keep an open mind."

"Okay." Keeping an open mind seemed easy enough. "And the second promise?"

"That you'll let me finish talking before you start freaking out."

That one wasn't as easy. My gut churned. "How do you know I'll freak out?"

He looped the piece of clear string through the needle. "Because you will."

Jeez. How bad was it going to be?

I swallowed the lump in my throat. "Alright, I'll try not to freak out until you're done talking."

He raised his eyebrows. "You'll try?"

I suddenly felt very aware that I was about to hear something very bad. "Fine. I won't freak out until you're finished." But after that, all bets were off.

He held the needle just above my ribcage. I flinched — I absolutely, one hundred percent hate needles. With all their sharpness and being pointy — their sole purpose was to stab you.

"I'm not even sure where to begin with all of this," he muttered, and let a hiccup of silence go by. "Do you remember that story I told you about? The one about the fallen star?"

"Yeah...I remember."

"Hold still," he said as he tipped the needle down and vigilantly guided it through my skin.

It stung...*Bad*. My eyes snapped shut, and I clutched on to the edge of the couch.

"Breathe," Alex reminded me.

My eyes flew open and I sucked in a breath of air.

"You good?" he asked after a second had ticked by.

"Yeah, I think so." But my voice trembled.

"Are you sure?"

"Yeah...but can you get this over with quickly? *Please*."

He nodded, and then weaved the needle into my skin again. "So, where was I?"

"You were talking about the fallen sta—" I gasped as he pressed the needle into my skin again.

"Oh yeah, the fallen star. All of what has happened has to do with that."

"How?"

"You remember the story, right? Twenty years ago a star fell from the sky."

I nodded. "But that doesn't mean I believe it."

He paused, the needle a mere sliver of air away from piercing into my skin. "You promised me you would keep an open mind, remember? And you need to believe in the fallen star story, otherwise the rest of this is going to sound like a lie."

"But you are a liar, right?" I asked, knowing I was treading on thin water here. He was the one holding the needle, after all. But still, it needed to be said.

"Liar's such a strong word. I prefer to think of it as me omitting some of the details."

I rolled my eyes.

This time when he snaked the needle through my skin, he placed his free hand on my stomach. My bare stomach. All of my focus centered on how his fingers were touching my bare skin. The warmth. The buzzing. It even numbed out the pain a little.

"Gemma?" His voice pulled me back to him.

I blinked dazedly. "Huh?"

He stared down at me, his forehead creased. "Did you hear what I said?"

As much as I hated to do it, I shook my head. "Umm...no."

"I asked if you remembered when I mentioned the secret group that hid the star."

I nodded, still somewhat distracted by his warm hand touching my stomach. "Yeah, I remember."

"Well, the secret group is called *Custodis of Vita*."

There was so much electricity. "The awhata?"

"The *Custodis of Vita*," he repeated, sounding irritated.

That's it. It was too hard to focus with his hand touching me like that. I reached down and lifted it off me.

He gave me a strange look, glanced at his hand, then back at me.

"What is that? Like Latin or something?" I asked, hoping to distract him.

160

"Yeah...it means Keepers of life. But for short we call ourselves The Keepers."

"Keepers of life." I raised my eyebrows. "It sounds like a cult."

A soft laugh escaped his lips. "It's not, though. We actually protect the world from dangerous things"

"We?" I studied his expression; so serious and, at least as much as I could tell, so not the expression belonging to someone who was lying. However, Alex was an excellent liar. "So you're saying that you belong to this *Keepers* group?"

He nodded. "And Aislin. And..." His voice got quieter. "Marco and Sophia."

I lay there, motionless, letting his words sink in. "So, what you're trying to tell me is that Marco and Sophia, the people who've raised me since I was one, belong to some secret group that protect the world from evil?" It sounded way too fictional. All saving the world from evil and demons and vampires. Yeah, I know, he hadn't actually mentioned vampires but...God, what if there were actual vampires? "No. There's no way. You're lying. You have to be lying."

"That's the second time you've said that in the last five minutes, which is really frustrating since this is one of the few times I've ever told the truth." He seemed so angry it was hard not to believe him. Besides, something else had just occurred to me. Something that might back up part of what he was saying. "Is that why you and Sophia were talking the other day? Did it have something to do with all of this?"

He gave a slow nod. "That night we were discussing....something."

I felt a sharp tug as the needle snagged my skin. I let out a whimper and my hand instinctively flew toward the pain. Luckily, Alex caught my fingers before they touched the stitches.

"Whatever you do, don't touch it," he warned.

I drew my hand back and cradled it against my chest. "So, if you're telling me the truth—which I'm still not one hundred percent certain you are—then why hasn't anyone mentioned this to me before?"

He hesitated, looking stressed. "I don't even know how to begin to explain the rest of this to you." He let out a frustrated sigh as the needle slipped through my skin. "Okay, so that star I was telling you about held a lot of power. That's why we—the Keepers—went and got it in the first place. If it fell into the wrong hands then..."

Silence grasped the air.

"Then, what?" I wished he would just spit it out.

He shook his head. "Nothing." He paused, seeming torn about something. "Okay, let me try this again. There are these people who have the ability to see into the future. Kind of like psychics, but we call them Foreseers. But, anyway, one of these Foreseers made this prediction—or a prophecy, I guess you could call it—that this fallen star would prevent the end of the world from happening." He picked up the scissors and trimmed the end of the string off. "You're into astronomy, right? So I'm sure you've heard of December 21, 2012?"

I stared at him, dumbfounded. *End of the world.* WTF.

"Gemma?"

"Um...yeah...Dec. 21, 2012? Aren't the planets supposed to align or something?"

He nodded. "At the exact same moment the winter solstice takes place." He tossed the scissors back into the box and pulled out a roll of tape and gauze. "When I say 'end of the world', what I mean is there's this portal that's supposed to open up at the exact moment the planets align."

"A portal," I repeated with skepticism. I mean, I've heard theories on what people believed was going happen on December 21, 2012, and a couple of them had discussed the possibility of the world ending. But a portal? Really?

He cocked an eyebrow. "You still seem like you don't believe me." He positioned the gauze over the stitches and secured it with two strips of tape. Then he set the roll of tape back into the first aid kit and snapped the lid shut. "I'm all done now, so you can sit up if you want. Just be careful, though. And don't move too fast or you might rip them open."

I tugged the edge of my shirt down and slowly sat up. My side felt all strange and tight, and the skin burned.

Alex set the kit down on a nearby table and dropped down on the couch beside me, his knee brushing against mine and making my muscles tense as electricity coiled up my thigh.

"So, what is that?" I asked abruptly. "That electricity thing I feel whenever I'm around you?"

He shrugged. "I have no idea."

I eyed him over suspiciously. "You have no idea what it is?"

He shook his head. "Nope. I've never felt anything like it until you came along."

"Yeah, me neither," I muttered. "Until the first time I was by you."

He looked surprised. "Really?"

"Yes, really. Why do you look so surprised? You just said the same thing."

"Because it's different with you." Before I could yammer out a bunch of questions about that, he shifted the direction of the conversation. "But anyway, back to the portal. See, if it opens up, it will let out a ton of Death Walkers. So I'm sure you can imagine how the end of the world is supposed to happen."

I stared down at my hand, remembering the bluish-purple color. "By ice."

"Exactly."

"So how come I started freezing to death, and my fingers turned all funky and blue, but you seemed completely unbothered?"

"Eventually mine would have turned out the same way," he explained. "Your reaction to the Death Walkers' chill is just a little worse than mine."

"Why?" I asked. "I mean, is there something weird about me?"

"I'm getting to that." He fiddled with a loose string hanging off one of the throw pillows. "There's this guy named Demetrius, who is the leader of all the Death Walkers, and he wants this portal to open. And basically, this fallen star is the only thing that has enough power to keep the portal from opening, so you can imagine how important it is to keep the star away from him."

"Do you still have it?" I was confused by how weird it sounded. It had to be some twisted, freaky dream. Or maybe I'd had a meltdown and created my own personal fantasy world inside my head. There was no way this could be real. But then, why did it feel like there was more truth to his story than anything I had ever been told?

A funny look flickered across his face. "Yeah, we still have it." He kept his eyes on me for an instant longer, before forcing them away. "We kept it hidden so Demetrius couldn't find it and destroy it. For the first few years, we had a Shifter transfer the star's energy into different objects to keep its location a secret." He stopped. "Do I need to slow down? You look lost."

"Kind of lost. Kind of overwhelmed," I admitted. "But you can go on."

"Okay, but just so you know, the next part is going to be very hard for you to hear. And you need to stay as calm as you can."

I swallowed hard, my stomach churning. "I'll try."

He took a deep breath and surprised me when he reached over and took my hand. "An accident happened three years after we found the star. Theron, the Shifter I told you about, was attacked by Demetrius while in possession of the object that was holding the star's energy. He ended up panicking and accidently shifted the power into something it should have never gone into." He paused. "It went into a woman."

"A woman?" My eyes widened "What happened to her?"

"Well, the energy didn't end up in her exactly. She was pregnant when it happened, and it ended up going into her unborn child."

I froze. Why did this seem so familiar? And why did the incident back at the telescope—the one where I had been sucked away to the field—pop into my mind? "So what happened to the mother and the baby?"

"They both lived and everything, but the star's energy got trapped inside the baby. And it's still there. For some reason—and no one knows for sure, because no one's ever come across anything like it before—no Shifter could transfer it out of her." He pressed his lips together, his hand tightening on mine. "A few years after it happened, the mother ended up passing away. But her death had nothing to do with the star." He watched me closely. "She was a Keeper, and her name was Jocelyn."

"Jocelyn," I repeated. "Why does that name sound familiar? Did I know her?"

He nodded. "You did, and very well."

"How?" But before he could answer, I realized why. Because I had seen the name before on my Birth Certificate.

Jocelyn was my mother.

Chapter 14

Neither of us spoke. The only sound was the clock ticking back and forth. Alex was still holding my hand, his skin warm and flowing with static. He never actually answered my question. But I think he might have sensed I figured it out.

"Gemma, are you okay?" he finally asked.

I nodded slowly.

"You do know who she is, right?"

I nodded slowly again.

"Then you understand what that means, right?"

I pressed my lips together. Yeah, I understood what it meant. He was saying that for the last eighteen years, I had been harboring a fallen star's energy inside of me. Some piece of a freaking solar system's sun. But as crazy as it sounded, it kind of made sense. I mean, I had been hollow and emotionally numb until an invisible prickle had released my emotions. Add that to the violet color of my eyes, and my ability to either sense or cause electricity to flow by being around Alex....I really was a freak. Literally. I probably wasn't even considered human.

"So what am I?" My voice sounded so numb.

"What are you?" His eyebrows dipped down. "What are you talking about?"

"Well, I can't be human." I choked on the words. "So what am I?"

"You're human," he assured me. "Just a human with a lot of power in her."

I could feel that power right now, and it was making me feel sick. I tried to ease my hand away from Alex, but he clutched onto it.

"Look," he began in a guarded yet determined tone. "I know this all sounds crazy. And I understand that you're probably freaking out right now, but there's more I have to tell you."

"There's more!" I cried. A few hours ago I wanted nothing more than to hear the truth. But after what I heard, part of me wished there was a rewind button so I could go back in time and choose not to hear it.

He gave a slow nod. "And I think I should probably warn you that it's just as bad—if not worse—than what I've already told you."

My hands shook, and it felt like I was suffocating. How could anything be worse than getting told I was carrying around the power of a star that could possibly save the world from an apocalyptic portal? I ripped my hand away from his and let my head fall into my hands. "This is a lot to take in. I'm not sure if I can take any more."

"Well, if you want me to stop then—"

My head snapped up. "No." I sat up straight. I was going to have to tough it out. "I need to hear the rest; otherwise it will drive me crazy."

He sighed. I think he might have been hoping I would tell him to stop. He looked reluctant, but continued. "Well, we lucked out because Demetrius never discovered the location of the star's power. A few months after you were born, though, a Foreseer told Stephan another prophecy about the star. The prophecy said that if your emotions weren't controlled, then the power of the star would weaken and eventually die, which would make it useless to stop the portal from opening." He placed his hand on top of mine, which I thought was kind of weird. He sure seemed determined to touch me. "So to keep that from happening, and to keep Demetrius from ever finding out, Stephan made the decision for you to go and live with Marco and Sophia in the real world."

"How old was I when I went to live with them?" I asked.

"You were one when you went to live with Marco and Sophia," he replied in a flat tone that puzzled me. His palm felt sweaty on my hand, and it was kind of gross. "And they were under strict orders to make sure you stayed unemotional."

I didn't say anything for awhile. I had hit some kind of eerie calm or something. Or maybe I should say an "unemotional" calm. I knew right then and there that any doubts I had about Alex telling the truth were gone. How could I deny it when he knew about my unemotional issue? But the problem was that I was made to be that way.

Intentionally.

"Gemma," he said.

"How?" I asked in the same lifeless tone I had used up until I felt the prickle.

He cocked his head to the side in confusion. "How what?"

"How did they do it?" I tried to wiggle my hand free from his, but he wouldn't let go. "Make me unemotional."

He fixed his gaze on the floor and shrugged. "I don't know. I guess by shutting you off from any kind of emotional contact. If someone doesn't ever know happiness, sadness, or love, then how can they ever feel it?"

The inability to make eye contact was the first sign someone was lying.

"You're lying," I accused.

"No, I'm not," he said, his eyes still locked on the floor.

"Yes, you are," I insisted. "You can't even look at me."

He shook his head and looked at me with a tolerant expression. "There. Are you happy?"

My dulled calmness abruptly faded, and a wave of panic and anger thundered through me. I tugged and pulled and yanked my hand, desperately wanting to get the heck out of here. All I wanted to do was get away and hide; curl myself in a tiny ball and cry until my eyes ran dry. So I did the only thing I could think of to get him to

171

let me go. See, over the last few weeks, I had caught on that Alex liked to be in control of the situation. So I needed to make him think he was losing the control. There was only one thing I could think that might do that.

Lie.

"But I have been able to feel," I told him.

"Yeah," he said, unsurprised. "Marco and Sophia noticed a change in you over the last few months. That's one of the reasons why Ailsin and I enrolled in school. We were trying to figure out what caused the change. And we were also keeping an eye on you."

I shook my head. I was going to have to let that one go for now, otherwise I would get sidetracked from my plan to escape. "That's not what I meant. I've been able to feel for more than a few months. Awhile ago, I found a paper in one of Sophia's trunks that had this list of dates on it." I caught a hint of understanding pass over his face—he knew what paper I was referring to. "After doing a lot of searching around, I finally figured out what it meant." I was going out on a limb here because I wasn't sure if the list of dates had anything to do with this. It was just a hunch I had, but I was going with it. "After that, the being-able-to-feel thing became simple for me."

I searched for a sign that he was buying my lie. At first, he looked completely lost. Then his expression shifted to anger. Moments later, worry washed over his face. I felt his grip loosen on my hand, and I seized the opportunity. I yanked my hand as hard as I could, and his hand fell off mine. I was on my feet in a heartbeat, bolting for the door, ignoring the pain tearing up my side.

"I wouldn't do that if I were you," Alex called out.

Ignoring him, I threw open the door.

"The Death Walkers will find you," he said. I could hear him moving toward me, his footsteps scuffing lazily against the hardwood floor like he was so sure I wasn't going to run away. "Now that they know the star's in you, they'll always be searching for you."

All I had to do was go. Find the front door and run my little heart out. But my fear made me hesitate. What if they did find me and I was all alone? Was it worth the risk?

I turned to face him, my hand still clasped on the doorknob. "How can you be so sure they know I have the star's energy in me?"

"Oh, trust me, they know." He came to a stop in front of me. "After what happened on the bus, there's no way they don't."

I was trapped. Either I could run and risk the chance of getting killed by a bunch of hypothermic-inducing monsters, or I could stay here with Alex, a liar who had caused me to suffer through most of my life as a walking emotionless corpse.

I stayed still, even when he placed his hand on mine.

"Running away would be a very stupid thing to do," he said in a low voice. "Don't ever try to do it again." I frowned as he removed my hand from the doorknob. "You

173

were lying, weren't you? About being able to feel earlier than we thought?" he asked.

I stared at him impassively.

"I know you were," he said. "If it were true then Marco and Sophia would have known."

"Would they?" I twisted my hand out of his. "She didn't seem to notice when I stole the list of dates from her trunk."

We stared at one another. I wasn't sure what to believe. And I had a feeling he felt the same way, which was what I wanted.

"Well, since this is going nowhere, I might as well call Stephan," he suddenly announced.

I folded my arms across my chest. "Fine. Do whatever you want."

"I was planning on it." He walked by me and motioned for me to follow him.

Even though I really didn't want to, I did.

Chapter 15

Alex led me down a hallway lined with doors. He finally came to a stop in front of a closed door at the very end of the hall. My head was hurting so terribly, and my ribs were aching big time. I felt more empty and alone than I had ever felt in my life. Although Marco and Sophia had never been that great of grandparents, they were still my grandparents. And what they had done to me felt like the ultimate betrayal.

Alex didn't open the door right away. He just stood there, staring at it as if he were trying to compel it to open with his mind. Needless to say, it didn't open. Then, unexpectedly, he whirled around to face me.

"There's something else I need to tell you before we go in here," he blurted out.

I sighed, "What now?"

"Relax, it's not about you. It's about Laylen, the guy who lives here." He leaned against the door and crossed his arms. "He's not exactly human."

"What does that even mean?" I asked. "If he's not human, then, what is he?"

"Well," he wavered, "a few years ago he was bitten by a...vampire."

I gaped at him. "So you're saying he's a vampire?" Was he kidding?

He moved away from the door and stepped toward me. "I know what you're thinking: that there's no way vampires are real. But they're about as real as the Death Walkers."

I pressed my lips together and stared down at the opposite end of the hallway, at a door with a small stained glass window on it. Light spilled through the glass, casting misshapen reflections across the floor and walls. It had to be the front door. And just on the other side of it was the warm and sandy desert. The complete opposite of where I had been no more than a few hours ago.

"You're not thinking about running away again?" Alex's voice tore through my thoughts.

I turned my head back to him. "No."

He cocked an eyebrow. "Are you sure about that?"

"Yeah, I'm sure," I said, sounding unconvincing.

He opened his mouth and started to say something but, changing his mind, clamped it closed again. He had been doing that a lot over the last few hours—starting to say something then stopping. Who did that remind me of? Hmm...Let me think. How about Marco and Sophia? Coincidence? Who knew?

"Do I have to worry about him biting me?" I asked tensely.

He laughed. "No, you don't have to worry about him biting you. Since he was a Keeper before he was changed, things work a little differently. He's more in control of his blood lust."

"And what about vampires that aren't Keepers to begin with? What are they like?"

He hesitated. "Let's just hope you don't ever have to find out."

And with that, he opened the door.

On the other side was a room that had the same red walls and ash-black hardwood flooring as the room we just left. There were bookshelves everywhere. The only noticeable difference was a long mahogany table that trailed down the middle of the room. In one of the eight chairs bordering the table, Aislin sat, staring down at her cell phone.

She immediately jumped to her feet when she saw us. "Oh, good. I was just about to come get you." She hurried over to Alex and asked in a barely audible voice, "Did you get everything taken care of?"

"Yeah." Alex's bright green eyes flicked in my direction. "I did."

Aislin gave me a wary look before returning her attention back to Alex. "I can't get a hold of Stephan." She tapped her cell phone in the palm of her hand. "It goes straight to his voicemail."

"That's odd," Alex mumbled. "Did you try Marco and Sophia?"

The mentioning of Marco and Sophia made my stomach ping.

Aislin nodded. "They didn't answer either."

"Where the heck could they be?" he asked. "They weren't going anywhere, were they?"

Aislin shook her head. "Not that I know."

"Do you know if Marco and Sophia were going somewhere?" Alex asked me.

I gave him an are-you-kidding-me look. "Yeah, because they tell me what they're doing."

Alex frowned. "Gemma, this isn't a joke. It's important."

"Oh, I know it's not," I assured him. "I was being very, very serious."

He stared at me, clearly irritated. I held his stare until the buzzing became too intense, and I had to turn my head away or else I might explode. "Stare all you want, but I still don't know where they are."

He heaved a frustrated sigh and looked back at Aislin. "Why would *all* of them not answer their phones? It doesn't make any sense."

"I don't know." Aislin twirled a strand of her golden blonde hair around her finger. "You don't think that something happened to them, do you? Like maybe the Death Walkers showed up at the house or something."

"I highly doubt it. The Death Walkers have no reason to go after them. They want Gemma."

I rolled my eyes. *Lucky me.*

"And even if they did go to the house," Alex said, starting to pace back and forth across the floor, "Stephan can take care of himself."

"Of course he can." A voice floated up behind me. It was a guy's voice and he sounded about as resentful as I felt. "Because we all know Stephan can do anything."

Aislin's gaze shot over my head. "Laylen, please don't start. That's the last thing we need right now."

I froze. Laylen, the vampire, was standing right behind me. Slowly, I turned around, my stomach rolling with nervousness.

He was about five or six inches taller than me, which meant he was really tall—six foot four at least. His blond hair swept across his forehead, the tips dyed a bright blue that matched the shade of his eyes. A silver ring hooped the bottom of his dark red lips. He wore a grey t-shirt, black jeans, and biker boots. Black symbols tattooed his forearm. They looked like a foreign language of some kind. Greek maybe?

His gaze dragged up me and came to a stop at my eyes. "You know, the last time I saw you, you were maybe about four years old. You've grown up a lot since then."

I scrunched my forehead. "Do I know you?"

He laughed a very gentle, non-vampire sort of laugh. "Yeah, kind of."

I forced a small smile. *Okay?*

"So," he said, directing his attention to Alex, "Aislin said you got yourself into some trouble?"

"I didn't get us into any trouble," Alex corrected him. "So don't get too excited."

"That's not what I was told." The smug look Laylen was giving Alex made me wonder if there was some kind of bad history between them. "From what Aislin said you,—"

"Laylen," Aislin hissed. "Shut up."

Alex folded his arms, and his glare sliced into Aislin. "Alright, so what have you been saying?"

She bit her lip, looking guilty as charged. "Well, it's just that I think...maybe the little thing that happened between you and Gemma on the bus was what helped the Death Walkers discover that the energy is hidden in her."

Alex shook his head. "There's no way that could have been the reason."

Ailsin raised her eyebrows. "How can you be so sure?"

"Because I can," Alex said easily. "There's no reason *that* could have given her away."

By *"that"*, did he mean when we barely kissed? I had to wonder since he said it with such regret.

Well, guess what? I regretted it too. I swear I did. Well, okay, whatever. It was kind of a lie. But I wished I was capable of regretting it, and that had to count for something, right?

"Alex, you didn't see it from my point of view," Aislin said. "From what I saw, it was far from ordinary. The lights were flashing on and off while you two—"

"Alright, I get it," Alex snapped.

"Wait a minute." Laylen held his hands in front of him. "What exactly did you two do?"

Was he joking? I didn't know him at all, so I couldn't tell if he was being serious or not. But it almost seemed like he was purposefully trying to cause trouble; like he was trying to embarrass us. And let me tell you, if that's what he was doing, then it was working. I have never been one to get embarrassed easily, but I could feel my cheeks getting warm. I squirmed around uncomfortably and fixed my gaze on the floor.

"It was nothing important." Alex's tone was flat. "So you don't need to worry about it."

A lump swelled in my throat. It felt like my heart had been ripped out and stomped on. I wished it didn't feel that way though. But despite how much I wanted to hate Alex—because, let's face it, nine times out of ten he was a Class A jerk—I couldn't.

"I need a break," I announced. "I'm going outside."

"Like hell you are," Alex said.

"I'm not a little kid." I stood up straight and raised my chin, hoping I appeared more confident than I felt. "If I want to go outside then I will. I need some fresh air."

Alex started toward me. "Gemma—"

Laylen stepped between us, creating a barrier. "How about I go out with her? That way she won't be alone." His bright blue eyes locked on me. "That is, if you don't mind?"

181

Did I mind? He was a vampire, at least according to Alex. It seemed like I should have felt untrusting toward him. But honestly, at the moment I couldn't have cared less what he was or wasn't. I couldn't see any blood thirst burning in his eyes or anything.

I shrugged. "Nope. I don't mind."

"Fine. Do whatever you want." Alex waved his hand, dismissing us, and turned back to Aislin. "Let's keep trying to get a hold of someone. We really need to know what's going on."

I heard Aislin mutter something in reply, but didn't hear exactly what because I was already out the door.

Outside, the deliciously warm desert air dusted my cheeks and swept through my hair. The sky had shifted grey and the stars sparkled across it. The sandy desert drifted aimlessly in front of me, shadowed by the nightfall. It was a relief not to have goose bumps speckling my skin. It was nice to be able to breathe without seeing it cloud out in front of me. It was so nice to be warm. So, deciding I might as well enjoy the warmth, I shoved the reason I was here far back into my mind and tried to let myself relax.

I sat down on the cement steps and stretched my legs out in front of me. The warm cement pressed through my jeans. The porch light shined from behind me and cast my shadows across the stairs below. Laylen seated himself beside me and leaned back on his elbows.

For awhile we just sat there, gazing out at the desert, listening to the crickets chirping in the distance. The stars were really dancing tonight, and I could clearly make out the constellation of Cassiopeia. I wondered if that's where my fascination with stars came from. Perhaps, deep down inside me, I knew what I really was and that some bits and pieces of me belonged up in the sky with them, not down here where I never felt like I belonged.

"So," Laylen's deep voice rang through the silence, "how's life been with Marco and Sophia?"

"Oh, just great," I replied, my tone sarcastic. "It's been a real blast."

He laughed. "They never have been the most pleasant people to be around."

I swatted at a bug that landed on my elbow. *Gross.* "So you know them then?"

"Yeah, but I haven't seen them in a really long time." He stared off in the distance, looking like he was lost in a painful memory. "I haven't seen any of the Keepers since...." He trailed off and looked at me. "Alex told you what I was, didn't he?"

I nodded. "But it's kind of hard to believe. All of this is kind of hard to believe."

"I imagine it would be." His voice was sympathetic. His blue eyes held such loneliness in them.

I propped my elbow on my knee and rested my chin in my hand. "So....what exactly is it that makes you a vampire?"

183

"What do you mean?"

"Well..." What was the correct way to ask someone how they were considered a creature of the night; the living undead; a blood thirsty monster? "I've read a lot of books and everything. Nothing that was actually factual, though. They all say different things about vampires, and I was just wondering which—or if any—had some truth to them."

He rubbed his hand along his jawline. "You want to know what it is that makes me a monster? Whether I bite, kill, or drink blood? If I can run at an inhuman speed or if I have super strength?"

It sounded like such a stupid question when he put it that way. "I guess that's what I'm trying to ask. Well, minus the whole monster thing, because I don't think that about you."

He cocked an eyebrow. "You don't think that I'm a monster?"

I shook my head. I didn't know him or anything, but he definitely wasn't sending out an I'm-a-demon-and-I'm-going-to-kill-you vibe.

He pressed his deep red lips together. "If that's true then you're probably the first person to ever think that." He gave a pause. "The whole hungry-for-blood thing doesn't apply to me. I don't drink blood. I don't kill."

"But it applies to other vampires?"

He nodded. "Other vampires are probably a lot like what you've read. And I'm not talking about the ones who drink blood, and do it by killing animals. They like to kill."

A chill crept down my spine. "Why haven't I heard anything about them existing?" I mean, if people were dying because their blood was being drained, wouldn't the news have mentioned something about it?

"For the same reason you didn't know what you were. People are excellent at keeping secrets."

"Yes, they are," I agreed.

He brushed his blue-tipped bangs away from his forehead. "I do have some traits that normal vampires have. I'm immortal. I'm stronger than the average person. I have fangs."

I gaped at him. "You have fangs."

He nodded. "They're retractable and I don't use them. *Ever.*"

I couldn't help but stare at his mouth. I know staring is rude and everything, but I just couldn't seem to look away. The guy just told me he had retractable fangs, for crying out loud.

He laughed, and I got a full view of his flat, white teeth. "Staring at them isn't going to bring them out."

I quickly turned my head away, feeling stupid. Could I really be sitting in the desert next to a vampire, all while harboring the energy of a fallen star inside me? There was so much wrong with that statement, yet, in a bizarre, twisted way, it felt right.

It felt true.

The howl of a coyote cut through the air, and I jumped.

"I can also sense when a person's afraid," Laylen remarked.

"I'm not afraid," I told him.

"I know." He stood up and dusted off his jeans. "Which makes you kind of weird."

I sighed. "Weird seems to be my middle name."

He chuckled. "So it does."

Everything seemed strange. Here I was, having barely discovered my life was a web of lies, and yet I still found myself able to laugh. A quiet laugh, but nonetheless still a laugh.

I heard the front door creak open, and Alex stepped out with a displeased expression on his face. "Are you two having fun?"

What? I wasn't allowed to laugh? Well, I guess technically laughing was an emotion, but, whatever.

I looked up at Laylen, who winked at me before extending his hand out to me. His hand felt cold against mine as he helped me to my feet. Truth to another myth, I wondered.

I let go of his hand and followed him up the stairs, where Alex was waiting impatiently for us. He shot Laylen a glare as he walked by, but didn't even so much as give me the benefit of a scowl, staring out into the darkness as I stepped by him.

Chapter 16

When we were back inside, Alex informed us that he hadn't been able to get a hold of anyone, which I found odd. I mean, how was it that three people wouldn't be answering their phones at the exact same time? It couldn't just be coincidental. There had to be more to it. And by the way Alex looked—all stressed out and confused—I was guessing he felt the same way as I did.

I sat down at the table and watched Alex pace back and forth across the room. He continued to do so for awhile, not saying anything, and I was starting to grow restless. The silence was driving me nuts.

Finally I couldn't take it anymore and decided to take matters into my own hands. "So, what are we supposed to do now?"

Aislin, who had parked herself in the chair across from me, was tapping her cell phone anxiously on her knee—apparently, no one could sit still. "We try to find them."

Alex stopped pacing and shook his head. "That's easier said than done."

"I'm just trying to help," she said. "There's no need to be rude."

"Did you two ever consider that maybe they don't want you to get a hold of them?" Laylen asked.

Alex tossed his phone down on the table. "Laylen, whatever it is you're trying to say, just say it."

Laylen crossed his arms and leaned back against one of the bookshelves, the muscles of his arms flexing beneath his shirt. I had to admit, the guy was cute. I wonder if it had anything to do with him being a vampire. Vampires were supposed to be cut, weren't they? Then again, Alex was the same way, so maybe it was a Keeper thing—being perfectly built. Because, trust me, that's what they both were.

My gaze wandered over to Alex. The sleeves of his long sleeve grey shirt were pushed up, the muscles of his forearms visible. I wondered what it would feel like to have those arms wrapped around me.

Suddenly I realized Alex was staring at me. Why was he staring at me? Because I was staring at him. He cocked an eyebrow and gave me a curious look.

I quickly looked away. I was such an idiot. Here I was, in the middle of a chaotic mess, my life in danger, and all I could do was stare at Alex's muscles.

"You want to know what I think?" Laylen said. "I don't think it's just a coincidence that Stephan, Marco, and Sophia are all unreachable at the exact time all hell breaks loose. There's got to be more to it than that." He moved

188

away from the shelf and walked over to Alex. "For all we know, they could be working with Demetrius and the Death Walkers."

"Why would they be working with the Death Walkers?" I asked.

"Gemma, just ignore him," Alex said, glaring at Laylen.

"Why should I?" I asked. "From what I know, there are two liars in this room. And he's not one of them."

Laylen pressed his lips together to hold back a grin. Aislin frowned, looking hurt. And Alex sauntered over toward me, a cynical smile on his face as he leaned across the table and looked me right in the eyes. He kept his voice low, making my body hum. "I'm not sure what's bringing on this new attitude of yours, but you know what? I think I kind of like it. It makes things more interesting."

He was mocking me. I got that. But I couldn't seem to think of anything to throw back at him. My brain had spaced out on me.

Stupid brain.

He backed away from the table, looking disappointed.

"Maybe we should go back to Afton and check up on things," Aislin suggested. "There might be something back at the house that could help us figure out where they are."

Alex stared at her, dumfounded. "Are you crazy? There's no way we're taking Gemma back there. It's too dangerous."

"What? Am I never going back there?" I sounded upset. But I don't know why. Escaping the snowy mountains was what I always wanted. But I never pictured I would have to leave because my life was in danger.

"You can't go back. Not when the Death Walkers know what you are." He arched an eyebrow at me. "Does that upset you or something?"

I considered this, thinking about going back to the mountains, to the snow, to living with Marco and Sophia. I shrugged. "I don't know. I guess not, but where am I going to go?"

Alex dragged his fingers through his dark brown hair. "That's a question only Stephan can answer."

What was it about this Stephan? And why could he make decisions about my life?

"I don't think—" I started.

Alex talked over me. "We need to get a hold of them." He picked up his cell phone and checked the screen. "Otherwise we're lost."

"Well…" Aislin tapped her phone against her chin. "What we could do is leave Gemma with Laylen while you and I go back."

Alex scowled at her. "There's no way in hell I'm leaving her alone with him."

Laylen laughed, but it was a laugh underlined with hurt. "What? Am I not even considered a person anymore?"

Alex's pause lasted one second too long. I could feel the tension bubbling, about to erupt.

"That's not what I was trying to say," Alex said unconvincingly. "I'm just worried that something might happen while I'm gone, and you won't be able to protect her."

Laylen rolled his eyes. "That's a bunch of crap. I'm just as capable of protecting her as you are, and you know it. You just don't trust me." They stared at one another like two angry dogs about to break out in a fight. Then, to make things worse, Laylen added, "I just might be even more capable than you."

For a second I thought they might kill each other. I had the feeling that there was more to their fight than what was being said. Like maybe something had happened in the past. I mean, there had to be more to their little argument than who was more qualified to protect me. If they did end up fighting, considering Laylen was a vampire I would guess the odds were in his favor. As much as Alex had pissed me off, I really didn't want to watch him get hurt. Plus, it would have been a great tragedy for that gorgeous face of his to get messed up.

I looked at Aislin, hoping she would do something to stop it. But she was chewing on a strand of her hair, staring down at the table.

I guess I was on my own.

"So, do I not get a say in any of this?" I said in a voice loud enough to break the tension.

Laylen and Alex tore their eyes away from one another, and I had to hover back from the burning anger in their faces. Losing some of my confidence, my voice quieted a little. "It's my life, so I think I should have some say in this."

"No," Alex said. "You don't get a say in any of this."

My anger boiled. So this was how it was going to be from now on? I wouldn't get a say in anything? I clenched my hands into fists, almost regretting that I had interrupted the fight between Laylen and him.

Shrugging off my death stare, Alex turned to Aislin. "Can you get us to Afton and back quickly?"

She raised her chin with confidence. "Of course I can."

"Then fine. We'll leave her here with Laylen." He aimed his finger at Laylen. "But if anything happens to her, it's on you."

Laylen rolled his eyes. "Nothing's going to happen to her."

"I'll believe that when I see it," Alex said.

Another eye roll from Laylen. "Thanks for the confidence."

"I have to go back into the library and grab my candle and crystal," Aislin announced. "Then we can go."

I cocked my head to the side. "Crystal? What crystal?"

"The one I used on the bus to transport us here," she explained. "It's how I'm going to get us back to Afton."

"Oh." I remembered; the purple amethyst, the burning candle, and the glowing yellow eyes. I shivered.

192

She started to get to her feet, but then dropped back down in the chair, smacking her hand on her forehead. "Crap! Crap! Crap! I completely forgot that the Death Walkers' ice ruined it. We were lucky just to make it here."

"There's no way you can do it without a crystal?" Alex asked.

"No." She wrapped a strand of her hair around her finger, thinking. "Well, there are other ways, but I haven't learned how to do them yet."

The room grew silent, except for the cracking sound Alex's knuckles made as he popped them.

Laylen twisted his lip ring from side to side. "What kind of crystal is it?"

"It's the one that looks like an amethyst." She propped her elbow on the table and let her chin fall into her hand. "Now what are we going to do?"

"Is it a Vectum Crystal?" Laylen asked.

Aislin raised her chin out of her hand, a hopeful expression on her face. "Do you have one?"

"No, but I know where we can get one." He gestured over his shoulder at the window. "There's this place in Vegas that sells things like that. I bet they have one."

Alex shook his head. "There is no way we're taking Gemma into Vegas. It's way too dangerous."

"So I can't go to Vegas. And I can't go home," I said, counting down on my fingers. "Is there anywhere I can go?"

"Not really."

I glared at him, but he didn't even so much as blink. He placed his hands on the table, leaned toward me, and spoke in a low voice that made my body hum. "Do you have to argue about everything?"

I ignored the flutter my heart did. "Maybe."

"Alex, can we please just go get the crystal and get this taken care of?" Aislin begged. "Sitting here and arguing about it isn't going to get us anywhere."

He shook his head, his green eyes fixed solely on me. "I said it's too dangerous for Gemma to go."

I took an exasperated breath. "Please stop say—"

He placed his hand across my mouth. My lips sparkled underneath his warm, electric skin. God, it felt good. Mind numbingly good. I was supposed to be mad at him...wasn't I?

"It's too dangerous." His voice flowed out like velvet.

For a brief second, I had this really strange thought. What if things were different? What if he wasn't a Keeper and I wasn't carrying a world saving star inside me? What if we had met under normal circumstances? What if I was allowed to have those kinds of feelings for him? The ones I was feeling right now, but knew I wasn't supposed to be feeling. Would things have been different between us? Maybe. Or maybe I would have been just a silly girl with a crush that ended up with a broken heart. Alex really did seem like the heartbreaking type.

Blinking myself back to reality, I shoved his hand away from my mouth. He looked momentarily stunned,

194

blinking a few times like he was just waking up from a dream.

"Alex, going into Vegas isn't any more dangerous than sitting around here," Laylen pointed out. "In fact, we'll be on the move, so it might be safer."

Alex backed away from the table and turned to Laylen. "Are you sure about that?"

Laylen shook his head and sighed. "Look, this place is very low key. We'll go straight there and straight back. Trust me, there won't be any problems."

Alex deliberated this. "You promise you won't try to make any other stops? Just straight there and straight back?"

Laylen stared at him incredulously. "Are you kidding me? Where else is it that you think I'm going to try and take us? McDonalds? Walmart? Oh, wait a minute, I do need to make a quick stop by the cemetery."

Trying to choke back a laugh, I ended up letting out a snort. I had to give the guy props. He was pretty funny.

Alex shot me a dirty look. "What? You think this is funny?"

I choked back another laugh, luckily without snorting this time, and shook my head.

Laylen did laugh, though. And Aislin sighed, dropping her head down on the table in an I-am-so-over-this way.

"Well, I'm glad you two find this so funny." Alex grabbed the back of a chair, his gaze pressing into me.

"Don't underestimate the Death Walkers, Gemma. They will kill you if they get the chance."

I swallowed the huge lump that had wiggled its way up my throat. A blanket of fear wrapped its way around my body. He was right. It wasn't funny.

"Alex, knock it off," Aislin warned. "You're scaring her."

"Good," he said. "She should be scared."

After that, all arguments came to a halt. The decision to go to Vegas was made with the stipulation that there would be no stopping except to get the crystal.

Because of the whole glass-stabbing-into-my-side thing, Ailsin insisted I needed to change before we left. Apparently there was no way I could go anywhere with blood all over my shirt. It was a fairly small spot, but whatever. I was tired of arguing.

I guess Alex and Aislin used to make frequent visits to Laylen's house, and Aislin had a room packed with a bunch of her stuff, including clothes. I was skeptical about wearing anything that belonged to Aislin. I mean, her whole wardrobe was so...pink. But right now, I guess fashion wasn't important.

Then again, was it ever?

The room she took me back to looked just like a normal girl's room should look; pink floral wallpaper, rose colored carpet, a white four post bed covered with tons of fluffy pillows.

Aislin marched up to an armoire in the corner and threw open the doors. "The only problem is you're about five inches taller than me," she said, assessing the selection of clothes hanging up. "But I guess we'll just have to make something work."

I dropped down on the bed. "So, you guys used to come here a lot?"

She took out a pink t-shirt and tossed it on the bed beside me. "Yeah, this house actually used to belong to Laylen's parents, and we used to come up here to take a break from everything." She threw a glittery scarf onto the bed. A scarf? We were in the desert, for crying out loud. "Things change though." She sighed, staring down at the pair of jeans she was holding in her hand. "We haven't been up here in a really long time."

There was such sadness in the way she said it, and it made me wonder why they stopped coming up here. But I didn't ask.

She started rummaging through the clothes again, every once in awhile tossing something onto the bed. Covering the walls was an array of photos. I got up and walked around, looking at them. One in particular caught my attention. It was of Laylen, standing out in the desert, his arm wrapped around Aislin's shoulder in an affectionate way that gave the impression they might have been a couple once. Next to Laylen stood Alex, and cuddling next to him was a pretty blonde-haired girl. All of them were smiling. They looked so happy. It made my heart hurt a little. Happy. Had I ever been happy?

"That was taken a couple of years ago," Ailsin said.

I tore my eyes off the photo and found her watching me.

"I think I was about fourteen or so," she said. "So about five years ago."

I did the math and something didn't add up. "Wait. How old are you?"

"Nineteen." She tossed a skirt onto the bed. "Alex is actually twenty. We lied about our ages so we could enroll in school."

"Oh." The saying *liar, liar, pants on fire* ran through my head. Even something as simple as their age was a lie. It made me question how many more lies I was in store for. "What about Laylen? How old is he?"

"Well, he would've been twenty-two, but after he got…um…." She trailed off and then shook her head. But I knew what she was going to say: before he was bitten. "But yeah, he's stuck at nineteen now, so…" She tossed a shirt onto the bed, then came over and stared down at the pile of clothes with a look of sheer determination on her face. "Okay, let's see if any of these fit you."

Spotting a black t-shirt at the top of the pile, I snatched it up immediately.

Aislin sighed. "Gemma, would it kill you to wear colors that aren't so depressing?"

"It might."

She sighed again. "Fine. But could you at least wear a skirt or something?"

I shook my head. "I hate skirts."

"You know, when you were little, you used to run around in dresses all the time."

I stared at her, confused. "I don't remember this."

Her bright green eyes went wide. She just said something she wasn't supposed to.

"What?" I asked. "What is it?"

"Nothing." She quickly shook her head. "It's nothing." She started to search through the pile of clothes again.

"It's something." I stood up, hugging the black t-shirt to my chest. "Whatever it is, you need to tell me. It's not fair that—"

She cut me off, shoving a pair of denim shorts at me. "Gemma. Please just drop it."

"How do you expect me to—?"

"Please," she said in a quiet but firm voice.

I grinded my teeth and snatched the pair of shorts out of her hand. "Fine." I turned for the door. "Where should I change?"

"There's a bathroom down the hallway. It's the third door on the right."

Dazed, and a little out of it, I ended up passing the bathroom and had to retrace my steps. Aislin's strange behavior had me puzzled. I couldn't figure out why she freaked out. Why was it so bad for her to mention I liked wearing dresses when I was a child?

I carefully slipped out of my blood-stained shirt and pulled on the black tee. But when I went to tug the shorts on, I realized the "shorts" Aislin gave was actually a denim skirt. By accident, I think not. I might have loved to wear dresses when I was little, but that didn't mean I did now. I stuck my tongue out at the skirt before reluctantly putting it on.

When I finished getting dressed, I splashed some cold water on my face in a pathetic attempt to bring myself out of this dream that I was sure I was stuck in. Vampires, witches, and secret groups who saved the world weren't supposed to exist. It was all too unreal—too science fiction. They key word here being "fiction."

But after I patted my face dry and opened my eyes, the same navy blue walls of Laylen's bathroom still surrounded me. I glanced into the mirror hanging above the sink and sighed at the sight of my freakish violet eyes staring back at me. I wondered if it was the star's energy that had created the color. How was I supposed to know how much of my reflection was me? And how much of it was the star's?

A knock at the door startled me.

"Gemma, are you ready to go?" Aislin asked.

I blinked one last time at my reflection before turning away from it.

Chapter 17

Laylen drove a 1960s Black Pontiac GTO with white racing stripes streaming down the middle of the hood. Apparently he and Alex had this thing for classic cars. Something I picked up on during a brief guy bonding moment between the two of them, when Alex had first seen the "beautiful" car.

I was starting to figure out that guys were kind of weird.

Their bonding moment quickly came and passed, and a few minutes later we were driving down the dirt road with nothing more than the roar of the engine to fill the silence.

Laylen's house was located in the middle of nowhere, so it took awhile just to get to the freeway. I was sitting in the back seat, watching the stars streak across the sky in shades of violet and silver. Alex had insisted that no one else could sit by me but him, muttering something about it being safer that way in case the Death Walkers tried to ambush us or something. But being in the back seat of a two-door vehicle during an ambush, I could see no advantage to the seating arrangement.

To make things even more complicated, being confined in the car was causing the electricity to crackle like a wildfire. My skin was getting hot and sweaty, and I felt like I was burning up with a fever. Fortunately, I discovered that even in the desert, the air cooled during the night and chilled the windows. I had my cheek resting against the glass, on the verge of falling asleep, when Alex asked, "What are you doing?"

"Trying to sleep," I mumbled crankily.

"You look like you're burning up," he remarked.

I heard him shift in the seat, and the next thing I knew he was pressing the palm of his hand to my forehead. It sent a shot of heat through my body, causing me to jump. Great. It was already so freaking hot—the last thing I needed was for him to touch me.

I turned my head to look at him. He had narrowed the distance between us so drastically that, even through the darkness, I could see his eyes assessing me.

"What are you doing?" I asked, raising my face away from the window.

"I'm checking to see if you have a fever."

"I don't have a fever," I argued, sliding my forehead out from under his hand.

But his hand followed me. He dragged it gently along my temple, letting it come to rest on my cheek. "Your skin feels really warm."

"That's because I am warm," I said, my voice sharp. "And you touching me just makes it worse." I tilted my face and his hand fell to his lap. "You're too hot." As soon as I said it, I immediately wanted to slap myself on the forehead. *You're too hot. What's wrong with you, Gemma?* "I-I didn't mean it like that," I stammered.

It didn't matter though. The damage had already been done. The corners of his mouth tugged upwards into a beautiful yet smug smile. "I'm too hot, huh?"

"Oh, shut up." Through the darkness, I fixed him with my angriest glare. "You know that's not what I meant."

"Do I?" His eyebrow teased upward.

I shook my head, frustrated. The last thing I needed was for him to think I had some kind of crush on him, because I didn't. I swear. Well, fine. Whatever. But he didn't need to know that.

"What I meant to say was your skin feels too hot," I said.

"Okay, whatever you say."

I heaved an angry breath. "You are such a—" I snapped my jaw shut as the city suddenly blistered over the horizon.

The sight was breathtaking. Flashy neon lights of every shape and color dazzled so vibrantly against the blackness of the night that I wondered if staring at it for too long would make me go blind. Giant billboards lit up the sides of the road, and uniquely shaped buildings stretched godly toward the sky. As we emerged closer to the city, the sidewalks became packed with mobs of people, the air buzzing with excitement. Now I understood why its nickname had been deemed The City that Never Sleeps. Everything was so alive and awake. *Literally.*

Awestruck by the sight, I pinched my arm to make sure I wasn't dreaming and winced from the sting I undeniably felt.

Alex must have seen me do it, because he leaned over and whispered, "You're not dreaming. It's real."

I rubbed the pinched spot on my arm. "I was just making sure."

He smiled. Clearly I was entertaining him.

We drove by a massive glass pyramid, a giant pirate ship, and a small replica of the Eiffel tower, finally hitting the heart of the city. Laylen made an unexpected veer to the right, and the atmosphere abruptly shifted. The lights faded away, and the crowds of people thinned out. The buildings shrank from the sky, looking worn out and less exciting. I caught Aislin reaching over and locking her door. The place was definitely sketchy.

I chewed nervously on my bottom lip and scooted away from the window to distance myself as much as I could from the outside.

"You do realize it's almost one o'clock?" Aislin informed Laylen. Back at the house, she had changed her clothes. She was wearing a frilly skirt and a lacy trimmed camisole. On her shoulder blade was a tattoo of a crescent moon outlined by a black star. "Is this place even going to be open so late?" Aislin asked.

Laylen flipped the signal light on. "Yeah, it'll be open. It's only open at night."

What kind of place was only open at night? Probably one as creepy as the street we were on.

Laylen made another turn, this time to the left, and any signs of life died instantaneously. The buildings looked dead and broken and most of the windows were boarded up. As Laylen slowed the GTO to a crawl, all I could think was, "Yes, *of course this is the street we're stopping on.*" We couldn't have just stopped back in the land of the living, where the lights shined brightly and it didn't feel like as soon as I stepped out of the car someone was going to jump out and stab me with a knife. Or jump out and freeze me to death.

I choked on the last thought.

Laylen parked the car in front of a gloomy building with dingy windows. The words "Angel's Fortress of Tattoos and Piercing" were painted sloppily across the window. No lights were on inside it or in any of the nearby buildings. The only proof of human existence was when a person wearing a black hooded jacket, cargo pants, and army boots darted out in front of the car, scurried down the street, and disappeared down a dark alleyway. It scared me so badly I seriously about peed my pants.

Alex leaned in toward me. "Are you okay?"

"Umm..." Did he just ask if I was okay? He even sounded like he was being sincere, which was weird. "Yeah, I think so."

205

Laylen turned off the engine, and the radio and the lights shut off. It got quiet and very dark.

"Are you sure you're okay?" Alex asked me again, his voice low and deep. "Because you look scared."

"I'm not," I lied, clicking my seatbelt loose.

"You don't have to be scared," he whispered in my ear. The heat of his breath made me shiver in a good way. "I promise I won't let anything happen to you."

What was with the sudden nice guy act? Maybe the electricity was becoming too much for him too and was messing with his head or something.

"Okay," I said, sounding confused.

Aislin scanned the ominous buildings surrounding us. "So which one is it?"

Laylen didn't reply, his eyes glued to the front window as he fiddled with his lip ring.

Aislin turned and looked at him. "Laylen, which one is it?"

When he finally spoke, his words dragged out. "It's none of them."

Alex scooted forward in the seat and rested his arms on the console. "What do you mean, it's none of them?"

"I mean it's none of them." Laylen dropped his fingers from his lip ring. "I needed to make an extra stop."

Oh boy. Here we go. Alex had been very specific about going straight there and straight back. And here we were, taking a detour. I squeezed my eyes shut and massaged the sides of my temples, waiting for all hell to break loose.

"What!" Alex shouted, slamming his fist down on the console. "I thought I told you we weren't supposed to stop anywhere else!"

Laylen slid the keys out of the ignition and kept his voice calm. "Before you start freaking out, hear me out first. Trust me, you'll want what I stopped for."

"Trust you?" Alex let out a cynical laugh. "Are you kidding me?" He made a gesture at the window. "I already trusted you and look where it got us."

No one said anything. I could hear dogs howling, and a loud bang like a garbage can toppling over echoed through the air.

Alex threw his hands in the air. "Fine. What did we stop for?"

Laylen tapped his fingers on top of the steering wheel. "The Sword of Immortality."

One...two...three seconds ticked by.

"Dammit, Laylen!" Alex exclaimed. "You've had it this whole time."

Whatever this Sword of Immortality was had to be something important. It was obviously a sword—*duh*—but what kind of sword? An immortal one? That didn't make any sense.

"Had it," Laylen corrected him. "I lost it during a poker game a few months ago."

Alex grinded his teeth. "So, let me get this straight. You stole it from us just so you could lose it."

"I took it for a good reason," Laylen said. "I didn't want to leave it in the Keepers' hands after I turned immortal." He paused. "You know this is why I didn't want to tell you about to begin with. I knew you would overreact."

"I'm not overreacting." Alex flopped back in the seat. "You didn't just take something insignificant like a car. You took the Sword of Immortality."

No one so much as uttered a word.

Feeling as though I might burst from the drawn-out silence, I asked, "What's the Sword of Immortality?"

"Exactly what it sounds like—a sword that can kill an immortal," Alex said, still aggravated. "And it would have been real handy to have while we were on the bus being attacked by Death Walkers."

I gaped at him. "The Death Walkers are immortal?" No one had ever mentioned *that*.

Alex dragged his fingers through his hair and nodded. "The sword is one of the few things that can kill them."

I shuddered at the thought. "So back on the bus, when we were being attacked, you couldn't have killed them?"

Alex shook his head. "Nope."

My eyes widened at the reality of the fact that a few hours ago I could have very easily died.

"So how do we get it back?" Alex asked, his voice ringing hotly.

208

"Well, it's inside there, in a display case on the second floor." Laylen pointed at an old brick building. "It's unguarded and everything. The only problem I can think of that we might run into is breaking into the display case. It doesn't just have a normal lock you can pick. In fact, I don't think it even has a lock, and I'm pretty sure breaking the glass would set off an alarm."

Aislin bounced up and down in her seat. "I might know a spell that would work."

Alex leaned forward and held up his hand. "Hold on just a second. First, I need to know where *here* is?"

Laylen didn't reply, staring off of at the brick building he pointed at earlier.

"Laylen," Aislin said. "Where are we?"

Laylen let out a tired sigh. "The Black Dungeon."

Alex cursed a sequence of too-inappropriate-to-repeat words, and then stared pensively at the building Laylen wanted us to go into. "Aislin, how quickly do you think you could do the spell?"

"I'll do it as quickly as I can," she told him. "But there's no guarantee on how fast I can get it unlocked. Magic takes time. You know that."

Alex pointed a finger at me. "You'll have to stay by me at all times."

"I already made that promise back at the house," I reminded him.

"Yes, but it's more important now." He paused, his expression shifting from anger to worry. "There are things in there that are very…dangerous."

My heart thrummed loudly. "What kind of things?"

He rubbed the back of his neck tensely. "Things that are—you know, maybe you and I should just wait in the car."

"I'd rather not." My gaze drifted to the building and then to the dark alley trailing to the side of it. "This place gives me the creeps."

"I don't think she's going to be any safer sitting out here than she would be inside." Laylen shoved the car keys in his pocket. "This neighborhood is pretty unsafe."

Alex glanced around, assessing the danger. "Fine, but we need to make sure we hurry." As Laylen and Aislin climbed out of the car, he muttered, "This is such a bad idea."

I should have guessed we would end up having to walk down a dark alley to get to the entrance of the Black Dungeon. Why wouldn't we, since the idea made me shiver? The only light was from the moon illuminating the puddles that spotted the asphalt. I didn't even want to know what the puddles were, seeing as how it wasn't raining. The air reeked of mold and wet dog. The garbage cans spilled over, oozing the ground with papers and boxes and filth that crunched beneath my shoes as I walked.

It was gross.

Laylen led us through the mess and stopped in front of a rusty metal door. Alex stayed close by my side, arms folded, very I'm-your-bodyguard style. The electricity was gyrating, but at least we were in open air now, making it less smothering and almost tolerable.

Laylen held up his fist to the door. "Are we ready?"

"Probably not," Alex grumbled, waving his hand at the door. "But go ahead."

Laylen let his hand fall against the door and waited a minute before knocking again. A couple of seconds later, a small flap at the top of the door slid open, and a pair of dark eyes peered out.

"What's the password?" a deep voice rumbled.

Laylen raised his forearm up to the flap, showing it to the pair of eyes.

"Very well," the voice grunted. A soft *click* and then the door swung open.

I'm not sure what I expected to see standing behind that door, but it wasn't this. A man barely my height, with bony arms and greased back hair, standing in a small, dimly lit room that had nothing but a metal fold-up chair to accompany it.

Laylen greeted the little man with a nod. "Doug."

The man—aka Doug—muttered an unfriendly, "Hey."

I stared quizzically at Doug, trying to figure out how he obtained a job as a bouncer or guard or whatever the title was for this place—I wasn't really sure, since I was still confused about what kind of place the Black Dungeon was. And not knowing terrified me to my very core.

Doug glared at me with his dark eyes. Apparently he was a firm believer in the whole staring-is-rude thing.

Alex gently nudged me in the back with his elbow, urging me to get a move on. I turned my attention to Laylen.

There was only one door in the room, and Laylen strolled up to it and jerked it open. A slender hallway extended out the other side. Black lanterns hung from the dusky walls, illuminating a trail of light across the stone floor and arched brick ceiling. Laylen and Aislin started down the hallway, and I stepped through the doorway after them, Alex following closely behind me.

The moist air dampened my skin as we zigzagged farther and farther down the hall. With every noise, my sense of fear heightened. My heart pounded in my chest, anxiously anticipating what was waiting at the end.

As I passed by one of the lanterns hanging on the wall, I noticed it had the same black symbols that were tattooed on Laylen's forearm. When I got a chance—hopefully I made it out of this place alive to *get* a chance—I would have to ask him what the symbols meant.

Music reverberated from somewhere, a low beat that grew louder the farther down the hallway we got, until it thumped so loudly it vibrated the floors and rattled the lanterns.

"This was such a stupid idea," Alex mumbled from behind me, "so stupid."

I peeked over my shoulder at him, and he met my gaze. Hatred was not shining from his bright green eyes like it normally did whenever he looked at me. Nothing but worry filled them. He was scared.

So was I.

I bit down on my bottom lip and kept walking. Laylen took us around a corner and a door popped into view. It looked like an ordinary door, but I had a feeling that whatever was on the other side of it was anything but ordinary.

"Okay." Laylen rubbed his hands together. "Is everybody ready for this?"

No one responded. Aislin and I both shared the same dumbfounded expression. Alex looked annoyed. Were we ready? Ready for what exactly?

I tugged down on the hem of my skirt while Ailsin straightened up her posture. Alex cast a glance back down the hall, bumping his shoulder into mine and erupting a fire underneath my skin. I was getting good at hiding my reaction, though. I didn't even gasp.

"Let's hurry up and get this over with," Alex said.

Laylen nodded, turned the doorknob, and the door creaked open.

It was a club. Like, an actual full-on dance club. And except for the gothic trend that seemed to be everywhere, everything seemed normal. I couldn't see anything slimy, glowing, or dead. Part of me had expected to walk in and find the whole place packed with demons and monsters of all shapes, sizes, and colors, feeding off humans. But that didn't seem to be the case.

Dangling from the ceiling were the same black lanterns that lit the hall. People were crammed on the dance floor, swaying hypnotically to the low beat of Nirvana's "You Know You're Right." Scarlet lights sparkled across the midnight marble floor. Black curtains draped across the upstairs balcony. Dark clothing trended the room. Laylen, Alex, and I blended in fine with the gothic ambience, Alex in his dark grey t-shirt and black jeans, Laylen all in black, and me in my black t-shirt and a dark denim skirt. Ailsin, however, was another story. In her lacy camisole top and frilly white skirt, the girl stood out like a sore thumb.

Laylen shoved his way through the crowd, heading for the dance floor. We all trailed behind him, the pokes and prods of stray elbows banging me in the back and sides. I cradled my arm protectively around my stitches to keep any stray body parts from jabbing them.

The air smelled of incense overlapped by cigarette smoke and sweat. In the middle of it all was a bar, raising the question of if we were even old enough to be in here.

At the edge of the crowd, swinging from the ceiling, was a giant life-sized bird cage. As I pushed my way out of the last of the sweaty bodies, I caught sight of what was inside the cage and came to a slamming halt. A woman was twirling gracefully around a pole. Her wavy black hair hung all the way down to the bottom of her back. A leather corset dress fitted her body, and thigh high boots laced up her legs. A velvet choker wrapped her neck, and snaking up her arm was whip. A pair of striking black-feathered wings sprouted out of her shoulder blades.

She spun around the pole, and then locked her haunting grey eyes on me. I felt my breath catch. My body suddenly felt so warm, like I was liquefying. My limbs, my muscles, everything centered to her. I knew what I needed to do. I needed to go to her. Right now. It was imperative that I did…A matter of life or death.

My leg lifted up and, like a puppet bound to its strings, stepped down, inching my body closer to the cage. A silent warning breezed my mind, screaming at me to *stop*, but my other leg rose up and touched back down to the floor, moving me to her. Another step…I was just within reach of the lock that bolted the cage's door shut. The feather-winged woman watched me with hungry eyes as my arm extended forward, my fingers brushing the cold metal —

Someone grabbed my arm. A zap of electricity hummed through my body.

"Don't," I heard Alex say as he guided me swiftly away from the cage.

I blinked dazedly at him.

"What do you think you're doing?" he asked crossly.

215

"I-I," I stuttered. What had I been doing? Was I trying to let the woman out? It seemed like such a good idea a few seconds ago, but now…

"If you open that up—" he pointed a finger at the cage—"you'll be the one trapped in there with a pair of wings growing out of your back."

I cringed. "I didn't mean to…I mean, I don't know why I was going to do it. I just couldn't…think." I glanced back at the cage. The woman's pale blue lips curled into a snarl, and she let out a hiss. I jumped back, slamming my shoulder into Alex's chest. Big mistake. Caught off-guard, I gasped from the electricity that shot through my body.

"Sor-ry," I stammered, stumbling away from him.

He pressed his lips together and rolled his shoulders and neck, as if he was trying to shake off my touch. "Please watch where you're going."

"I said I was sorry," I snapped.

He sighed and turned around, heading off in the direction of a spiral staircase. Aislin and Laylen stood at the top of it, staring down at us.

"So what is she?" I asked, climbing up the stairs after Alex.

He glanced over his shoulder at me. "What?"

"The woman back there." I gave a nod back at the cage. "She's obviously not human. So what is she?"

He came to an unexpected halt, and I almost ran into him. *Again.* "She was probably human once, until she

216

opened up the cage for the previous Black Angel that was locked inside."

"A Black Angel? What, like a Fallen Angel or something?"

"Not quite." He shook his head. "Look Gemma, as much as I would love to stand here and explain everything to you, I really think we should get going." And with that, he turned his back to me and trotted up the stairs.

I sighed and grudgingly followed after him.

"How much longer is this going to take?" Alex asked Aislin, pacing impatiently in front of the doorway of the room where the Sword of Immortality was locked inside a display case.

"Not too much longer," Aislin replied. "I think."

I was standing just outside the doorway next to Laylen. He was keeping a look out for...well, anything basically. A hallway extended out on each side of us. The florescent lighting of the lantern lights was hitting the maroon walls and tinting everything a dark shade of red. It reminded me of blood.

And what part did I play in all of this? Absolutely nothing. I served no more purpose than the vase perched on the table in front of us. It took up space and nothing more. All I did was make the situation even more dangerous, especially if a Death Walker showed up, which Laylen informed me was a possibility. I wasn't sure if Alex knew this or not, but I wasn't going to be the one to break it to him.

Laylen and I had been quiet for the most part. It wasn't necessarily an awkward silence, though. I think we both spent our fair share of time being lonely, and silence wasn't an unsettling thing.

"So...do you think he's going to wear a hole in the carpet or what?" Laylen asked, breaking our not unsettling quiet.

I had been watching the staircase intently, waiting for someone to unexpectedly pop into view and take us by surprise. "Huh? Who?"

"Alex."

I glanced at Alex. He was still pacing the floor, his eyes fixed like a hawk on Aislin.

"Maybe," I answered.

Laylen laughed. "I'm almost certain he's going to."

I laughed softly, the air tickling at my lungs.

Laylen leaned against the wall and folded his arms, his muscles flexing and making his skin ripple a little.

I stared at the tattoo tracing his forearm. "What does that mean?" I asked, pointing to his tattoo.

He raised his arm. "What, this?"

I nodded. "I noticed you put it up to the door outside so we could get in. And it's also on the lanterns that are all over this place, so I'm just wondering what it is."

He pressed a grin back. "A tattoo."

218

I rolled my eyes. "I got that, but does the tattoo mean anything?"

He traced his finger across the tattoo. "It's actually the mark of immortality."

"Then it's not a tattoo?"

"Not exactly. It appeared on my skin when I turned into a vampire." He paused, his Adam's apple noticeably bobbing up and down as he swallowed hard. "It happens to everyone that turns immortal."

"So why did you have to show it to the man at the door? Is this place like an all exclusive club for immortals or something?"

He laughed. "Yeah, I guess you could put it that way."

"So…" I snuck a peek at Alex, making sure he wasn't listening. He was still pacing the floor and cussing at Aislin to hurry up. Aislin was hissing at him to shut up, her hand pressed to the display case where the sword was locked, the jagged silver blade and dragonhead handle glistening in the light. I leaned in toward Laylen and kept my voice low. "What's a Black Angel?"

Laylen cocked an eyebrow at me, surprised by my question. "Where'd that question come from?"

I shrugged. "There was one downstairs in a cage and I asked Alex what it was, but he said he didn't have time to explain it to me."

"That doesn't surprise me." He backed up a few steps so that he was out of view from Alex and Aislin and gestured at me to do the same. "The thing with Alex," he

219

began as I moved closer, "is that he has it in his head that everything is a secret."

"So there's nothing important about a Black Angel."

"Only the fact that they're angels from hell and not heaven."

"Wha—" I started to exclaim, but Laylen stopped me with a quick shake of his head. I glanced over my shoulder to check if my loudness had brought any attention to us. Both sides of the hallway still remained vacant. I turned back to Laylen and dropped my voice down a notch. "Sorry, but an angel from hell. The two, like, completely contradict each other."

"In this world—"he motioned around us— "a lot of things do. Take me, for instance. A Keeper turned vampire. A complete contradiction. One stands for evil, the other for good."

I eyed him over. His beautiful blue eyes, his warm smile. "I highly doubt you're evil."

He forced a small smile. "Depends on who you're asking."

I felt bad for him. He seemed so...in pain. "I don't think you're—"

"Are you two enjoying yourselves?" Alex's voice interrupted over mine.

Laylen rolled his eyes, and I let out a tired sigh as I turned around. Alex held his classic irritated expression as he leaned against the doorway, watching us.

"At any moment during your little huddle up, someone could have strolled up, and I'm pretty sure neither one of you would've noticed," Alex said.

"Yeah, we would've," I protested. "Both of us have a clear view of each side of the hall."

"And it sure looked like you were keeping a close eye on them, all cuddled up with one another, talking about God knows what," he said scathingly.

"Alex, just relax." Laylen's voice was calm, but firm. "We weren't cuddled up, and we weren't talking about anything important." Laylen slid me a sideways glance that I hoped Alex didn't notice. "Jesus Christ. You can be so uptight sometimes."

Alex strolled up to us very cat-on-the-prowl like and pointed a finger at Laylen's chest. "I think you're forgetting why I'm uptight. She's not supposed to get close to anyone."

"Hey," I fumed. "That's not—"

Alex held a hand up, cutting me off. "This doesn't concern you."

I breathed heavily, placing my hands on my hips. "If it's about me, then it concerns me. You can't control me just because you want to."

A lethal stare-down broke out between us. I fixed him with my best glare, trying to summon up as much fire in it as I could. Of course, Alex looked unbothered, his face set in a tolerant expression.

"You know what," Laylen said to Alex. "I really think that your being uptight has nothing to do with me at all."

I gave Laylen a funny look. What was that supposed to mean?

"What exactly is it you're trying to get at?" Alex asked sharply.

"Oh, I think you know what it is I'm getting at," Laylen said. "This isn't about me talking to Gemma, or Gemma getting close to anyone. It's about you wanting what you can't have."

Alex's expression faltered. Laylen had obviously nailed whatever was bothering him. But what a gorgeous, self-confident—and yes, extremely cocky—guy like Alex would want but couldn't have was beyond me.

I noticed that Laylen was watching me closely. Alex wasn't looking at me at all, his eyes fixed on red tinted carpet. He appeared at a loss for words, which was strange for him. He was never at a loss for words. In fact, he usually had too much to say.

I opened my mouth. "I'm sorry, am I missing some—"

"Got it," Aislin announced as she bounced through doorway with the Sword of Immortality gripped in her hand. "Now, let's go."

Alex let out a breath of relief. "Sounds good to me."

Laylen took a balled up navy blue duffel bag out of his pocket. Back at the car, he had stuffed it in there so we could smuggle out the sword without it being noticed. He shook it out and unzipped it. "Here, put the sword in here."

Aislin placed the sword inside the bag. "Are you sure no one's going to be suspicious of us carrying out a bag?"

"They would be far more suspicious if it *wasn't* in the bag," Laylen pointed out, zipping the bag up.

"Can we just get going?" Alex snapped, backing down the hall.

Aislin sighed. "Yeah, let's go."

Laylen slid the handle of the bag over his shoulder, and then he and I followed them down the hall. The air dipped colder the closer we got to the stairs. Goose bumps polka dotted my skin. I shivered, rubbing my hands up and down my arms.

"Are you cold?" Laylen asked, adjusting the handle of the bag.

"Kind of," I replied, my breath rising out in a cloud. *Well, that can't be good.*

Laylen stopped dead in his tracks, his already pale skin draining to a ghostly white.

"What is it?" I asked him. Before he could answer, I slammed into the back of Alex.

"Go back," he hissed, shoving me in the direction we just came from. "They're heading up the stairs."

He didn't have to explain who "they" were. I already knew by the icy brittleness that had strangled the air. My heart hammered as we ran back into the room where the sword had just been locked up.

Aislin bounced up and down on her toes. "Oh my God, how did they find us?"

Laylen shrugged. "I have no idea."

"Is there another way out of here?" Alex asked Laylen.

"There's a fire escape at the end of the hall," Laylen told him. "But it'll probably set off the fire alarm when you open it."

"Well, if there's no other way, then I guess we'll have to risk it." Alex crept over to the doorway and peered out into the hall. "There are two of them standing at the top of the stairs....What we need is a decoy." He turned around, his eyes locking on Laylen. "Someone to distract them while I get Gemma out of here."

"And I'm assuming you want me to be that decoy." Laylen's tone didn't sound bitter, but empty.

It made my stomach ping.

"Laylen, I'm sorry, but I just don't see any other way," Alex said. "I think it would be best if I was the one with—"

Laylen cut him off. "Just go."

Alex hesitated, but only for a split second. Then he grabbed a hold of my hand, throwing me off balance as he yanked me toward the doorway. "Come on, Aislin."

Aislin didn't budge. "No."

Alex stopped and gaped at her. "What do you mean, no?"

She crossed her arms and raised her chin defiantly. "I'm not going to leave Laylen here to fend for himself. I'll stay and help him."

Knots tied in my stomach. They were staying behind to fend for themselves all because of me.

Alex shot her a warning look. "Aislin, there's no way—"

"This is not a debate," Aislin interjected. "I'm staying. Now hurry up and get out of here before you can't."

It took another second of hesitation before Alex agreed. "Fine, but promise me that neither one of you will try to kill them. Just distract them long enough for me to get Gemma out of here, and then make a run for the car, okay?"

Aislin nodded and shooed us toward the door. Alex cast one last look at Aislin and Laylen, then he tightened his grip on my hand and tugged me after him as he sprinted down the hall, leaving Aislin and Laylen behind to fight the deathly ice monsters by themselves.

Chapter 18

Guilt. What a feeling, like rotting eggs spoiling inside my stomach, the stench seeping out through my pores. It sucked, and I wanted to get rid of it. But I couldn't. Leaving Aislin and Laylen behind had created the horrid feeling, and I was pretty sure it wouldn't go away until I knew they were safe again. So add the guilt with the possibility that I might die pretty soon, and my chances of vomiting were getting pretty high.

And my guilt continued to fester the farther and farther Alex dragged me down the hall. I was desperately struggling to keep up with him, clumsily tripping over my own feet. I was scared but trying not to freak out.

Lining the sides of the hall were paper-white shoji doors. On some of them I could see shadows of human-shaped figures moving around on the other side. But I feared what they belonged to weren't human. They could have been anything. Death Walkers, Black Angels, vampires, take your pick. All were scary in their own way.

Unexpectedly, the hallway came to a fork, and Alex slowed to a jog.

"Which way is the fire escape?" I asked in a shaky voice.

He started for the left, and then, I guess, changing his mind, took off down the right.

My feet stumbled in protested as he pulled me after him. "How do you know this is the right way?"

"I don't," he said simply.

I gulped. Was I allowed to throw up yet? Because I'm pretty sure the foul taste gurgling in the back of my throat was vomit.

Alex breathed a sigh of relief. "There it is."

And sure enough, at the end of the hallway was a door with the words "Fire Escape" printed at the top. My heart leapt. I had never been so excited to see a door in my life. That was until the stupid thing opened.

The alarm went off, blaring deafeningly down the hall as a black-hooded monster emerged from the door.

"Son of a—" In the snap of a finger Alex had me twirled around and was pulling me back down the hall.

A cold breeze rushed up against the back of my legs, and I knew the Death Walker was coming after us.

"What are we going to do?" I cried, in an unnaturally high-pitched voice.

We rounded a corner and then, without any warning, he screeched to a halt. And for the third time today, I smacked straight into him. I didn't care though. Nor did I react. At the moment, who the heck cared about the electricity?

He did a quick scan of our surroundings. "We need to find a place to hide."

"A place to hide?" I repeated, glancing around like there actually might be the possibility of a secret door lurking by us.

"Yeah, a place to hide." He let go of my hand and grabbed the handle on a nearby shoji door.

I hadn't realized how bad my palms were sweating. I wiped them on the front of my skirt as Alex jerked the door open. Behind it was a man lying on a bed. His eyes were shut, and a woman wearing an old fashion corset dress was kneeling over him. Her blond hair curled down her back and tracing her neck was a tattoo—the mark of immortality.

Noticing us, the woman rose up and bared her fangs.

A vampire. My mouth dropped open. "Holy—"

Alex slammed the door shut.

I stared at him with wide eyes. "Wh-what was that?"

Alex brushed me off, already rushing to the next shoji door.

I dared a glance back down the hall, wondering if I would find a Death Walker charging at us. Surprisingly, I found it empty. But that brought no comfort to me. At least if I had been able to see it, then I would know where it was.

Alex slid another door open, and thankfully no one was inside. He pushed me through the doorway and slammed the door shut behind us. The room was dark; only a trickle of light seeped through the screen door.

"Now what?" I breathed.

I heard a soft *click* as he locked the door. "I need to find a place to hide you."

"Hide *me*? What are you going to do?"

He felt his way around in the dark, moving across what I could make out as a bed, a dresser, and then coming to a stop at what looked like a room divider.

"Over here," he whispered. "Get behind the screen."

"Why? What are you going to do?"

"I'm going to kill the Death Walker," he hissed. "Now get over here."

"Kill the Death Walker." I inched my way toward him. "But you said they couldn't be killed. Not without the sword, which you don't have."

He took me by the arm and gently shoved me behind the divider. I couldn't see his face, but I sensed he was afraid. "I know that," he said softly.

I pressed my quivering lips together, feeling like I might cry.

"Look." His voice was gentle. "I promise everything will be okay, just as long as you stay behind here." Then, he did the strangest thing ever. He brushed his fingers across my cheek. The touch was as light as a feather, but the electricity still tickled down my cheek. "Promise me you won't come out until you know everything is okay."

My thoughts were fluttering all over the place, and I wasn't thinking clearly. "Okay."

And then he was gone. Just like that. And I was alone. That's when I realized what I had done.

Chapter 19

I stayed behind the divider for what felt like an eternity. I swear the world could have been ending and I wouldn't have known; the room was too dark and quiet to get any kind of sense of what was going on.

All I had were my thoughts to pass the time. They brought me no sense of comfort whatsoever. All I kept thinking about was how Alex had said to wait here until I knew it was safe, but he never mentioned anything about coming back. So what did that mean? That he wasn't coming back?

I was so going to throw up.

Plus, I wasn't exactly sure how I was supposed to know when it was safe enough for me to come out. So I did the only thing I could think of doing. I waited until I felt like I was going to burst—until I couldn't take it any longer—and then I made up my mind that it was time to step out from behind that divider.

I crept to the edge of it, my adrenaline pounding at such a rate that it just about knocked me to the ground. I paused, taking a deep breath, and…*1…2…Bam!* The lights flipped on. And before I even had time to react, fog was swirling all around me. I panicked. What was I supposed to do?

Holding my breath, I backed away from the edge of the divider. Logically, the best thing to do would be to stay calm, analyze the situation, and make a plan. But how the heck was I supposed to stay calm when there was fog everywhere, clouding everything, including my brain? So instead I freaked and jumped out from behind the divider, preparing to run. I quickly realized just how big of a mistake I made. I couldn't see anything but fog. It was like being in a haunted house on Halloween. The only thing missing was the strobe lights.

Okay, okay, think. I searched the room for any sign of yellow eyes. When I didn't see any sign of them, it opened up a tiny glimpse of hope, and I bolted in the direction of what I prayed was the door. Bumping my knee on the dresser and catching the tip of my shoe on the leg of the bed, I finally touched the wall with the palm of hand. I felt around for the door, the chill of the fog seeping into my bones.

I found the bulge of the board trimming the doorway, and a rush of excitement charged through me. I reached for where the doorknob should be, but instead of touching metal, my fingers touched fabric. Ice-cold fabric. I looked up and found a pair of glowing, soulless eyes staring down at me.

I was so dead.

I gaped at the murderous monster, frozen with terror, unable to move. Its eyes burned into me like they were trying to burn into my soul. I needed to go. I needed to move away from it. I willed my legs to move and staggered backward until the backs of my legs pressed into the side of the bed. I skittered around it and inched back into farthest corner, putting as much distance as I could between me and the Death Walker.

The fog opened up, creating a hollow tunnel between the Death Walker and me. I waited for it to charge, but it just towered in the doorway, its eyes blazing yellow from beneath its black hooded, ankle-length cloak. It was the first time I ever saw one up close, and I instantly wished I could erase the sight from my mind. Its long, bony fingers stuck out from the sleeves of its cloak. The corpse-like skin that covered its hands almost made me gag. The face looked like it was rotting, the flesh peeling away, revealing bits of raw muscles and jagged bones.

I pressed my back against the wall, wanting to get as far away as I could from the hideous thing. I let out a shiver, longing to disappear, wishing to be anywhere else but here.

The Death Walker's eyes fired up to a bright gold, and it opened its mouth and let out a screech that sounded like a dying animal.

Then it charged.

I screamed as I realized I should've never trapped myself in a corner. I was such a goner. There was nothing I could do but wait for it to kill me.

Trembling with fear, I sank to the floor, catching one last glimpse of those haunting yellow eyes before I closed my own. I hugged my knees to my chest and waited for the cold to suck the life out of me. This was the end of me.

I wished I had been able to live a less lonely life.

A loud bang, followed by a shriek, and then something fell, hitting the floor with a heavy thud.

Buzzing filled my head as I cracked open my eyelids. I let out a gasp. Sprawled out on the floor, just in front of my feet, was the Death Walker, either unconscious or dead—I couldn't tell since it looked dead even when it was alive.

"Gemma, are you okay?"

I raised my chin and met Alex's bright green eyes. I nodded. My throat felt as dry as the desert air, and I swallowed hard, trying to hydrate it enough so I could form some sort of words. "Yeah."

Alex hopped over the body of the Death Walker and extended his hand out to me. I took it, catching my breath at the sight of the bluish-purple shade my skin had taken on.

"Don't panic." Alex wrapped his hand around mine and pulled me to my feet. His skin was so warm it burned against my overly chilled skin. He kept a hold of my hand and began rubbing it in attempt to create friction and bring warmth. Then he took my other hand, pressed my palms together, and cupped his hands around mine.

"It'll be okay," he said, and breathed on my hands, deluging my skin with warmth.

"Why does it always happen to my hands?" I asked, my body shaking from the cold that still lingered in the air. Or maybe it was from my nerves.

"It's where you lose your circulation first," Alex explained with another breath. "The Death Walker's cold works the same way as normal cold air does. It starts at your fingers and toes, and works its way up. The only difference is theirs works much quicker."

"Toes?" I flitted a glance down at my DCs, frightened at the idea of what was in them. Purple and blue toes? Toes that would need to be amputated?

I really wanted to keep my toes.

"You'll be fine," Alex assured me. "Let's just get you to the car." He breathed one last breath on my hands, and then let them go. Then he yanked the Sword of Immortality out of the Death Walker's back. The jagged blade was covered in sticky black goo—the Death Walker's blood, I assumed.

"Where did you get that?" I asked.

"Laylen and Aislin. They're pulling the car around right now so we can get out of here." He wiped the blade on the cloak of the Death Walker, cleaning off the goo. Then he held out his hand to me. "Come on."

I took his hand, trying to ignore the flutter in my heart. "What about the other Death Walkers?"

"They're dead."

I tried my best not to look at the foul creature as I stepped over its body, but I still caught a hint of its rotting face and felt my stomach churn. "You killed all of them?"

"There were only two." He pulled me toward the door. "And this—" he lifted the sword into the air— "makes killing them easy."

I followed Alex down the hall, my legs shaking the whole time. I think I entered some kind of state of shock or something. My body felt numb and strange, and the way the world swayed in beautiful bright colors and shapes wasn't normal. To be honest, I barely remember making it to the car. But somehow, a little while later, I was sitting in the back seat of Laylen's GTO with the warmth of the heater blasting across my skin, and the sound of tires screeching as we peeled away from the Black Dungeon.

Chapter 20

There was something wrong with my head. It wasn't like anything had physically broken; it was more like I had mentally cracked. Whether it was from the shock of barely escaping my death, or the last few hours finally catching up with me, I didn't know. But for whatever reason, I couldn't seem to focus. Everything kept spinning and spinning, like I was trapped on an out-of-control merry-go-round. I was starting to get nauseous when Alex had me lie down and elevate my legs, mumbling something about how it would keep me from going into shock.

I was lying down in the back seat of the GTO, with my legs resting on Alex's lap. It didn't occur to me until later that lying down in a skirt and putting my feet on a guy's lap may not have been the greatest idea.

When I started to grasp a hold of reality again, I realized that, if he really wanted to, Alex could see straight up my skirt. Luckily, he seemed fixated on staring out the window. And really, who was I kidding? There was no way Alex wanted to look up my skirt.

I sighed, tugging the hem down.

Alex turned his head and looked down at me. "Oh, good, you're awake."

"Was I asleep?" I asked.

His eyes skimmed over my face like he was checking for visible signs of my head being broken. "Are you sure you didn't bump your head?"

I thought back to when I had just about been killed. "No...I'm pretty sure there was no head bumping."

He glanced at Aislin. They both exchanged a look I couldn't interpret.

"What?" I asked, starting to sit up. Whoa. Can you say head rush? I pressed the heel of my hand to my forehead. "Ouch."

"Gemma, you need to lie back down," Alex insisted.

I slid my legs off his lap and sat up straight. "What's going on?"

They exchanged another look, and this time I thought I saw a hint of disappointment in Alex's expression.

"Why do you two keep giving each other weird looks?" My head had stopped spinning, and I realized not only had the car stopped, but Laylen wasn't in it. "And where's Laylen?"

"He's inside." Aislin pointed out the window at a red-brick building with the words "Adessa's Herbs and Spices" printed across the door. "He went in to check things out and make sure everything was okay before we all went inside."

"Oh...well, why do you guys keep looking at each other like that?" I asked.

"Like what?" Alex asked so casually I knew he was playing dumb.

I looked back and forth between the two of them. Neither of their expressions gave anything away. But still, I could sense something was up.

"Are you sure you didn't hit your head?" Alex wondered. "You're acting kind of funny. Are you feeling okay?"

Hmm...Am I feeling okay? Suddenly, I had an epiphany. "Wait just a second." I held my hands up in front of me exasperatedly. "Did you guys think I had gone back to not being able to feel again or something?" Aislin shifted uncomfortably in her seat, and I could tell I guessed what they were thinking. "Why would you think that?"

"Because you were acting weird," Alex replied in a laidback tone.

"You were so mellow," Aislin added in an unsteady voice.

"Oh." I raised my eyebrows. "So, you guys thought that I bumped my head and knocked the old unemotional Gemma back in."

Neither of them said anything. Aislin fiddled with the visor above her head, and Alex stared out the window. I knew he was only trying to avoid making eye contact with me, seeing as how we were in a dark, desolated area, and there was nothing particularly fascinating to look at outside.

"Well, that's nice," I muttered, slumping back in my seat.

Aislin slowly turned around in her seat and looked at me with sad eyes. "Gemma, we didn't mean it like that. We just thought…"

"That I stopped feeling," I finished for her grudgingly. "Well, sorry to break it to you, but I don't think a bump on the head is going to knock me back to *that*." Then I crossed my arms and pretended like I was harboring this huge secret about what had caused the sudden onset of my emotions, which, strangely enough, felt very gratifying.

"Gemma, if you know something…" Alex began, but I turned my back to him and stared out the window, tracing the lines of the surrounding buildings with my eyes.

I tried to brush off the fact that Alex seemed disappointed that I showed emotion. Who cared what he thought. I could feel and that was all that mattered. Okay, well, that was a lie. But I was going to try my best not to focus on how Alex felt about me because, if I did, it would probably eat away at my insides.

As I stared at Adessa's Herbs and Spices, I noticed a crescent moon outlined by a black star sketching the window of the door. I glanced at the tattoo on Aislin's shoulder. It was exactly the same as what was on the window.

"What is that?" I asked, pointing at her shoulder.

She traced the lines of the tattoo with her finger. "It's the witches' mark. After I became a witch, it appeared on my skin."

"Like the mark of immortality?" I inquired.

Her eyebrows dipped down in perplexity. "How do you know about that?"

"Laylen told me while we were at the Black Dungeon," I explained.

"Oh great," Alex scoffed. "What else did he tell you?"

"Nothing," I lied. "So does everyone have a mark?"

Aislin nodded. "I actually have two. One because I'm a witch." She lifted her foot onto the center console and flipped the ceiling light on; a black circle trimmed by fiery gold flames tattooed the side of her ankle. "And one because I'm a Keeper."

"And, what? They just all of a sudden showed up?"

"Yeah, my Keeper's mark appeared when I was about twelve. It was also about the same time I really started learning about what it is to be a Keeper. And my witch's mark showed up when I was about fifteen, which is when I first found out I possessed Wicca magic."

I wondered how many marks Alex had. Was he more than just a Keeper?

"If you're wondering if I have one, the answer is yes," he said, like he read my mind.

Hold on. What if he could read minds? I mean, with everything else I learned over the last twenty-four hours, I wouldn't be a bit surprised if there was such a thing as

241

mind-reading abilities. If Alex could read minds then that would totally suck, considering how my thoughts tended to center around him and his beautifulness.

"I only have one mark, though," he said, meeting my eyes "The Keeper's mark."

Phew. What a relief. "Does it look the same as Aislin's?"

He nodded. "Same mark, just in a different spot."

Why, for the life of me, his remark fired up the electricity was beyond me. I chewed on my bottom lip, severely distracted by my thoughts of where his mark could be.

A sly grin spread across his face. "If you want, I can show you where it is."

"Alex," Aislin hissed. "What are you doing?"

"Relax," Alex said. "There's no need to get all wound up. I was just teasing her."

I came to the conclusion right then and there that maybe Alex had some kind of a bipolar disorder or something. First he hated me. Then he kissed me. Sometimes I irritated him. And sometimes he was teasing me. For someone who didn't want me to feel, he was sure sending my emotions all over the place.

Looking out the window, Aislin heaved a huge sigh of relief. "Oh good, we can go in."

I followed her gaze and saw Laylen, standing in front of Adessa's, waving us in.

***

Inside of Adessa's Herbs and Spices, the air smelled of sage and a few other spices that I couldn't identify. Black and white tile checker-boarded the floor, the witches' mark painted in the center. Glass countertops displaying simple things like jewelry, candles, and incense outlined the room. There were, however, some things inside the display cases that looked rather questionable. A black pot with a creepy looking eye painted on it (I swear the thing was watching me), a miniature figurine of an Egyptian pyramid, and a statue of a cat with two heads. I couldn't help but wonder what these strange objects did. Were they merely for display? Or did they hold some kind of magical power to them?

"So..." Aislin skimmed about the room with a puzzled expression. "Where's this Adessa?"

"She'll be down in just a minute." Laylen leaned back against a display case and rested his elbows on top of it. "She had to run upstairs to get something."

I walked around the room, trailing my finger aimlessly along the glass countertop as I gazed down at all the peculiar looking objects. On one of the counters, I spotted a crystal ball that looked like what Fortune Tellers used to see into the future. I peered inside it, curious if I would be able to see what my future held. Violet ribbons floated gracefully in a sea of shimmering water. Through it, my reflection stared back at me. Apparently I possessed no psychic abilities. Either that or this particular ball was a dud.

"If you're not careful, you might get stuck inside it," Alex said, appearing out of thin air and scaring the crap out of me.

I threw my hand over my accelerating heart. "Jesus. You scared the heck out of me." I paused, catching me breath. "So what were you saying about me getting stuck inside something?"

"Stuck inside here." He tapped his fingers on the crystal ball. "It's a Foreseer's crystal ball. The kind they use to see visions. But to see the future, they actually have to go into the future." He flicked the ball with his finger again. "By going inside."

"But why would *I* get stuck inside it? I'm not a Foreseer."

"Yeah, but you're...different. I don't think you should touch it."

"But you keep touching it," I pointed out.

"But I don't have the power of a star flowing around inside me, do I?" He rapped his fingers on the crystal ball again, trying to prove his point. "Who knows what might happen if you touch it? You might set off its power or something and get sucked into a vision. In fact, you probably shouldn't touch anything at all."

"Including the floor," I said with sarcasm. "Because that seems like it would be very tricky."

Most people would have gotten aggravated by my smart mouthed comment. Not Alex though. It was like a game to him.

"That does sound pretty tricky." He leaned in toward me and lowered his voice. "I think you know that's not what I meant."

I took a few slow deep breaths because I had to. With how close he was, the electricity had ignited and forced me into a tug-o-war with my emotions. Part of me wanted to slap him, while the other part of me wanted to press my lips against his.

I tore my eyes away from him and looked over at Laylen and Aislin to distract myself from my insane feelings. They seemed to be engulfed in a very serious conversation. Laylen had his eyes fixed on Aislin, who kept waving her hands around in a heated kind of gesture.

"Well, if it's that big of a deal if I touch something," I mumbled, "then maybe I should go wait in the car."

"You can't go back to the car," Alex said sternly. "Not by yourself."

We stared at each other, as this giant bubble of electricity built around us.

Finally, Alex broke his gaze away. He kicked the floor with the tip of his shoe. "So yeah, just make sure you don't touch anything, except for the floor."

A few moments later, a woman around thirty years old or so waltzed into the room. She had golden cat-shaped eyes and wavy black hair that flowed all the way down to her waist. She wore a navy blue velvet dress, large gold-hooped earrings, and her skin was the color of honey.

"I'm Adessa," she said in a voice as smooth as silk. "Now, Laylen told me that one of you is a witch and is looking for a Vectum Crystal." Her cat eyes landed on me. "And let me guess, is it you?"

I glanced around nervously and then shook my head, lost as to why she'd think that. I pointed a finger at Aislin. "No, not me—her."

"Hmm…that's interesting." She focused her attention on Aislin. "So what particular one are you looking for, dear?"

"Well, I've been using the purple amethyst." Aislin paused. "But since we have to travel a long distance, I think maybe the gold one would work better."

Adessa twisted a necklace that hung around her neck. "How long of a distance is it, dear?"

"Oh…I think about 500 miles," Aislin said. "Give or take a few."

Adessa wandered behind the counter and waved at Aislin to follow her. "I think I have something that would work even better than the gold one." She raised her hand and drew an invisible rectangle in the air. One of the shelves lining the purple walls shifted backwards, sinking into the wall like it had been drawn back by an invisible force; or a magical force. My mouth dropped agape as the shelf disappeared altogether and revealed a solid black door hidden behind it. Adessa flicked her hand like she was shooing a fly away, and the door swung open. From where I stood, I couldn't see what was inside. I tried to casually lean to my left to get a better look, but no such luck—Adessa and Aislin were blocking my view.

Adessa motioned at the doorway. "After you, my dear."

Aislin bit down on her lip and tentatively stepped inside. Adessa followed behind her. A bright red flash sparkled throughout the room, and the door slammed shut.

Then they were gone.

"What the heck?" I was resting somewhere between being completely fascinated and absolutely terrified. "Where did they go?"

"To a secret place where Adessa keeps certain things hidden," Laylen answered.

"What kind of things?" I asked, intrigued.

Laylen came over beside me, his hands tucked in his pockets. "The dangerous kind."

"Laylen," Alex warned.

"What?" Laylen gave him an I'm-so-innocent look. "She asked a question, and I answered. What's wrong with that?"

"Everything's wrong with it," Alex said forthrightly.

I sighed. Would the secretiveness ever end? I could cross my fingers and hope so, but I wasn't holding my breath—I'd probably die from lack of oxygen if I did.

I traced my finger along a crack in the display case. "So why did Adessa think I was the witch?"

Laylen cocked his head to the side, his forehead scrunched over. "I'm not really sure."

Alex spun the Foreseers' crystal ball in its stand. "Probably because of your eyes."

I absentmindedly touched the corner of my eye. "Why would my eyes make her think that?"

"You've seen them, right?" he said derisively. "The color's anything but normal—a dead giveaway that there's something *different* about you."

"Yeah, I've seen them," I snapped.

"I'm not trying to be mean." He sounded like he meant it, but who could tell for sure? "I actually like the color. It's a nice different."

Confused if he was teasing me or not, I opted to keep my mouth shut. That way nothing stupid would escape it.

Laylen wandered away from us and started fiddling around with a set of black and blue ceramic boxes on a nearby shelf. Electric sparks started kissing at my body, moving from the tips of my toes to the top of my head. It wasn't too hot or too strong, and I had to admit, I liked the way it made me feel. But I wondered if there would ever be a time where I could just freely enjoy the feeling. Or freely enjoy my life. Would I ever just be normal? Maybe after I stopped this end-of-the-world thing from happening, I just might be able to live freely.

But what was even going to happen to me after I stopped the end of the world from happening?

"Can I ask you something?" I asked Alex.

He fixed his gaze on a tiny black stone inside the counter. "Depends on what it is, I guess."

I shook my head. I highly doubted he was going to give me a straight answer—or any answer at all—but I had to at least try. I took a deep breath and quickly threw my question out there. "What happens to me after the portal closes?"

Okay, so I have learned from past experiences that Alex was a good actor. He could lie like a real pro. Pretend to be something he wasn't. Manipulate my thoughts. So when his face drained of all its color, my heart stopped. Whatever the answer was, it had to be horrible.

"What is it?" My words rushed out of me in a panic.

He shook his head, his skin still very pale. "Gemma, I'm not sure we should be talking about this right now."

"What do you mean you don't think we should talk about this right now?" I stomped my foot on the floor—yes, like a two-year-old, but considering the circumstances, I think it was called for. "Just tell me."

"I'd rather not," he said flatly.

"Well, I'd rather you did," I retorted.

"No, this isn't something we should be discussing right now."

And that's when I knew it. I was never going to be normal. I was never going to be able to enjoy things, be happy, and do whatever I wanted with my life.

"I'm going to die, aren't I?" I choked.

"I don't know." He hesitated. "No one knows, really. You could just go back to normal or...." He drifted off.

"Or I could die," I finished for him.

He didn't answer, but he was looking everywhere else except at me.

Freaking out, I whirled around on my heels, preparing to make a mad dash for the door, but my elbow bumped into something cold and hard—the Foreseers crystal ball. It bounced out of the stand, rolled off the counter, and hit the floor with a loud clank.

"Crap," I said. Without even thinking, I bent down to swipe it up.

Alex and Laylen yelled, "No!"

As my fingers grazed the glass, I felt my body being pulled. And then I was spiraling down a dark tunnel.

Chapter 21

The fall seemed endless, like I was being sucked into an abyss. Fear set in as I realized that an abyss might be exactly what this was. Of course, if there was a bottom and I hit it at the speed I was falling, then...well, I didn't want to think about it right now.

Below my feet, I saw a white light twinkling through the blackness. As I plunged closer to it, it began to shimmer brighter and brighter, eventually becoming so bright I had to shut my eyes or else I might go blind. Warmth blanketed around me, and I sucked in a breath as my feet hit the ground hard.

I toppled forward, landing face first onto a surface that felt scratchy and dry like grass. I quickly leapt to my feet. Sure enough, the scratchy, dry surface was grass, and I had a mouth full of it.

I spat a few times, clearing out my mouth. My head was throbbing and my stitches ached. Worried I had torn them open, I lifted up the bottom of my shirt and carefully peeled back the bandage. My skin looked red and swollen, but there was no blood and the stitches still seemed to be holding my skin together.

I pressed the bandage back down and glanced around, seeing if I could recognize my surroundings. Bright orange and pink leaves danced through air, and the wind whispered against my hair. Tall trees trimmed a translucent lake. The place felt strangely familiar, like I had been here before but couldn't quite remember when. It was the same feeling I experienced when I had been sucked away back at the field trip.

For a moment I just stood there in the sunshine and breathed in the cool fall air. Then suddenly it dawned on me. I obviously had been sucked into the Foreseers' ball like Alex had warned might happen. He also warned me that I could get stuck inside it. All of my calmness was ripped away in the blink of an eye.

Okay. Okay. Don't panic. Yeah, that was easier said than done. I gazed around frantically, crossing my fingers that somehow a magical door would materialize out of thin air. Magic existed, right? So why couldn't I just conjure up a door? Because I'm not a witch, that's why. And, of course, no door appeared.

That's when I really started freaking out.

"Help!" I screamed at the top of my lungs. "Someone! Anyone!"

Tears stung the corners of my eyes. Great. Now I was crying. I hated to think it, but not being able to feel right now would have come in real handy, because I was becoming hysterical. And being all frantic and crazed wasn't going to get me anywhere.

I took a deep breath and tried to relax. *Okay, you can do—*

A stream of purple whipped past me. I jumped back, my hand pressing against my heart, my breath fumbling to regain its steadiness. My gaze darted after the purple blur, and I realized it wasn't a blur but a little girl wearing a purple dress. She had to be around four or five years old. Her long brown hair whipped in the wind as she stood at the edge of the lake, staring out at the water.

Unsure of how a Foreseer's vision's worked, I approached her cautiously. Would I be able to communicate with her? God, I hoped so.

"Excuse me." I went to tap her on the shoulder, but my hand slipped through her like I had just tried to touch a ghost. Great. I raised the volume of my voice. "Hello!"

Nothing. The girl just stood there, completely unfazed by my loudness as she stared out at the lake.

Great. If I couldn't communicate with anyone, then how was I ever going to figure out a way out of here?

The little girl started twirling in circles, and I gasped as I caught sight of her face. It was all hazy, like bad reception on a television screen. I blinked my eyes and rubbed them with the heels of my hands, but the haze stayed.

"Don't get too close to the lake," a voice called out from behind me.

I spun around just as a boy ran past me. He looked a few years older than the little girl and had dark brown hair. His face was hazed over as well.

"You need to be careful or you might fall in," he warned.

"Don't worry," the little girl replied, teeter-tottering near the edge of the water. "I won't fall in."

"Please just move away," he begged, his hand extended out to her. "You don't know how to swim."

She took hold of his hand, and he guided her away from the lake.

I was having another weird *déjà vu* moment, just like when I disappeared into the field during the fieldtrip. The peoples' faces had been blurry then too. So were the two linked somehow? This had to be a vision, and the fieldtrip…well, I didn't know what that was. It couldn't have been a vision, though. It wasn't like I touched a Foreseer's ball.

"You two get over here right now!" a man barked from somewhere behind me.

His voice made the atmosphere alter into a-graveyard-in-the-middle-of-the-night kind of setting. The kind of setting that made the hair on my arms stand on end, and my stomach churn.

Before I could even turn around, the man appeared beside me. He was tall, husky, and had jet black hair similar to Marco's. He wore a black button-down shirt, grey slacks, and a gold chain dangled around his neck. His face was also hazy.

I quickly caught on that he was intimidating with the way he shook at my nerves. Even the kids seemed to back away from him.

"It's time to go," his voice iced out.

"Where are we going?" the little girl asked, gripping little boy's hand tightly, like her life depended on it.

"That's none of your business!" the man roared.

Even though I couldn't see the girl's face, I knew she had to have flinched. I flinched. The fear that he might hurt the two of them howled through me. And what was I supposed to do if he did? Stand by and watch helplessly?

I heard the soft treading of approaching footsteps. Then a figure rushed by me. It was a woman with long brown hair and a face as hazy as the others.

She swept the little girl up in her arms and hugged her protectively. "You stay away from her!" she shouted at the man.

Her presence brought warmth that mixed with the chill the man sent out. The two combined created a mixture of emotions that buzzed through the air and made me nauseous.

"This is not your decision," the man rumbled at the woman. "You knew when she was born that things like this had to happen."

"Mommy, I'm scared," the girl whispered.

The woman—the mother—smoothed back the little girl's hair and kissed her on the forehead. "It's going to be okay. You don't need to be scared. I promise I won't let anything happen to you."

The man laughed the kind of laugh that sent fear soaring through my body. "I'd like to see you try." He turned to the little boy. "Go inside, right now."

The boy didn't move.

"Now!" the man ordered.

"Yes, Father." The boy's voice shook. He trod up a hill, heading toward a castle-like building made of grey stone and tall towers.

After the boy disappeared inside the castle, the man turned back to the woman. "Now, we can do this the easy way or the hard way."

She stood defiantly, holding the little girl tightly in her arms. "You're not taking her anywhere. She's my daughter, not yours."

"So it's going to be the hard way, then." He lunged at the woman and snatched the little girl away.

The woman desperately fought to get her back, tearing and clawing at the man's arms.

The girl reached for her mother, kicking and screaming with all her might. "I want to stay with you! Don't let him take me!"

But their efforts were useless. The man stood strong, entirely unaffected by their attempts. And when he plucked a small black bag out of his pocket, the woman froze. Silence choked the air, and I could hear my heart thudding.

Balancing the little girl in one arm, he dangled the bag in front of the woman. "Now, like I said, we can do this the easy way or the hard way."

"You wouldn't dare," whispered the woman.

"Wouldn't I?" He looked down at the little girl in his arms. "Hey, sweetie, how would you like to go for a swim in the lake?"

The girl hovered back. "But I can't swim."

"You'll be fine," the man coaxed. "Someone will be there to help you."

"Knock it off!" screamed the woman, clenching her hands into fists. "I know you're bluffing. You need her too much."

The man laughed wickedly, making the hairs on my arms stand on end. "There are ways to get her back when I need her. She would probably be better off down there anyway, until it's time."

The woman's breathing faltered. "Please don't do this. *Please.*"

The man laughed again. "Oh, I won't just as long as you get into the lake yourself."

Go in the lake! Why! Was he going to try and drown her?

"You'll never get away with this." Her voice was edging near a sob. "I know the real reason why you want her, and sooner or later, someone else is going to figure it out. You'll never be able to get away with it."

"Oh, I highly doubt it. I have everyone wrapped around my little finger." He set the girl down on the ground, pointed his finger at the castle, and ordered the little girl to "Go inside."

She didn't budge.

"Go!" the man hollered.

Again she didn't budge. She was a brave one, because I'm pretty sure I would have been running for my life.

"Go ahead, honey," her mother urged in a soothing voice. "It's alright. I'll be okay."

It took the girl a second, but she finally walked away, casting one last glance back at her mother before starting up the hill toward the castle.

My heart broke for the little girl and the mother. Somehow—and I don't know how—I knew it would be the last time they would see each other. She would grow up motherless, perhaps even hating the people who would be chosen to raise her. There would forever be an empty hole resting in her heart.

"Now it's time to deal with you," the man said, turning back to the woman. He let a pause drag out, like he was trying to instill fear with his silence. "Get in the lake. *Now!*"

I shook my head, trembling. *No! No! No!*

"You've been planning this all along, haven't you?" Her voice quivered. "Every single word that's come out of your mouth has been nothing but a lie."

"You know me very well," he said. "Now quit stalling and get into the lake."

Shaking her head, she backed up toward the water. The man followed after her, matching her every step.

I chased after them, desperately wishing I could do something to stop the man from forcing the woman into the lake.

"You're wrong about not getting caught." She reached the brink of the lake, the waves rolling against her feet. "There are people who you don't have wrapped around your finger."

"Then I'll have to take care of them as well." He tugged open the black bag, scooped out a handful of something that looked like ash, and sprinkled it into the lake, making the water turn a cloudy dark grey.

"Don't think you've won." She raised her chin high and stepped back, submerging her legs into the water. "Someday it will all catch up with you."

Another few steps and the water was waist deep on her. The lake lay dead calm, like the calm before the storm. Then came the loud *swoosh*! Water splashed up and she plunged down.

I let out a blood curdling scream.

The man turned his back on the drowning woman and strolled away, whistling some funky tune that sounded like a combination between "It's a Small Word After All" and "Twinkle, Twinkle, Little Star."

Without even thinking, I ran into the water, forcing myself to go farther as the cold water ascended higher. But when it reached waist deep on me, I realized two things: 1) like the little girl, I couldn't swim, and 2) I couldn't actually touch the woman, so how was I supposed to save her?

Shortly after these thoughts crossed my mind, a third reason why I shouldn't have gone into the water dawned on me. Obviously there was something wrong with the lake. I heard the swish. I saw the splash. I saw the man dump some creepy ashy stuff into it.

I should have known better than to go running into it.

But I didn't, and it was too late now. A bony hand had already grabbed me by the ankle and was trying to jerk me beneath the water. I kicked and screamed and fought with every ounce of strength I had, but whoever the hand belong to was strong. It pulled me under the ice-cold water and kept dragging me deeper and deeper underneath the water.

Chapter 22

I gasped for air as my eyes shot open. Purple walls and glass counters surrounded me. I was back at Adessa's. I made it. I wasn't dead. My skin was dry. My feet were planted firmly to the checkerboard tile. The Foreseers' crystal ball was cupped in my hand.

"Ah!" I shrieked and dropped the ball. It hit the ground hard, causing it to crack down the center.

"Gemma."

I looked away from the broken ball and found Alex standing right next to me. His green eyes were wider than usual, and his mouth was set in a worried line.

Behind him stood Laylen with the same worried expression on his face.

I breathed heavily. "What the heck happened?"

"What do you mean, what the heck happened? You touched the Foreseers' ball after I told you not to touch it." His voice, although full of anger, slightly shook.

"It was an accident," I snapped. "I didn't mean to touch that—" I waved my hand at the broken Foreseer ball—"*thing.*"

All three of us stared down at it. Water was seeping out through the crack, forming a puddle on the floor.

"Well, what happened?" Alex asked, his voice a little calmer now, but he still looked concerned.

What happened? I thought to myself. Well, let me see. I got sucked into a tunnel, hit my face on the ground, and watched a woman being murdered. All I got to come out of my mouth, though, was, "I-I…"

"Did you go into a vision?" Alex asked, speaking slowly like I was incompetent.

"Yeah. I mean, at least I think I did."

"And you were able to come back," he stated with amazement.

A loud crash suddenly echoed through the room, scaring me to death. I jumped and ended up ramming my shoulder into Alex's chest.

"Sorry," Laylen apologized, as he swept up a black ceramic candlestick he apparently knocked onto the floor.

I let my breathing slow down.

"I'm going to take her outside and see if I can get her to calm down," Alex told Laylen.

Laylen nodded, and Alex led me to the front door. He made me wait there while he checked inside the GTO to make sure everything was safe. Once he gave me the go ahead, I went outside, and we climbed into the back seat of the car.

Both of us were quiet for awhile, the night spilling through the cab of the car. I could barely see anything, which did nothing for my nerves.

"So what did you see?" Alex finally asked.

"Um…" I fumbled for some sort of words that could explain the horrible scene I had just been forced to watch. "Something….You know, I'm not sure I really want to talk about it."

"Well, you have to," he said. "If you saw a vision, I need to know what happened. It's important."

I massaged the sides of my temples and sighed, "Fine."

I gave him a recap of every detail I could remember about the vision.

"You know you were really lucky, right?" Alex asked when I finished.

"Lucky? How?" Did he not get that I just witnessed a woman being murdered?

"Well, for starters, you were lucky you even made it back. I've heard stories about people getting stuck inside visions and never returning. And you were also lucky you didn't get captured by the Water Faerie."

"Water Faerie," I repeated, mystified. "What's a Water Faerie?"

"It's what pulled both you and the woman down in the lake. Water Faeries are the Guardians of The Underworld."

"The Underworld?" I said "As in the place where the Greeks believed people went after they died?"

"Kind of." He seemed hesitant to embellish on the subject, but I wasn't going to let him get away with keeping any more secrets.

"Tell me," I demanded. "Or I'll just go ask Laylen to explain it to me."

I thought that might make him angry, but instead, he just stared at me with what I thought looked like a trace of hurt in his bright green eyes. What he had been hurt about, though, I had no idea. I probably just imagined it or something.

"Fine." He threw his hands in the air and gave in, which shocked the crap out of me. "The Underworld is the land of the dead. It's also a prison. After we—the Keepers—capture someone like, say for instance a vampire that had been on a killing spree, we sentence them to a life down in The Underworld as a form of punishment."

I questioned whether he used a vampire as his example intentionally, as a way to get back at me for threatening to go ask Laylen.

"But why wouldn't you just kill them instead?" I asked. "I mean, you killed that Death Walker. Why can't you kill a vampire too?"

"Trust me, death is a milder punishment than getting sent down there. Most go insane from the torture after only a few weeks' time."

Something suddenly occurred to me. "Hold on just a second. Does that mean the woman I saw get dragged down into the lake is going to end up in The Underworld?"

"Maybe," he answered reluctantly. "The Water Faeries usually don't kill the people or the things they capture. They are under strict orders to take whatever they catch straight to the prison."

"But why do they want prisoners?"

"Because they feed off the prisoner's fear. It's what keeps them thriving even in their dead form."

I swallowed hard. "So if the vision I saw really ends up happening, then the woman's going to end up being tortured down there."

"Maybe. But she also might already be down there." He sighed. "Sometimes when someone inexperienced tries to see into the future they just end up seeing something that has already happened."

"So she could be down there right now!" The loudness of my voice made us both glance around nervously.

Alex gave me a look that stressed for me to keep my voice down. "She could be down there right now, but if she's been down there for awhile, then she may have already died. Depending on how strong she is, she could be able to survive the torture for up to a few years without it driving her mad. But if she's already lost her mind, the Queen would have had her killed."

265

"Why would the Queen have her killed? And who's this Queen, anyway?"

"The Queen of the Dead. She's in charge of everything that goes on in The Underworld. After a prisoner goes insane, they no longer produce the right kind of fear for her people to feed off, so she gets rid of them."

I gaped. "By killing them?"

Alex sighed and ran his fingers through his hair. "You have to understand that most of the things—or people—we send down there have committed horrible crimes; the kind of crimes that haunt people's nightmares."

"Yeah, well, considering the Death Walker's haunt my nightmares…" I really shouldn't have mentioned that.

He cocked an eyebrow. "You've dreamt about them?"

I nodded. "A lot, actually."

"Why didn't you tell me this before?"

I shrugged. "You keep secrets—"and *probably still are*—"so why can't I?"

He shook his head, irritated. "Did you dream about them before you ever saw them in real life?"

"Yeah, I started having the dreams a couple of months ago, and the first time I saw something that I thought might be a Death Walker was only a couple of weeks ago in the school parking lot. But I wasn't one hundred percent sure if I had actually seen one. I thought I might have imagined seeing it or something."

"It was back when I had to chase you down in the parking lot so I could give you your book, wasn't it?" he said. "When you were freaking out and wouldn't tell me why."

I nodded. It seemed like such a long time ago.

He stretched his arm across the top of the seat. "So you started dreaming about them around the same time you started to experience emotions?"

A touchy subject for me. "I don't know." I turned to the window. "Maybe."

Electricity tickled up and down my spine. Being alone with Alex in the poorly ventilated car was driving me absolutely insane. Not necessarily in a bad way though. In fact, I think my body was building up a tolerance to the electric sensation, because it was no longer making me feel like I had a fever. Warm and sparkly, it felt kind of good.

"So," I began, turning my head back to him. "If it was a future vision I saw, would we be able to change what happened?"

He shook his head. "Prophecies are very hard to change, and I don't have a clue as to how we would even be able to find out if it was a past or future vision. That is, unless we want to go to the City of Crystal and chat it up with the Foreseers."

"*City of Crystal?*"

"It's where most of the Foreseers live, but you can't get there without this special kind of crystal ball, which happens to be very hard to come by."

I felt like I just might cry. If I had seen a future vision, how was I supposed to just sit around and let the woman

267

get taken away to The Underworld for real? The place sounded awful and...well, I couldn't shake the feeling that I knew the woman somehow. "I don't get it. You say that prophecies are hard to change, but isn't that exactly what you guys are trying to do with me?"

"That's different though. We knew yours was a future prophecy right from the start, and a lot of energy and time has gone into trying to change it." He sighed. "Besides, you *are* emotional so we haven't done a very good job."

"But you're still trying to, right?" I picked at a loose string hanging off the hem of my denim skirt. "I mean, I'm sure you have a backup plan."

"No, we don't," he said too quickly.

A red flag immediately went up. "What is it you're not telling me?"

"I'm not keeping anything from you." His voice smoothed out like honey

I let out a cynical laugh. "I highly doubt that because, first off, it's *you* we're talking about. And second, you freaked out when I just asked you if you had a backup plan. So what is it? What's your big backup plan? Are you going to put me up in some super-secret chamber and lock me away from everyone and everything until the only emotion I can feel is loneliness?"

"Actually, that's not a bad idea," he said. "I'll have to pass that one on to Stephan."

Furious, I searched for the handle that moved the seat forward.

Alex caught me by the elbow and drew me back. "I don't think so. You're not going anywhere."

Wanna bet?

I tried to shuck off his hand. "Let go of me."

He tightened his grip. "No."

"I'm not going to just sit here and listen to you talk about turning me back into a walking zombie." I reached for the seat with my free hand, hoping if I could grab hold of something then maybe I could jerk away from him.

Still grasping onto my arm, he snaked his free hand around my waist and pulled me back.

"You're hurting my stitches," I whined, even though his hand was on the opposite side.

He pulled me closer to him. "No I'm not."

I put up quite a fight, but in the end he still managed to pin me against him, with my back pressing against his chest. This was both good and bad. Bad because I was really pissed off at him, and the last thing I wanted was to be near him. But it was also good because…Well, because it felt good. Nice and warm and effervescent.

Ugh.

"This is so stupid," I seethed. "You can't have control over everything I do."

"Yeah, I can." He held me so tight my skin warmed like melting butter, and I thought I might actually melt into him. "Especially when you're trying to do something stupid. Do you think what happened back at the Black Dungeon was a game? Do you not realize how close you came to being killed? Because let me tell you, if I wouldn't have shown up when I did, then you and I wouldn't be sitting here having this argument."

I froze, slowly taking in his words. With every breath he took I could feel his chest rising and falling against my back. My own breathing lifted and fell, rhythmically matching with his. The electricity seemed to be synchronized with it, as if it were trying to create a harmonious song or something. It was weird and strangely comforting. Like, if I closed my eyes, I would drift off into a peaceful, Death-Walker-free dream.

"Gemma," Alex whispered in my ear, sounding breathless. "I think that—"

I never got to hear what he thought, because the passenger door swung open and the interior lights clicked on.

It was Aislin. She held a small gold box in her hands, which I assumed held a crystal inside. She started to climb in, but stopped when she caught sight of us. "What are you two doing?"

I can only imagine what this looked like to her; me practically sitting on Alex's lap, his arms wrapped around me, obviously trapping me against him. Yeah, I'm pretty sure more than a few question marks were popping up in her head.

A few question marks were popping up in my head.

"Gemma was getting out of hand," Alex replied coolly. "She needed to be dealt with."

"I wasn't getting out of hand," I said indignantly. I tried to jam my elbow into his side, but it didn't go very far since I could barely move. "You are such a—"

Alex threw his hand over my mouth. I thought about biting it, but then decided against it. I'm not sure why.

"Alex!" Aislin exclaimed. "You can't just do whatever you want with her."

Alex dropped his hand from my mouth. "Aislin, she was trying to jump out of the car and run away."

Aislin frowned as she slammed the door. The lights shut off, and I could barely make out the outline of her face. "You two really need to figure out a way to get along. This whole fighting all the time thing is not helping the stress level in this already way too stressful situation."

"Well, if she would behave," Alex started at the same time as I said, "If he would leave me alone—"

Aislin lifted her eyebrows at us.

"Fine," Alex surrendered. "I'll stop."

"I'll stop too," I told her, "just as long as he lets me go."

I guess to prove a point that he could still have some control over me, Alex waited about twenty more seconds before finally letting me go. And he refused to sit anywhere else but in the middle of the seat so he could be close enough to me in case I made an irrational decision to "jump out of the car while it was moving," as he so bluntly put it. Yeah, even I wasn't that crazy, but okay.

By the time the seating arrangement was all settled, Laylen emerged from Adessa's looking somewhat happy. Hmmm....I wondered what was up with that.

He climbed in the car. "So, what happened?" he asked me.

I furrowed my eyebrows. "What? You mean with the crystal ball?"

He nodded. "Did you get sucked into a vision?"

"What!" Aislin shouted. "She got sucked into a vision and no one told me?"

I felt like I was getting strangled to death—that's the effect the vision had on me.

"I'll explain it on the way back to the house," Alex said. If I wouldn't have known better, I would have thought he said it because he had sensed my lack of comfort with the subject. But I did know better, so...

"Okay." Laylen started the car, and the engine roared to life.

Aislin was more reluctant to give up on the discussion. She remained turned around in her seat, continuously eyeballing Alex and I until Laylen merged the car back onto the busy main street of Vegas. Then the dancing lights and throngs of people distracted her attention away from us.

After we made it back onto the highway and the last of the lights had fizzled away, I rested my head against the window, and without even meaning to, I fell asleep.

Chapter 23

I was plummeting deeper and deeper into the murky water. I couldn't breathe. I couldn't see. So this is what drowning feels like, I thought numbly.

I kicked my legs, trying to fight my way back to the surface. I refused to drown. I could not drown.

"Gemma." A feathery voice floated up from beneath my feet. Huh? Was I hallucinating?

I kicked harder and paddled with my arms, giving a very lame attempt at doggy paddling.

"No, Gemma, down here," the voice rippled up through the water.

And then I knew. The voice didn't mean me any harm. I was supposed to listen to it.

I was supposed to go to it.

I let my legs and arms fall limp, allowing my dead weight to sink me downward to the sandy bottom of the lake.

"Good," the voice purred. "Now keep coming. I need your help."

What do you need my help for? I thought, because speaking would do anything but get me a mouth full of water.

To my shock, the voice responded inside my head. I need you to save me.

How?

Just trust me.

I don't know why, but I did. I do trust you.

Good. Now whatever you do, don't panic.

Why would I panic?

The voice didn't answer, but I figured out why as fingers wrapped around my ankles and yanked me down. Despite what the voice said, I panicked and clawed at the water, frantically trying to get away, but it was useless. I tried to scream, but water flooded my lungs. If I didn't get away, I was a goner. If I didn't get away, I would end up a prisoner in The Underworld, at least until I went insane and they killed me.

I needed to get away…

Shaking…huh….someone…shaking…my shoulder. My eyelids shot open. Disoriented and groggy, I jerked away from whoever was touching me.

"Jeez, Gemma," Alex said with his hands held up in front of him in an I-mean-you-no-harm kind of way. "Settle down."

I did a quick scan of my surroundings and realized I was still in the back seat of the GTO, which was now parked in the garage. Laylen and Aislin were nowhere to be seen. It was just Alex and me…Why was it just Alex and me?

274

"Where are Aislin and Laylen?" I asked, rubbing my sleepy eyes.

"Their already inside." He gave a nod in the direction of the garage door. "Getting things set up."

Yawning, I stretched out my arms. "So why are *we* sitting out here?"

"Because you fell asleep and I couldn't get you to wake up." He paused, looking as though he was considering something. "Were you having a nightmare?"

A nightmare? That was putting it mildly. "Why do you ask?"

"Because you were getting all squirmy and making these moaning noises."

Oh—my—word. I was absolutely mortified. "Oh."

He waited for me to explain further.

I didn't.

"Alright." He sounded a bit irritated. "Let's go inside."

Oh, whatever. He could be irritated all he wanted. I was under no obligation to tell him about my dreams.

Inside, Alex immediately jumped *into get a hold of Stephan* mode, hitting redial on his phone over and over and over again.

Several failed attempts later, he started banging his phone against the table like he thought beating the crap out of it would somehow make Stephan miraculously answer the phone. Yeah, all that resulted from that was the back of his phone popping off and the battery shooting out

275

across the table. After that, he gave up his redial mission and tucked his phone away in his pocket.

Feeling tired, I plopped down in one of the chairs at the table. The box Aislin had gotten from Adessa wasn't too far off on the table in front of me. It looked so much like a jewelry box, with its tiny encrusted jewels and shimmering shade of gold, that I half expected it to be full of pearl necklaces and diamond earrings. But inside the box lay a glinting red crystal. I had the urge to reach out and touch it, let my fingers brush along the jagged edges and see what it felt like. But after getting sucked into the Foreseers' crystal ball, I decided to resist the urge.

"So, this is it." Alex came over with his hands stuffed inside his pockets and leaned over my shoulder to get a better look at the crystal. "That's what's going to get us to Afton and back?"

Aislin, who was sitting across the table from me, nodded enthusiastically. "Adessa said it would work better than any other crystal."

"I sure hope so," Alex uttered under his breath.

Aislin either didn't hear him or chose to ignore him. "So we should probably get going."

Alex reached over my shoulder to collect the gold box. "Where do you want this?"

Aislin made grabbing gestures with her hands. "Here, give it to me."

Alex handed it to her and she took out the crystal. She retrieved a lighter out of her pocket and lit the wick of a black candle. Then she set the candle, the lighter, and the empty gold box down on the table.

With her eyes fixed on the glittering red crystal, which she now had grasped in her hand, she asked Alex, "Are you ready?"

"Just a sec." Alex pointed a finger at Laylen. "Before I go, you better be absolutely certain you can handle this."

Laylen rolled his eyes. "I'm *absolutely certain* I can handle this. Now go."

"You better be," he told him, and whipped a finger in my direction. "And you need to promise that if something does happen, you'll make sure to get away no matter what."

"Okay, I will," I promised with zero hesitation.

He looked surprised by my cooperation.

Hey, I may be a stubborn brat sometimes, but when it came to not getting killed I was more than willing to cooperate. Well, I did have to minus the whole trying-to-run-away incident back at Adessa's. Oh yeah, and the time I tried to run away when I first found out about what I really was. But other than that…oh, fine. Most of the time, I was a brat. But at least I wasn't being one now.

Alex still looked taken aback. "Well, good."

"Now, are you ready?" Aislin asked, dipping the tip of the crystal into the flame.

Alex picked up the Sword of Immortality. "Yeah, I'm ready. Let's go."

Without taking her eyes off the crystal, which had now started to smolder a rose tinted cloud of smoke, Aislin instructed Laylen and me to "Move back a ways unless you want to get taken with us."

I followed Laylen over to the farthest corner.

As soon as we made it over there, Aislin started whispering, "Per is calx EGO lux lucis via."

The smoke rising up from the candle slowly shifted to the shade of blood red.

Alex became more fidgety the further Aislin got with the whole transporting process. He kept throwing nervous glances at Laylen and me, along with a couple of strange looks I couldn't quite decipher.

"Per is calx EGO lux lucis via." Aislin's voice grew louder.

Another strange look from Alex, this time directed solely at me. His bright green eyes held so much worry that, for an instant, I thought he might run over to me. The look made me feel edgy. It pushed worried thoughts into my mind, and had me questioning just how high of a chance the Death Walkers showing up was. High enough for him, Mr. Stoically Calm In Frightening Situations, to look uneasy.

He kept his eyes glued on me as Aislin screamed, "Per is calx EGO lux lucis via!"

A flash of red, a thunderous burst, and then, just like that, Ailsin and Alex were gone.

I stared at the spot they vanished from, the electricity fizzling out of my body and leaving a giant empty void in its place. *Weird.*

I shook my head, tried my best to tuck the feeling away, and turned to Laylen. He was watching me with an expression that could only be translated as curious.

"What?" I asked, curious as to what was up with his strange look.

"Oh, nothing." He shrugged. "It's just that you look so much like her."

I tilted my head to the side, perplexed. "Like who?"

"Like your mom."

Whoa. That threw me for a loop—a big, giant, excited loop. I perked up. "I do? Really?"

He nodded. "Yeah—well, except for the color of your eyes."

I frowned. Of course it would exclude the color of my eyes since no one else had violet eyes. I was really going to have to consider getting some colored contact lenses.

"What is it with you and your eye color?" Laylen asked, semi-amused. "You know, the color's not that bad. In fact, it's pretty awesome."

"Awesome, huh? I would say more like different." *And freaky.* I sighed. "When you've been as different as I have, the idea of being normal sounds nice. But you can't be one hundred percent normal when you have freaky violet eyes."

"Yeah, I can understand how you would want to be normal, considering everything you've been through," he said as he started for the table. "But being normal is way overrated. Trust me."

"Oh yeah." I followed the Keeper/vampire over to the table and sat down.

He laughed, dropping down into a chair. "Yep, or at least that's what I've been told."

"So..." I began, wanting to go back to talking about my mom, "did you know my mom very well?"

He nodded, stretching out his legs in front of him. "I knew her pretty well."

"What was she like?" I asked eagerly.

"Well, she was really nice. There was no bad in her at all, and she was also one of those people who you knew you could trust."

I was soaking up every word he said like it was the oxygen that kept me alive.

His forehead creased over. "You know, I'm really surprised you don't remember anything about her."

"How could I?" I wondered. "I was only a year old when she died."

He stared at me, dumbfounded. "No, you weren't. You were four."

I shook my head. "No, I was one."

"No, you weren't," he insisted. "A few weeks after you turned four, you went to live with Marco and Sophia." He paused. "Who told you you were one?"

"Everyone." I was trying not to get riled up. "Marco, Sophia…Alex."

"Why would they do that?" Laylen mumbled. "Why would it make a difference whether you were one or if you were four?"

I was thinking the exact same thing. And if I really had been four, why would I have no memories of my mom at all? Yeah, I know four is a little young and everything, but still…I should have been able to remember something about her.

Laylen remained quiet, fiddling with his lip ring. "I'm sorry," he finally said.

"You don't need to apologize," I reassured him. "It's not your fault all of this happened."

"It's partly my fault." He rubbed his forehead and let out a stressed sigh. "I knew what Stephan was planning to do to you, and I didn't do anything to stop it."

"You were like, what, eight when all this was going on? And besides," I said, trying not to let any bitterness sneak into my voice, "it had to be done to me, right? I mean, so that the world could be saved and all that."

"I don't know." He looked lost in thought. "Maybe, I guess."

I wondered what he meant. Was there another reason why my emotions had been shut down? Or had it never been necessary for them to be shut down in the first place?

He tapped his fingers on the table, thinking. "Gemma, what exactly have they told you about yourself?"

281

I gave him a quick recap of everything Alex had told me while he had been stitching me up. I also told him about the things I picked up on myself; the list I found back at Marco and Sophia's, and the bizarre vision thingy I had been pulled into back at the field trip. I even told him about the prickly sensation. I poured my heart and soul out. It felt really good too, like an enormous weight had been lifted off my shoulders. However, there was one thing I never mentioned. The electricity. That detail I just didn't feel like explaining. It was too complicated...and too personal.

After I finished yammering Laylen's ear off, he stayed silent for awhile, and I started to worry if I had bored him to death or something.

But finally, after what seemed like an eternity, he said, "I don't even know what to say Gemma. I'm so sorry,"

That's when I realized that he had just been being a good listener and taking in what I was telling him. I was so used to being the quiet one and never talking that when it came to being the one talking rather than listening, I was clueless.

"I didn't realize how bad things were for you," Laylen continued. "You know, what I find strange is that Stephan made this big plan to seclude you from everyone to keep you from feeling, but I never thought the plan would actually work. I mean, how can you force a person to become emotionally detached?"

"Alex told me it was because if you raised a person to never know what happiness and sadness and love are, then they wouldn't know *how* to feel them. And it was working well, too. That is, until a couple of months ago when I suddenly snapped out of it."

"But if Alex's little theory is true, then why would you suddenly start to feel?" He paused. "And why would they lie to you about how old you were when you went to live with Marco and Sophia? It just doesn't make sense."

"Maybe so I wouldn't try to remember my mother," I suggested. I mean, it made sense; them telling me I hadn't been old enough to remember her so that I wouldn't try to remember her. But still, they had created such a tangled maze of lies, who knew what was true and what wasn't?

"I guess that could be why, but it still doesn't explain why you suddenly started to feel." He brushed his blue tipped bangs off his forehead and sighed. "Gemma, regardless of what Alex tells you, Stephan can't be trusted."

"How come?"   But really, did I even have to ask? Stephan was, after all, Alex's father.

"Well, there have been a lot of things Stephan's done that are questionable. One of the worst, though, was when your mother disappeared."

My heart thumped loudly in my chest. "What do you mean, she disappeared? I-I thought she died?"

"Well, that's what Stephan told everyone." He scooted his chair in closer so that we were huddled together. "Right after she went missing, I overheard my parents

283

talking about how Jocelyn had this huge fight with Stephan over you. She didn't want to give you up, and from what I understand, she was going to make a run for it. When she did, Stephan went looking for her, but when he came back, he only had you. He told everyone he couldn't find Jocelyn anywhere. The Keepers searched for her and everything, but no one could ever figure out what happened to her. After awhile, they just assumed she died."

Blood howled inside my ears. "They just *assumed* she died? How can anyone just *assume* someone died?"

"Mysterious deaths are very common in the Keeper's world because we are constantly encountering so many dangerous things."

"But do you think she died?"

He shook his head. "And neither did my parents. I only heard bits and pieces of their conversations, but from what I understood, my parents didn't believe Jocelyn just up and died. And they had their suspicions that one of the Keepers might have played a part in her disappearance."

"And you think it's Stephan," I said, feeling like I might throw up. My mom hadn't just died in a car accident. My mom had disappeared. And someone might have made her disappear.

"I can't say for sure because I don't have any proof, but...." He twisted his lip ring back and forth. "Okay, this is what I know about Stephan. First, he is very power hungry, and he likes to be in control of things at all times. If anyone gets in the path of what he wants, he'll do whatev-

284

er it takes to get rid of them. And because he's the leader of the Keepers, no one questions the decisions he makes."

"So you think that he might have gotten rid of my mom so he could have control over me and the star's power?" My voice sounded strangely off pitch.

"I think that's one possibility. But since I have no proof, I can't say for sure."

"Well, maybe you could ask your parents," I suggested. "They might know more about it."

His bright blue eyes saddened as he leaned back in the chair. "My parents are dead, Gemma. They died in a car accident a few months after this happened."

"Oh." I felt so bad for bringing it up. *Nice one, Gemma.* "I'm so sorry."

"Don't worry about it. It was a long time ago." He was acting like it wasn't a big deal, but I knew it really was.

"Does Alex know about any of this?" I asked, shifting the subject away from his parents.

He seemed hesitant to answer. "The thing about Alex is that he's kind of been brainwashed. Like how you were with your emotions. He's got it in his head that Stephan can do no wrong. But yeah, I have mentioned it to him, and he didn't believe me."

Everything was so confusing; a bunch of questions with no answers—cliffhangers without endings. I sighed, my mind spinning.

"Hey, I have an idea." Laylen scooted his chair away from table and got to his feet. "Why don't we take a break from all of this deep talk and go into the kitchen and get you something to eat?"

Hmmm...I was kind of hungry. "That actually sounds like a good idea." I yawned. Apparently I was kind of tired, too.

He laughed. "And then maybe you should get some sleep."

I glanced at the window. The sun's pale pink glow spilled through the glass. Sunrise had arrived and I really did feel tired, but I didn't want to stop our conversation. I wanted to figure out as much as I could before Alex returned. "Yeah, I guess I could sleep."

Hearing the reluctance in my voice, Laylen said, "Don't worry. We'll finish talking about this. I promise."

I sure hoped so.

We went into the kitchen and Laylen began cooking me some eggs. Yes, a vampire/Keeper was making me eggs. Crazy, right? I was sitting on one of the barstools that encircled the midnight blue countertop island, waiting patiently. I would have been helping him cook, but he refused to let me when I offered.

The pan sizzled as Laylen dragged the spatula through the eggs. It had been quiet for awhile now, so when he spoke, it startled me.

"Gemma, do you still have that list of dates you told me about?"

Instinctively, I reached for my pocket, but quickly realized I was wearing Aislin's skirt. The piece of paper with the list of dates was tucked away in the pocket of my jeans, which Aislin had thrown into the washing machine. "Ah, crap."

Laylen turned, spatula in hand. "What's the matter?"

"The list is in the pocket of my jeans," I explained. "The ones Aislin threw in the washing machine."

He cursed under his breath. "Well, I think it's probably a goner."

"Crap!" I said again. "Now what am I supposed to do?"

The pan hissed, and he swiftly turned the stove temperature down. "Do you remember any of the dates on it?"

"Just one of them." I sighed, frustrated that the list of dates was gone forever. "February 8th. And I only remember that one because it was the first day I felt the prickle and started to experience emotion."

He moved the pan off the burner. "Okay, that's weird. Was there anything that seemed significant about any of the other dates?"

I shook my head. "Nope. They all seemed random except for the February 8th one."

Shaking his head, he took a plate out of the cupboard. "It just doesn't make sense; the list of dates; the prickling sensation. If Alex's theory about how you lost your emotions is true, then how would a prickly feeling be able to jump-start your feelings?" He scooped some eggs onto the plate. "You know what it sounds like, right?"

"No."

"Like magic."

"Magic," I said slowly. "Like *witch* magic." Like Aislin's *witch magic?*

He slid the plate of eggs across the counter. "Maybe, but it could be something else. In our world there are a ton of things that would be able to wipe out a person's ability to feel."

I was just about to take a bite of my eggs, but his words made me drop my fork. "You think they *wiped* out my emotions?"

"It's possible, but like I said, there are tons of possibilities. With what you've told me, though, I'm starting to think that some kind of magic was involved."

I wasn't hungry anymore. With all the stomach aches I was getting lately, I wondered if I was getting an ulcer.

"Gemma, are you okay? You look a little pale."

"I'm fine." I swallowed the lump in my throat. "My stomach just feels a little queasy."

"Food looks that bad, huh?" he joked, trying to lighten the mood.

I summoned a small smile. "No, it looks really good." I took a bite. It did taste good.

Laylen scrapped the leftover bits and pieces of egg out of the pan and into the garbage, and then rinsed the pan off in the sink.

"You're not eating?" I asked, scooping up another forkful of eggs.

He shut off the faucet. "No. I don't eat."

"Oh." I felt so stupid. Of course he didn't eat. He was a vampire, after all. "Gotcha."

I ate my eggs and watched him with curiosity as he wiped down the countertops and stove. If someone would have asked me a day ago whether I would've ever thought that I would be sitting in the kitchen with a vampire, eating eggs, all while trying to unravel the secrets that belonged to a group of people whose mission it was to save the world, I would have told them no. Then I would have run for my life because I would have thought they were a total psychopath.

"Laylen." I dragged my fork through my eggs. "Can I ask you a question?"

He tossed the towel aside and turned to face me. "Sure. What's up?"

I hoped I wasn't crossing a line. "How exactly did you get turned in to a vampire?"

He crossed his arms over his chest, muscles flexing, and leaned back against the counter, looking confused. "I don't….I can't remember."

"Is that how it normally works?" I shoved another forkful of eggs into my mouth.

He shook his head. "Memory loss isn't a side effect from getting bitten. Something else had to have happened to me. The only thing I can remember about that night is coming out of a club alone and thinking I heard a noise from behind me. When I turned around, everything went black. I'm not sure if I blacked out or what, but when I did come to, I was sprawled out in an alley with a bite mark on my neck." He pointed at the immortality mark on his forearm. "And of course, this lovely little thing was on my arm. It took me a few days before I figured out I had been bitten by a vampire. I started getting all of these weird...cravings. But luckily, because I was a Keeper to begin with, the cravings were fairly easy to control." He made his way around the island and took a seat on a barstool next to mine. "What's really strange is that I've been told by other vampires that the change is supposed to be this big, memorable experience, yet I can't remember a single thing about it."

I had a flashback to when Alex had opened up one of shoji doors back at the Black Dungeon and I witnessed the vampire about to bite the seemingly willing man. My gut instinct told me not to ask, but curiosity got the best of me. "Do humans let vampires bite them?"

His eyes widened. "Wha—why would you ask that?"

They say curiosity killed the cat. "Because when we were in the Black Dungeon and Alex and I were running from the Death Walkers, he opened a door and there was a woman vampire getting ready to bite a man. And the man seemed...well, he seemed really relaxed for someone who was just about to get bitten."

I was making him uncomfortable. "Yeah...some people do," he said.

"Why?" I scraped the last of my eggs off my plate. "Wouldn't that mean they would turn into a vampire themselves?"

He shook his head. "That's not how it works. They have to bite you, and then you have to drink their blood. Really, it's this whole big ordeal. See, and there's another problem with me turning into a vampire. I know I wouldn't voluntarily drink a vampire's blood."

"That does seem strange..." About as strange as me not being able to remember the details of my life. "So when you turned into a vampire, did you have to die or anything?" The reason I asked was because in a few of the vampire-themed books I've read, the humans who would drink the vampires' blood would have to die right after in order to turn into one.

"Yeah, I had to die," he said charily.

I choked on my eggs, bits and pieces spewing from my mouth and nose. Eww...so gross. "You died?" I coughed.

"Yeah, but I don't remember that part either. I just know that I had to die in order to be what I am now," he said with a matter-of-fact attitude.

I eyed him over, taking note of his pale skin, his extremely red lips, and his abnormally bright blue eyes. As bad as this was going to sound, I had to admit, for a dead guy, he looked pretty good.

291

I wiped my mouth with the back of my hand. "So, I still don't get it. Why would someone let a vampire bite them?"

He gave a quiet laugh. "You really ask a lot of questions, don't you?"

"Sorry," I said, feeling stupid.

"No, it's okay." He took a deep breath, which puzzled me. I mean, if he was dead, then why was he breathing? "Humans let vampires bite them for a few different reasons. There's the whole thrill of the danger that being bitten brings. Sometimes it's out of sheer curiosity. But most of the time, people do it to stimulate their...desires"

Okay, so I've felt embarrassed before, but never absolutely mortified. Wow. It had been awhile since I felt the prickle. I could feel my face heating up, so I let pieces of my hair drift across my face.

"Yeah. So, anyways," Laylen said, in an attempt to change the subject and remove the awkward silence that had gripped the air. "Going back to that prickle sensation thing you were talking about. Do you feel it every time you experience an emotion? Or does it just happen every once in awhile?"

"It only happens when I experience a *new* emotion," I told him, and then shivered, suddenly feeling cold.

He considered this. "Hmm...I don't think I've heard of anything like that. But seeing as there are hundreds of different forms of magic out there, there are a lot of things I haven't heard of yet."

"So how can we find out?" I shivered again.

He cocked an eyebrow at me. "Are you cold?"

I rubbed my hands up and down my arms. "I'm freezing. Aren't you?"

"I always run cold." He glanced around the kitchen, and then he jumped up from the stool and sprinted over to the window.

"What are you looking at?" I stood up and walked over beside him. "Is there something out there?"

"What the—" He jumped back, curse words flying. "How the hell did they find us?"

"What are you...Oh!" I panicked. "The Death Walkers are here!"

He looked at me, his beautiful bright blue eyes flooding with a sea of fear. "Yeah, they're right outside."

Chapter 24

"Shouldn't we be hiding?" I asked Laylen.

After discovering a swarm of Death Walkers marching across the desert toward the house, Laylen had grabbed me by the arm and sprinted down the hall back to the room where Alex and Aislin had transported to Afton from. Then he started throwing books off the shelves. What the purpose of this was, I didn't know. Maybe he was having a momentary lapse in sanity—too much stress or something. I don't know.

"Laylen!" I hollered over the thudding of the books hitting the floor. "What are you doing?!" A book flew straight at me, and I had to dodge to the side to avoid getting smacked in the face by it.

"There's a key somewhere around here..." He glanced inside a book and tossed it on the floor. "To a trapdoor just below that rug." He nodded at a black and red checkered rug on the floor. "We can hide you there until..." He chucked a book over his shoulder and it landed on the floor in front of my feet.

"Until what?" I asked anxiously.

He ripped an old leather-bound book from the shelf and flipped it open. "Until I can lead them away from here...get you out of dan—" His blue eyes lit up as he plucked a small silver object out of the inside of the cover. He dropped the book on the floor and hurried over to me. "Here we go." He held up the silver object, which was a key.

"What's it for?" I asked, my voice taking on that high, pitchy sound that seemed to come out whenever I was in a stressful situation. I threw a quick glance at the window, wondering how close the Death walkers were, but couldn't see anything because of the curtains. "Laylen, I really think—"

"Just a second." He went over to the rug and flipped it over. There was a small square carved in the hardwood floor that had a key hole and an indent for a handle. It looked like one of those trapdoors used on stages back in the olden days. He knelt down and slipped the key into the keyhole. *Click.* Then he raised the door up. "Hurry up and get inside."

I stared down at the mysterious dark hole, my feet glued to the floor. "You want me to do what?"

"Get inside and hide."

I stole a glance back at the curtain-covered window. The air was getting chillier by the second. Goose bumps dotted my arms and legs. They had to be getting close.

"Gemma!" The sound of Laylen's angry voice snapped my attention away from the window and back to him.

"But what are you going to do?" I asked.

He gave me a *duh* look, and I understood. He was going to stay up here and fight while I hid like a coward. My gut twisted with guilt just like it had back at the Black Dungeon when Alex and I had run away and left Aislin and Laylen behind.

I started to argue. "But I—"

He cut me off. "Look, I know it's hard—always being the one who has to hide. But that's the way it has to be. You can't change who you are no matter how much you want to. Trust me."

"This isn't right," I told him.

Ignoring what I said, he held out the key for me to take. "This key also locks the door from the inside. Make sure you lock it when you get in."

Frowning, I snatched the key from him, and stomped over to the trapdoor. "I still don't think this is right," I said as I lowered myself down into the hole.

It was dark inside, and the ceiling brushed the top of my head. If I was a sufferer of claustrophobia, I would have been in trouble.

I looked up at Laylen and he reached down. In his hand was a golden-handled, silver-bladed knife.

"If something does happen," he said, "take this and aim it straight for their heart. It might weaken them enough to give you a chance to run away."

I reluctantly took the knife, the handle feeling cold against my skin. "And where exactly am I supposed to run?"

"To the car. The key's in the ignition. Try to find your way back to Adessa's. She'll be able to help you, at least until someone gets there."

Yeah, fat chance that was ever going to happen, seeing is how it was dark when we drove to Vegas, and I had a bad sense of direction.

A loud thud. It sounded close—maybe even inside the house.

"Don't come out until you know it's safe," he whispered, before dropping the door shut.

Darkness suffocated me. I reached up and fumbled around until I found the lock. It took me a minute to get the key in it, but I managed. Above me, I could hear a lot of banging. The cold had crystallized the air and was biting against my skin. I shivered and chattered and every one of my senses felt hyperaware. I couldn't see the outcome of this situation ending well—Laylen up there alone, trying to fight who knows how many Death Walkers without the Sword of Immortality, while I hid down here, freezing to death. Even if the Death Walkers didn't kill me, the cold probably would.

With absolutely no light, and no way to see above me, I had no clue as to what the heck was going on. There was a lot of thumping and scrapping, and all I could do was stay hidden, crossing my fingers, hoping that by some miracle Laylen would suddenly throw open the door and tell me it was okay to come out.

Of course, that never happened.

The noises did start to dwindle, which made me start to consider coming out. I mean, I couldn't just hide down here forever. Laylen said to wait until it was safe. Quiet had to mean safe, right? Yeah, that might have been a little bit of a stretch, but I was going with it.

I took a trembling breath, trying to calm my nerves. My hand quivered as I felt around and found the lock, the metal frosting my fingertips. So not a good sign. I slid the key in and unlocked the door. *Okay, you can do this.* I let out a breath and pushed on the door. It didn't budge. I tried again. Nothing. Something was on top of it. That something I hoped was the rug. I put the knife back into my pocket, and using both my hands I shoved as hard as I could against the door, grunting and cursing, until the thing finally flew open, hitting the floor with a loud thud, which was not a good start. My gut twisted, and I could feel the eggs I had eaten on the verge of forcing their way back up. I waited a second, listening for any warning sounds, but everything had grown eerily still. A good sign or a bad one, I wasn't sure. But there was only one way to find out. With shaky arms, I heaved myself out of the hole and scrambled to my feet. I did a quick scan of the room. The window was shattered and the bright sunlight was seeping inside. Books were strewn about the floor, but Laylen had done that. Most terrifying were the icicles hanging from the ceiling, long and pointy and sharp.

I needed to come up with a plan, and quickly. I knew what I was supposed to do—run out to the car and go to Adessa's—but the thought of leaving Laylen behind was gnawing at my insides. So instead I did something really stupid. I started for the door to go find Laylen.

I took the knife out of my back pocket and cracked open the door. As I peeked out into the hall, my breath rose in a cloud in front of me.

Another bad sign.

I inched the door open and glanced up and down the hallway. The coast looked clear. I opened up the door the rest of the way and stepped out.

The floor was glazed with ice, giving it a skating rink effect. Now, I am not Miss Coordinated by any means, so I had to brace my hand against the wall as I slowly crept down the hall, my feet slipping with every step. I made it about halfway when it occurred to me just how dumb of an idea this was. Why was it a dumb idea? Well, because a Death Walker had suddenly appeared at the end of the hallway, and at the pace I was moving it was going to take a heck of a lot of time for me to make it anywhere.

I spun around as quickly as my legs would allow me. I lost my balance for a split second and almost ended up face planting it. Keeping my hand pressed to the wall, I glided across the icy floor, making my way back down the hall.

The front door wasn't that far off, but when I turned to check on the Death Walker, it was darting effortlessly toward me, and I knew there was a slim to none chance I was going to make it to the front door. Panicking, I made a hasty decision to go back inside the room. I slammed the door behind me and locked it, knowing full well that locking it wasn't going to do much to stop the monstrous beast. All I could hope for was that it would slow it down enough for me to make it out the window and to the garage.

But I only made it halfway across the room when the door came crashing in. I took off, running as fast as I could. I made it to the window and started to climb out, but then I heard a crackling sound float up from underneath me. I knew what that sound belonged to. Ice. And it was crawling up from beneath me and webbing its way to the window. I had to jump back to avoid being frozen over with ice.

Seconds later, the window was completely sealed off by a thick wall of ice. I tried chipping away at the ice with my knife, but it was useless. The wall was way too thick. I was trapped.

A cold chill shot up my spine, and I slowly turned around. The Death Walker towered ominously in front of me. My breathing faltered as I stared my death in the eyes—its yellow, soulless eyes that held the passion to kill.

No. I couldn't give up. Not with the fate of the world resting in my hands. Or inside me, I should say. I had to save myself in order to save the world.

I could feel the cold handle of the knife pressing into the palm of my hand, and without a glitch of hesitation, I swung it forward, aiming the blade straight at the Death Walker's heart, just like Laylen had told me to do. And to my utter shock, the knife actually drove into the monster's chest.

The Death Walker let out an ear-clawing shriek, and its eyes fired up beneath its black cloak before burning out into black holes.

I did it. I freaking did the impossible. I was able to take one of them down.

Or at least that's what I thought.

Moments later, the Death Walker lunged at me, huffing out a fog of frost-bitten air that hit me directly in the chest. Every ounce of oxygen was sucked out of me. Struggling to breathe, I collapsed to the floor, my body paralyzed with cold and fear. Lightheaded and unable to move, I waited for it to attack again, this time finishing me off.

The monster staggered toward me, swaying like a drunken man as it tipped backwards, then forwards, before finally losing its balance altogether and toppling to the ground, landing only inches away from me.

I let out a wheeze. Was it dead? Had I killed it? *No, don't assume anything.* Laylen said that stabbing a Death Walker would only slow it down. I needed to get my butt off the floor and make a run for the car while I still could. Problem was, my legs and arms weren't having any part of it. What on earth had the thing breathed on me? Was that what was causing me to be paralyzed? Or was I just freezing to death from the cold?

I needed help.

I opened my mouth to scream but only a croak escaped. I tried to get to my feet, but it was useless. Every ounce of my strength had slipped away. I was so sleepy.

My eyelids drifted shut.

"This was not part of the plan," a man's voice snarled. "We were supposed to keep her secluded from humanity. That was the deal."

*What the...*My eyes shot open. I was no longer at Laylen's but curled up in a ball behind a chair in an unfamiliar, dark room. The walls were carved of stone, and underneath where I lay was a Persian rug. Fear skyrocketed through me. This was just like the telescope incident.

I slowly sat up and strained my ears to listen to the voices yammering away on the other side of the chair.

"I understand what the plan is, Demetrius." It was from a different man's voice, deep and low. "But you need to understand that there are obstacles I have to work

302

around. Some of the other Keepers are becoming suspicious of me."

Demetrius? Keepers? From what Alex had told me, these two were complete enemies. Demetrius was the one who wanted me dead, and the one who controlled the Death Walkers. So why was a Keeper talking to him?

"Yes, the Keepers," the first man—Demetrius—replied. "So what is it you've done to make them suspicious of you, my good friend?"

"Well, it seems that the girl's mother has disappeared," the other man—the Keeper—said. "And there's been some speculation that I might have had something to do with her disappearance."

"Has there?" Demetrius replied thoughtfully. "Well, isn't that interesting."

"Very," the Keeper replied with laughter in his voice.

Every part of my body tightened. Could they...could they be talking about my mother and me?

No. There was no way. Was there?

I had to know what this Keeper looked like. In all the other vision things I had been sucked into, no one had been able to see me. I was hoping it was the same here.

Very carefully, I peeked around the side of the chair.

Standing in front of a fireplace were two men. One significantly taller than the other one, with dark hair that brushed his shoulder tops. He had on a long black cloak that looked like the ones the Death Walkers wore. The other man—the shorter one—was dressed head to toe in

303

black, and his black hair was slicked back. The fire cast an orange glow onto their faces, which were blurred over by a sheet of haze.

I should have known.

"I need you to be patient, Demetrius," said the shorter man—the Keeper whose name I didn't know. "I'll make sure the girl stays safe until the time is right."

"You better," the man wearing the cloak—Demetrius—warned. "Otherwise you're out."

"Watch who you're threatening," Mr. No Name Keeper replied, pointing his finger sharply at Demetrius. "You're walking a very thin line right now."

A sudden snap of light blazed across the Keeper man's face. The haze covering his face momentarily flickered away before returning to a blur again. But the flicker lasted just long enough for me to see a faint white scar scuffing his cheek. I gasped. It was the man from my nightmares. The one who always stepped out of the shadows of the forest right after the Death Walker captured me.

"Did you hear that?" the man with the scar asked.

Demetrius shook his head. "Hear what?"

Scar man held up his hand, and his head turned in my direction.

I threw my trembling hand over my mouth and sank back behind the chair. He wasn't supposed to be able to see me.

Heavy footsteps trod toward me. My body shook with fear. If he caught me, I knew he would kill me, just like he did in my nightmares.

"I could have sworn..." his voice drifted over the back of the chair.

I shut my eyes. Please wake up. Please wake up. Please....

"Gemma, wake up."

Electricity sparkled across my skin. I cracked open my eyes. I was back at Laylen's, and Alex was there, standing over me, looking utterly terrified. But why was he looking at me like that?

"What the heck happened here?" His voice cracked.

I opened my mouth to speak, but nothing came out but a wheeze. What was wrong with me? Then it all came rushing back to me. The Death Walker; its breath hitting me in the chest; being paralyzed.

Panicking, I tried to will my cold limbs to move.

"Stay still," Alex told me, and turned to...Aislin—I hadn't even noticed she was there until now. "Go see if you can find Laylen."

Her bright green eyes were wide. "What are you going to do?"

"I'm not sure," Alex said, glancing down at me. "Her skin's already turned blue."

Blue! I struggled to lift my hand up so I could check out the damage, but I couldn't move.

Aislin had a purple duffel bag draped over her shoulder, and she let it fall to the floor. "Alex, are you going to be able to stop it from...because you know if you can't then—"

"Just go!" he yelled.

She flinched and dashed out the door.

Alex immediately went into "save Gemma mode." He slipped off his jacket and knelt down on the floor beside me. "Okay," he mumbled as he assessed me. He wrapped his arms around me and helped me sit up, every bone in my body feeling as though it was going to snap like a twig. Then he leaned me into him.

Right away, the electricity started working its magic, thawing my frozen body and lifting the cold away. I could breathe again and even wiggle my fingertips a little.

"It's going to be okay," he whispered.

Well, this was a nice change. Put me on the verge of dying and he was all for being nice to me. And as strange as it was, I actually felt content. All of my problems, big or small, seemed irrelevant at the moment.

Seconds later, my breathing returned to normal. And I was shivering, which was a good sign because that meant I was no longer paralyzed.

He rubbed his hand up and down my back. "Well, at least you're moving again."

"Yeah, at least there's that," I croaked.

He laughed, his breath tickling at my neck.

I was starting to feel better, but I made no effort to move away from him. I sat there and let him rub my back and whisper that it was all going to be okay because...well, because it felt nice. I still hadn't forgotten about all the lies and unsolved mysteries that seemed to center around Alex. It was just that his arms being around me felt so comforting. And hey, I was only human...or at least partly human...I think.

"Gemma," Alex murmured.

"What?" My voice sounded strangely euphoric.

"Did you do that?"

"Do what?"

"Stab that thing."

I raised my head away from his shoulder and followed his gaze to the Death Walker sprawled on the floor, a knife sticking out of its chest. "Yeah, I did. Laylen told me if I ran into one of them, to stab it in the chest and run. But it breathed this cloud on me, and I couldn't move my body anymore."

"That cloud is called the Chill of Death," he said, then muttered, "I can't believe you actually stabbed one of them."

Chill of Death. Well, that sounded lovely. "I think I took it off-guard or something."

"Still, it's not—"

Aislin walked into the room. When she caught sight of us, she hit a dead halt and pressed her hand over her heart. "Oh my gosh. I'm so glad you're alright. I thought—"

"Aislin," Alex warned.

I knew what he was trying to do. He was trying to stop her from breaking the bad news to me that I almost died. But I figured that out the moment the Chill of Death had hit me.

"Where's Laylen?" Alex let go of me and rose to his feet.

I tried not to act too disappointed about him letting me go as I struggled to get to my feet. My legs wobbled and the room spun and I almost fell right back down. Fortunately I was getting good with being dizzy, and worked my way through the spinning without falling on my butt.

"He was just behind me," Aislin said at the very same moment Laylen ran into the room.

He slammed the door behind him, the icicles on the ceiling rattling in protest. He went to lock the door, but the lock was broken. "Son of a—" He smashed his fist against the door. "We need to get out of here! Now!" He hastily shoved one of the bookshelves against the door—a very heavy bookshelf, which he was able to pick up very easily. So he was strong.

"There are more of them!" Alex cried, and I was suddenly aware that he had the Sword of Immortality gripped in his hand.

Laylen gaped at him. "Yeah, there's more. What did you think, that one single Death Walker showed up?"

Alex glared at Laylen and took a threatening step toward him.

"Guys!" Aislin stepped between them. "You can fight all you want later. Right now we need to get out of here before the rest of them find us, or that thing decides to wake up." She pointed at the unconscious Death Walker lying on the floor.

"That one isn't ever going to wake up," Alex said, yanking out the knife I had stabbed into its chest. He tossed the knife aside, the blade covered with thick black goo. Then he raised the Sword of Immortality into the air and drove it deep into the Death Walker's chest.

Honestly, I was expecting this big ordeal. Like the Death Walker's eyes would shoot open, or it would jump to its feet and let out one of those horrible screams I heard it do before. But nothing happened.

Alex heaved the sword back out and wiped the black goo off on the Death Walker's cloak. "Can you transport us out of here?" he asked Aislin.

"I don't know. Four people are a lot to do at once." She paused, mulling it over. "But if I made two trips it might work."

"Okay..." Alex's gaze drifted over to Laylen, then me, before landing back on Aislin. "You should take Gemma and me first since she's the most important one to get out of here. Then you can come back and get Laylen." He turned to Laylen. "Is that okay with you?"

Laylen shrugged. "Whatever. But you might want to hurry up. There were a bunch of them heading across the desert right for us. I've already taken care of two of them, but when the rest show up, even the Sword of Immortality isn't going to help."

Alex nodded and gathered up two duffel bags—one black, one grey—from off the floor.

"Why does Laylen always have to be the one to stay behind?" I asked Alex as he swung the black duffel bag over his shoulder.

"Because I need to be the one watching you," he answered simply. "I leave for only a couple of hours and all hell breaks loose."

"That wasn't Laylen's fault," I argued. "I was the one who came out of the hiding place that he told me to stay in."

"He was the one responsible for you, therefore it's his fault," Alex said, loud enough for Laylen to hear.

Laylen didn't say a word.

I opened my mouth to protest, but Laylen gave me this look that told me not to even bother. I sighed. "Oh, fine. Whatever."

Alex gave Laylen a dirty look—I had no idea why, though, since he was the one being rude—and tossed a grey duffel bag at me. Instead of catching it, I hopped to the side. Like I've said, I'm not coordinated and know not to even try.

"We picked up some of your clothes while we were at your house," he told me, his tone clipped.

Frowning, I swiped up the bag. The idea of Ailsin and him digging through my clothes made me squirm. "So, did you find Marco and Sophia?"

He shook his head. "Nope."

"What about Stephan?"

"Nope."

He was being a total jerk so I just stopped talking.

So Aislin and Alex hadn't been able to find anyone back in Afton. I thought back to the conversation Laylen and I had about Stephan and my mom's "disappearance," and how Laylen had said Alex was brainwashed. What if they had really found Marco and Sophia? What if they had really found Stephan? What if this was all a ruse to get me somewhere where they could force me to stop feeling?

"Gemma." Alex's voice ripped me out of my daze. He moved over beside Aislin and motioned for me to come over.

I scurried over as Aislin dipped the tip of the candle into the flame.

"Wait a sec." She pulled the crystal back out. "Where are we going?"

"To the Hartfield Cabin," Alex replied. "No one ever goes up there, so it should be safe for now."

She nodded and started twisting the crystal in the flame. "Per is calyx EGO lox lucid via," she whispered.

Red smoke rose up from the candle.

I glanced back at Laylen, who was leaning against the bookshelf that was holding the door shut. I hated to leave him behind. I barely knew him, but out of everyone in my life, he was the only one who was truthful with me. And now I had to go off with Alex, the Guru of Lie Twisting.

Laylen mouthed for me to be careful.

I nodded, letting him know I understood what he meant—watch your back.

"Per is calx EGO lux lucis via!" Aislin shouted. The crystal was glowing bright red. Smoke was rising wildly in the air.

Alex unexpectedly slipped his arm around my waist, shocking me, and my muscles tensed up.

"So you don't fall on your face like the last time we transported," he explained to me with a small amount of amusement in his voice.

It was a good idea, I guess.

I closed my eyes and grasped on to the handle of my bag. I heard a loud bang and then...I was falling. Or flying?

I wasn't exactly sure.

When I opened my eyes, I was in a different room that had dusty white sheets draped over all of the furniture. A grey and tan stone fireplace layered one of the walls, and the rest of them were made of logs.

Alex instantly let go of my waist. He had been right. Holding onto me had kept me from falling.

Aislin relit the candle. "I'll be right back."

Alex took me by the arm and guided me away from her. "Hurry, please," he told her in an anxious voice.

She gave him a small smile and plunged the crystal into the flame. "Per is calx EGO lux lucis via," she said. This time she disappeared quickly.

I dropped my bag on the floor and sat down on a marble step that extended out from the fireplace. Alex sat down too. Neither of us spoke as we waited for Aislin and Laylen to return. We waited and waited. About ten minutes ticked by, and Alex got to his feet and started pacing back and forth across room. I kept my eyes glued to the spot where Aislin had vanished and chewed on my fingernails, which was so weird since it hadn't been a previous habit of mine.

An old grandfather clock towering in the corner struck the hour of ten, devastatingly announcing that way too much time had gone by. They should have been here by now.

Alex stopped pacing and stared vacantly at the clock.

I hated to say it—I hated to even think it—but I had to know. "They're not coming back, are they?"

With the most heart-wrenching look on his face, he said, "No, I don't think they are."

313

Chapter 25

I had been sitting at the foot of the fireplace, watching Alex tug sheets off the furniture, for about fifteen minutes now. I think it was his way of trying to distract himself from the fact that something terrible may have happened to Laylen and Aislin. He had tried to call them but couldn't get a signal on his phone from "all the way up here," wherever that was.

I hadn't said anything to him because I had no idea what to say. I could have tried to be positive and tell him reassuring things like, *Hey, maybe Aislin has just broken her crystal again.* But we both knew there was a slim to none chance that was the case. We just weren't that lucky.

"So…" I began, still in the middle of deciding what to say. "What is this place, anyway?"

He yanked a sheet off a forest green couch that had tiny moose embroider on it. "It's a cabin I used to come to when I was little." He drew a sheet off a lamp and dust flew everywhere.

I sneezed. "So what do we do now?"

"We're going to drive into town so I can get a signal on my phone." He unzipped his duffel bag. "Then, we'll try and get a hold of someone."

I was biting my fingernails. "So where exactly are we?"

He nodded at a window masked by a curtain. "The middle of nowhere, basically."

"The middle of nowhere." I stood up, went over to the window, and threw back the curtain. Then I grimaced. Steep mountains and pine trees everywhere. And yes, of course, a thick blanket of crisp white snow was covering it all.

"Yuck," I muttered and let the curtain fall. Why oh why couldn't we have gone somewhere warm? Like, say, Hawaii. I sighed. Man, I sounded like a selfish brat, complaining about being in the snow when Laylen and Aislin could be in some serious trouble. *Okay, suck it up, Gemma.* "So, where is here? What's the place called?"

"We're in Colorado." He looked up from his bag and raised an eyebrow. "What's with the disappointment?"

"Oh, nothing," I sighed. Apparently I failed miserably at sucking it up. "I just really hate the snow. That's all."

"Oh, yes, you and the cold," he remarked as he drew a tan hooded jacket out of his bag.

I picked up my bag from off the floor. "So, is there somewhere I can change?" I really wanted to get out of this skirt and into my own clothes.

"Yeah, follow me."

315

He took me back to a bedroom with light blue wallpaper and grey carpet, and then he left me alone to change.

I set my bag down on a massive log bed and started searching through it for something to wear. Fortunately, I wasn't a girl who was really into fashion because I was pretty sure whoever packed this mess of a bag was in a hurry. Everything in it was so random; two mismatched gloves, three different socks, and one boot. I decided on a pair of black jeans and a grey and black striped hooded Henley. I kept my DCs on because...well, what good was one boot?

After I finished getting dressed, I realized how heavy my eyelids felt. I barely got any sleep over the last twenty-four hours, and I think I might have been running on an adrenaline high or something and was now starting to crash.

There wasn't a blanket or sheet on the bed, just a mattress. Even though it was kind of gross, I thought about lying down on it and letting my eyes close for a few minutes. But then I thought of Aislin and Laylen and told myself to suck it up.

Now wasn't the time for sleeping.

I opened the door, only to find Alex standing there on the other side. He scared me, and I almost bolted off in a mad sprint.

"Holy crap," I said, catching my breath. "You scared the heck out of me."

"Yeah, I can tell," he said, his voice cautious.

316

He had put on a tan hooded jacket and a black baseball hat. He looked perfect. He always looked perfect. There was no use trying to deny it.

He scaled me over from head to toe. "We need to get you some kind of disguise in case we run into trouble."

I fidgeted with the edge of my shirt. "What kind of trouble?"

"The same kind we've been running into." He sighed tiredly. "The Death Walkers are going to be all over the place now that they've discovered you."

I sighed. "Okay, so what do you want me to do?" I pointed at my bag of clothes. "Because there's not a whole lot in there."

"Yeah, I think Aislin basically just dumped a drawer of your clothes in it."

"And then added one boot?"

He scrunched his forehead. "Huh?"

I shook my head. "Never mind....So yeah, I don't think I have anything very disguise-like." I paused and pulled my hood over my head. "Does this work?"

He gave me a doubtful look.

Oh, don't you give me that look too. I wasn't some secret agent/master of disguise who could create a new identity out of some string and tape, so cut me some slack, would you?

He ran his hand over his face and sighed. "Well, I guess it'll have to work. Do you at least have some sunglasses to cover those up?" He pointed at my eyes.

"No, I don't have any—hey, I thought you said you liked the color of my eyes. You said it was a nice different."

"I wasn't saying that to be mean. There just aren't a whole lot of people walking around with violet eyes. It'll give you away." He zipped up his jacket. "And I do like the color of your eyes. They reminded me of these flowers you used to pick when you were...." He trailed off, his bright green eyes widening.

"When I what?" I pressed.

He cleared his throat. "Nothing, it wasn't important. Let's go." He turned his back on me and started down the hall.

"What? Were you going to tell me some story about when I was four years old and not living with Marco and Sophia?" I called out, chasing after him.

His froze. "Who told you that?"

"Laylen."

He said nothing and went into the living room.

I followed after him. "What? You don't have anything to say?"

"Gemma, I don't have time for this right now." He opened a door that led out to the garage. "We need to get to town."

He was right, but this was *so* not over.

Chapter 26

We drove to town in a black Jeep Wrangler which, by the layer of dust on the dashboard, had most likely been sitting out in the garage for quite awhile. The snow on the road was deep, and Alex had to drive incredibly slowly.

I had come up with this brilliant plan to try and catch some zzz's during the drive, but the second my eyelids closed, Alex decided it was chat time.

"So, what else did Laylen tell you?" he asked.

I slowly opened my eyes. "What do you mean?"

"Well, he told you about how you weren't really one when you moved in with Marco and Sophia." He practically bit at the words, which made me feel bad...for Laylen. If and when Laylen returned, Alex was probably going to rip into him for telling me. "I'm just curious what else he told you."

"Nothing really," I lied. I wasn't going to get Laylen into any more trouble.

Alex slipped me a sideways glance. "He told you nothing else at all?"

I shook my head, acting as cool as the snow on the road, "Nope."

He shot me a skeptical look. "Yeah, I'm not buying it."

I shrugged. "Well, it's the truth."

"So, then, what did you two talk about while Aislin and I were gone?" he asked. "I mean, we were gone for at least an hour. So what did you two do?"

"I don't know." It felt like I was walking into a trap, so I had to make sure I chose my words very carefully. "We sat around. Ate. Almost were frozen to death by a bunch of murderous Death Walkers. You know, the usual."

"And you didn't talk at all?"

"Not really...I mean, we did a little, but it was mostly about him?"

He shook his head, his knuckles whitening as his grip tightened on the steering wheel. "Fine, Gemma. Don't tell me."

Okay, I won't.

Alex rounded a sharp corner and a town rose into view. Log cabins dotted the snowy hills. Trees canopied the yards. I frowned, thinking of Nevada's golden desert sand and delicious warm air, which also made me think of Aislin and Laylen. Were they alright? Or had the Death Walkers gotten them? After all, the Death Walkers had come close to killing me on more than one occasion. I shuddered, remembering how it felt when the cold was sucking the life from my body; the helplessness I felt lying paralyzed on the floor; the vision thing I had been pulled into right afterwards. The vision. Through all of the chaos, I had completely forgotten about it. How could I forget

320

about something so important? I mean, this man with the scar—the Keeper—I had to know him somehow, otherwise why would I have dreamt about him. From what I picked up on in the vision, he might have had something to do with my mother's disappearance, and why I had spent most of my life emotionless. I had to find out who he was.

Somehow.

Another thing I wondered was why I kept slipping into the vision things. I hadn't touched a crystal ball or anything when I witnessed the Keeper and Demetrius chatting it up, just like I hadn't when I had been pulled away back at the telescope and saw the mother and daughter walking in the field—the daughter who might be me. But if that was the case then the vision had to be from the past, so why couldn't I remember it actually happening? If it had already taken place, I should have some memory of it.

Ah! I was so confused.

I pitter pattered through my thoughts, trying to make sense of everything, but ended up feeling more lost than ever. There was only one way I could think of to get some answers to my endless list of questions. But whether he would tell me the truth or not, who knew? I at least had to try, though.

"Alex," I said so abruptly it made him jump.

"What?" he asked breathlessly.

I ignored the warning in my gut begging me not to ask. "Is it possible to see a vision without a Foreseer's crystal ball?"

He gave me a funny look. "Why do you ask?"

I shrugged. "I was just wondering."

He thought about it for a second. "I don't know... I think there might have been one Foreseer who was powerful enough to do it, but I don't know anything about him."

Oddly enough, he sounded like he was telling the truth. "Oh. Okay."

I turned and looked out the window, thinking about the Keeper and Demetrius's discussion about the woman that they conveniently made disappear, and the girl who they said needed to be kept away from humanity. They had to have been talking about my mother and me. Either that or there was another poor unemotional girl roaming around the world somewhere. God, this was some heavy stuff. I really needed some answers. What I needed was Laylen. He would help me figure all this out.

Alex stopped the Jeep at a stop sign. "Do you think you saw a vision without a crystal ball?"

"Huh?" How was I supposed to answer? With the truth? My gut instinct told me not to. "No, I was just curious. That's all."

He stared at me, his bright green eyes weighing heavily on me, causing the intensity of the electricity to spark up. "Gemma, it feels like you're keeping something from me. Are you? Because if you are, whatever it is, you can tell me."

I wanted to tell him, but I was afraid he would freak out. I had to tell someone, though. It was important. And since he was the only one here... "I don't know...Well, it's just that back at Laylen's house I thought—"

Alex's phone rang, interrupting me. He slid his phone out of the pocket of his jeans, and relief swept across his face as he glanced at the screen. "It's Stephan," he said, then answered it.

I could hear Stephan's voice murmuring on the other end. Alex pulled out onto the main road, and we drove by a sign welcoming us to Mountain View, Population 523. Wow, a town smaller than Afton. Who would have thought?

"Yeah, hold on," Alex said into the phone. He parked the Jeep on the side of the road, in front of a cedar-sided house that had a giant sculpture of a moose decorating the yard.

"What are we doing here?" I asked, but he was already climbing out of the car. "Stay here," he told me, and slammed the door shut. Then he walked around to the back of the Jeep and stood there with the phone pressed to his ear.

Obviously they were discussing something that they didn't want me to hear. That meant I needed to hear it, right? I mean, it could be something important, maybe something about me. Oh no. What if they were making a plan to remove my emotions again?

One good thing about an old Jeep is that the windows aren't automatic. This allowed me to crack the window without all the noisy buzzing pressing a button would have brought on. I leaned my head toward the window and tried to listen, but the engine was running and I could hardly hear a thing. I eased the window down a sliver more and put my ear up to the opening, the cold air biting at my skin.

"Well, what do you want me to do until then?" I heard Alex saying. A pause and then, "I know, but she's growing suspicious. You don't know how she is…She asks a lot of questions…" Another pause, this time longer. "I know, but it's hard for me to do that with her. She just…I just can't…I don't know. I have a hard time lying to her."

Well, that was news to me. Not the lying part, but the part about him having a hard time lying to me. Hmm…maybe I could use it to my advantage.

"Alright, fine. I'll see you in a bit," Alex said.

I fumbled to roll the window back up and barely got it up in time, my hand dropping from the handle right as Alex opened the door.

"Stephan's on his way," he told me, slamming the door closed. "He'll be here in a bit."

Oh, yippee, I thought sarcastically. "Oh, yeah."

He pulled the Jeep back onto the road. "Yeah, Marco and Sophia are with him, and he said that Laylen and Aislin are alright."

I would have felt relieved except for the sick feeling in my stomach, warning me that it was a bunch of crap.

"So we should probably get some food," Alex said, turning into a parking lot that belonged to a brick building that had a huge sign that read, Edmund's Groceries. "Then we'll go back to the cabin so we'll be there when everyone shows up."

"So where are Aislin and Laylen?" I asked. "I mean, why did they never transport back?"

"Stephan said that he sent them on an errand," he said, not really answering my question.

"What kind of an errand?" I asked, trying to keep my voice neutral, not wanting to let on that I was suspicious.

"I don't know—he didn't say." He parked the Jeep and shut the engine off, then turned in his seat so he was facing me. "Gemma, what exactly is it you're getting at here?"

I shrugged. "I wasn't getting at anything. I was just wondering where they were. That's all."

He studied my face. "No, that's not all....Okay, what did Laylen tell you?"

I unbuckled my seatbelt. "I already told you, we didn't talking about anything."

He kept his eyes on me. Despite my urge to hover back, I stayed where I was and kept my face expressionless. I don't know what he was expecting—me to break down and pour my heart and soul out to him—but finally he gave up, took the keys out of the ignition, and opened the door. "Let's go."

So I know this is going to sound totally weird, but I've never actually been inside a grocery store before. All through my childhood, Sophia and Marco rarely took me anywhere, and never to a grocery store. So strolling through a store full of food was a whole new experience for me.

But I wasn't basking in the it's-like-I'm-a-real-person experience. I was too distracted. The whole vision thing was really bugging me. I wanted to piece everything together. Every ounce of my body was telling me I had to know.

And fast.

There was also something else troubling me; the whole Marco-Sophia-and-Stephan-are-on-their-way-thing. There were so many holes in the story Stephan had told Alex. Like for instance, why hadn't anyone answered their phones during the millions of times Alex had tried to call them? And why did Alex have to get out of the Jeep to talk to Stephan? I hadn't heard anything suspicious during my eavesdropping investigation. However, I couldn't hear what was being said on the other end of the phone either. The only thing I'd really heard—and it only seemed semi-important—was that Alex had a difficult time lying to me.

So, maybe if I asked Alex enough questions, he just might let something slip out that he didn't want me to know.

As we roamed up the snack aisle, I put on my best poker face. "So...I have a question."

Alex stopped pushing the cart to eye over the selection of granola bars. "Okay. What's your question?"

"Where were Marco, Sophia, and Stephan when you couldn't get a hold of them?"

He selected a box of granola bars and dropped it in the cart. "They were up at a lodge in Jackson. I guess their car got stuck or something and they ended up having to stay longer than they expected to stay."

There were so many things wrong with his answer. "Yeah, but why didn't they answer their phones?"

He motioned behind me where the chips were. "Grab a bag of Doritos, would you?"

I snatched one up and tossed it in the cart.

"Because you know how it is up there," he said, inching the cart forward again.

I shook my head. "No. How is it up there?"

"Well, the phone service is really crappy. There are just too many mountains or something, and most of the time you can't get a signal." He arched an eyebrow at me. "Haven't you ever tried to call anyone up there before?"

I gave him an are-you-kidding-me look. "Let me think." I tapped my finger on my lip. "Since calling people usually requires having someone to call, I would say no, I don't know how it is."

He stopped pushing the cart abruptly, looking taken off-guard; a little sad even. And perhaps...wait a minute...hold on...guilty.

It occurred to me that my snide remarks were probably not the best way to get him to open up and tell me the truth. "Sorry," I apologized, starting down the aisle again.

He followed, the wheels of the cart squeaking with every turn.

"So what happened after they got back and realized what was going on?" I asked, sidestepping around a cupcake display.

He paused at the soda section. "They headed straight to Vegas. And they made it there just in time to stop Laylen and Aislin from getting killed. I guess when Aislin trans—" He stopped talking as a middle-aged woman with overly-bleached hair walked by us. A Death Walker in disguise perhaps. Yeah, I don't think so. "After Aislin went back to get Laylen," he continued, after the woman had disappeared around the corner, "more Death Walkers showed up. There was this huge mess, and I guess she ended up breaking her crystal." He grabbed a twelve pack of Coke and set it in the cart.

If what he just told me had been a story in a book, it would've been the part where everything seemed to play out a little too perfectly. "So Marco, Sophia, and Stephan just, what? Showed up and saved the day?"

328

"Yeah, basically." He picked up a loaf of bread from off a shelf. "Stephan's very good at the whole rescue thing. He has a gift for it."

I chose to ignore that comment. "So why didn't Stephan ever call you?"

He reached for a box of cereal, and then pulled back, glancing over his shoulder at me. "What do you mean?"

"When they were making the, like, eight-hour drive to Vegas—it seems like plenty of time to call and give a heads up that they were on their way, if you ask me."

"I don't know…maybe because they were in a hurry." He started to push the cart again, but quickly slammed on the brakes and spun around. "Gemma, what exactly is it you're getting at?"

I shrugged. "I don't know. I was just trying to point out the obvious, I guess. I mean, don't you think it's just a little bit strange that they didn't call right when they figured out what was going on?"

He scowled at me. "What did Laylen tell you?"

"I already told you, nothing."

"Then what the hell's wrong with you?"

"Nothing's wrong with me. What the hell's wrong with you?"

My plan was going so well….not.

"Just so you know," he growled, "most of Laylen's bitterness towards my father comes from the fact that he made Laylen give up his position as a Keeper after he was turned into a vampire."

329

"Stephan forced him to leave?" I asked, astounded.

"Well, we really couldn't let him stay a Keeper when Keepers are the ones who are supposed to be protecting people from vampires." He turned around and started pushing the cart down the aisle again.

It sounded completely cruel and heartless. How could they kick him out just because he was a vampire, especially when he wasn't evil? "That sounds really harsh."

"Yeah, it is," he said in a flat tone. "But that's the way things have to be in order to do what's right."

"Do you really believe that?" I asked. "Or are you just repeating someone else's words?" *Like, say, hmm...your father's.*

He whirled around again, his eyes burning with fury. "Isn't that what you're doing right now—repeating Laylen's words?"

"Well, Laylen's words are the only truthful ones I've heard in the last fourteen years," I snapped with anger. *So much for keeping calm.*

"And how do you know that for sure?" He glared. "You've only known him for like a day."

"What does knowing someone for a certain amount of time have to do with whether or not they tell the truth? I've known you for like a month, and Marco and Sophia for like seventeen years." I held up my hands in front of me, my voice dripping with bitterness. "Oh no, wait, I mean fourteen years."

We were standing so close to each other that I could feel the warmth of his breath against my cheeks. Electricity was rushing passionately through my veins. Alex opened his mouth, about to snap something back at me, but clamped it shut as his gaze wandered over my shoulder.

I turned around and then cringed. I wasn't sure how loud we had been arguing, but apparently pretty loud because we had drawn in an audience. At the end of the aisle, watching us with wide eyes and a curious expression, was a teenage boy wearing a yellow Edmund's Groceries apron. The middle-aged woman that had passed by us earlier also stood there, staring at us, along with a younger girl that had fiery red hair.

"Whoops," I muttered, turning back to Alex.

He gave me a yeah-no-kidding look, took me by the arm, and guided me down the aisle in the opposite direction of our little audience, pushing the cart along with us.

And that was about the end of our little conversation, as well as our grocery shopping expedition. Alex grabbed a few more things, and then we headed to the checkout stand. Neither one of us said anything. I could tell he was still mad, but so was I. I was bummed out too, because I hadn't gotten a single useful thing out of him. In fact, I think I ended up even more confused. It's a good thing I wasn't planning on going into a career as a detective, because I really sucked at the interrogation thing.

At the checkout stand, I helped Alex empty the cart onto the conveyer belt. Then we waited as the cashier—a perky blonde girl wearing too much makeup—scanned each item. She kept batting her eyelashes at Alex, then started babbling to him about her job being a total drag, all while throwing in the occasional giggle and hair flip.

She was totally flirting with him.

It sucked.

As much as I hated to admit it, I was jealous of her flawless flirting ability that I so did not possess. The last and final straw was when Alex flashed her an award winning smile, leaned over the counter, and started flirting back. I almost lost it. Yeah, I know, I had no claim over him, and I was supposed to be mad. And I was. But when you feel some unexplained intense electricity thingy every time you're around a guy, being territorial is kind of a given.

To avoid watching the painful scene—and also to avoid doing something really stupid—I wandered over to a nearby magazine stand and distracted myself by reading through the headlines.

I picked up a magazine and flipped to the page with an article titled "The Top 10 Greatest Hits of All Time." Most of the songs were totally old school, but I appreciated the distraction.

"Interesting read?" A stranger's voice, soft and melodious like velvet, floated over my shoulder.

I instantly put my guard up as I slowly turned around. Standing a little too close for comfort was a guy probably a few years older than me with sandy blonde hair and eyes as gold as the desert sand. Immediately, I sensed something was off about him, but couldn't place exactly what.

He smiled, flashing a set of perfectly straight white teeth. "Hi. I didn't mean to scare you or anything. I just haven't seen you around here before. Are you new here?"

"Umm...yeah," I said guardedly. It was so bizarre. People hardly ever approached me like this.

Unsure of what to do, and figuring Alex would freak if he saw me talking to someone, I set the magazine down on the rack and started to walk away.

"So are you just visiting someone then?" he asked, halting my getaway.

"Yeah. I'm just visiting."

He paused, seeming like he was choosing his next words carefully. "My name is Nicholas. And you are?"

"Gemma," I replied automatically, and then realized I probably shouldn't have told a complete stranger my real name. I mean, who knew who this guy really was? Yeah, he could be just some guy from Mountain View, Colorado. But he could be something else.

"Gemma. That's a pretty name." He brushed a strand of his sandy blonde hair out of his eyes, and the sleeve of his navy blue shirt slipped up just enough for me to catch a glimpse of a tattoo on his wrist; a black S wrapped by a small circle.

Just a tattoo?

I wasn't sure.

My instincts told me to get away from him, so I forced a smile and started to walk away again. "I gotta go."

He stepped in front of me and nodded in the direction of where Alex stood, still chatting it up with Checkout Girl. "Is that your boyfriend over there?"

My pulse sped up. "No."

His mouth curled into a smile that sent a shiver down my spine. And not the good kind of shiver either. "Well, if that's not your boyfriend, then maybe you and I could go out sometime."

Yeah, like he really wanted to go out with me. I would have laughed if I hadn't been so freaking terrified. Something wasn't right. The guy was showing way too much interest in me. And that questionable tattoo on his wrist....I needed to go. *Now!*

I moved to go around him. "Look, I really have to—"

Alex suddenly appeared by my side, and I felt a rush of relief sweep across my rattled nerves. "Ready to go?"

"Yes," I said, wanting to get the heck out of here and away from this guy. "Let's go."

As Alex pulled me toward the exit doors, I thought I heard Nicholas mutter, "Not your boyfriend, huh?"

For most of the drive back to the cabin, Alex and I stayed quiet. I was beginning to think this was how things would always be between us. Either we were biting each other's heads off, or ignoring one another. I wasn't sure which one

I preferred. Neither really. I wished things could just be normal.

Finally, after what seemed like forever, Alex spoke.

"Can you please explain to me why you thought it was okay to talk to a complete stranger like that?" he asked, his voice sharp with anger.

"Excuse me?" I said incredulously. "It wasn't my fault. I was just standing there, minding my own business, when he came up and started talking to me."

"It was your fault." He paused as he turned the Jeep around a sharp, slippery corner. "You should have just walked away."

I forced my anger down the best I could. "I tried to leave, but he wouldn't stop talking."

"I don't care if he wouldn't stop talking. You should have walked off. Do you not understand how dangerous that could've ended up being if that guy wasn't just some guy?"

"Yeah, I understand that," I grinded through my teeth. "But like I said, I tried to walk off, but he—"

He cut me off. "There are no buts. You should have left."

He was being so irrational that I swear I could have slapped him. I clenched my hands into fists, telling myself to stay calm.

"And I thought I told you to put on some sunglasses." He was practically yelling at me now.

"What the heck is *your* problem?" I snapped.

"What the heck is your problem?" he bit back.

I glared at him. It was one thing for him to lecture me over something that was my fault. It was another thing for him to sit here and chew me out over a situation I had no control over. "Well, if you wouldn't have been so busy flirting with that stupid cashier girl, then maybe you would have noticed a little bit earlier what was going on." Yeah, I regretted that one right after I said it. I sounded like a jealous girlfriend.

He gave me a funny look. "I wasn't flirting with her. I was being polite. When a person talks to you, it's rude not to talk back."

"Whatever. It doesn't matter to me whether you were flirting with her or not." I folded my arms and turned my head toward the window. "I was just pointing out that if you'd been paying more attention, then you would have noticed a lot sooner that the guy had cornered me."

"So it doesn't matter to you whether I was flirting with that girl or not?"

"Nope," I lied. "You can flirt with whomever you want."

"Yeah. I'm buying it. You don't sound very convincing. In fact, you can't even look at me when you say it."

I squirmed uncomfortably in my seat. Then pulled myself together and looked over at him. "I don't care whether you were flirting with her or not."

He locked eyes with me. "You don't?"

"I don't," I said, unable to break my gaze away from his.

He raised his eyebrows. "Whatever you say."

"I don't." My voice sounded strangely high. "I really don't."

He suppressed a smile as he pulled the Jeep into the driveway. His cocky attitude was really starting to get under my skin. He was so sure of himself; so convinced I had some big crush on him, which I didn't. I swear.

Oh, whatever.

As soon as he parked the Jeep inside the garage, I jumped out, preparing to storm inside, but ended up slipping on a patch of ice. I had to grab onto the door handle to catch myself from falling on my butt. Regaining my balance, I slowly made my way into the house, not bothering to help Alex carry in the groceries. I was too irked to care.

The moment I stepped into the living room, I knew something was off. The air felt heavy, putting my senses on high alert. I glanced around the room. Everything looked fine. The sliding back door was closed. The lights were off. I shook my head. *Strange.* This whole Death-Walker-trying-to-kill-me thing was making me paranoid.

I flipped the light on and started for the room where my bag was. I figured I would go back there and take a nap. Some sleep might help me relax.

As I passed the kitchen, the hairs on the back of my neck stood straight up.

"Hello, Gemma," said a soft and melodious voice.

I didn't have to turn around to know who that voice belonged to. Nicholas—the creepy guy from the grocery store.

Before I could even attempt to run away, an arm caught me by the waist and jerked me backward. I opened my mouth to scream, but a hand came down over it, silencing me.

"Shhh," Nicholas purred in my ear. "You don't need to be afraid. I'm not going to hurt you."

Yeah, he couldn't have sounded less convincing if he tried.

Chapter 27

So maybe Alex was right. I shouldn't have been talking to anyone in the grocery store. I still stood by what I said though—it wasn't my fault. He had come up and talked to me. But it was too late to do anything about it now. Nicholas had me trapped and was holding me against him like a hostage.

I didn't think he had a weapon on him or anything. Well, aside from his strength, which felt inhumanly strong. And he had gotten up to the cabin so quickly; too quickly for any human to pull off. Even if he had driven, I still don't think he would have been able to beat Alex and me up here. Besides, I hadn't noticed a car parked anywhere, so I was guessing that he might have another way of traveling—like say, hmm...transporting. That was just me going out on a limb though. I couldn't be sure since I had only the vaguest clue about other means of transportation besides by vehicle.

Nicholas' skin felt warm against mine, but not in the same sense as Alex's felt—all buzzing with electricity. Nicholas' was more a damp, earthly kind of warm. He also had this strange smell to him, like lilacs mixed with forest and freshly fallen rain. The smell was intoxicating, and I had to wonder if he had recently stepped out of a rainforest.

Breathing heavily against the palm of Nicholas' hand, I heard the treading of Alex's footsteps heading up the cement steps of the garage. There was a soft thump, and he stepped into the living room, his hands full of grocery bags. He took one look at us and the blood drained from his face. The bags slid to the floor, and a tub of mayo rolled out of one of them. For a second, we all just stared at it.

Alex folded his arms across his chest. "Okay, so who are you?"

Nicolas moved his hand away from my mouth and pressed me so tightly to his chest that I could feel his heart beating through my back, slow and rhythmically, like the beat of a drum. He didn't answer Alex, and I found the quietness very unsettling.

Alex stared Nicholas down, and Nicholas let out a soft laugh, his grip on me loosening a little. Seizing the opportunity, I jabbed my elbow into his stomach. His muscles tensed, but he didn't let go of me.

"I'm hurt that you don't remember me, Alex." Nicholas' voice dripped with sarcasm.

Whoa. Hold up. Alex knew him?

Alex processed what Nicholas said, recognition slowly showing in his expression. "Nicholas Harper."

"Aw, so you do remember me," Nicholas said with a hint of amusement. "I'm so touched."

340

Alex shook his head, looking irritated. "What do you want?"

"Hmm...What do I want?" Nicholas mused, stroking his fingers through my hair. "She sure turned out to be a pretty little thing, didn't she?"

Okay. That was enough. If Alex wasn't going to do anything to get this guy off me, I was going to have to take matters into my own hands. I gradually lifted up my leg and then kicked him in the shin as hard as I could, while at the same time slamming the back of my head into his face.

"Son of a—" he cursed and let go of me.

Alex looked stunned as I sprinted over to him. He jumped in front of me, acting like a barrier between Nicholas and me.

"Jesus, that hurt," Nicholas groaned, rubbing his nose. He took a deep breath and shook his shoulders out like he was shaking off my attack. His lips curved into a grin. "Wow, she's quite the wild thing, isn't she?"

Alex glanced over his shoulder at me, a trace of a smile teasing at his lips. "Perhaps." He quickly shook his head, and his face fell into a dead serious expression as he turned back to Nicholas. "Did you come here because you want something? Or was it just so you could be annoying?"

Nicholas rolled his eyes. "It's amazing how over the course of ten years you haven't changed a bit."

Alex sighed, losing patience. "Just tell me what you want."

Nicholas held up his hands. "Fine. My word, you have no sense of humor."

"When it comes to you I don't," Alex said flatly.

That wiped the smile right of off Nicholas' face. "What I've come for is her—" he pointed at me—"on behalf of the Foreseers."

"What!" I cried out.

"Don't say a word," Alex hissed at me.

How on earth was I supposed to not say anything when a thousand questions were bursting inside me? Still, I bit down on my tongue and kept quiet.

"And why do the Foreseers want her?" Alex asked calmly.

Nicholas crossed his arms, the sleeve of his shirt slipping up, displaying the circle with an S on his wrist. "So she can be trained to be a Foreseer."

My jaw dropped. "Trained to be a Foreseer."

Alex took my hand and gave it a squeeze, a warning to be quiet. "And why does she need to be trained to be a Foreseer?"

Nicholas stared bewilderedly at him. "Um... because she is one."

"No, she's not," Alex said.

Nicholas shook his head, looking frustrated. "Did she or did she not use a crystal ball to see a vision?"

Well...crap. How did he know about that?

Alex hesitated. "Listen, there's been a misunderstanding. Gemma, she's...well, she's different."

I shook my head. *Different*. There was that word again.

"Look, I don't care what she is. The law says if a person can see a vision, then they belong to the Foreseers. She saw a vision, therefore she belongs to *us*." He put a little too much emphasis on the word "*us*," if you asked me. "But you're a Keeper, so you should already know that."

"I know what the law says," Alex snapped. "But like I said, she's..."

"...Different," Nicholas finished, making air quotes. "Doesn't matter. She has to go back with me. She can try and plead her case when she gets there if she wants to." His gaze bore into me, making my skin crawl. "But personally, I would prefer if she didn't."

I shrank back behind Alex. The room grew so quiet you could have heard a pin drop. Or even a grandfather clock ticking, since I could.

Finally, Alex threw his hands in the air. "Fine, she'll go."

"What!" I exclaimed in outrage. "Are you kidding? You can't let him take me."

"She's definitely a wild thing," Nicholas commented with a smirk.

Alex shot me a look, cautioning me to keep my mouth shut.

"You can't let him take me," I hissed.

Be quiet, he mouthed and turned back to Nicholas. "But just so you know, I'm going with her."

"You can't," Nicholas said. "It's not allowed."

343

"There are no laws that forbid Keepers from entering the City of Crystal," Alex informed him. "So I'm going."

Nicholas glowered at Alex, his golden eyes smoldering like ambers. "Nothing has changed with you. You still just do whatever you want."

"Yep," Alex replied. "I sure do."

And really, he did. But that was fine by me in this case, because there was no way I wanted to go off alone with this Nicholas guy. He was creepy. And I especially didn't want to go off alone to some city filled with people who could see the future.

"Let's go then," Nicholas said, and he headed toward the coffee table.

I looked at Alex. "You really want me to go?"

He nodded. "You don't have a choice. There are certain laws that we all have to abide by, and one of them states that when someone possesses the Foreseer ability, they have to be trained by the Foreseers."

"But I don't want to," I complained.

Alex leaned in. "I'll get you out of this, I promise. But we have to go."

Of course he would get me out of this, but not out of the kindness of his heart or anything. It was because I had the star's power inside me.

Grudgingly, I followed Alex over to where Nicholas stood.

Nicholas retrieved a miniature crystal ball from his pocket and balanced it on top of the table. "Ladies first."

My stomach twisted into a billion knots. "What exactly am I supposed to do?"

Nicholas nodded at the crystal ball. "Put your hand on it."

I glanced at Alex and he gave me a nod, giving me the go ahead. I swallowed hard and reached out for the crystal ball, hesitating briefly before letting my fingers brush the glass.

There was a bright burst of light. Then I was spiraling down a dark tunnel once again.

Chapter 28

I tried very hard not to fall smack dab on my face when I landed, but we all know how great I am at avoiding falls. So yeah, basically I ate it. I did, however, manage to keep my head from hitting the ground, which I was grateful for since it was made of crystal; hence the name, City of Crystal.

Pushing myself up from the ground, my wrist let out a loud pop. I winced as the pain spread up my arm. I cradled my injured wrist against me and glanced around. I was standing in a cave. A very unique cave. The high arched ceiling was dusted with what looked like glittery charcoal, and dark red crystals hung down from it. Rubies ran in a wavy pattern across the snow-white crystal walls. Through the translucent crystal floor, a river as dark as the midnight sky elegantly flowed, flakes of gold speckling in it like stars. I had to admit, the place was absolutely beautiful. Unrealistically beautiful, though. I mean, how many times have you found yourself stumbling around in a cave made of glass and crystal?

Probably never. That is, unless you are a Foreseer.

I heard a faint *swoosh*, and then Alex dropped down from above, landing gracefully beside me.

Startled, I jumped back, pressing my hand to my heart. "You scared the crap out of me," I said breathlessly.

Alex put a finger up to his lips. "Shhh."

Huh? "Why?"

Before he could answer me, I heard another *swoosh*, and Nicholas dropped down next to me.

"Well, that was fun," Nicholas remarked with a grin. "Wouldn't you all agree?"

"Oh yeah, super fun," I muttered.

Alex shook his head. "Can we just get this over with? The quicker we get out of here, the better."

"What's the rush?" Nicholas slid his hands into his pockets and rocked back on his heels. "No matter how long you're down here, they're never going to let Gemma leave until she's trained." He winked at me. Yes, actually freaking winked. "Which gives you and me plenty of time to get to know each other."

"Yeah, no thanks," I told him. "I would rather just go back with Alex."

Nicholas' expression slipped into scowl, and Alex worked hard to suppress a grin.

"Let's go," Nicholas said in a clipped tone as he waved at us to follow him down a glass path.

We made our way over a bridge paved with broken pieces of porcelain. And just on the other side of the bridge towered two massive pillars. They peaked, forming an entryway to a set of silver doors that stretched to the ceiling. The handles of each door were twisted in the shape of a circle that wrapped an S; the same exact shape as the tattoo on Nicholas' wrist.

"Wait here," Nicholas told us and pushed through the tall silver doors.

I leaned over, trying to catch a glimpse of what was on the other side of the door, but it snapped shut too quickly, like it had been yanked by some kind of magnetic force.

Alex turned to me, his words rushing out in a jumble. "Okay, here's the deal. When we get in there, let me do most of the talking. It's going to be a problem getting them to let you go because of the laws."

"That's what I don't get." My wrist was throbbing, so I cuddled it closer against me. "How are you supposed to get them to let me go when you keep talking about these laws that won't allow them to?"

He considered this. "Well, the Keepers have a little bit of power over the Foreseers, so I'm hoping that will help."

I gaped at him. "You're hoping that will help. But you promised you would get me out of here."

"I will," he assured me. "I'm just hoping that it will be easier with Keepers having some power over the Foreseers. But if that fails, we'll just go another route."

I eyed him suspiciously. "What kind of route?"

"Trust me, you don't want to know."

"I always want to know."

"This time you don't."

Silence.

"So, do they know what I am?" I asked.

"No," he replied, keeping his voice low. "And it needs to stay that way."

I leaned closer to him. "But wasn't it a Foreseer who made the prediction of what was going to happen to me and the star?"

"The Foreseer that saw the vision was a close friend of Stephan's," he whispered, his breath hot against my cheek. "And they've worked really hard to keep it a secret from the rest of the Foreseers, so let's not ruin it now by talking about it, okay?"

"But they might already now," I pointed out. "Since the Death Walkers do."

"They might, but they might not. And let's hope they don't, because it will make it a lot harder to get you out of here if they do know."

I rubbed my aching wrist, considering the idea of being trapped down here. The place was beautiful, but it was also creepy. And empty—I hadn't seen a single person yet. Then, of course, there was Nicholas. He heightened the creepy factor by like a billion notches.

"Did you hurt yourself?" Alex asked, eyeballing my wrist.

I shrugged. "It's not a big deal. When I landed, I fell and my wrist popped."

"Here, let me look at it." He reached for my wrist, pausing before gently taking hold of it. My first instinct was to jerk back and tell him not to touch me. Still, and I don't know why—I guess I had a weak moment or something—I let him take my wrist in his hand and examine it, sparks lighting up like lightning during a thunderstorm.

"Really, it's not that bad," I told him, flinching as my wrist let out another pop.

"Sorry," Alex apologized, tracing his finger lightly along the inside of my wrist. It tickled to the point that I had to bite my lip to keep from giggling. "I don't think it's broken or anything. You probably just popped it out of place." He let go of my wrist. "If it still hurts when we get back to the house, I can wrap it up."

I nodded, cradling my wrist in my hand. "Okay." *If I ever get back to the house.*

"How about your stitches?" he asked. "How are they doing? They're not coming loose, are they?"

I shrugged. "I don't think so."

He stared at me incredulously. "You haven't check on them?"

"I glanced at them after I went into the vision and face planted it on the ground," I said. "Everything seemed to look okay, I guess."

He lifted an eyebrow. "You guess."

"Well, since I've never had stitches before, I'm not sure what qualifies as them looking okay. But they don't hurt or anything."

"They could have loosened up when you fell. Or they could be getting infected. You never know." He moved his hand toward the bottom of my shirt.

I backed away. "What are you doing?"

He looked at me like I was an idiot. "Checking to make sure your stitches are okay."

"I don't think that's such a good idea."

"So you would rather get an infection and end up in a hospital?"

"No." I sighed, inching into his reach. "Fine, go ahead."

I held my breath as he raised the corner of my shirt, peeled back the gauze, and peered underneath it. The way his fingertips kept grazing my skin tickled. Man, life could be so unfair sometimes. There should be a law banning Alex's touch to feel this good. It was practically torture.

"So what's the symbol on Nicholas' wrist mean?" I asked in a pathetic attempt to distract myself.

"It's the mark of a Foreseer." His fingers worked their way along my skin.

I tensed as he touched a tender spot on my ribs. "Then why don't I have one?"

"I'm not sure…Things seem to work differently with you. You might get one and you might not." His fingers lingered on my skin for an instant longer before he pressed the gauze back into place and tugged the corner of my shirt back down. "They're good. Completely intact and infection free."

351

"Good," I said. And then, being the polite girl that I was, added, "Thanks for making sure."

"Whoa. Hold on." He smiled, cupping his hand around his ear. "Did I seriously just hear you say thanks?"

"I've said thanks to you before," I said.

He raised his eyebrows accusingly.

"Well, maybe not to you per se, but I've said the word before."

"Oh yeah?" he laughed. "Is that so?"

I nodded. "But I only say it when I truly mean it, so it doesn't come out a whole lot."

He laughed again, and I felt my own smile breaking through.

Okay, were we seriously having a moment here? *So weird.* Although, I wasn't going to lie and say that I wasn't enjoying it. The moment gave me a brief glimpse into what things might have been like if I was normal.

However, when one of the tall, silver doors opened up, our little moment slipped away, just like that.

"He's ready for you," Nicholas said, holding the door open. "You can come in."

As I stepped through the doorway, I had to catch my breath. The place made the glass cave look completely ordinary. Shiny cutouts of silver and blue porcelain paved the way through green gemstones that mimicked blades of grass. The blue sky glimmered like a giant diamond, the cotton ball clouds floating across it like a mirage.

Alex and I followed Nicholas down the porcelain path, winding back and forth until we arrived at a silver throne perched on top of a sapphire platform. A short, plump man with curly elf shoes and dark brown hair stood beside the throne. Nicholas approached him, whispered something in his ear, and the little man nodded.

While Nicholas was distracted, Alex placed his hand on my arm and whispered, "Oh yeah. You need to be careful around Nicholas. He's part faerie, so he can't be trusted."

Before I could even react to the word *faerie*, or the combusting electricity his breath and touch brought on, a man appeared from behind the throne. He was maybe in his sixties, give or take a few years. He was tall, with pale skin and grey shoulder length hair. The silver shade of the robe he wore matched the silver shade of his eyes.

He took a seat on the throne, curling his thin fingers over the edges of the armrests. "Welcome to the City of Crystal. I am Dyvinius, leader of the Foreseers." His voice came out in slow, motionless syllables—very monotone-like. "I understand that you were able to use the Foreseers' power to channel up a vision yesterday. Am I correct?"

I glanced around idiotically and then it clicked—he was probably talking to me. "Umm...yeah."

"Good." Dyvinius tapped his fingers together, seeming pleased. "Well, I'm not sure if you know much about what a Foreseer does, or what we are, so I'll explain. What we do is we use the energy of the Divination Crystal to see

353

visions of either the past or the future. But mostly it's the future. Once the vision is read, it becomes permanent. There is no changing it."

Maybe he should explain that to the Keepers, since they seem to think differently. Most of my life had been centered on trying to do just that, and here he was saying it was impossible. What if he was right though? Would that mean there was no hope to stop the portal from opening up? That there was no hope for humanity?

Wow. Talk about slapping reality across my face. And reality seemed to be forming a giant lump in my throat that was making it super hard to swallow.

"Now, from what I understand, you saw a past vision, which isn't too uncommon of a thing to happen with beginners," said Dyvinius.

I felt like I might cry. The vision I had seen was from the past. Which meant what? That the woman in it couldn't be saved?

That lump in my throat nearly doubled in size.

"When a person goes into their first vision, they usually don't know what they're doing," Dyvinius continued. "However, typically the Foreseer's ability is discovered in a person before they see their first vision. That way we are able to monitor them. Occasionally, someone does end up slipping through the radar undetected. Sometimes we're lucky enough to discover them later on, but sometimes we aren't." His silver eyes locked on me, his expression blank. "We have a radar system that lets us know when there has

354

been an interference with a Divination Crystal. Now it's not necessarily a bad thing—what you did. Although I have to say, you are very lucky you were able to come out of it. Sometimes people do get stuck." He paused. "Even though the vision you saw was from the past, it does need to be read correctly. Otherwise it can alter the human world as we know it." His face suddenly lit up. "And so we have brought you down here to re-see your vision and be trained as a Foreseer."

I cast a frantic glance at Alex.

"Is something wrong?' Dyvinius asked me. "You look upset."

"Umm…" I struggled.

Alex stepped forward. "I don't think her staying here is going to be possible right now. There are certain circumstances that require her to stay with the Keepers."

Dyvinius stared at Alex, seriousness shadowing his silver eyes. "The Keepers…Tell me, boy, what is your name?"

"Alex Avery," Alex responded calmly.

"Any relation to Stephan Avery?" Dyvinius asked.

Alex nodded. "He's my father."

"Oh, I see," Dyvinius said, and it was clear he wasn't pleased. "Tell me, Alex, what are these circumstances that are keeping Gemma with the Keepers?"

"I can't answer that," Alex replied coolly. "As you know, like the Foreseers, the Keepers have certain things they have to keep to themselves."

"Yes, I do understand. However, there are also laws we're all supposed to follow. I'm sure you know the law that states that if a person is able to use the crystal ball to see a vision, then they have to be trained in the City of Crystal by the Foreseers." His mouth sagged down into what I assumed was supposed to be a frown, but a frown on his expressionless face just looked creepy. "If Gemma doesn't stay here then she could end up altering the future. Or end up getting trapped inside a vision if she tries to enter one again."

My heart raced. Oh no. He was going to make me stay. I looked over at Alex, my eyes pleading with him to do something.

"I understand that. I really do," Alex said. "But there has to be something we could work out."

It was amazing how calm Alex was being. Not me. I was freaking out. And I had started the nail biting thing again.

Dyvinius's sliver eyes darkened, sending a chill down my spine. "Yes, maybe we could work something out... If you were to make a promise that she would never use a crystal ball again until she has been properly trained, then I don't see why I can't let her go back with the Keepers for awhile." He paused. "Of course, after these circumstances that are keeping her with the Keepers are gone, she would have to come back."

Okay, now I was really panicking. I never wanted to come back here. *Ever.*

Alex stayed quiet, arms crossed, jaw set.

"Otherwise I'll have to have *her* make the promise." Dyvinius's eyes glinted. "But I have a feeling you would probably rather make the promise."

Was I missing something here? Was something bad going to happen if the promise was broken?

"I guess a promise could be arranged...by me," Alex gritted through his teeth.

"Very good." Dyvinius beamed. "You understand that you're making that promise in the City of Crystal. And I assume you already know what the consequences are if you break this promise."

Alex nodded slowly. "Yeah, I understand."

Dyvinius leaned forward in the throne, his eyes glowing with eagerness. "Then I need you to say the words out loud."

Alex glared at him. "I promise."

Dyvinius leaned back in the throne, looking satisfied. "Good. Now that that has been taken care of, I need one more thing from Gemma before I let you both go back."

Oh, yippee. "Okay," I said warily. "What do I need to do?"

"I need you to go back into the vision and correct it," he told me.

"Correct it?" I asked. "How am I supposed to do that?"

"Well, I'm guessing that when you went in the vision, either some clips were missing, or things might have been blurry."

"Yeah…the people's faces were blurry."

"Good. That will make it a little easier to correct. You see, Gemma, every vision has to be seen clearly," Dyvinius explained. "Otherwise, if left unfinished, it could end up altering past or future events, and the world as we know it could shift."

I was confused. "So how exactly do I correct it?"

"You go back inside the crystal and see the vision again." Dyvinius looked over at Nicholas. "I'll send you with her to make sure everything goes correctly this time."

What!? So not only did I have to go back and suffer through the vision again, but I also had to go with a creepy half faerie—whatever that meant. I've read books about faeries that were able to put up some kind of glamour so they looked human. Looking at Nicholas, I wondered if what I was seeing was real or not. Were his blond hair and golden eyes just an illusion? A trick of the eye?

Catching me staring at him, Nicholas flashed me a sly smile and winked.

I blasted him with a fiery glare.

"Well, let's get started then." Dyvinius snapped his fingers and the chubby little man with elf shoes ran up to the throne. He was carrying a crystal ball identical to the one back at Adessa's. He placed it in Dyvinius' hands, bowed, and disappeared behind the throne.

Dyvinius held his hand out, the crystal ball balanced in his palm. "Whenever you're ready, Gemma."

Sucking in a shaky breath, I stepped up to the podium. I stared down at the crystal hesitantly, the violet ribbons dancing around inside almost tauntingly. "So I just put my hand on it?"

"To start with, yes." Dyvinius waved his hand at Nicholas. "Nicholas, take her hand."

Nicholas grabbed hold of my hand. His skin still felt exceedingly warm, and it took a lot of effort for me not to cringe away from him.

"Now close your eyes and picture the vision you saw," Dyvinius said, his silver eyes twinkling in the pale violet glow of the crystal. "Then hold the picture in your mind while you place your hand on the crystal."

I shut my eyes and focused on the lake...the grey stone castle...the blurry faces of the people. I held the image as I reached out and let my fingertips skim the glass.

I was jerked forward.

Then I was falling.

Chapter 29

I really wanted to be done with the whole traveling-through-a-crystal-ball thing, because it sucked. Big time. The falling part made my stomach churn, and don't even get me started on the landing.

My feet hit the grassy ground with a thud, and I tripped forward, rolling my ankle. "*Ow!*"

"Are you alright?" Nicholas stood beside me, still holding my hand. Which I guess was good, but only because it kept me from falling onto the ground.

"Yeah, I'm good." I slipped my hand out of his.

The castle towered behind us, the lake rippling in front. The sight of it tugged at my memories of the last time I was here.

"So what do I do now?" I asked Nicholas.

"You wait until the vision starts," he told me. "You'll have to tell me when it does, though, so I can help you see things clearly."

I gave him a funny look. "You can't see when it starts?"

He shook his head. "It's your vision, so only you can see it. That's the way things work."

I gestured around us. "So what does this look like to you?"

He leaned in, his shoulder bumping into mine. The smell of lilacs, forest, and rain flooded my nostrils. "Everything looks grey. There's a little haze and color here and there, but everything's distorted."

I backed away from him and focused on the scenery. It really was a beautiful place. Well, if you liked the whole outdoorsy thing that is. But there was the connection it held to the woman getting yanked away to The Underworld, which basically ruined any possibility of me liking the place.

A streak of purple suddenly rushed by me—the little girl.

"Okay, it's starting," I told Nicholas.

The little girl twirled in circles, just like she did the first time, her face still all hazy.

"What do you see?" Nicholas asked.

I wondered if I was allowed to tell him "Um..."

He frowned. "I can't help you if you don't tell me what you're seeing."

I sighed. "I see a little girl twirling in front of a lake."

"Can you see her face?"

I shook my head. "Nope. It's still all blurry."

"Then you need to focus harder," he said, as if it were that simple.

But it wasn't that simple. "Focus harder on what exactly?"

361

"Hmm…" He gave me a look that immediately put me on edge. He strolled around behind me, standing way too close for comfort. And the smell of flowers and rain was killing me. I mean, I don't mind breathing in the smell of lilacs every once in awhile, or taking in the scent of freshly fallen rain right after a storm, but he was a guy that smelled like flowers. It was too weird.

"Right now your mind is trying to adjust to the power of the crystal, but it can't quite figure out how to get there." He leaned over my shoulder, breathing into my ear. "The first thing you need to do is take a deep breath. Then, try to relax."

What was it with him and invading my personal space? Maybe it was a faerie thing or something.

I took a deep breath and tried hard to ignore the flowery smell. "Okay, I'm relaxed. Now what?"

"Let your mind focus," he said, still breathing into my ear. "The images are already there; they just haven't connected with your mind."

I inched away from him as casually as I could and sighed. "Yeah, I still don't get it."

He placed his hands on my shoulders. "Have you ever looked at one of those magic eye images before?"

My shoulders stiffened under his touch. "Uh, yeah, I guess."

"Well, this is kind of like looking at one of those." He pressed his fingertips into my shoulder blades, massaging them gently. "Relax your eyes and let your mind make sense of the images."

I shrugged off his hands and concentrated on the images.

The little boy had come up during Nicholas' little tutoring session and was now guiding the little girl away from the lake. Their faces were still blocked out by a sheet of haze, so I took a deep breath and let my eyes relax. Gradually, a tunnel started to form, fading away the rest of the surroundings so that the only thing I could see was the blurred image of the little girl's face. Slowly, her face began to focus like a lens on a camera. Clicking and clicking, getting clearer and clearer.

I was getting so close to being able to see who the little girl was. Only a few more seconds and I probably would have had it. But then the man stepped into view, and all of my concentration shattered.

I kicked the ground with the tip of my sneaker. "Crap."

"What?" Nicholas asked. "What's wrong?"

"I just about had it and then this man....I don't know. When he appeared, he ruined my concentration or something."

"Well, don't look at him then. Try to pretend he's not there."

Easier said than done, since I knew what the man was going to do pretty soon. I shook my head, frustrated, and returned my gaze back to the vision. I put my concentration on the boy this time, letting the tunnel form again. But right before his face snapped into focus, the woman ran up, and again my concentration shattered.

I was getting discouraged. "So what happens if I can't do it?"

"You can," he assured me. "All you have to do is catch a glimpse of each of their faces, and in the end your mind will put it all together."

"And what if I can't see all of their faces before the vision ends?"

He laughed. "Then I guess I'll have to keep you down here until you do."

His words filled me with determination.

The little boy was getting ready to head to the castle. *Okay, you can do this, Gemma.* The dark tunnel took shape, zoning in on the haziness of his face. Bits and pieces shifted together. Just as he was slipping out of my view, his face clicked into focus. His eyes were green, his hair brown.

I so had this.

I flung my attention to the man, who was yanking the little girl from the woman's arms. I paid attention to nothing else but the girl's blurry face. This time the haze disappeared much quicker. But I must have seen it wrong. There was no way that could be right. I blinked, and blinked again. But nothing changed. Her eyes—the color—violet. The exact shade of my eyes. My heart pounded inside my chest. Seeing the vision clearly suddenly became much more important.

The woman was heading down to the lake. Time was running out. I ran for her.

"Hey! Where are you going?!" Nicholas called out.

Ignoring him, I let the tunnel zoom in on the woman's face. Her bright blue irises, her warm smile, everything became clear, and I knew I had seen her before. But I had already figured that out as soon as I caught sight of the little girl's eyes. If this little girl in the vision was me, then the woman had to be my mother.

Tears streamed down my cheeks as I watched the woman get yanked underneath the water. I spun around to the man, shaking with anger. He was walking away, a sickening, satisfied grin on his face. His dark grey eyes, his black hair, I grabbed onto every little detail I could, right down to the slight crookedness of his nose and the scar grazing his left cheek.

My mouth dropped. "Holy—"

A hand came down on my shoulder, and I whirled around, my breath whipping out in frantic gasps.

Nicholas held up his hands. "Whoa. What the heck happened? What did you see?"

"Nothing," I choked. "It wasn't important."

"It had to be something important since you're all worked up."

"I'm fine," I snapped. "Can we just go back? The vision's over."

He eyed me over with his golden eyes. "Yeah, I know. I can see everything now that it's complete. Beautiful place, by the way—the Keepers' castle."

"This is the Keepers' castle?" I said, stunned. Alex had mentioned that the lake was the entrance to The Underworld, but he never said anything about the castle belonging to the Keepers. Why would he keep that from me?

"Hmm…I thought you would have known that since you're a Keeper."

A…Was I? "Um…yeah, but I've never been here before," I told him, and then added, "I've lived a very sheltered life."

He stared at my eyes. "Really? Is that so?"

I was getting nervous. "So can we go back?"

"What did you see exactly?" he asked, dodging my question. "Was there any meaning to it?"

"I don't know. Is there supposed to be a meaning?"

"Sometimes." He shrugged. "Sometimes not. Normally Foreseers use the crystal to see a vision that has a purpose." He inched closer to me. "But your vision was started by accident, so maybe there's a reason you saw it and maybe not. Regardless, you had to finish the vision just in case there was some kind of significance to it."

Oh, there was a reason I saw it. Here was the problem, though. If the little girl was me, why couldn't I remember any of this happening?

"Can we go back, please?" I asked Nicholas, trying not to sound anxious.

Nicholas ran his fingers through his hair. "Are you sure you want to go back?" He moved toward me until the tips of his black and red sneakers clipped against the tips of mine. "Because, if you want, we can stay here a little bit longer."

I kept my voice steady. "Thanks, but no thanks. The vision is over. There's no reason to stick around."

His mouth curved into a devious grin. "I could give you a reason."

Okay, faerie guy, it was time for you to back the heck down. "Yeah, I'm going to have to pass on that."

His eyes were all over me. "If that's what you want."

"Oh, it is," I assured him.

He looked disappointed as he held out his hand. "Let's go then. But might I add that you are awfully nervous for a Keeper."

I shook off his comment and took hold of his hand.

"Ready?" he asked.

I nodded. I was more than ready.

Returning to the City of Crystal was as simple as tying my shoe. There was no crystal ball to go through. No falling. I just blinked and we were back, surrounded by grass made of glass and a sky that shone like a diamond. Dyvinius was gone, which I thought was odd. But I was grateful for his absence and anxious to get back to the cabin, because there

367

was something I needed to ask Alex. See, something occurred to me during the split second I was being pulled away from the vision. And if I was right about what had occurred to me, then Alex telling me about the star was going to seem mild.

Alex, thank goodness, was waiting for us in the Palace, and he rushed over as soon as he saw us appear.

"Everything good?" he asked, giving me a cautious once over, like he expected me to return broken or something.

I nodded. "But I'm ready to go."

"So am I," he said.

No one spoke as Nicholas took us back to the spot where we had entered the city.

Nicholas retrieved the tiny crystal ball from his pocket and held it out in front of me. "Are you sure you want to leave? Because, personally, I would love for you stay down here."

I rolled my eyes. "I'm good with going back, but thanks."

"Well then." He winked. "Until we meet again."

Which hopefully was never.

I placed my hand on top of the crystal ball with zero hesitancy, and the next thing I knew, I was tumbling down the tunnel *again*.

I landed in the living room of the cabin with the gracefulness of a drunken person, stumbling and banging my knee on the corner of the coffee table. I don't know what it was—if the falling threw off my equilibrium or something—but I just couldn't land normally when traveling by a crystal, or by teleporting, or when walking on ice. Oh, fine. Maybe it was just me.

I was rubbing my soon-to-be-bruised knee when Alex appeared beside me.

"Alright, what happened?" he asked immediately. "And why are you rubbing your knee?"

"Because I bumped it on the table." My voice came out sharp.

"Okay, jeez. Sorry for asking." He paused. "So what happened?"

I stared at him, wondering if what I was thinking could be true.

He gave me a strange look. "Did something happen...I mean, with Nicholas? Did he...um...try something?"

"Huh?" It took me a second to get what he meant. "What? Yuck. No. Why would you even ask that?"

"Because that's the way he is," he said. "It's the faerie inside him."

"Well, nothing happened." I sat down on the edge of the coffee table. "Not really, anyway."

"Not really anyway." He gaped at me. "What does that mean?"

"It means he was acting creepy."

He cocked an eyebrow. "Acting creepy how?"

"He was just..." I shook my head. I was getting off track here. "That's not important right now. Okay, I'm going to ask you something, and I want you to tell me the truth, okay?"

He gave me a doubtful look. But before he could protest, I stood up, trying to appear confident.

"No, you're not going to wiggle your way out of this one," I told him. "I want the truth, and you're going to give it to me. None of that 'I can't tell you' crap. No more lying. Just the truth." I had no idea where that boost of confidence came from, but it felt kind of good.

He held my gaze with sheer intensity, and I had a flashback of the two of us sitting in the astronomy classroom, staring each other down. "What's your question?"

I took a deep breath and prepared myself for the worst. "Has my memory ever been erased?"

Chapter 30

I didn't even have to hear his answer. His expression said it all.

"Why?" I cried. "Why would you do that?"

It took him a second to respond. "Why would you think your memory has been erased?"

"For two reasons," I said, my voice shaking uncontrollably with anger. "First, because I'm almost certain the little girl in the vision was me."

His bright green eyes widened. "What! It was *you*?"

I let out a derisive laugh. "Oh, like you didn't know that already."

"I didn't," he said. "I swear. But why do you think it was you?"

"Because of her eyes...they were violet. And if the little girl is me, then I'm pretty sure the woman that was forced to go to The Underworld is my mother."

He swallowed hard. "Gemma, I don't even know what to say. I am a little confused as to why this would make you think your memory was erased."

"Because of the second reason." I couldn't believe I was going to tell him this. I mean, I wanted to have some

371

secrets of my own. But in order to explain everything clearly, I needed to tell him. "Do you remember when I was looking through the telescope back at the field trip, and I suddenly ran off?"

"And I found you crying on the bus," he said, nodding.

"Well, the reason I ran off is because, while I was looking through the telescope, I went into something similar to a vision. Although I had no idea at the time what the heck was going on. But anyway, I ended up out in this field. There was a little girl and a woman there, and both of their faces were blurred out."

He stared at me impassively, but I caught his Adam's apple bobbing up and down as he swallowed hard. "So, what happened?"

"Nothing really; they just stared up at the stars for awhile, talking."

"And you don't know who they are."

"Well, the mom had called the girl Gemma, which puzzled me, because if she was me, then, why couldn't I remember the scene from my own memories? I mean, I know I would have been only like four at the time, but still…you would think I would be able to remember something. I also thought the same thing when Laylen told me I was four when I left my mother." I paused, taking a deep breath. "And then, on my way back from correcting the vision, something clicked, and I knew that the mother and daughter in the field, and the mother and the daughter by the lake, were me and my mother. It was like my mind suddenly was able to retrieve some of my lost memories or something."

He looked like he was struggling to stay calm. "I still don't understand why this would make you think your memory has been erased. Sometimes people just forget things."

I shook my head. "No. This is different. I can feel it. I know there's got to be more to it than that. I mean, I can barely remember anything about my life at all."

"Gemma, I really think that—"

I threw my hands in the air exasperatedly. "Just tell me. Has my memory ever been erased?"

He shook his head. "No. Your memory has never been erased."

"You're lying!" I yelled. "I know you are. There's no way I could forget her."

And now I was crying. But there was too much agonizing pain inside me to care.

"Gemma, please just sit down for a minute and hear me out," Alex said in the shakiest voice I have ever heard come out of his mouth.

"*No!*" I cried. "I'm not doing anything else that you tell me to do. I'll never listen to you again!"

He rubbed his forehead, looking tense. "If you'll sit down and listen to me, then I'll try to explain everything the best that I can."

"Yeah, right." I sniffled. "You're like the mastermind of lying."

He pressed his lips together, trying really hard not to laugh at my remark. "I know I've lied to you a lot, but this time I won't. I promise."

I stared at him through tear-drenched eyes, searching his face for signs that he was lying. He looked so sincere it was startling.

"You promise." I sniffed. "You'll tell me the truth?"

He gave a slow nod. "But I have to warn you that what I'm going to say is way worse than what you're imagining."

I wiped the tears from my face with the sleeve of my shirt and sank down on the couch. "It doesn't matter. I still want to hear it."

He sank down on the couch beside me, slipped off his baseball hat, and dragged his fingers tautly through his hair. "I don't even know where to begin. No matter where I start, it's going to sound really bad."

I liked that he was nervous. He was usually so calm, cool, and collected—he was usually lying. "Start, anywhere, then. If it's all bad, then what does it matter?"

He contemplated this. "Okay, so you remember the prophecy I told you about, right?"

I sighed. "How could I forget it?"

"Well, I left out a few parts of the story. See, while Stephan was trying to figure out a way to keep the prophecy from happening, your mother had just disa—or if what

374

you say is correct, was thrown into The Underworld." He paused, gazing, lost in thought. "You were extremely emotional—crying all the time."

"I had just lost my mother," I pointed out, annoyed. "Of course I was emotional."

"Yeah, I know. And I'm not saying that it wasn't understandable; I'm just trying to explain why Stephan did what he did." He shifted uneasily in the chair. "A lot of Keepers are born with gifts. There are a lot of different kinds, some more useful than others. The one Sophia has is called *unus quisnam aufero animus,* or one who removes the soul."

"One who removes the soul," I repeated, my eyes widening. "You took my soul! Are you freaking kidding me?!" I leapt up from the couch, my adrenaline pulsating into overdrive. He was right. It was way worse. At least the star's energy could be construed as adding to a person's life. But taking away a soul—it was like ripping away the very essence of being human.

My legs wobbled and the room swayed. I grasped onto the edge of the coffee table, gasping for air. Was this what a panic attack felt like?

Alex got up and placed his hand on my back. "Gemma, calm down and listen to me. That's not what I am saying."

I tried to shake off his hand, but he held it steadily in place.

375

"Get—away—from—me," I gasped between shallow breaths.

"No, I won't get away from you. You need to listen to me. We didn't take your soul away."

"Huh?" I let go of the table and stood up straight. Alex's hand fell off my back. "Then what did you do to me?"

"I'll tell you, but let me finish before you start freaking out, okay?"

I nodded, but it still didn't mean I wouldn't freak out. In fact, I wasn't even sure I had any control over my reactions at the moment.

"So, like I told you a few times, we didn't take your soul. *Unus quisnam aufero animus* is mostly used as a form of punishment. But in your case, we weren't trying to punish you or anything. You were just a little girl and Jocelyn's daughter. So, instead of taking your soul, Sophia did something a little less severe. She detached your soul from your emotions. And since emotions have such a huge connection with memories, it made it so you couldn't remember anything about your past."

An annoying buzzing noise had developed inside my head. Alex watched me closely, waiting for me to react. But all I could focus on was the buzzing. Had a family of bees suddenly taken up camp in there or something?

"Gemma." Alex's tone was cautious. "Do you want me to continue? Or do you need a break?"

"What?" I blinked and shook my head. "No, you can go on."

"Are you sure? Because I can give you a break."

"No," I said determinedly. "I want to hear the rest."

He didn't want to tell me, but went on anyway.

"After Sophia detached your soul, she and Marco took you to Afton to keep you hidden from the Death Walkers. There was something about the snow that made it difficult to track the star's energy. I think the cold might reduce the heat the energy produces or something, but I'm not exactly sure."

"Maybe that's why I hate the cold so much," I joked in an eerily humorless tone. God, I sounded as dead and hollow as the Death Walkers looked.

He gave me a small smile. "Perhaps, but that's not really the point I was trying to make. The point is, your soul is still there, along with your memories. You just can't connect with either of them. Or couldn't, I guess I should say."

He gave me a look that made my skin feel hot and fiery, and it wasn't just the electricity. No, this was something else; something more. The prickle on the back of my neck was confirming that. I hadn't felt that sensation in awhile, and I wondered if somehow my soul was trying to reconnect with me.

Or maybe I was just hoping.

I had to slow my breathing down before I spoke. "So why did I all of a sudden start to feel again?" I asked.

"No one really knows the answer to that." He shut his eyes and massaged his temples. "Sophia tried to detach it again, but it didn't work."

Breathe, I told myself. "What do you mean she tried to do it again? When?"

He opened his eyes back up. "She tried it a few months ago, after you started showing signs of feeling emotions. You don't remember because she did it while you were asleep."

No wonder I have nightmares. Imagine some old lady sneaking into your room late at night and trying to detach your soul. You'd probably have nightmares too.

"So, what do they plan on doing to me now that it didn't work?" I snapped. "Lock me away somewhere and throw away the key?"

"No," he said, avoiding eye contact with me.

"Then what? Tell me! What are they going to do?"

There was a hint of pity in his bright green eyes. "There's someone else with the same gift as Sophia that's headed here right now. He's supposed to be more power-ful than Sophia, and Stephan seems convinced it'll work."

I couldn't believe what I was hearing. Well, I actually could, considering all the other crap I had been told over the last few days, but…"Why?"

His eyebrows dipped down. "Why what?"

"Why didn't you guys have this detaching soul person detach my soul sooner? I have been feeling for a few months now! Why wait and let it get worse?"

378

"Because—"he faltered"—they couldn't find the guy. I guess on the night of the field trip, Stephan finally found him. That's why we couldn't get a hold of them. They had gone to pick up this man."

No wonder Alex had gotten out of the Jeep to talk to Stephan. "I-I can't believe this. You guys are so—so—"

"Gemma, you need to calm down," he said. "You're freaking out, and I can't understand what you're saying."

"Of course I'm freaking out!" I yelled, clenching my hands into fists as I jumped to my feet. "You just told me that I have to go back to being Hollow Zombie Girl."

I'm not sure how he expected me to react, but by the look of shock on his face, I was guessing he probably anticipated a more mellow reaction.

I started to back away from the couch. "I won't do it. There's no way. I can't go back to being like that—*ever*."

"You don't have a choice," he said, getting to his feet. "This isn't just about you. It's about the safety of the world and everyone in it. Do you want to be responsible for people dying?"

"No," I said, sidestepping around the coffee table. "But how do you expect me to just let them detach my soul and take away everything? Do you know what it was like living that way for—for—I don't even know how long it was, because time felt nonexistent. Every single day was nothing. There was no point in even waking up. Yet I did, every single day. And even though my emotions were gone, it was still torture. And it's going to be worse now

379

because I've experienced what it's like to feel things and be human. You guys may think it's okay to do it, but it's not. Yes, it may have to be done to save the world, but it's still horrible, because aside from what you guys may think, I'm not just *something* carrying around a star inside of me. I'm human too. Or at least part human."

Okay, that was by far the biggest speech I've ever made.

"I know you're human," he snapped. "You don't think I understand how wrong it is? Do you know how much I wish there was another way to fix it?"

"That's such a load of crap," I said, my voice hot with anger. "You've hated me since the first day we met."

"I've never hated you." His voice had softened. "Not once."

I glared at him. "You are such a liar."

He grabbed me by the arm and reeled me to him, crashing me into his chest. "I've never hated you."

I had to remind myself to *breathe*. Every part of my body felt hot and electric, and my head was spinning.

"Well, it's good to see that your wrist is feeling better," he said.

"Yeah…" It felt so nice when he touched me.

"Just forget about everything for a minute," he whispered.

Maybe I could…forget about…everything.

His eyelids drifted shut as he leaned in to kiss me.

That slapped me back to reality. "Forget about everything?" I yanked my arm away from him and shoved him back. "What is this? Are you trying to distract me or something?"

"No." He looked stunned, but like I've said before, he is an expert liar. He stepped toward me. "Gemma, that's not what I—"

I backed away from him. "Stay away from me."

He kept coming at me. "I'm not—"

"Stay away from me!" I cried and sprinted down the hall.

I wasn't sure if he followed me or not. I never checked. I stormed into the room that held my bag and locked the door. Then I threw myself on the bed and cried and cried and cried until I ran out of tears.

Chapter 31

"Gemma, wake up," a voice whispered.

I groaned. My eyelids were too heavy to open.

"Gemma." The voice rose louder

I let out a grunt and opened my eyes, only to realize that not only was I lying on the floor, but I was lying on the floor in an entirely different room. I sat up, rubbed my eyes, and peered around at the purple walls pinned with drawings, photos, and a...galaxy map?

"Okay," I whispered. "Where am I?"

"I want to tell you something."

I recognized the voice instantly and jumped to my feet. Sitting in a bay window, gazing up at the night sky, was a woman with long brown hair and blue irises—my mother. Sitting next to her was a little girl with violet eyes—me.

And I could see their faces. Apparently, memories or not, getting rid of the haze in one of them had cleared them all up.

"Look at the stars Mama." The younger me pointed at the sky. "They're so pretty."

"Yes, they are," my mother agreed. "And it's very important that you remember that, no matter what happens."

The younger me looked up at her. "Why? What's going to happen?"

"That's for me to worry about." My mother smoothed the younger me's hair back.

"I'm scared," the younger me whispered, getting teary eyed. "I don't want you to leave me."

"I know. And I don't want to leave you. But in case something does happen, I need you to know that I love you more than anything." My mother wiped a tear away from the younger me's eye. "And I always will. Never forget that."

The younger me nodded and hugged my mother tightly. "I promise I'll never forget."

"Yes, you will," I whispered, tears trickling down my cheeks. "You'll forget everything."

My eyes shot open. I was back at the cabin, lying on the bed. My eyes and cheeks were damp with tears. My neck was sore and hot—I must have been sleeping in a weird position or something. Whatever these things—visions, resurfacing memories, or maybe just dreams—were, I still had managed to cry in real life. My guess, though, was that they were memories.

I tried not to think about how heartbreaking the scene between me and my mother was as I wiped my tears away with the sleeve of my jacket. It was just too painful to think about.

Unsure of how late it was, I scooted off the bed and trod over to the window. Pulling back the curtain, I saw that it was nearing dark. The hills were shadows, the sky grey. But it was still early enough that the stars had not yet awakened.

So what was I supposed to do now? The last thing I wanted to do was to walk out and find Marco, Sophia, Stephan, and Detaching Soul Guy waiting for me. I needed to find out if they arrived yet.

I tiptoed over to the door, cracked it open, and listened. The only noise I could hear came from my own breathing. Crossing my fingers that no one was here yet, I opened the door the rest of the way, went out into the living room, and almost jumped with joy when I found it completely people-free.

But where was Alex?

I searched the house, checking the kitchen, the dining room, even going out into the garage, but there was no sign of Alex anywhere. *Is that necessarily a bad thing?* I asked myself, and sighed because the answer was yes.

I was just about to sit down on the couch and wait it out when I spotted Alex through the sliding glass door. He was sitting in a porch swing on the back porch. Beneath the dim porch light, I could see that he had ditched the black baseball hat, his dark brown hair sticking up in its messy, yet perfectly done, way. He was staring down at his hand, and I couldn't help but feel nervous about what he might be holding in it.

I made my way over to the sliding door, and paused before gliding it open. I stepped out into the cold night air, my breath puffing out in a cloud.

He glanced up at me, and then returned his gaze back to whatever was in his hand.

"It's freezing out here." I tugged the hood of my jacket over my head, tucked my hands up into the sleeves, and tromped through the snow over to the swing. "What are you doing out here?"

"Just thinking about stuff..." He clasped his hand around something shiny and silver and looked up at me. "I'm surprised you came out of the room. I was pretty sure that you were going to lock yourself in there and refuse to come out."

"It wouldn't have done me any good." I sat down on the swing, and it rocked beneath my weight. "You guys probably would have just broken down the door and dragged me out."

He didn't say anything.

I let the tips of my shoes trace across the snow as the swing swayed back and forth. "So...what do you have in your hand?"

He hesitatingly opened his hand, and a necklace rested in his palm. A violet stone carved the center of a silver heart-shaped pendant. The color of the stone reminded me of the color of my eyes.

I stared at the necklace, mesmerized by its beauty. "What is it?"

A smile teased at his lips. "A necklace."

I rolled my eyes. "Obviously, but why are you showing it to me?"

"Because it was yours." He slipped the chain of the necklace through his fingers and dangled it in front of me. "Your mother gave it to you when you were little…before everything happened."

"It was mine? Really?" I asked excitedly.

He nodded. "It really was."

I pressed my lips together, my eyes starting to burn from the tears that were threatening to break through.

"Are you okay?" he asked.

I nodded because I couldn't speak. I don't know how to even begin to explain just how much this meant to me. I'm not even sure there are any words that would fit what I was feeling. Okay, imagine if every ounce of who you are was ripped away and there was nothing left but a lost version of yourself struggling to find a way back to a life you never knew—a life you knew had to be better than the empty one you were living. That's what this necklace was. A piece of my past that reminded me that I once had a good life, with a loving mother, free to do and feel as I pleased.

"So…" I began after I found my voice again. "Why are you showing it to me?"

"I have no idea," he said, not in a rude way, but in a confused one.

"Okay…" I said, sounding as confused as he did. "Do I get to keep it?"

He eyed me over. Then he took my hand and placed the necklace in it, the metal warm against my frostbitten skin.

"So…that's a yes then." I wanted to know before I got too excited.

He leaned back in the swing. "Yeah, you can keep it."

"Thank you," I said in the softest voice.

"Wow, two thank you's in a day. That's impressive."

I smiled, but it was forced. I just wasn't feeling it at the moment. I was excited about the necklace, but sad at the same time, because I knew at any given moment, my recollection of it, along with everything else, would be gone forever. And that stole away all of my wittiness.

"Gemma, are you alright?" He furrowed his eyebrows quizzically. "You're acting kind of… strange."

"So are you," I said, clamping my hand around the necklace.

"How so?"

"You're being too nice, giving me the necklace and everything. It's weird."

"Yeah, you're probably right," he agreed. "Maybe I should take it back." He reached for the necklace.

I wrenched my hand back. "I didn't mean you had to take it back. I want it, and I'm not giving it back to you."

"Relax, I'm just teasing you," he said. "Look, I know things have been up and down between us, but just for a moment, can we try to be normal?"

I frowned. "The last time I thought things between you and me were headed to Normalville, you were playing me for a fool so you could try to find out if I knew why my emotions had started up again."

"And I'm sorry for that," he said sincerely.

"Oh, my word, did you just say sorry?" I widened my eyes and did an over exaggerated look of shock. "Holy crap, I think the world just stopped spinning." He grinned and I added, "Is that normal enough for you?"

A moment of silence passed between us. I stared at the necklace, the silver and purple sparkling almost like the stars that had now dusted themselves across the sky.

"Aren't you going to put it on?" he asked, nodding down at the necklace in my hand.

"Yeah, good idea." I started to unfasten the clamp when it hit me. What if there was something wrong with the necklace? "You know, I'm not sure if I should. I mean, what if this is a trick or something? For all I know, putting this on could be part of the process of detaching my soul."

He shook his head and sighed. "It's not and I can prove it." He reached over and flipped the pendant to the back. Flawless cursive engraved the letters GL—my initials. "See, GL—Gemma Lucas."

I smiled a real smile. It really did belong to me. I flicked the clasp open and wrapped the chain around my neck.

Okay, so I am not a jewelry wearing kind of girl. Putting on a necklace was a whole new experience for me, and I couldn't get the sucker to hook shut.

"Need some help?" Alex asked, looking like he was enjoying watching me struggle.

"No," I refused stubbornly. "I got it." But after a few more minutes of trying to get the dang clamp closed, I gave up. "Oh, fine. I guess I need your help."

He laughed, making a circle in the air with his finger. "Turn around."

I did, and he took the necklace from my hands, his fingers grazing mine. I tried my best to ignore how hot his touch made me feel as he fumbled to secure the clasp of the necklace closed.

But like me, he seemed to be struggling.

"Hmmm…" He paused. "Well, that's interesting."

I glanced over my shoulder at him. "What's interesting?"

"Well, it looks like you got your mark."

"A Foreseer's mark?"

He nodded, tracing his finger gently along the back of my neck. "I can see the outline of it forming right here."

"What does it look like?"

"Exactly like Nicholas'," he said. "Each group's mark looks the same."

"So does that mean I might actually be a real Foreseer?"

"Yeah, probably, but I still don't know how. I never thought you were a Foreseer. I thought it was just the star's power setting off the crystal. Usually possessing Foreseer ability requires coming from a line of Foreseers."

"My mother wasn't one?"

He shook his head. "Jocelyn was just a Keeper."

"What about my father?" I asked. "Maybe he was."

"Maybe, but I can't say for sure since I don't know who he is."

"You don't know who he is!" I exclaimed. "How is that even possible?"

"Because Jocelyn would never tell anyone who he was. For some reason, she insisted she had to keep it a secret."

Well, that sucked. I really was all alone in this world, wasn't I?

I choked back my tears.

He sighed. "Here, let me put this thing on you, and then you can go look at the mark in the mirror." I nodded slowly and turned back around.

He started fiddling with the clamp again, his fingers teasing me with their touch. I gazed off into the darkness of the night, thinking of my mother and father and how I hardly knew anything about them. And that seemed to be creating this giant hole inside my heart.

"You're nervous," he remarked.

"Huh?" I shook my head. "No I'm not."

"Your foot's shaking like crazy."

I looked down at my foot and realized I was tapping it crazily against the snowy ground. Apparently, I channeled all the hot energy that Alex's touch was bringing on down to my leg. "I'm not nervous. It's just that…"I felt the necklace fall against the back of my neck—he had gotten it hooked. Finally.

"Just that what?" he asked, his mouth extremely close to my ear.

"Nothing." I started to move away. "Never mind."

He caught me by the waist, making my body heat hotter. "Just tell me."

"It's nothing." I kept telling myself to breathe as a mixture of heat and confusion swirled through my body. "It's just the electricity. It sometimes makes me a little…squirmy."

"Are you sure that's all it is?" His breath was hot against my skin, making every part of me go crazy. A moment later, I felt his lips press against the back of my neck. I froze, and I was pretty sure that my heart even stopped beating for a second. I tried to tell myself to get up and walk away. *Don't do this. It wouldn't be worth it. You wouldn't even know if it was real or if he was playing you.*

But then he whispered my name, and I turned around. After that, all my thoughts floated away, because he kissed me. And not like the little peck when we were on the bus. This one lasted a lot longer and was full of fire.

At one point I wrapped my arms around his neck, and he pulled me closer to him so that are bodies were touching. There was so much heat that the snow was probably melting on the ground beneath us.

Okay, so you're probably wondering how I could kiss him after everything that happened. But please, try not to judge me too harshly. I know things haven't been the best between Alex and me, but I am only human. Or at least part human, anyway. I have things I want to do, like kiss the guy that can make my skin sparkle. And unlike most people, my time to do so is going to run out, like any second, so this is probably my one and only chance to get kissed.

I'm not sure how long the kissing went on, but eventually we did break away from each other. Which was kind of good, if only to keep me from passing out from lack of oxygen. But I did feel a ping of longing for my lips to be touching his again.

Alex gazed up at the night sky, rocking the swing back and forth. The serious expression that he usually carried had faded, and it made him even more gorgeous.

The pendant of the necklace pressed warmly against my skin. I absentmindedly rubbed my thumb against the violet stone as I stared up at the sky, thinking about the kiss and trying not to think about the fact that soon I would remember nothing about it. I spotted the constellation Andromeda, Cassiopeia pointing at it like a target. I thought about the other people in the world staring up at the stars. I hoped they were happy and grateful to be alive.

I felt a small crack running along the edge of the pendant. I looked down and realized that it wasn't just a pendant, but a locket.

I snapped it open. Framed inside was a small photo of a group of people. I squinted down at the photo, examining each of their faces, and then…"Oh my God."

"What's the matter?" Alex asked.

"Is that my mother?" I asked, pointing at a woman with long brown hair and bright blue irises—the woman I had seen in so many visions, dreams, and memories.

He nodded. "Yeah, that's her. Is she the one you saw in the vision?"

I didn't answer, sliding the tip of my finger to the man that stood beside her. "So who's this next to her?"

"That's my father." He gave me a funny look. "Why?"

I jumped to my feet, panic firing through me as wildly as the sparks did when Alex had kissed me. "Because he's the one I saw force my mom into the lake."

Chapter 32

"No. There's no way," Alex said, shaking his head. "It's gotta be a mistake."

We had gone into the living room because the temperature had dipped so cold that our butts were almost freezing off. He had said about a thousand times that there was no way his dad could have forced my mom to get into the lake.

But I knew what I had seen.

"It's not a mistake," I told him. "I know what I saw. I know it was him."

He glared at me. "You don't know that for sure."

"Yeah, I do," I assured him with confidence. "I've seen the vision twice."

"But you were only able to see his face in one of them," Alex pointed out. "So there's a possibility that you might be mistaking him for someone else. I know my father would never do anything like that. *Ever.*"

Tell that to Laylen. "How can you be so sure?"

He stared at me, dumbfounded. "Because he's my father."

I chewed on my lip, mulling over my options here. Should I tell him about my dreams? If I did, I ran the risk of giving away too much information, and I still wasn't sure if I completely trusted Alex. "You were there, you know? In the vision. There was a little boy with the same bright green eyes you have." I wasn't sure if I was right or not; it was just a guess. It made sense though.

"No. There's no way," he said firmly. "I would be able to remember it happening if I was there."

I raised my eyebrows at him. "Perhaps your mind has been tampered with too."

"No. There's no way," he repeated, but the firmness from his voice had slightly faded. He ran his fingers restlessly through his hair. "Look, Gemma, maybe you saw it wrong. Maybe it was someone else who forced your mom to go into the lake. I mean, Dyvinius said that you didn't see the vision correctly the first time. Who's to say you didn't see correctly the second time either?"

I bit back my irritation the best I could. "I saw it correctly both times. The only problem with the first one was that I couldn't see the people's faces." He still looked unconvinced, and it made me so angry that I kept going. "Besides, the vision isn't the only time I've seen him."

He blinked, looking lost. "What do you mean?"

"Well..." There was no backing out now. I had already opened Pandora's Box. "Before I learned anything about who I was, I was having these nightmares where I was being chased through the forest by the Death Walkers."

"Yeah, I remember you mentioning that." He sat down on the couch and rested his arms on his knees. "But what does that have to do with my father?"

"Because at the end of every dream, the Death Walkers capture me and a man appears and orders them to finish me off." I sighed and sank down into the couch beside him. "The man in my nightmares had the same scar as your father." His eyes widened as I continued, "And back at Laylen's, when I was lying on the floor freezing to death, something happened to me—something similar to what happened to me back at the field trip. I went into this vision, and there was a man and Demetrius chatting it up about how they got rid of some poor woman that was a Keeper."

He gaped at me. "Hold on. So what you're telling me is that you went into a vision without a crystal ball not once, but twice. Why didn't you tell me this before?"

"I did. At least, I did with the first one."

"Yeah, but I just assumed that was some resurfacing memory or something. But if you're seeing something that has Demetrius in it…" He let out a loud breath. "There's no way that could be a memory. You've never seen him before." Silence choked the air as he considered all of this. "How is it even possible for you to do that?" he muttered to himself. "How can you see a vision without a crystal ball? It's just not possible."

"When I asked you about it before, you said you weren't sure if it was possible for someone to see a vision without a crystal ball," I reminded him. "You even said that you may have heard of someone who could."

He stared down at the floor, contemplating what I said.

"Alex," I said, a little too loudly, and he jumped. "That's not important right now. What's important is that this other man chatting it up with Demetrius had a scar on his cheek."

He swallowed hard, looking...well, really vulnerable. I had to admit, I didn't like how it looked on him. It made me feel anxious and had me questioning whether he was going to fall apart. He couldn't fall apart. Not if his father was secretly working with Demetrius and was the one who had gotten rid of my mother, and was heading here right now.

"Look, I know this has to be hard to hear," I said.

"Has to be hard to hear?" He laughed an unsettlingly kind of laugh. "What you're telling me is that not only did my father send Jocelyn to The Underworld, but that he's working with Demetrius."

"I understand that it's hard to hear, but do you think it wasn't hard for me to watch my mother get sent to The Underworld?"

"Yeah, but you don't even know her," he mumbled.

397

"Hey." I sprang from the couch and threw my hands on my hips. "That's not fair. The only reason I don't know her is because of you."

"You can't be right about my father," he muttered, ignoring me. "There's just no way."

"If that were true, then how would I know all of this? What? Do you think I just made it all up or something?"

He shrugged. "How do I know? Maybe you did."

I was fuming. "I'm not the one who's a liar."

He glared at me.

I glared back.

I'm not sure how long our argument would've gone on—probably awhile—but I never got to find out because the air suddenly froze over with a deathly chill, and we both stopped talking.

Great. Not again.

Chapter 33

"How did they find us here?" I was standing in the dining room, watching Alex dig frantically around in a secret cabinet that had been hidden behind a massive china cabinet. I hadn't realized just how strong Alex was until he slid the enormous thing out of the way like it was made of air. "And what the heck are you looking for in there?"

I was still pissed off about his refusal to accept that his father was responsible for my mom being trapped down in The Underworld, but my fear that the Death Walkers were heading here was overriding my anger. After we felt the air freeze over, Alex had checked out the window, and sure enough, a flock of Death Walkers' eyes lit up the night like a swarm of fireflies.

"This is what I'm looking for." Alex held up the Sword of Immortality. "And this." He held up another sword, a much smaller one with a less jagged blade. He shoved the handle of it at me. "Here, take it."

"Why?" I backed away. "It wouldn't do me any good."

"You've stabbed one before."

"Yeah, but that was a freak accident."

He nudged the small sword toward me. "Take it."

I sighed and took it. "What are we going to do now?"

"We're going to make a run for it," he said, and rushed out of the room.

I chased after him. "How though? They're practically here already."

Heading for the garage, he shot me a look over his shoulder that told me to quit being difficult. "So what? You would rather stay and wait for them to get here?"

"No," I said dumbly. "That's not what I meant. It's just that how are we supposed to get out of here?"

He opened the door. "In the Jeep."

"Will we be able to outrun them?"

He shrugged as he headed for the Jeep. "Hurry up and get inside."

I ran over and jumped in, my nerves bubbling so badly that my hands were trembling. I was so afraid that just on the other side of the garage door the Death Walkers would be waiting for us, all yellow-eyed and hungry to kill. I quickly buckled my seatbelt and started chewing on my nails as the Jeep's engine roared to life.

With one hand gripping tightly on the steering wheel and the other grasping onto the shifter, Alex sucked in a deep breath. "Ready?"

"No." My voice shook.

"Okay, hold on." He pushed the garage door opener that was clipped to the visor, and the door slowly inched open. It seemed like it took forever for it to rise up all the way.

Alex threw the shifter into reverse and started to back out. He only made it a few feet, though, before he hit the brakes.

"What's wrong?" I followed his gaze to the back window, and I had my answer. Tons and tons of glowing yellow eyes bursting through the darkness.

A moment later, someone emerged from around the corner of the garage. When the light hit the person's face, it felt like someone had punched me in the stomach. It was a man with black hair, dark eyes, and a scar on his left cheek.

We were so screwed.

Chapter 34

"Stephan." Alex took the keys out of the ignition and grabbed hold of the door handle, about to climb out.

"Alex," I hissed. "*Please* don't. We still need to get out of here. There are Death Walkers everywhere."

"Alex," Stephan called out in a commanding voice.

The door handle made a *click* as Alex started to push the door open. Panicking, I reached out and clutched onto his arm. He glanced down at my hand clutching his arm, and then looked up and gave me this strange look.

"*Please*," I begged and released his arm. "If this isn't proof that your dad's working with Demetrius—" I did a gesture back at the driveway, where dozens of yellow eyes glinted at us through the darkness—"then I don't know what is. We have to…"

He pressed a finger to my lips, shushing me. Then he slid his fingers around my necklace and tucked it down in my shirt. My mouth dropped open. *Huh?* "Whatever you do, keep that hidden. Don't let anyone know you have it."

"Why?" I asked, but he had already turned away and was climbing out of the car, the Sword of Immortality clutched in his hand.

I sat there for a second, confused about why I had to keep the necklace hidden. Then it hit me. Because I probably wasn't supposed to have the necklace to begin with and Alex didn't want to get in trouble for giving it to me. Nice, really nice, Alex. And now I had to climb out of the car and not only face the monsters that wanted to kill me, but also face the man who was responsible for my mother's disappearance and the whole crappiness of my life.

So with wobbly legs, I dragged my butt out of the car, tucked the small knife Alex had given me into my back pocket, and made my way over to Alex and Stephan. I stayed several feet away from them, because seeing Stephan in real life was about a million times more frightening than seeing him in my dreams.

When I approached them, Stephan had been telling Alex something in a low voice, but shut his mouth when he saw me.

"Gemma," Stephan said in an eerily calm voice. "It's so nice to finally meet you."

Well, look at him. Pretending like he had never met me before. What a jerk. As much as I wanted to spit every foul word that was running through my mind right in his face, I didn't. Just being there, in the same room with him, felt like I was suffocating, and my voice was getting strangled inside my throat. So instead, I just stood there like a coward, nervously eyeballing the Death Walkers that were gathering in the driveway.

"Well, Alex, you've done a good job keeping her out of trouble and everything," Stephan said. "But I'll take it from here."

What did that mean? Detach my soul? Sick the Death Walkers on me? I eyed the door that led back inside the cabin, contemplating whether or not to make a run for it.

"Okay," Alex told Stephan, and I wanted to smack him in the back of the head.

"Traitor," I muttered.

He shot me a look and shook his head once as if to say *"be quiet."*

"Look," Alex said to Stephan, "I understand that there are some things that need to be done here. But what I don't understand is why they're here." He pointed at the Death Walkers.

"That is a very good question," Stephan said in a condescending tone. "But right now, all I need for you to do is give me the Sword of Immortality and keep your mouth shut. You know better than to question anything that I do."

Wow. I couldn't help but wonder if there was some kind of "How To" class that Keepers were required to go to in order to be such crappy parents/guardians, because Stephan reminded me a lot of Marco and Sophia

Speaking of Marco and Sophia, weren't they supposed to be gracing us with their presence too?

Stephan held out his hand and tapped his foot impatiently as he waited for Alex to surrender the sword over.

"Okay, I'll give you the sword," Alex said, and my gut clenched. "But I have one small thing I have to ask you before I do."

"Make it quick," Stephan grumbled.

The next thing I knew, Alex's fist was slamming into Stephan's face. After that, everything moved by in a blur. Stephan staggered back. Alex yelled for me to run. Suddenly, I found myself running inside the house and out the back door into the forest.

Definitely not the brightest thing I had ever done.

Chapter 35

I made it a little ways into the forest before the entire severity of my situation hit me. I was running through the forest, being chased by Death Walkers and Stephan. *Great thinking, Gemma. Way to set yourself up for a cold death. Didn't your dreams teach you anything?*

Yep, I was a real genius.

Debating whether to head back and get the heck out of the trees, I slowed to a jog. What were my options here? I mean, I could either head back to the cabin and face whatever was waiting for me there, or I could keep going farther into the trees, probably end up lost, and eventually get captured if this played out anything like my nightmares, which I was beginning to think might be a big possibility.

In the midst of my indecisiveness, I heard a twig snap from behind me. I reeled around and did a quick skim of my surroundings. I could barely see a thing. The only light I had to go by was the faint light trickling down from the moon.

My heart hammered in my chest as I slid the knife out of my back pocket and held it out in front of me like I was some kind of Sword Fighting Master or something, which, of course, I so wasn't. Another snapping twig, and then I saw it—my imminent doom. My grip tightened on the handle of the knife, my life flashing before my eyes as Stephan and a handful of Death Walkers ascended from the trees. Ice crackled over the snow, moving straight for my feet. The temperature descended. My body glazed cold, and I was hit with a spine chilling sense of *déjà vu.*

My breathing was heavy. My hand trembled. And, I swear, everything moved in slow motion as Stephan trampled up to me, and I swung the blade at him. He flicked it out of my hands effortlessly, and it fell to the icy ground with a clank. Then he bent down, scooped it up, and tucked it into the pocket of his jacket.

"Hello, Gemma." He grinned a spine chilling grin. "Going somewhere?"

Chapter 36

Dragging me behind him like a ragdoll, Stephan trampled through the snow back toward the cabin. The Death Walkers' chill nipped at my heels, and my breathing had slowed due to the cold. I wasn't going to lie and say I wasn't scared. I was downright terrified. But on a positive note, unlike my nightmares, he hadn't commanded the Death Walkers to finish me off.

"You know, things were never supposed to come to this," Stephan said, jolting me to the side as he swerved around a dead pine tree. "This wasn't part of the plan."

"What plan?" I asked in a shaky voice. "The one where you kill me?"

"Kill you?" He laughed like it was the silliest thing he ever heard. "Oh Gemma, no one wants to kill you. In fact, you being alive is very important."

"Important to whom?" I whimpered as my shoulder scraped the bark of a tree. My skin burned beneath my jacket, and I could feel the warmth of the blood bleeding out.

"And my son," he continued, shaking his head with disgust. "He should know better. Let's just hope no permanent damage has been done."

"Permanent damage to what?" I asked.

He laughed wickedly. "Oh, you'll soon find out."

That did not sound good.

And where was Alex? Had something happened to him? I guess I was about to find out, because the cabin came into view.

By the time we reached the back door, a small part of me felt grateful. My body had practically gone numb from the cold, and I knew that the inside of the cabin would be warm.

Other than that, I had nothing else to look forward to right now.

Stephan paused at the sliding glass door, his hand still grasped tightly onto my arm. With his free hand, he reached inside the pocket of his jacket and drew out the sword he had stolen from me earlier, the blade glinting dangerously in the porch light.

"Just to make sure you don't run away again." He lifted the sword, and I screamed as he sliced the blade across the upper part of my leg. It slashed through my jeans and stabbed into my skin. Tears stung at my eyes as blood seeped out.

"I think that should teach you a lesson not to ever run off," he said, wiping the blood soaked blade off on his jeans.

The world swayed around me. I thought I was going to pass out. The pain…it was excruciating.

I teeter-tottered on the border of consciousness as Stephan yanked me inside the cabin.

I felt a tiny rush of relief when I saw that Alex was in the living room. At least he believed me now—about his father being bad—and was on my side. At least I wasn't in this alone. That's what I thought, anyway, until I realized the he was just sitting on the couch, completely unguarded. There was no reason for him to be here. Why hadn't he run out into the forest to save me?

Alex's bright green eyes went wide as he caught sight of the gaping wound on my leg, which looked even worse underneath the bright lighting of the living room.

"Jesus Christ, Stephan." He jumped to his feet. "What the heck did you do to her?"

"She needed to be taught a lesson," Stephan told him in a serene voice. "Running away is not an option for her, and you should know better than to tell her to do so."

I noticed a spot of dried blood beneath Stephan's nose and wondered if Alex had made him bleed when he clocked him one.

"I said I was sorry about that. I didn't understand the situation," Alex said apologetically, staring down at the floor.

"The situation," I repeated, my confusion swirling just about as bad as the room was. "What situation?"

410

Stephan shoved me onto the couch, and Alex winced as I stumbled and landed on it awkwardly. But he didn't try to help me.

"She needs to be alive," Alex warned. "She won't be useful if she's dead."

Gaping at Alex, I pressed my hand to my leg, trying to get the bleeding to stop. I didn't understand. It seemed like whatever evil thing was about to take place here, he might actually be a part of it.

"We need to do it now," Stephan told Alex "Before things get worse."

"Do what?" My voice sounded weak and pathetic. "What are you going to do to me?"

"Gemma." Alex gave me a sympathetic look. "I already explained to you what was going to happen."

"You're going to let him detach my soul," I said, flabbergasted. Sparks were pouring through my body, and I suddenly despised them more than I ever had. "After all of this, after he sent my mom to The Underworld, after he showed up with them." I pointed to the window, where the glowing eyes of the Death Walkers were peeking in.

Stephan clapped his hands together. "Bravo. Very impressive—discovering what I did to your mother." He gave a dramatic pause. "But how on earth did you do it?"

I waited for Alex to tell him about my Foreseer ability, and the visions I saw with and without the crystal ball. Surprisingly, though, he kept his mouth shut.

I raised my chin defiantly at Stephan. "Wouldn't you like to know?"

He glared at me. "Your mother needed to be gotten rid of. She was getting in the way. And she went like a coward—crying the whole way to take you instead of her. She didn't seem to understand that the world's fate is depending on you and your inability to feel."

So not true, but I couldn't tell him that. "If the world's fate depends on that, then why are you working with the Death Walkers? I just don't see them being in a on a plan that has anything to do with saving the world."

"What I do is really none of your business," he snapped. "But if you must know—they *are* working with me to protect the world."

I gave Alex a pleading look. "You can't be buying this. Not when it's Death Walkers that will come out of the portal and destroy the world. How could they be working to help protect the world, when they're the ones who will be destroying it?"

Alex swallowed hard, but still didn't say a word.

"Alright, that's enough questions." Stephan raised his hand in the air and snapped his fingers. "Bring me the *memoria extracto*."

I glanced around the room. Who was he talking to? And what was the memario extracta or whatever the heck he said? Well, I was about to find out. A single Death Walker strode through the back door, carrying a small black box with a red eye painted on it.

It handed the box to Stephan and then left the room, taking all the warm air with it.

My body felt heavy and numb, but I wasn't sure if that was from the cold air or from the significant amount of blood I lost.

Stephan's dark eyes lit up as he opened the box and took out a grey rock.

"What is that?" I asked, not sure whether I should freak out or not. I mean, it was a rock for crying out loud. How bad could the thing be?

But any trace of humor I possessed slipped away as the rock turned black and started puffing out smoke.

"This is the most magnificent thing I've ever discovered." Stephan held the smoking rock up for Alex and me to see. "It is so much better than detaching your soul, because not only will it rid you of all of your memories, but it will wipe away everything inside your mind. You won't even be able to function anymore."

Vomit burned at the back of my throat. And even though I didn't want to, I started to cry hysterically. My tears had no effect on Stephan whatsoever, which I assumed as much. But I caught a glimpse of guilt flash across Alex's face.

Maybe, just maybe, it wasn't over for me yet.

"Alex, you can't let him do this," I cried. "*Please*. This is so much worse than detaching my soul, and you know it."

413

I could see in his eyes that he could feel my pain, and for a moment I thought I had him.

Tears streamed down my cheeks. *"Please."*

And then....he turned his head away from me.

My heart broke. How could I have kissed him? As beautiful as he was, and as wonderful as his kisses felt, a part of me had always wondered if everything he did was a rouse.

And now I knew. That part of me had been right.

The prickle traced up the back of my neck, releasing an overwhelming sense of pain. And I'm not talking about the pain I felt when my leg was cut. This was a whole new level of pain; the kind of pain that grips at your heart and rips it apart; the pain that comes when someone betrays you.

Stephan walked up to me, the rock smoking madly in the palm of his hand. "It's time."

With tears streaming down my cheeks, blood dripping down my leg, and my heart breaking, I shook my head. This was it. This was the end of my life. As sad and short-lived as it was, I didn't want it to come to an end.

Stephan held the rock in front of my face. For a split second I thought I felt my skin glow warmly beneath the locket. But it happened so quickly that it was probably just my imagination. The sparks of electricity were going insanely wild, after all. They were probably heating up the metal.

"It's time," Stephan repeated.

I took one last look at Alex. His bright green eyes seemed to have lost a little of their shine. When I turned back to Stephan, a rush of warmth swept through my body. Funny, I would have guessed it would be cold.

Stephan grinned as I let out a painful gasp. I clutched onto the edge of the couch as my head started to hum. I was slipping away. I could feel it—the life leaving my body. I tried to think of my mom, her bright blue irises, and her warm smile.

I tried to picture the life I never knew.

The humming in my head rang louder and louder until I couldn't think anymore—couldn't feel. The last thing I saw was Alex's horrified expression before my eyes slipped shut. He had no right to be horrified. He let this happen.

I thought I heard a loud crash, but my eyelids were too heavy to open. Everything shifted black, and then...

I was gone.

Jessica Sorensen lives with her husband and three kids in the snowy mountains of Wyoming, where she spends most of her time reading, writing, and hanging out with her family.